All this time music had been playing in the background, not that anyone had been listening, but when it stopped the talking began to subside. Quickly the hall fell silent as the lights were slowly doused. Vivaldi was replaced by the sound of a single sitar. The audience listened quietly. There was the odd rustling, a sneeze, a cough or two. The stirring ceased. The people sat silent and then even the plaintive notes of the sitar faded. The low lights dimmed further until there was nothing but blackness.

Ginnie felt for Selina's hand and squeezed it. Sitting quietly in the darkness she realised that the excitement she had been feeling was evaporating, to be replaced by a strange calm.

'Remember this,' a melodic, disembodied, but beautiful, male voice intoned, 'remember this. You are no longer alone.'

From the packed audience a collective sigh rose to the rafters ...

Anita Burgh was born in Gillingham, Kent. She is the author of several novels, including *Distinctions of Class* which was shortlisted for the RNA Romantic Novel of the Year Award.

THE
CULT

Anita Burgh

ORION

An Orion paperback
First published in Great Britain by Orion in 1997
This paperback edition published in 1997 by Orion Books Ltd,
Orion House, 5 Upper St Martin's Lane, London WC2H 9EA

A CIP catalogue record for this book is available
from the British Library.

ISBN: 0 75280 929 6

Typeset by Deltatype Ltd, Birkenhead, Merseyside

Printed and bound in Great Britain by
Clays Ltd, St Ives plc

For my son Alexander Gregory Leith,
with love and admiration

EXTRACT FROM THE
DIARY OF H.G. – THE MASTER

The truth should be told before it is too late, for I fear I shall soon be killed.

Fear! What an odd word for me to choose when I have expended so much energy telling you, my followers, that death is but a step to be taken. It is not death I dread – at seventy-two I am familiar with the idea. No, it is the manner of my dying that fills me with foreboding.

I spend much time wondering how it will be, a knife, a push in the dark, poison, a gun.

I hope it is not a gun. I've spoken often of my abhorrence of them; it would be a cruel irony, then, if one were used.

This line of thought startles me. If the irony strikes me there is no reason it could not do the same for him. But such a question has no answer – not, that is, until the end.

I shudder at the idea of being shot. It's not the degree of pain that worries me, it is how I would look. I should so hate to appear ugly!

Are you laughing at an old man's vanity? Those who really know me would evince no surprise at my reaction. They are aware of how vain I am. I glow with pride at compliments and find great happiness when others call me beautiful. How I look has been important to me in life, so why should I not be the same in death?

I write you, but I wonder who you are, who has found these scribblings of mine, the notes and ramblings of a condemned man. So dramatic! I do ramble these days, I admit. It makes it so much harder for those who have to transcribe what I say. Maybe they should stop now. Maybe I've said all there is to say and what we are left with is repetition and inconsequential meanderings.

What do I want you to read? The truth, as I have said. My apology for the untruths. And I want it known what he has done and how he has begun to corrupt my life's work and besmirch all that was so clean and good.

Where to hide these confessions so that he won't find and destroy them bothers me. I hope my chosen place is secure enough that he does not find them, but obvious enough that you do.

I must work quickly. The fear is mounting. Yet I'm to blame. If only I'd taken notice of so many discrepancies. The noises in the night. The vacant expressions in their eyes. My fault! But knowing it does not help me come to terms with my own stupidity. I must get on with this!

The truth, then?

The truth is, of course, there is no truth. Doesn't that sound just like me? An ideal thought for the day. I shall, undoubtedly, use it, and all of you will worry at it and debate it and meditate upon it and record it, as you do everything I say.

That last is not kind. It reads as if I despise your diligence, your method. That is far from the truth, which is that I love and respect you all – well, those who are left whom I know.

Everything recorded: except this. My secret ...

chapter **one**

1

A couple of times a month, always on a Wednesday for that was early closing in Finchester, Ginnie Mulholland had lunch with her friend, Selina Horne.

Once she had parked the car, Ginnie walked the short stretch past the Bishop's Palace and into the Close. To get to Selina's bookshop she had to walk the length of the Close, looking in the windows of the expensive china, gift and clothes shops that lured the thousands of tourists who visited Finchester every year. She stopped to look in the Jaeger shop and waved at the manageress, whose face lit up at the sight of her – though more likely at the thought of her Gold Barclaycard, she thought.

It was a lovely, crisp October day, and the leaves on the trees which dotted the Cathedral Green were still in colour. There was a good sprinkling of people walking their dogs on the grass – despite the signs telling them not to. Ginnie didn't notice the massive cathedral, its pale stone golden in the sunshine, for, in the way of things familiar, she took it for granted.

There was a lightness in her step that had not been there yesterday or for some time past. Ginnie had had a problem – her husband, Carter. She loved him deeply, jealously, suspiciously. Ever since they married, twenty-two years ago, Ginnie, not really believing in her good fortune, had expected the relationship to end. If he was late returning home she was convinced he had met someone better than her. When he was away she just knew he was with another woman. And she could, and did, torture herself imagining their bodies entwined, thrashing sweatily about in some distant hotel bed. Although for years he'd had money enough for the Ritz, she'd noticed when checking his Visa statements that he tended to patronize Trust House Forte.

Her life was a perpetual quandary: always fearing the worst, yet afraid to ask him the truth.

Ginnie's suspicions irritated him for Carter was an artist with an artist's love of freedom. She told herself that she could not expect him to be as other men, that this was how he'd been when she'd met him so she must accept it. Only she couldn't, and still fondly nurtured the notion that she was the one woman who could make him change.

The problem this last time had been that Ginnie had convinced herself he was in love with Anna Tylson, someone Ginnie met socially, often enough for the situation to be fraught with difficulties. Sometimes she liked to imagine the relief she might feel if she confided her fears to someone – Selina, perhaps. But confidences, she felt, might come back to haunt her, or be used against her in some way.

Today, however, was a new beginning, for last night Carter had come home for dinner on time, with a bottle of Pol Roger – her favourite – an enormous bouquet of flowers that bordered on the vulgar, the latest bestseller and a happy grin on his face as he told her of his Christmas plan for them. And she'd reasoned that a man who was planning to leave was hardly likely to spring such an exciting surprise. Anna Tylson was history, she was certain – well, almost.

When Selina had woken and realised it was Wednesday, she had thought how nice it would be to have the day free to do what she wanted. She *could* phone and cancel her lunch – but she knew she wouldn't. Ginnie looked forward to them in a way that Selina never did, and she hadn't the heart to let her down.

Selina's last customer finally left the shop without buying – one of the many, these days, who came in from the cold for a free browse. She bagged up the money from the till and decided to count it later, but registered that there seemed to be more than most mornings' trading recently. She marked the till roll with date and time and tidied up the paying area.

Then she collected the coffee cups and took them into the back kitchen to wash up. There had been a near riot this morning when she had explained to some regulars that they were going to have to pay for it in future: 'Times are hard, I'm sorry.'

One of the problems Selina had with these Wednesday lunches was that, because of the wine, she was in a daze for the rest of the afternoon, and nothing else got done. Of course, the simple solution was to refuse the wine but she could never make herself do that. And Ginnie, when it was her turn to pay, never stinted on quality. Without doubt Ginnie was the most generous person she knew. But there were times when the open-handedness reminded Selina of an unpopular girl at school who had tried to buy friendship with sweets.

It was a one-sided relationship: Selina had an army of friends while Ginnie seemed to have only her. But Selina could not bring herself to distance herself from Ginnie and perhaps hurt her.

She worried that Ginnie's reliance on her might become worse: the other woman had never had enough to do and with her daughter, Tessa, newly away at college she'd have even less to occupy her. Maybe she'd want to have lunch every Wednesday from now on.

Selina had introduced Ginnie to myriad occupations and, for a time, it had looked as if aromatherapy might grab her interest. She had started the training but, as with so many other things, she'd quickly given it up. It had been the same with astrology, tarot reading, night classes in A-level English, a French Linguaphone course and yoga.

And Ginnie was not the easiest of people to get on with. A perfectionist, she tended to be dogmatic and could be highly critical of others' failings. There was an edginess to her, which was disconcerting. It was as if she was about to break down, or was, perhaps, holding some great sadness inside her. Not that Selina would ever know what it was for Ginnie was not the sort of person to confide in her. In fact, that was probably the reason they had become friends in the first place: Selina herself never told anyone about her deepest feelings. Not that sometimes she hadn't wanted to, imagining what it would be like to unburden herself to a sympathetic soul. But she never could. 'We want no flaunting of untidy emotions here,' her mother had said, sharply and frequently to her son and daughter, at the first sign of any emotional trauma and Selina had learnt to hide that which hurt, but she felt sometimes as if there was a dam inside her holding back the problems of her life – it was a dark place which her mother's training had taught her was best ignored.

Although they called themselves 'best friends', Selina knew that she and Ginnie were not – or, at least, not in the conventional, confiding sense, and probably never would be.

'Am I interrupting?' Ginnie's voice and the shop bell sounded at the same time. 'You look deep in thought.'

'Nothing earth-shattering.' She felt confused, almost afraid that Ginnie might sense what she had been thinking.

'I love this shop.' Ginnie sat gracefully on one of the wing chairs arranged round a low oak table where customers could sit, drink coffee and decide which books

6

to buy – well, that was the theory. She looked up at the low ceiling with its massive old beams. 'Lovely, unique,' she said.

'Used to be. Not any more, though, with all that clutter.' Selina pointed to the display of ouija boards and the pyramid of handcrafted burners for the aromatherapy oils which she now stocked in the hope that they would save her business.

'Still, the clutter, as you call it, brought us together, didn't it?'

'That's true,' Selina said, for Ginnie had come into the shop one day looking for books on Tantra – not that Selina had ever plucked up the courage to ask her if it was Tantric sexual practices that had interested her. 'Do you fancy a drink before we go? I've some wine.'

'I booked us a table at the Buckingham for one thirty,' Ginnie said hurriedly, preferring an aperitif there than the cheap, acidic wine that Selina served nowadays.

Selina flicked the switch on the CD player, stopping the Mozart in full flow, turned off the lights, threw her sage-green wool poncho over her head, patted her hair which, since she had a mass of tightly packed natural curls, had no effect on it, and said, 'Right, I'm fit.'

2

Selina and Ginnie walked towards the old coaching inn where horses never came since now it was marooned in the pedestrians only Close. Both were aware of how different they were in appearance and had often joked about it, especially when people looked curiously at them, wondering what on earth they could have in common.

Ginnie's pale complexion was that of a natural blonde,

even if the colour of the chin-caressing bob was helped now by her hairdresser's skills. She was tall, slim and with good facial bones. Her skin was fine with only a faint tracery of lines. Her mouth was thinnish, her grey eyes large, but with a wary expression. She was always dressed expensively and stylishly with never a crease, dropped hem or broken stitch. Her clothes, make-up, figure, hair and style were the result of the rigid control that ruled her life.

Selina bobbed along a good six inches shorter, feet clad in sturdy ankle boots, her skirt brushing the tops. Her clothes were a mish-mash of different fabrics, colours and layers. She put on whatever was at hand in the morning and forgot about it for the rest of the day. She was far from overweight, but her lack of height and the loose-fitting clothes she preferred conspired to make her look plumper than she was. Her hair was allowed to grow in whichever way it chose so her face was framed by an abundance of brunette curls tinged with red. She had an intelligent face, more expressive than beautiful, with particularly fine hazel eyes which, fortunately, since she wore no make-up, had naturally thick black lashes. Although ten years separated the women, they looked the same age: expensive creams and clever make-up helped Ginnie look younger while a broken marriage and money worries had taken their toll on Selina.

In the entrance hall of the Buckingham their way to the bar was blocked by a group of smartly dressed elderly women, who were fussing stridently as they checked whether everyone in their party was there.

'Oh, no!' Ginnie said, under her breath at sight of her mother-in-law, Joan Mulholland. 'Has she seen me?' she whispered to Selina.

''Fraid so,' Selina smiled and waved.

'Is she coming over?' asked Ginnie, looking in the opposite direction.

''Fraid so,' Selina repeated. 'She's almost reached us.'

'Selina, how lovely to see you. And Virginia.' She nodded curtly at Ginnie.

'Joan,' they said in unison, and both looked down at the floor, like schoolgirls who'd been caught out.

Joan Mulholland's satisfaction with her position in society gave her a smugness born of a conviction that she was envied for it. To those she deemed of a lower order, the category in which Ginnie was certain she'd been put, she spoke with a studied slowness, in the belief that her superior status gave her a superior intelligence.

'Are you here for one of your luncheons?'

'We are, the Wednesday ritual,' Selina answered, since it was obvious that Ginnie wouldn't, or couldn't.

'How delightful. So are we – the cathedral flower girls!' She laughed in a coquettish way that sat uncomfortably with her years.

Selina was not sure what to say next. 'Well ...' she ventured, unsure where it might lead her, but she was interrupted.

'As you're lunching in the restaurant,' Joan said, 'perhaps you'd care to join us?'

'How kind – but, sadly, we're booked in the carvery,' Selina excused them deftly.

'Next time, then, dear Selina. And now I must be getting back to my party.' She smiled patronisingly at both women and swept off.

Once they were safely in the bar – safe since Joan was of a generation who would never be seen in a hotel bar – Selina asked, 'Is she for real? She was so rude to you.'

'You were a brick. You think so fast. Will we get into the carvery now?'

'Sure. I'll nip and check.'

'I'll get the drinks in. G and T?'

'Spritzer, please. I'm giving up spirits.' Selina pulled a face as she left to arrange their table.

When she got back, she found seats for them in the crowded bar with its worn leather sofas, faded Turkey carpet, sporting prints, nicotine-stained ceiling and surly barman, who seemed determined to ignore Ginnie as she waited to order the drinks. Selina wondered why she put up with his rudeness, just as she had Joan's. If Selina's mother-in-law had behaved like that, she wouldn't have stood there and taken it. It revealed a weakness in Ginnie that a bully like Joan would latch onto immediately.

It could not have been easy for Ginnie, marrying into that relentlessly proper middle-class family. She doubted if Joan had ever forgiven her for marrying her precious Carter – no one in the world would have been good enough for him. Selina remembered her own mother saying tartly one day that it was a shame Joan Mulholland hadn't devoted as much time and dedication to her husband, Patrick, as she did to her son. Then the old boy might not have been the groping menace he was to the other women in the town. She might tell Ginnie that – perhaps it would cheer her up. On the other hand, perhaps she'd better not: people were odd about their families and anything that could be construed as criticism.

'Promise not to laugh – but do you ever think you sound like your mother?' Ginnie asked later, when they were half-way through their lunch.

'It's not a joking matter. It happens all the time. Creepy, isn't it?'

'Horrible! The other day I saw my shadow and nearly shrieked – it looked so like my mother's!' Ginnie shuddered as she spoke.

'Your mother's alive. I warn you, it gets even worse when they're dead. I believe I'm even beginning to think like mine – God forbid!'

'Then you didn't like yours either?' Ginnie asked, and

then looked flustered as she realised she had inadvertently betrayed herself.

'We couldn't stand each other – ever. When Chris and I split up she told him she understood why he wouldn't want to live with someone as difficult as me. Charming! We never spoke again.'

'You must have been so hurt.'

'Not particularly. Still, that said, some loyalty would have been nice.' She picked up her glass to end this topic of conversation. She might put a good face on it, but it *did* hurt. Sometimes, when yet another relationship bit the dust, Selina wondered whether it had been her mother's coldness towards her that had made it impossible for her to sustain any relationship, that the love never lasted because to her it was never real. She knew now that one needed to be loved as a child to know how to love. It was an interesting theory and she realised, since she was an honest person, a cop out. But she had never elaborated on this to Ginnie – that went too deep.

'How's Carter?' Selina asked, more out of politeness than interest. She did not like Ginnie's husband, who, she felt, was too full of himself by far.

'He's fine. Painting away,' Ginnie answered, smiling brightly, and then, as if she could not contain herself, 'He's giving me the most fantastic present for Christmas.'

'What's that?'

'A trip on Concorde to New York for a week.'

'That's some present!' Selina said, but could not stop herself wondering who was paying for it.

'Isn't it just! Right out of the blue too!' She looked as if she was about to hug herself from sheer happiness. 'Just the two of us and Tessa.'

'Nice.'

'How's Geoff?' Ginnie asked then, dutifully. She did not like her friend's partner, thinking that he did not appreciate Selina enough.

'He's away until Friday but he's fine. I'll tell him you asked.' Selina trotted out the words, the neat social gloss of pretending all was well, which was far from the truth. A relationship that had started so promisingly was, she knew, heading fast for the rocks of familiarity and boredom. She could have told Ginnie of the humiliation that was sidling towards her at the idea that he might be seeing his ex-wife again – and not just for the sake of the children. She wanted to but, of course, she didn't. 'And Tessa?' she asked instead.

'She's home next week for Carter's birthday. I miss her so much, now she's at university. The house seems empty without her.' She congratulated herself on how easily she spoke the words that were expected of her when the truth was that she liked having her daughter away at college and being alone with her husband.

'Quieter, surely?' Selina grinned.

'I'll never complain about her music again, or her feet – she has such noisy feet.'

They paused as they waited for the waiter to serve coffee.

'Was it hard living on your own?' Ginnie asked, but even as she did she wondered what had made her say that. She'd never been on her own, she thought happily, so there was no need to know.

'Not really,' Selina answered, with a carefree shrug that camouflaged how awful she found it. 'Why do you ask?'

'Nothing, just being nosy, I suppose.'

When she was with Ginnie Selina often felt that she was in the middle of the conversational equivalent of a minuet. They would touch on something that verged on intimacy, and then shy away to the safety of polite *non sequiturs*, just as dancers touched then swooped away from each other.

The Rector of Witham – Ginnie's village – was passing

their table and stopped, taking the opportunity to confirm that Ginnie would be helping at the Christmas Fayre.

'Do you do a lot of that stuff? You know, Lady of the Manor,' Selina asked, as the clergyman fussed away.

'What a thing to say!' Ginnie laughed. 'I do what I can. After all, if you live in a village I think you should help out.'

'Remind me not to move to a village. I couldn't deal with that.'

'I quite enjoy going to church, it's comforting. Not that I go that often, I don't like most of the stuck-up congregation.'

'What do you mean, *comforting*?' asked Selina, curious.

'You know, that there might be something there. Don't you ever wonder?'

'No.'

'Don't you want to believe in something?'

'What? God on a cloud, angels and all that Rossetti stuff?'

'Of course not. Don't be silly. No, a force greater than us.'

'Doesn't sound very C of E to me.'

'No, I suppose not. But I think everybody needs something.'

'Not everybody. *I* don't,' Selina said emphatically.

EXTRACT FROM THE
DIARY OF H.G. – THE MASTER

There are times when I waffle somewhat – not that anything is said, my followers' adulation sees to that. But I like to think I'm honest about myself and I admit it. So since I don't know who you are, or even if you are one of my devotees, I shall try to curb this irritating habit.

He has been away, which has lightened my mood considerably. He will be back tomorrow and the thought agitates me.

I must get on and tell you everything. The truth, or rather untruth, began over sixty years ago on a beach in Ceylon.

The official version of that morning has been told many times but never how it seemed to me. As you undoubtedly know, I was lying in a hollow in the sand, hovering in that place between sleeping and waking. I was enjoying those precious moments that those who have lived in a hot country will understand – those minutes of comfort when the chill of night has disappeared and the cauldron of the day's heat has not yet commenced.

A distant jabbering pulled me awake. I peered over the ridge of my little trench and saw some people, about fifty yards away, moving purposefully in our direction. The group was led by a stout, upright white woman. Her parasol was held aloft. Dressed in white she looked ghostlike. She never faltered in her step, although the sand was soft and deep, but marched purposefully on, those with her bowing obsequiously and darting about her like shoals of fish around a great whale.

That is how the Honourable Bay Tarbart found me

that morning just as the documents she had found in the sandalwood box had said would happen – or, rather, as she had interpreted their words. Who would argue with her? Since Miss Tarbart was of that breed of imperious upper-class Englishwoman who is suffused by her own sense of rightness, that her interpretation of events would not be accepted had probably never entered her head.

Unusually, for the times, Bay Tarbart had renounced her religion. No doubt this decision was helped by the loss of her fiancé in the carnage of the Great War, ended only nineteen years before: the memories and horror must still have been crystal clear.

I have often pondered on how different our lives would have been without that tragedy – she a wife, mother, chatelaine of a stately home, titled. And me? Well, who knows? Dead, probably, long ago.

Still, as is my habit, I digress. What could fill the void with which this loss of religious belief had left her? Humanism, Christian Science, a soupçon of Buddhism combined with a love of animals, that's what. In other words, a rare old muddle.

She needed something to believe in and found it in an ancient parchment manuscript, hidden in her precious sandalwood box. It told her when and where she would find her prophet. She had set out to find him. And she did. Me!

I shall be honest, for the first time, about the writings: I find them somewhat implausible. They remind me of the words of Nostradamus – riddles within riddles – which seem to mean anything you want them to.

Bay Tarbart's interpretation was that in the third decade of this century on a 6 July, close to a town whose name began with a C, by the sea in a land where elephants roam she would find a holy man, dark of skin and with eyes of blue. Vague, isn't it? Except for that last bit, for I am famed for the colour of my eyes. Many

15

towns close to the sea must begin with a C. Elephants helped narrow the search. No one pointed out to her that 6 July was the day her fiancé had been killed on the Somme.

By the time her party had reached me I was fully awake and had scrambled out of my sandy hollow and stood, looking somewhat woebegone, in my dirty clothes, with no shoes on my feet. My friends had also emerged and we stood agog.

'Ask him his name.' She pointed imperiously at me with her parasol.

'I'm known as Harry, but ...' I didn't finish for the woman had gone as white as the clothes she wore; she seemed to sway like a mighty tree and her young, pretty companion screamed.

'Haré – just as it said!'

'Harry ...' I began, then stopped. She seemed so happy to think I had a holy name that I let it be.

'He understood me! He speaks English.' She clutched at her throat and I noted the fine rings she wore on her chubby fingers – poverty makes the eyes alert to such baubles.

'It's divine intervention,' the younger woman gasped.

'Hyacinth, it is no such thing! What have I been telling you? It's in the Sandalwood Manuscript. The child with the holy name and with eyes of blue who speaks many tongues. Can you speak other languages, boy?'

'Si, señora. Guten Tag. Et comment ça va?' I replied, with insufferable smugness.

'It's a miracle,' Hyacinth exclaimed, undeterred by Miss Tarbart's irritation. Behind her stood a short, fat Indian. He was watching us nervously, his glance darting back and forth like a humming-bird's and his tongue licking his lips with the speed of a lizard's.

I grinned, proud of my own cleverness, and hoping my gang of beggars was astonished and impressed with my smartness. I was fairly low in the pecking order, I could do with a leg-up: the more senior one was, the more one kept from the daily take – and the better, of course, one ate.

From her voluminous bag she took a small black velvet pouch and handed it to the fat man. It clinked, most invitingly, of money.

'Take this, Sanjay. Find his parents. Persuade them. Sign whatever papers are necessary. He's coming with me,' she said.

I was about to tell her that there was no need, that I had no parents, and I'll never know what stopped me – the second untruth. Instead I winked at Sanjay and jerked my head ever so slightly, hoping he'd realise that I'd like to come to some arrangement with him over the money.

The Englishwoman took my hand. I shouted to my chums, told them goodbye with no heaviness in my heart. When alone in the world, one is always waiting for the next opportunity to arise, and one has no time for sentiment.

So, I held tight to the dough-like hand and trotted along beside this strange, commanding woman and into my new life ...

It's almost time for tea. Some things in life are immutable and the Edwardian notion of tea at four, which I inherited from Miss Tarbart, is one of them. I shall return to this, later ...

chapter two

1

Tessa Mulholland was bored. She hadn't wanted to come home for the weekend, but she knew she could not cope with the ensuing histrionics if she didn't. She watched her mother fussing about the kitchen with mounting annoyance.

'Some birthday treat this is turning into. Where the hell is he?' Tessa asked Ginnie who, having prepared her husband's birthday dinner and having cleared and tidied the kitchen, was wiping down the perfectly clean work surfaces, a bottle of Dettox in one blue-gloved hand, a J-cloth in the other. 'Mum, you've already done that once. Can't you sit down? You never relax.'

'I like to leave things clean.' Ginnie rubbed the ceramic tiles on the work top, concentrating especially on the grouting.

'You could do open heart surgery in here with confidence. Any more gin?'

'Do you think you should? I never drank –'

'Until long after you married – I know, I know. You've said it often enough!' Tessa interrupted, with youthful exasperation at the straitlaced ways of the older generation. 'And if it's escaped your notice, I'm eighteen and can drink what I like when I like. It's got nothing to do with you any more.'

'It's not good for you,' Ginnie said evenly, so used to Tessa's irritability that it no longer registered.

'If it's not good for me then it can't be for Dad either.'

'That's different.'

'What's different about it? At college you'd be amazed at what I drink.'

'I'd rather not think about it, thank you very much, and that's there, not here.' She began to reclean the cooker. She had to keep busy: if her hands were active then, hopefully, she could keep at bay the despair that skulked so close.

'It's not very relaxing here with you farting about. I gave up a good party to be here, I'd like you to know.'

'He won't be long.' Ginnie rubbed non-existent grease off the halogen hob. She did not dare look at her watch: it would remind her just how late Carter was – and for his birthday too! This made her want to sob with unhappiness, but she couldn't. She didn't want Tessa to know anything about her suspicions – that the affair with Anna was back on track again. And, in any case, if Tessa found out, she could not be sure whose side her daughter would take.

'He's an inconsiderate sod!'

'Tessa! Your language!' She laughed, though, for she knew Tessa didn't mean it. She adored her father, was fonder of him than she was of Ginnie, but Ginnie didn't mind. To her it seemed normal for she'd had just such a close relationship with her own father. Once she'd thought herself lucky, but she had learnt since that, sadly, it had not been such a good thing that Harry Brown had loved her with such an unselfish perfect love. The problems had cropped up when her relationship with her husband had not matched that with her father – in fact, hadn't come anywhere near it. She sighed.

'Why are you sighing?'

'Was I?' she asked, though she knew she was. 'I was just thinking of your Grandfather Brown, and wishing you'd been old enough to really know him before he died.'

'Did he like Dad?'

'What an odd question. Of course he did,' she lied smoothly, and rubbed the cooker harder.

'*I could have wished you were to have a better start with a more stable partner,*' he'd said, when she'd told him she was to marry Carter and, at the same time, confessed she was pregnant. He had been methodically making a neat display of Jaffa oranges in his shop, a glowing orange pyramid until her news had made his hand shake and the edifice collapsed.

She'd tried to explain to him how she felt about Carter, how she was sure he'd settle down – he was only twenty-five – and how nice he was.

'*Nice* never built a marriage!' her father had exclaimed. 'Does he love you?'

She could remember how she'd blushed and laughed as if the question was of no importance.

'He hasn't said he loves you, has he? He's doing this out of duty because of the baby.' There it was. Stated. What she knew. What she did not want to acknowledge.

'But I love him, Dad, enough for both of us. It'll be all right,' she'd said, with a trace of desperation. She wanted him to believe her, needed him to. Longed to take away the sad expression on his face. But she'd never achieved that. Her father had gone to his grave still sad and worried for her ...

'Yoo hoo – anyone in there?' Tessa shouted, waving her hand close to Ginnie's face, bringing her back to the present when, on days like this, she'd much rather stay in the past.

'Sorry, I was miles away. Maybe I'll have a gin with you.'

'Christ! Are the heavens about to fall in?' Tessa cupped her hands over her mouth. 'Attention, everyone! Ginnie Mulholland's about to have a gin.'

'You are silly. Mind your feet.' Ginnie had a broom in her hand as she tracked invisible dust.

'If I pour you a drink, will you sit down? You're worse than you normally are. What's up?'

'Nothing. I just wish your father would come.'

'Don't we all? I'm starving. Where did you meet Dad?' Tessa asked abruptly.

'I must have told you.'

'You have, often, but you like telling it and I like hearing it and maybe it'll make you sit down.'

Ginnie laughed but sat at the table and took the glass in her hand. 'I was working in your Grandfather Mulholland's chambers and he just walked in and came right up to me and said, "You're new." And then he wanted to know my name and asked me if it was Brown with an "e" or the plain sort. And when I said plain sort he said, "In name only." I'd never been flirted with like that.' She smiled as she remembered the day, the time even, the atmosphere in the stuffy office. 'And then he took me out for an expensive dinner and I couldn't imagine what he saw in me. He was so tall and handsome and he had the most wonderful soft blue velvet suit with a flowered shirt and a floppy matching tie – Liberty, as I remember.'

'Sounds gross!'

'Oh, no. It was the height of fashion then. We talked and talked and I'd never listened to anyone with such interesting radical views. He believed that no one should work if they didn't want to. That dustmen should be paid as much as brain surgeons – if not more – since emptying dustbins must be so boring. That marriage was a bourgeois trap and the nuclear family a sick joke. I tell you, it was all news to me …' She trailed off, then went on. 'And then he took me to a party and that was that. We were in love.' She refrained from telling her daughter about the student party in a chaotic house, with purple walls and black-painted ceilings, on the outskirts of town. It had been crowded and noisy, too, with Pink

Floyd blaring out of speakers that looked like drainpipes. Cheap wine and beer had been freely available, as were cigarettes, lovingly hand-rolled and passed between people with red-rimmed expressionless eyes – no, that part would always be kept secret from Tessa.

Ginnie had looked out of place in her neat blue dress, with its crocheted Peter Pan collar and short A-line skirt, which her mother had fretted about, and her white plastic knee-length boots. The other women had wafted from room to room in long, loose, flowing dresses, stockingless feet in Indian sandals. They giggled rudely as they sashayed past her. And she could never tell her daughter how he had taken her hand, pulled her through the crowd and up the narrow stairs, stepping over those who lolled on the treads, into a small back bedroom. He'd locked the door and pushed her onto the bed, which was covered in a pile of coats. She lost her precious virginity painfully to a tattoo of knocking on the door and with her face pressed into the coats, which smelt musty and of unwashed bodies. Strange, how she could still remember every detail even after all these years ...

'At least he practised what he preached.'

'What do you mean?' Ginnie dragged herself back from the past again.

'He's never worked in his life.'

'Oh, no, Tessa, that's not fair. He works hard at his paintings. It's not his fault people can't see how good he is,' Ginnie said, with the well-oiled practice of years.

'Come on, Mum. He hardly tries these days, you know he doesn't. When did he last have an exhibition? You're too soft with him.'

Ginnie shook her head in bewilderment. This was not how the conversation was supposed to go. 'But, Tessa, you love your father.'

'Of course I do, but that doesn't mean I can't see his faults and acknowledge them.'

'It's not like that – it mustn't be,' replied Ginnie, to whom loyalty and love were inseparable. 'I don't like to hear you talking about him like this. It's disloyal.'

'He's disloyal to you.'

Ginnie put up her hand like a traffic policeman to ward off words she did not want to hear. 'I'd rather you didn't speak of your father in this way, Tessa.'

'Suit yourself.' Tessa shrugged. 'You know, Mum, you don't look anywhere near forty-four. Not a bit. Looking like you do, you could do anything.'

'Thanks for the compliment, but I don't think I could aspire to be a nuclear physicist or a biochemist. You need a bit more than looks for that. And, in any case, why should I want to change anything?' She felt happy at her daughter's approval: it made the hard work involved in keeping up her appearance that bit more worthwhile.

'You know what I mean!' The exasperation was back again. 'You can't go on as you are – the good little wife forever sitting at home waiting for *him* to deign to turn up. You've got to do something with your life, Mum. You're only here once and you're letting everything slip by, hiding behind Dad.'

'I don't. I've many interests,' Ginnie said, a shade defensively.

'Aromatherapy, yoga, crystals – all that New Age stuff you get from Selina. But, Mum, have you ever stopped and asked yourself why these odd things interest you? I'll tell you. Because you hate your reality, you're disappointed with life, you're looking for a safe alternative. Well, you won't find it with a load of superannuated hippies, I can assure you.'

'You do talk tosh sometimes, Tessa. You really do. Yoga keeps me fit and I've always been interested in alternative medicines.'

'And alternative lifestyles.'

'But I can't see what's wrong in that.'

'Because rubbish like that will hold you back from *really* doing something with your life.' Tessa thumped the table. 'Find a career other than wife and mother. I'm away, so that only leaves the wife role – and Dad's not exactly falling over himself to thank you for that, is he? So do something else. Find the real you. Be yourself.'

'Only someone as young as you are could talk such stupid nonsense,' Ginnie said sharply. But Tessa, she had to conclude, knew more about the true state of Ginnie's marriage than she wanted her to. 'Of course, it's all right for you to be selfish and self-obsessed but it's not fine for me.' She began to twirl her glass, feeling agitation mounting in her.

'Don't go ballistic on me! I hate to see you not reach your potential, that's all. You're still young – well, comparatively. You look great for your age. Do something!'

Ginnie laughed, irritations and fears momentarily blotted out by Tessa's cack-handed compliments.

'Promise me something, Tessa? You'll never try for the diplomatic corps.'

Tessa frowned, then grinned and pushed back her long, dark hair with a gesture so like one of her father's.

'You know, you get all your looks from Dad. I often wonder if there's any of me in you,' Ginnie said wistfully.

Again Tessa banged the table with her fist. 'There you go again, putting yourself down! There's a lot of you in me, I'm happy to say, but I hope I haven't inherited your ability to martyr yourself!'

'Tessa, please!' That was horrible, she'd intended to add, but didn't have time.

'Tessa, please, what?' Carter asked from the doorway, his presence immediately filling the room.

'Thanks for bothering to show up,' Tessa said sharply. 'We've eaten.'

'We haven't, Carter. She's teasing you.' Ginnie felt her spirits lift at the sight of him.

'Oh, Mum!'

'Sorry I'm late. I got held up – I've been introduced to some Germans who might be interested in mounting an exhibition.'

'Carter, that's wonderful!' Ginnie exclaimed, as she poured him a drink.

'Oh yeah, when?' Tessa said, cynically.

'After our trip to New York – in the New Year.'

'So soon?' Ginnie knew exhibitions normally took months to set up. It wouldn't be possible to arrange one so quickly.

'About Christmas, Dad, count me out. I'm going to France with a group of mates.'

'Tessa, no!' Carter said, his happy mood dissipating immediately.

'Oh, darling!' said Ginnie, but she couldn't stop the glimmer of joy at the news that she'd have her husband all to herself.

2

'Dad, don't you agree? Mum should find something to occupy her.' Tessa laid down her knife and fork as she spoke, the better to concentrate on the topic.

'I'd have thought she's pretty well occupied already.'

'You know what I mean. She should have an interest.'

'She has an interest. Me.' Carter raised an eyebrow at his daughter as he helped himself to more potato dauphinoise.

'Don't be obtuse, Dad. She needs a hobby that'll keep her mind busy.'

'She has a hobby—'

'If you say you I'll throttle you.' Tessa giggled and threw her napkin at him.

'I wish you wouldn't discuss me as if I wasn't here. You'll be asking your father if I take sugar next. More peas anyone? More meat?' Ginnie poked at the remains of the Beef Wellington.

'I'm stuffed. That was lovely, Gin, my best birthday dinner ever. Thank you.'

'I thought the meat was a little on the dry side.' Ginnie frowned.

'It was perfect.'

'You needn't pretend.'

'I'm not.'

'Now I wish I'd—'

'Mum, *please*, just for a minute will you listen to me and stop worrying about the food? It was a wonderful meal. You surpassed yourself. Now, can we stop dodging the issue – I'm serious. You should search for something to do or I think you'll have a breakdown.'

'I'll get the pudding – your favourite, Carter.' Ginnie smiled at him, happy for once – even if, as she was aware, it was a happiness helped along by the wine she'd drunk. She wasn't relaxed, but Ginnie was resigned to being one of those people who never were. She collected the plates on a tray and left the room.

'Aren't you worried about her, Dad?'

'Should I be?'

'Don't you see how tense she is? How obsessed she is with things – the food, the house?'

'That's your mother's way, she's always been the same. She likes things just so.'

'I know she's house-proud – hell, I had to live with it as a child.' Tessa snorted at the memory of her mother constantly tidying her things away or nagging her to do it. 'But she's getting worse. I sat in the kitchen when we were waiting for you to condescend to appear and I swear she cleaned those work surfaces at least three times. That's nutty behaviour. She'll be washing her hands every five minutes at this rate.'

'You do exaggerate, Tessa.' He poured more wine into their glasses. 'What do you think of this wine? It's a Château Cheval Blanc 1990. I picked up a couple of cases.'

'Dad, I honestly think you're the most egotistical, selfish person I've ever known,' she said.

'And I love you too, darling.' He blew her a kiss. 'Bloody good, isn't it?' He raised his glass.

'I wish you'd listen to me. Take me seriously for once.'

'Tessa, I do. Promise.' Playfully he put his hand on his heart. 'This time I think you're barking up the wrong tree. Your mother is very much as she's always been. You can't expect to change her just as you can't make me into a self-effacing saint. We're too old for any of that.'

'Do you love her?'

'What a question. Of course I do.'

'Then you've a funny way of showing it.'

'What's that mean?'

'She's always on her own. She's always waiting for you to show up. She devotes her life to you and you don't even seem to notice.'

'I notice.'

'When did you last take her out – I mean just the two of you?'

'She does all right.' He sounded short.

'When did you bring her flowers, a surprise present?' Tessa ploughed on choosing to ignore his tone.

'I gave her a huge bunch only the other day.' He looked smug. 'But in time you'll learn, young woman, that there's more to marriage than bouquets and prezzies.'

'I'm fully aware of that, but since you so rarely give her

flowers and hardly any companionship don't be surprised if one day she just ups and leaves you.'

At this Carter Mulholland laughed, a loud burst of noise, and held his side as if this was the funniest thing he'd ever heard. 'Hell will freeze first.'

'Then I hope she does, just to take that self-satisfied look off your face,' said Tessa, leaning across the table and hissing the words at him. 'Are you having an affair?' she asked abruptly.

Carter choked on his wine and flapped his napkin ineffectually at his face. 'If I was it's none of your business,' he finally managed. 'As it is, I'm not.'

'She thinks you are.'

'Really? With whom?'

'I don't know. She doesn't discuss it, but that's what she's thinking.'

'She hasn't said so, then?'

'No, but I'd lay money on it that's why she's so nervy and tense.'

'Tessa, Tessa. You must *not* go around saying such things. Stirring up trouble. You've too much imagination for the good of all of us. Where's your mother?' He looked round to the door and, as if on cue, it opened. Ginnie entered backwards carrying a large silver tray.

'Part of it collapsed,' she said mournfully. 'That's the trouble with using frozen fruit in Summer Pudding, there's too much liquid. I'm sorry.'

'It'll taste just as wonderful as always.' Carter smiled consolingly at her.

'Tessa, couldn't you have cleared the rest of the dishes?' Ginnie asked tetchily, placing her crumbling burden on the sideboard and beginning to collect them herself.

'Sorry. We were talking.' Tessa jumped up and began to help. Carter sat stolidly, watching them.

When they were finally seated with their pudding, Ginnie asked, 'So what were you talking about?'

'This and that,' said Carter.

'You,' said Tessa.

'Oh, Tessa! You weren't boring your father with your silly ideas?'

'That's it!' Tessa pushed back her chair abruptly as she stood up. 'I don't know why I sodding well bother!' She threw her napkin on the table. It landed in her bowl and the blood-red stain of the fruit juice quickly seeped into it. Ginnie was immediately on her feet fretting over the stain. 'Christ, you're turning into a bloody soap advert, Mum.' Tessa stalked across the room. At the door she turned to face her parents. 'Quite honestly I think you deserve each other,' she said, and before either could respond she was through the door and slammed it satisfactorily behind her.

'What has got into the girl? She's so ratty and rude.' Ginnie looked at the door with a puzzled expression.

'You can say that again! I never expected her to speak to me like that.' Carter was still reeling from the shock of finding his position as adored-daddy-who-could-do-no-wrong suddenly assailed. 'She asked me if I was having an affair. My own daughter, can you imagine?'

'She didn't? How dreadful!' Ginnie said calmly, but feeling sick with apprehension at what his reply might have been.

'Yes. She's got it into her head that you think I'm having an affair. You don't, do you?' he asked aggressively.

'What a silly idea!' Ginnie laughed nervously. She knew that this was the moment she should ask him the truth but, too afraid of his answer, she let the opportunity slip away.

'I thought she loved me.' He still sounded dazed.

'And so she does,' Ginnie hastily reassured him, but

was unable to prevent herself feeling glad that he also knew now just how unfriendly, aggressive and irritable Tessa could be when she wanted.

'If she carries on like this I'll be glad she's not coming to New York with us. It'll be pleasanter just you and me.'

At his words Ginnie's heart sang. 'It'll be different.'

'I do notice what you do for me, Gin. I do appreciate it. You're the best wife a man could wish for.'

'That's nice.' She smiled broadly.

'Tessa says I don't spend enough time with you but, hell, look at the time we've been married. We don't have to live in each other's pockets, do we?'

'Of course not,' she said, when she thought the complete opposite.

'We'd soon get bored with each other, wouldn't we?'

She managed not to reply to that by asking if he'd finished with his pudding and began again to clear the table.

'Do you feel more tense and anxious?'

'More than normal? No.' Ginnie congratulated herself on how light-hearted she sounded when she felt every nerve tightly coiled inside her. She longed for him to get up from the table and put his arms about her and tell her he loved her – something he never did. But instead he sat in his chair at the head of the table and asked her to fetch the brandy. Still, she told herself as she collected goblets and bottle from the drawing room, she should be happy and pleased with what he had said. She must stop herself constantly wanting more. And, in a way, Tessa had done her a favour: he was in the dining room thinking about their relationship, something he probably hadn't done in years. All in all, it had been a wonderful evening, and with Tessa in bed they could spend the rest of it alone.

'How many paintings do you need for the exhibition?' she asked, on returning with the brandy, determined to take an interest.

'Thirty. I've got twenty-five in the studio. I suppose it's one advantage to not selling them – at least I've got a stack when I need them. The rest we can have on loan from your personal collection.' His voice was bitter. Bitter at the rejections, the 'no sales' of the past.

'It's not your fault if people are stupid and blind and can't see what you do.' She put her hand on his shoulder. His came up to grasp hers, just as she'd planned.

'You're so loyal, Gin. I've been meaning to tell you – Oh, hell!' he said, as the telephone rang. He glanced at his watch.

'I'll get it.' She stepped towards the door.

'No, don't bother. It's for me. I was expecting a call about now.'

'Who from?'

'Anna Tylson.'

Ginnie felt the room rock, certain it hadn't been her imagination. 'Anna Tylson?' she queried inanely.

'Yes, she introduced me to the Germans. Anna's arranging the exhibition for me. Didn't I tell you?'

'No, you didn't,' she said, in a wavering voice, but he couldn't have heard because he was already out of the door heading for the phone. He was virtually running, she thought. 'He lied!' she said aloud to the empty room.

EXTRACT FROM THE
DIARY OF H.G. – THE MASTER

Such a busy few weeks. So many meetings. So much work to prepare. Once I never prepared anything. I just sat on my rug – that famous rug – and spoke. Those days are long gone.

He hasn't done anything untoward, and sometimes when I think logically I wonder why I have this fear, which makes my bowels feel they are made of water.

He is always polite – I can't even say he is too much so since one of the curses of my position is that everyone is always exquisitely courteous to me. Rudeness or lack of interest would stand out, not politeness. I have forgotten what it must feel like to be contradicted, not to be held in awe. What bliss it would be if someday someone would turn to me and say, 'H.G., you're a stupid old fart!' I laugh long and loud at this impossible dream.

It's very difficult to explain what is bothering me so. It's a feeling, as real to me as the wind on my face, that he despises me, that he wishes to harm me, to see me fail, to take over from me. He thinks me a fool. He is aware that there is far more money to be made from the movement than I am prepared to create.

Money, as is well known, is unimportant to me. Left to my own devices my needs are simple. Once I had met Miss Tarbart I had no need for it any more and my fascination with it, which had marked my early years, faded. As a child I had pursued money, hungered for it: its possession meant the difference between life and death. But once under her care, my belly was full, my thirst quenched, I had clean, decent clothes and a roof over my head. My love of money died and I have never given it another thought – until now.

But to return to my confession of the untruths.

Once I had allowed the lies to begin on that beach, so many years ago, I did not know how to set things straight. I was motivated by a fear that if the truth came out I would not be wanted and I would be cast out. So I remained silent.

When manhood came and, with it, the wisdom I had not expected, I was weak and I allowed the falsehoods to stand. Weakness, yes, but there was another reason. Over the years so much had been expected of me and I did not want to disappoint – so many wanted to believe in me and my philosophy that it would have been cruel for some if I had spoken out.

One of my favourite maxims has always been 'The Power of Silence'. Little did my followers know how literally I believed in that.

Haré Gan, of course, was not my real name. You know how the mistake over Haré came about. Gan was my nickname, short for Ganish, god of the elephants, creatures I loved. I shall reveal now, for the very first time, I am – Harry Peter Vicente! As you are aware I am known around the world as H.G.

I never told Miss Tarbart any of this. Until the day she died I was Haré Gan, or just Gan or H.G. Nor did I ever explain to her my ability to speak in several tongues, which, for her, was the most significant fact about me. Was I wrong to deceive her?

The explanation is simple. My English mother had eloped with my Italian father, who was her singing teacher. I was born in Paris, where I spent my early years, and there, since my father adored the works of Wagner, I learnt German from a fraülein he employed. By the age of four I was prattling in four languages. The explanation is prosaic but, then, the unembellished truth often is.

In India, my mother died of cholera. Memory can be a blessed thing, for I have no remembrance of her suffering or of her death. All I can recall is her sweetness, the beauty of her dear face, the loveliness of her mellow voice and her smell – lily-of-the-valley. Such an intense memory, this, that I can never smell that flower without feeling I could put out my hand and touch her.

I remember my father's grief. As a child of six, I saw my tall, powerful, adored father grow old in an hour. Within days he was like a husk from which the fruit has gone. I had lost him. He looked at me but through me, as if I no longer existed. I sensed he longed to die, to join her. I have never since felt such loneliness and isolation as I did then.

The German consul, alerted by my fraülein, contacted his British counterpart to say that a child of an English mother was being neglected. The consul arrived at our house, more out of duty than compassion, and was shown into my father's study. From my position, on the bottom step of the verandah, I listened as their greeting became a discussion which rapidly degenerated into an all-out row.

A short time later the door burst open and the man emerged, looking red and blustery and most certainly put out.

'Infernal cheek,' he muttered to himself as he set his clothing straighter. At which point he saw me. He stood over me, quivering with indignation.

'Remember, boy, you're a Woolston of Porthwood.'

'Yes, sir,' I said meekly, not understanding what he meant. He went off in a huff of dust, and I wandered off to find my father who, for once, was not crying. 'What is a Woolston of Porthwood?' I asked, and immediately wished I hadn't.

'Never say that name again – ever!' he screamed. He tore from the room and things began to crash and smash wherever he moved, and I was frightened. But, of course, his reaction ensured that I never forgot that name.

That night we packed, and in such a hurry that my few books, my toys and, worst of all, my pet dog were left behind. At last I began to understand how my father felt for I wept and screamed for that little animal just as he did for the return of my mother.

I think he feared that people would take me from him – that was what he implied. Maybe the mysterious Woolstons of Porthwood. But no one came and we left for Ceylon. I don't know why he went there, or for what he was searching. He no longer spoke much to me ...

It is time for the meeting and duty calls.

chapter **three**

1

If the telephone had rung two minutes sooner Selina and Geoff would still have been, as he put it, 'on the job'. It was a phrase she hated. They were lying side by side and had just lit their 'post-coital' cigarettes – another of his expressions that put her on edge.

'Hello, Ginnie,' Selina said sleepily.

'How on earth did you know it was me?'

'Because at this time of night it's invariably you. Joke!' she added, knowing how sensitive Ginnie could be. 'What's the problem?'

'Why should there be a problem? No, I just called for a natter.'

Selina blew out a column of smoke.

'Selina! You're smoking again! Oh, I *am* disappointed in you.' And Ginnie grabbed at the excuse to lecture her friend about smoking, rather than talking about what was really bothering her.

Eventually Selina hung up. Geoff put aside the book he'd been reading and looked at her expectantly. 'What did she want?' he asked, in the tone of one who did not like the person of whom he spoke.

'I don't know. Something's bothering her, but she never lets on.'

'Married to that scumbag Carter Mulholland then, of course, she's got problems. Nothing in a skirt's safe when he's around.'

'I've not heard any of that and Ginnie's never said anything.' She wished he'd drop it, gossip bored her.

'Perhaps she's that rare type of woman who doesn't need to blab,' he said, his voice drenched in venom from some experience in the past – Selina didn't know what. 'You don't seem very interested.'

'Ginnie's my friend, not him. He's someone who's always been around, that's all.'

'Stuck-up bunch,' Geoff said unpleasantly.

'Ginnie isn't stuck-up. Despite her money her feet have stayed firmly on the ground.' She lit another cigarette to cover a flash of irritation.

'Do you know what pisses me off? I can't stand the way women automatically allow a wife to claim what's rightly the husband's even in speech.' Geoff had recently been divorced and had come away from the experience reeling from the discovery of what had been hers when he'd fully believed it to have been his.

'That's where you're wrong.' She hated herself for feeling so smug at being able to correct him. She pushed the tangle of curls back from her face. 'It's all hers,' she said.

'You're joking! Everyone thinks it's Mulholland money.'

'Just shows you how sweet Ginnie is.' There it was again, that reprehensible smugness.

'You're not having me on? It really is hers?' He sat up, his face alight with the eager anticipation of the born gossip.

Selina knew she shouldn't be discussing Ginnie's business but for some time she had thought it grossly unfair the way Carter flaunted a wealth that wasn't his.

'Both their fathers died around the same time. People assumed it was Mr Mulholland who'd left them a fortune when it was Steve Brown.'

'What, the greengrocer? Had that shop at the bottom of North Street? Nice old boy, I remember him.'

'That's right, but he had a hobby – stocks and shares.

For forty odd years he'd been quietly dealing away, amassing an absolute fortune. He left enough to buy a flat in town for his wife, with a hefty annuity for life. Everything else went to Ginnie.'

'Then why ... ?'

'Because Ginnie loves Carter. He would hate people to know he lived off her, so she lets people think it was Mulholland money that bought the house, paid for the BMW and all the bits and bobs. She told me in confidence so don't repeat it, will you?'

'Well, she's a fool.'

'Maybe, but a nice one. Fancy a cup of tea?' she asked, regretting that she'd broken her promise to Ginnie. No doubt Geoff would repeat it to everyone. Still, she thought, as she slipped over her shoulders the antique tasselled shawl she used as a dressing gown, part of her wanted everyone to know.

'Nah. I've got a heavy day tomorrow.'

'I think I will. I'll try not to wake you when I come back.'

'You can wake me anytime.' He leered at her as he stubbed out his cigarette.

Her cat was not amused at being woken by the kitchen light going on. The Siamese peered cross-eyed and angrily at her from his basket in the corner of the room and made a deep-throated mutter. As she bent down to pet him he lashed out at her with sharp claws and then spat at her for good measure.

'You're *such* a foul-tempered creature, I don't know why I bother with you.' Selina sucked at the scratch on her hand. Like I don't know why I bother with so many things, she thought, as she made her tea. Then, carrying the mug and an unopened packet of McVitie's digestives, she flicked off the kitchen light and went into the small sitting room.

She looked about the untidy room with an expression

of distaste. The foil cartons of the Chinese take-away littered the coffee table. Newspapers and magazines lay where they'd been dropped. Cushions were on the floor rather than on the sofa and the fireplace looked a mess, as grates do when the fire is out. The mirror was askew and over all was the pervading smell of stale smoke. The room was too small for two people to pollute – one was bad enough.

'God, what a mess!' she said aloud. She hadn't always lived in this hateful muddle: when she'd a husband to worry about people marvelled at her ability to organise work, large home, demanding husband and self. In this small place it should have been easier, but somehow it wasn't. The house needed a clear-out from attic to cellar. At least she didn't have a garden.

The shop, in contrast, was immaculate. She never stopped work until everything there was ordered and shipshape. Looking after it, keeping it efficient and inviting, had never palled. These days, though, she always felt too tired to be bothered with the living part. She sat at the desk and pushed back some papers to make way for her mug and biscuits. Where to start?

Everything needed an overhaul. What, for a start, was she doing with Geoff?

Since her marriage break-up, six years ago, she'd had several boyfriends, but only three relationships she could call serious. She had begun each affair with such high hopes, with the conviction that this was *it*, and that true happiness stretched ahead.

Some happiness!

The problem, she knew now, was that when she met a fellow she fancied, sense and observation flew out of the window.

Tim had been a cannabis-smoking drop-out, a dreamer who talked of the book he would write while never being seen with a pen in hand. He was as handsome as any film star and she gloried in his looks, until the day she realised he did too.

Mark was a muscular commodity broker, with a fast car, a penchant for expensive wine and Jack Daniel's, and a lust to be rich at the expense of everyone else, which included her.

Geoff, in the book trade, had appeared the ideal companion. Both divorced and wary of marriage, he and Selina suited each other. He liked evenings at home with a simple meal and had no dreams of artistic fortune. He worked as a rep for a large London publishing house. His job took him away several nights a week, which gave them space in their relationship and something fresh to talk about. They had books in common and the world of writing and publishing to share. That's what she had thought but it hadn't turned out like that. 'I sell books, I don't have to read them,' he'd announced one day and she'd laughed, thinking it a joke rather than a warning.

Now the truth stared her in the face. They had nothing in common. How long would it be before the irritations that bothered her became full-blown rows? She hated scenes and she didn't relish the prospect of being alone again.

She sighed, drank the last of her tea and pushed away the bookwork, which she'd had some vague idea of tackling. She'd do it tomorrow. Meanwhile he was probably asleep now and it would be safe to go back to bed.

Her head jerked up. What a thing to think! It said it all, really.

2

The following Sunday, with Geoff away visiting his children, Selina was free to concentrate on the long-promised tidy of her flat.

Now, late in the evening, she looked about her at the spotless, tidy room with a glow of satisfaction at a job well done. The whole place smelt of furniture polish, loo cleaner, bleach and cleanliness. She must not let it slide into chaos again.

Carrying a tuna sandwich and a glass of white wine, she approached her desk, determined to round off the weekend with the bookwork as neat and tidy as her house.

She loathed doing her accounts, especially when after an hour it was apparent that nothing would balance. The best solution was to pack it all in a carrier bag and let Andy, her accountant, do it for her. That was a grandiose way to describe the lanky youth who did her books. Since she could not afford a proper accountant she used this moonlighting accounts clerk instead. But now she'd reached the point where she couldn't afford Andy either.

She was missing eight hundred and thirty pounds and fifty-six pence. An invoice had to be missing. She lit another cigarette – she'd been doing well, not smoking, until the last few weeks when, insidiously at first, the thought that had lurked for several months at the back of her head wormed its way to the front. She was going bust.

It was all right for Ginnie to lecture her on smoking, but Ginnie did not understand about the pressures of everyday life. Why, that eight hundred pounds odd wouldn't be enough to buy one of Ginnie's jackets.

'Now, now, Selina. Stop thinking that way – it's no help!' she said aloud and firmly. Her cat, attracted by the uneaten tuna sandwich, silently entered the room. He leapt up onto the desk and wound his body around Selina's arm, purring now as if apologizing for all the times he was bad-tempered. She nuzzled her head against his side and felt herself calming down.

It was odd that she should suddenly think about Ginnie and her money, which wasn't something that normally preoccupied her. It wasn't Ginnie's fault that she was rich and Selina was broke. And Ginnie was so generous – this cat was an example of that. One day Selina had said how much she loved Siamese cats and the next day Sabbie had entered her life in a fabulous cat basket tied with tartan bows and accompanied by a box containing everything a spoiled cat would ever need.

Ginnie's love of giving presents was endearing. In fact, sometimes she tried to give too much so that Selina had finally learnt never to say she liked something for fear that Ginnie would rush out and buy it for her.

If Ginnie knew of her current problems, she would immediately produce her cheque book and the problem would be solved.

Except that it wouldn't.

Remove this problem and how long before bankruptcy loomed again? Soon after taking on the shop she had realised that it was going to be hard to make a success of it. In a recession, books, for most people, became inessential so she'd diversified, slowly at first, into cards and wrappings, products that, made of paper, were related to books. She'd always had a strong selection on alternative lifestyles – health and food – and soon she was adding volumes on alternative cultures and religions, followed by others on the occult, crystallography, meditation, anything to do with New Age thinking. The aromatherapy craze had been a godsend and the oils and burners had been the next logical step. She could not remember when the ouija boards, crystal balls, healing crystals, tarot cards and amulets had crept in, but gradually there had been less and less room for the mainstream books which, until then, had been her mainstay. She had become neither one thing nor the other – neither fully a bookshop, nor yet a New Age specialist.

Through this diversification, however, she'd met some interesting people. Unlike anyone she already knew, they had different interests, attitudes, a freedom in their lives and thinking, which was what she wanted.

'Load of layabouts!' Chris, her husband, had dismissed them when, one evening at the tail-end of their marriage, she'd held a meeting of the Light People at their home.

'You don't know them.'

'No, thank God, and I don't want to. I heard enough of their gobbledegook. You'll ruin a good business. This is the only independent bookshop for miles around. You're a bloody fool, Selina.'

Now it was easier to see that his vehemence had not just been about the change in direction she'd taken in business, or even the new friends she'd made. Rather, it had been symptomatic of a marriage that was souring and should never have been. At ten years older, he had been too old and, as a solicitor, too staid. In her early twenties when they married, Selina had rapidly felt middle-aged. He approved of the bookshop but never read the books.

After six years Selina gave up the BMW, the detached house with paddock, the colour-coordinated décor and her charge-cards, and moved into the flat over the shop, complete with secondhand furniture. She'd refused anything from her past, reasoning that Chris had bought it and Chris should keep it. Quite the little paragon, she'd been, even if there were times now when she regretted her magnanimity.

No one from her old life understood why she had run out on Chris, least of all her parents. United, they had

43

taken his side and had never spoken to her again. Now they were both dead.

Four years she'd been on her own now, two as a divorced woman. The shop had been hers for six. Odd, that, her marriage had ended after six years and now, also after six years, she knew she was facing the end of the shop too. Six months with Tim and Mark, and now Geoff.

Six months! There it was again. The ominous six, which seemed to haunt her life. There was a book on numerology in the shop, she'd have to check it out.

It would be more normal, she thought, if she was upset at the prospect of yet another failure but she was not sure what she felt. Uppermost, though, was relief that she was finally facing the truth. An anticipation of freedom. The only blot was that if she finished with Geoff she must shelve any idea of having a child – until she could find another potential father.

She sipped her drink staring into space, unaware that Sabbie had removed the top slice of bread and was tucking into the tuna.

It was on her last birthday, her thirty-fourth, that she'd become conscious of time passing and her biological clock ticking in a way that hadn't bothered her before. She'd not told Geoff she wanted a baby – she'd known what his reaction would be, stark horror and a bolt for the hills ...

She suddenly sat upright and rested her glass on the table. Now *there* was a thought. Could it be possible that, subconsciously, she'd chosen Geoff because, knowing he didn't want to be a father again, she knew she stood a good chance of him leaving her alone with her child so that she wouldn't have to share it with him? Such an idea jolted the very roots of her upbringing. That was not the way it should be: people married, children must have two parents.

'Still, some chance,' she said aloud to Sabbie. Over the last six months she'd failed to take the pill so many times – whether by accident or design she preferred not to contemplate. Then she sat bolt upright. For six months she'd hoped to become pregnant and nothing had happened. Maybe with him it wouldn't. That was why she felt so edgy. Her biological clock was telling her to move on.

It was an almost pagan feeling inside her. In a way the decision to finish with him had been taken out of her hands. All she had to worry about now was whether to dump him before or after Christmas. She thought she preferred before.

'Yes, Selina, you're a cold fish,' she told herself, as she gave up on her book-keeping and pushed away the papers.

3

Ginnie sat at the table in her mother-in-law's house and, not for the first time, felt isolated and knew how the poor relation in a Victorian household must have felt. Tolerated.

The conversation swirled around the table, but Ginnie did not join in. Invariably when she put forward a view her mother-in-law would look coldly at her and through her, as if she and her opinions did not exist.

Tonight was different, though: tonight she was seething with so much anger she doubted that she could have spoken even if she had wanted to.

'Pudding, Ginnie? Ginnie, are you dreaming? Pudding?' Joan Mulholland sighed with annoyance.

'Oh, no, thank you,' Ginnie replied, startled out of her

thoughts. 'I'll get the cake,' she mumbled, and went out to the kitchen.

While the others ate their chocolate mousse, Ginnie carefully removed the birthday cake she had made from its box. She put it on the silver cake-stand and began to put the candles into their holders. Suddenly she remembered another time and another cake and her father lighting the candles for her so that she did not burn her fingers and experienced an almost physical longing for him.

'Oh, Dad. I wish you were here,' she whispered. With Steve Brown in the world she had always felt safe – and loved. Since the day he had died, ten years ago, there had been an emptiness in her life which she now knew would never be filled. God, what she wouldn't give just to feel her father's arms about her, the rumble of his voice as she pressed her ear to his chest and heard the strong thump of his heart – his treacherous heart.

'It'll be all right, you wait and see.' He would have kissed the top of her head, and the pain would have gone away, just as if she had had a bump or a graze. Somehow he'd have made everything better.

She folded up the cake-box neatly. Thinking like this was getting her nowhere. Dad was dead, she was on her own and, as her own mother frequently delighted in saying, she'd made her bed and now she must lie in it.

Not tonight! Tonight this family had gone too far. She had nearly dropped her glass of spritzer when the door had opened and the last guest for the birthday dinner had walked in. Anna Tylson.

From then on the evening had been a nightmare. Ginnie had sat silent among the chattering while inside her was a screaming vortex. She smiled while wanting to cry. She listened attentively while hearing nothing. And the panic began to turn to anger as a brick of humiliation was added to a brick of despair, jealousy and betrayal placed on top and the whole lot cemented together. The fury inside her felt like a physical burden.

His mother, she decided, knew about Carter and Anna, as she was sure everyone in their circle did. She'd seen the sly glances assessing her reaction when Anna had marched in. Was she last on purpose so that everyone was there and so that no one missed out on Ginnie's shocked expression?

Why should they hate her so? The question had rattled through her head all evening. Well, she wasn't going to make a scene – if that's what they wanted then they were in for a disappointment. She had her pride and she clung to it, all through dinner, resisting the ocean of self-pity and frustration into which she could so easily slip.

Looking at Anna across the table the endless questioning *why* mounted to a crescendo. Anna was overweight – a good size sixteen, Ginnie was sure. She had wrinkles, her make-up was anchored in the sixties of her youth and her hair was long and tangled, unsuitable on such a matronly soul. If Carter fancied that then Ginnie had wasted her time bothering with her appearance over the years. All those creams she'd used, the careful monitoring of her food and drink, the hours of massage, all the exercising to keep herself firm – she could have done whatever she wanted instead of the self-control she had forced upon herself – for him!

Anna was intelligent, though, she had to concede that. She was a good talker, funny too – Ginnie had laughed with everyone else at a couple of her stories, even though she wished she could have sat stony-faced. And Anna was nice to her, which made matters worse …

Ginnie glanced at her watch. Nine thirty, just the cake-cutting and a glass of champagne to go. With luck, they should be away by ten – quarter past at the latest.

Carrying the cake, she pushed open the swing door with her bottom and entered the dining room.

47

'We're all getting a bit long in the tooth – we welcome younger blood, my dear,' her mother-in-law was saying.

'Do we bring our own flowers or does the Cathedral supply them?' Anna asked.

'No, we contribute our own from our gardens, but most of us cheat now and then and go to the florist's.' Joan laughed gaily, her false social laugh, tightly controlled, not a laugh at all, really.

'I shall look forward to it. Wednesdays, you said—'

'How could you?' Ginnie asked. She stood in the doorway, clutching the cake with its lighted candles, her face as white as the icing she'd laboured over so long.

'Are you speaking to me, Ginnie?' Joan smiled up at her. 'Oh, my, what a lovely cake! You're so good with cakes, so clever with the icing,' she trilled.

'Like a bloody cook! I'm not your sodding cook!'

'Well, really!' Joan fluttered her hand uncertainly in front of her. 'How dare you—'

'I'll dare whatever I want. And as for this – cake – I – hell!' And with all her strength, words having failed her, Ginnie hurled it, candles spluttering, across the space between her and the table. It crashed and smashed on the highly polished surface, sending glasses, flowers and bottles of wine flying.

'Well! Really! Well!' Joan's vocabulary seemed to have deserted her.

'Ginnie! What the hell's got into you?' Carter was on his feet.

The other guests divided into two camps, those who found the scene embarrassing and acquired a sudden interest in their hands and those who found it inordinately funny and failed to control their sniggers. Anna fitted neither group but sat transfixed, her mouth slightly agape, one hand palm up, as if warding off the cake – And her teeth are all fillings, thought Ginnie, as, unsure now what to do, she swung round on her heels, grabbed her handbag from the hall table and, forgetting her coat, thundered out into the cold night.

She opened the car door and delved in her bag for the keys, which she knew she had since it was always she who drove home so that Carter could drink. She had just put the key into the ignition when the passenger door opened and Carter climbed in.

'What was all that in aid of?' he asked angrily.

'Get out!' she yelled.

'Don't be stupid.' He strapped on his seat-belt.

'I don't want you in this car.' She swung round in the seat and glared at him, but had to look away from the anger on his face.

'Don't be so bloody stupid. Now drive.'

'No. I want you out!'

'Well, I'm not getting out so I suggest you get a move on before I physically remove you and drive myself.'

'Oh, sod you. Suit yourself.' Furiously she switched on the engine.

'Charming! I didn't even know you knew such words. Watch out!' he yelled, as she swung the wheel and the heavy car narrowly missed the Rector's Twingo. 'I repeat, what the hell was all that about?'

'You damn well know,' she snapped.

'I *don't* know. One minute all's well and the next you're hurling cakes about the room.'

Ginnie drove on, clutching the steering wheel so tightly that her knuckles showed white. She was determined not to speak until she was in better control of herself. She didn't want to descend into a screaming row with her doing most of the screaming. Even now, clear of the city and two miles down the road, she was beginning to have a sneaking idea she would regret the cake.

'Are you going to explain that disgusting ill-mannered display? Or are you going to continue to sulk?'

'I don't wish to discuss it,' Ginnie said, through almost clenched teeth.

'I bet you don't, but I fear, my dear, you're going to have to. You don't think my mother isn't going to want an explanation. And the Rector and his wife, and the doctor and Ted and Jean ...' His voice droned on and on as they drove towards their house. He was questioning, astonished, angry, surprised, critical, curious, all in turn. She tried not to listen. Wanted to shut his voice out. Strange that she'd always loved his voice, loved listening to him. She could not recall ever having wanted before to shout, 'Shut up!'

'Aren't you going too fast?'

'No.'

'I think you are. Slow down.'

'Slow down yourself,' she said childishly, and pressed her foot down further on the accelerator. Maybe they'd crash and then everything would be resolved.

'Shit! Ginnie, for Christ's sake!' he shouted, as she swung the car to the left to avoid a motorcyclist who had hurtled round the bend in the narrow road, dangerous enough in daylight let alone now. She felt as though a bucket of cold water had been thrown over her. *She* didn't want to die, and she was horrified at the prospect of killing Carter. She wanted this resolved, wanted to wake up from this nightmare and find it all gone away.

She drove sedately now, until the turning into their own drive and the safety of her home. She dived from the car leaving the door open and hurtled into the house as if being chased by demons.

'So, are you going to explain yourself? I think I'm owed that, don't you?' Carter asked calmly as, five minutes later, he poured large brandies for them.

'I'd have thought you were the last person who'd need to be told. You've engineered the situation.'

'And what situation's that, Ginnie, my darling?' He

smiled his half-crooked smile at her, the one that always made her go funny at the knees. Not tonight, though.

'I don't want to be patronised. I want an explanation. Why did you invite that woman tonight?'

'What woman?' he asked, all innocence.

'You know damn well. Anna Tylson.'

'I didn't invite her. My mother did. Though why that should upset you so much—'

'Oh, come off it, Carter. I'm not a fool. I know. I don't know why you pretend with me.'

'Pretend what?'

Her temper was beginning to simmer again. 'Please, Carter. I don't want to play games. You know full well that I object to sitting at dinner with your mistress. And what I really want to know is, is your mother in on the conspiracy? Was this evening planned? Was I supposed to overhear her inviting Anna to help with the Cathedral flowers? God, that hurt, the flower rota of all things!' She fought her tears.

Carter spluttered into his glass, then turned his head so that she couldn't see his face. His shoulders began to shake and then, despite all his efforts, the laughter rocketed out of him and tears were rolling down his cheeks and he was speaking, but she couldn't hear what he was saying through the spluttering. She waited, stony-faced, for him to control himself.

'The flower rota ... I can't believe it. The flower rota!' she eventually heard.

'You don't understand anything, do you, Carter? Nothing.'

'I don't understand the fl—'

'Don't say it. Don't!' she shrieked, and hurled her glass into the grate.

'For God's sake, stop this hysteria, Ginnie!'

'How can I? How? When you treat me so. After all I've done for you and your family.'

'Ah,' he said, sitting down. 'I wondered when it would come to this. I always presumed you'd helped me because you love me,' he said smoothly.

'But your mother – when they lost all that money at Lloyds—'

'No one *asked* for your assistance, Ginnie, you *volunteered* it – so don't give me that crap.'

'I was happy to help!'

'Then if you were why don't you do me a favour and shut up?'

'But to invite that woman.'

'Anna is an old family friend who is helping me with my career – which is more than can ever be said of you. You don't even know if a fucking canvas is the right way up or not.'

'That's not fair, no one did. I checked. When I hanged it the wrong way I'd asked other people.'

'Hanged it? Hung it, Ginnie. Won't you ever learn?'

'Hanged, serviette, lounge, settee!' She was screaming the words he was always correcting, jumping up and down as she did so, knowing she was making a spectacle of herself but seemingly unable to stop.

'Ginnie, get a hold of yourself. You'd best get used to the idea. You know damn well that Anna is arranging my show in Munich in the New Year. We're flying out next week to finalise the arrangements. Understood?' he asked coldly.

'No! Please, no!' she shrieked.

'Quite honestly, Ginnie, I think you need a sedative – Valium or something. Or is it your age?'

With one sweep of her arm she knocked the half-dozen silver picture frames and enamel pill boxes on a side table crashing to the floor.

'My, my, we *are* in a throwing tantrum tonight, aren't we?' He stood up and walked to the door.

'If you go to Munich, Carter, you needn't come back.'

'Oh, Ginnie, stop playing silly arses.'

'I mean it, Carter. I really mean it!' But already she was talking to the closed door and she had no idea if he'd heard her.

EXTRACT FROM THE
DIARY OF H.G. – THE MASTER

I've not got very far with my diary of confessions, have I? But I've been travelling. After the recent large meeting here – over two thousand followers came, I'm proud to say – I went to Canada, then to California and, finally, home here to my beloved Cornwall.

I always enjoy my trips to California. I don't think I've ever lost my awe of the United States for, don't forget, when I was young, it was every man's dream to sail to that great country and become rich and famous. But in California the people, with their often strange ideas, always make me feel that anything is possible, that anything can be believed in. Which, in a nutshell, is what I've been advocating all along.

So, where did I get to? I've confessed to my name, that I'm not from the East, that I'm not who I'm supposed to be. Or have I?

After we left Bombay my father and I arrived in Ceylon.

I've never forgotten Ceylon – or Sri Lanka as I must try to remember to call it. For years I had a dream that I would retire there one day to a fine villa by the sea, close to the elephants. But teachers such as I don't retire, I've learnt that, we're expected to die in harness. Since I've had such a spectacularly comfortable life, it is a small price to pay.

The principle by which I've always stood is that all of us here at Fohpal are equal and each of us has an equal right to say what he thinks and wants. A true democracy. Would that it were. With myself revered as I am, a true democracy is out of the question. It's sad, and something I never intended.

I'm wandering again, but there's so much I want known – not only the record to be set straight but I'd so like everyone to know how I felt, how I saw through so many things, how I was just an ordinary man caught up in extraordinary circumstances.

My father calmed down in Ceylon. He began to plan again, to look to our future.

One day, to escape the heat of Colombo, we set out in an old Austin Seven intending to spend the next few months in the cool of the mountains in Kolbi. We sang as the small car rattled along the rutted road.

We'd been driving some time when the Austin stalled and smoke billowed out from beneath the bonnet. My father sent me to get water for the overheated radiator. I ran towards the trees, turned once to wave, dived into the undergrowth in search of a stream.

When I returned ten minutes later the car, the cases and my father had gone.

I waited. Of course I did. I presumed he was testing the engine and would return for me. I sat by the side of the road until night fell.

I was frightened. Seriously so, as the night filled with the sounds of barbaric nature, which echoed through the valley. I was cold too – all I had on were my cotton shorts and shirt. And I was bitten throughout the night by insects.

As dawn rose I used the water to bathe my swollen face and legs and set out to find my father. I'd walked only ten minutes when I saw him. I ran up to him crying, 'Papa! Papa!' relief flooding through me. He was asleep on his back. As I approached I disturbed the swarm of flies clustered about his neck, and they rose in a black, buzzing cloud. Then I saw that crawling things were feasting on the red slash in his neck ...

chapter **four**

1

'Hasn't your friend anyone else to phone?' Geoff asked, as soon as Selina replaced the receiver and sat down at the table where they were finishing their usual hasty breakfast.

'She's only called twice in the past two weeks. That's hardly a bother.' Selina did not smile: for one thing it was too early in the morning but also Ginnie had been unusually short with her and had hung up rather abruptly.

'The first time we were in bed and this time barely up. I call that inconsiderate. What did she want?'

'She cancelled lunch today, but—'

'Did you wash my blue striped shirt?'

'No, I haven't had time.'

'I asked in particular for that shirt. You never have time, these days.'

'Then you should have washed it yourself.' Dear God, she thought, they sounded like a carping married couple. This could not continue. They seemed to have a spat every morning. Still, morning was never his best time of day, or hers.

'You look deep in thought,' he said, more pleasantly now as if aware that he was being unreasonable.

'I was wondering if us both hating the mornings was a good or bad sign.'

'Good, undoubtedly.' He grinned at her, leant over and kissed her cheek and she let him stroke her hair as if she wanted him to, then immediately felt guilty at her weakness in not saying what she thought.

'Since she can't make today, Ginnie has invited us both to lunch next Sunday,' she said, suddenly wanting to make amends and puzzled by the dizzying swings of her mood and feelings towards him.

'Can't make it. I'm seeing the kids.' He picked up his newspaper and shook it open.

'But you looked after them last weekend.'

'Em's going away and I never mind stepping into the breach,' he replied. She wondered why he was not looking at her as he spoke.

'We could have them here and take them with us. Ginnie wouldn't mind – she likes children.'

'They're happier in their own environment.'

'They're nine and ten, Geoff, hardly toddlers who'd be disrupted.' She spoke with exaggerated slowness.

'Em wouldn't like it.'

'Why?'

'She doesn't think they should see me with—' He stopped abruptly.

'Your mistress? Is that what you were going to say? Is that how the sainted Emma regards me?'

'What else am I to call you?' He sounded defensive.

'I don't mind partner, companion, lover. I'm not too keen on girlfriend. But *mistress*, never!'

He laughed at this. 'Can't see the difference myself.'

'There's a huge difference. Being a mistress implies a kept woman – and that's one thing I'm not.' She began to stack their cereal bowls noisily.

'I think you're being over-sensitive.'

'Do you? Well, I don't. I resent I'm not considered good enough for your kids to be with.'

'I can't help what Em thinks.'

'What if I got pregnant? What then? Would Em stop your kids coming to meet their sibling?' What a daft question, she thought, but it was out now and she realised she was waiting with an almost morbid curiosity for his answer.

'You wouldn't get pregnant. For a start, you're far too sensible. And if by chance you were then I'd pay for half the abortion – so Em wouldn't be involved, would she?' He looked at her now, a hardness in his eyes she hadn't seen before.

'At least that tells me where I stand.' She sounded composed but she was seething inside, which was odd when she had not been surprised by what he had said.

'That's about it.' He was standing now, folding his newspaper so calmly that she wanted to scream.

'I think it would be better if you moved out, Geoff.' There, she had said it.

'I'd agree on that.'

'Fine, then.' She stood up, carried their dishes to the sink and wished he'd leave now instead of fiddling about with his papers. And yet why did she feel so miserable and empty inside?

Fortunately, after this conversation, Geoff had been in London for two days at a sales conference and there had been no further confrontation. Now that, at last, everything was out in the open, the last thing she wanted was endless analysis or arguments. While he was gone Selina had wondered if she should pack for him, but had finally rejected the idea. She would hate anyone to do that for her – it would be too intrusive somehow. He hadn't returned on the Friday evening but had shown up mid-morning on the Saturday while she was busy in the shop. The first day of her closing-down sale – another decision made.

'I'll get my stuff,' he said, as he passed through, not even pausing to ask if she had meant what she said. And that was that. He'd loaded his car before closing time.

'Where are you going?' she asked, feeling a degree of responsibility.

'My brother's, probably.'

'I'm sorry, Geoff.'

'Nothing to be sorry about. We ran our course, that's all. It was fun while it lasted.' He stepped aside for a customer. 'Good luck with the sale.' He waved and was gone.

2

Selina parked her car on the semi-circular driveway in front of Ginnie's pseudo-Georgian house, rang the doorbell and waited, gazing at the expanse of lawn in front of the house. The flower beds looked bare and forlorn in the winter drizzle. As no one answered, she rang the bell again, a long press for good measure, and was rewarded by the sound of bolts being drawn back. The door opened an inch and Ginnie peered out.

'Selina! I forgot you were coming. Could you come another day?' she said, in a thick, mumbling voice.

'What's the matter?' Selina asked, taken aback by her friend's honesty.

'Next Sunday, perhaps?' She began to shut the door.

'No, Ginnie. I can't. What's up?' And, putting all thought of manners aside, she pushed at the door, which Ginnie resisted.

Selina put her shoulder to the door and, this time with one foot in the hall, she won the undignified tussle and went in. 'Oh, my poor old love, what's happened?'

Ginnie was in her dressing gown, her normally immaculate hair dishevelled and unbrushed. She stood, arms hanging limply at her side, head bowed, a picture of defeat. She didn't answer but stood crying silently, the tears rolling down dried stains made by earlier ones. Selina put her arms round her and felt as if she was holding a wooden board, for Ginnie's body was rigid and the mute weeping was more heartrending than any howling could have been.

'Come on, sweetie. Let's go and sort this out.' She led her friend across the marble-tiled floor to the kitchen. The antique pine table was cluttered with unwashed dishes – this, if she'd needed one, was a true sign that things were bad, for Ginnie's kitchen was always pristine, the sort of kitchen other people dreamt of and never achieved.

'Tea? Coffee?'

'Nothing, thanks.' Ginnie dabbed at her eyes with a sodden tissue and suddenly laughed – it was quite small, but it was a laugh nonetheless.

'What's funny?'

'Isn't it odd that whenever something goes wrong we immediately shove things in our mouths as if that can make things better?' By the end of the sentence her voice was bitter and the tissue in shreds.

Selina picked up a roll of kitchen paper and plonked it in front of her. 'If you don't mind, I'd like a drink – if you'll tell me where it is. Fridge? White? Just a soupçon?' She was pulling faces as she spoke, not sure why but not knowing what else to do.

'There's some Chardonnay chilling – or champagne if you want.'

'Chardonnay's fine. Champagne always gives me indigestion.'

'It's the bubbles. You should swizzle them away.'

'Really? That's interesting. I'll remember that,' said Selina, knowing that they were making conversation to delay facing the problem. She collected two glasses and a corkscrew, took the wine out of the fridge, cleared a space on the cluttered table and sat down again.

Ginnie rammed the spike of the corkscrew into the cork. 'I'm never any good doing this.' She looked helplessly at the bottle. 'Carter always opens the wine.' She grabbed for the kitchen roll.

'I often say it's one of the few valid reasons for having a man about the house,' Selina said brightly, hoping a joke would make her laugh again, but Ginnie was crying. She leant forward and took the other woman's hand. 'Ginnie. You should talk about what's bothering you – it'll make it better,' she said, masking her distrust of this theory.

'He's left me,' Ginnie said baldly.

'Who? Carter?' Selina asked, realising she sounded half-witted. 'Join the club, then.' Selina held out her hand for Ginnie to shake. 'You and me – Geoff's gone too.'

'No! Really? Why?'

Selina was pleased that Ginnie was distracted so, most unlike her, she talked about the mounting irritations, the wife–mistress discussion. She poured herself another glass of wine. 'I don't know what I want. I mean, last night I felt so bloody mizz and alone. And yet he was driving me mental,' she explained.

'You never seemed much of a couple to me. It was always as if there was an invisible gap between you and Geoff. Even when you were together, it was as if you were apart.'

Selina picked up her glass and studied it for a moment. 'It's the loneliness. That's the worst. I mean, he's only been gone a day and I miss him, and yet I asked him to go. I don't understand myself.'

'Loneliness can be a scary thing,' Ginnie said wistfully, as if she knew a lot about it.

'But I thought you once said you liked being alone?'

'One says a lot of things one doesn't necessarily mean, just because they sound better,' Ginnie admitted bleakly.

'Even so, loneliness isn't excuse enough to continue with a relationship that's over, is it? Did you have a fight?'

'No, it was coldly civilized. I think I might feel better about it if we'd had a right old barney. It was something he said – that if I got pregnant he'd pay for half the abortion.'

'He said *that*?'

'I bang on about female independence, yet I was affronted.' Selina paused briefly and sighed. 'I suppose it's an equal opportunities situation.'

'If you had got pregnant would you have had an abortion?' Ginnie asked.

'No way. I'd have managed somehow.'

'But you wouldn't have married him?'

'I don't think so. Being pregnant isn't reason enough to marry, is it? Shotgun marriages rarely last, do they?' Selina looked up and, with dismay, saw the expression on Ginnie's face. 'Oh, Ginnie! I'm sorry. What have I said?'

Ginnie couldn't control her tears. Several minutes passed before the weeping lessened.

'Do you want to tell me?' Selina eventually asked. 'I'll understand if you don't.' Half of her longed for Ginnie not to want to. Selina knew she did not want to take on Ginnie's misery – she'd problems enough of her own. She wanted to remain detached. It was safer.

'Do you mind if I do? I mean, other people's problems – who wants them?'

'What are friends for?' Selina trotted out the well-worn cliché, and despised herself for her own shallowness. But it was evidently well hidden for Ginnie began to talk and once she had started she couldn't stop, not even to criticise Selina when she lit a cigarette in the non-smoking zone that was Ginnie's kitchen.

At first Selina listened with sympathy to the depth of her friend's unhappiness. But soon astonishment crept in that she had allowed the situation to last for such a long time, and as Ginnie continued her monologue of hurt and pain, exasperation set in. How could she have been so lacking in pride?

'... so I said if he went to Munich he needn't come back, and he flew out yesterday with *her*.' Selina waited, but Ginnie had finished.

'You can't go on like this. You'll have a breakdown or something – and life's too short. Have you talked to a solicitor?'

'I couldn't do that!' Ginnie looked at Selina with horror. 'He might tire of her. He might come back to me. He always has before.'

'There have been others?' Selina was shocked, until she remembered how Geoff had said that no female was safe with Carter.

'Yes.' Ginnie slumped in even greater despair.

'How many?' Selina found she had a grisly need to know.

'I lost count.'

'And he admitted as much?'

'No, he always denied it. Said I was neurotic. But *I* knew.'

'And you still want him back? You're mad! Have you thought that maybe *he*'s wanted out for a long time.'

'Don't say that!'

'But you've got to face facts. Maybe your threatening him brought it out in the open. Bit like Geoff and me. When I said I thought he should go there was almost a look of relief on his face.'

'But I don't want Carter to go. I didn't mean what I said to him. I thought it would bring him to his senses.'

Fat chance of that, thought Selina. Judging by the saga she'd just heard, Carter was the type of man who kept his brains under his zip. She dragged her hand through her hair. 'I don't understand you, Ginnie. How could you want to go on with someone who respects you so little? Who obviously doesn't love you as you love him.'

'Selina, don't—' Ginnie's hand shot to her mouth.

'Then why tell me?'

'I didn't want to. I tried to stop you coming in. But then you were here and suddenly I couldn't stop myself – it was what you said about having to get married. And he and Anna have so much in common – she even understands his painting, and I never have. I'm afraid he's fallen in love.'

'Ginnie, honestly, you're better off getting it over with and getting on with your own life – get a job.'

'He *is* my life – and I don't want a job.'

'He doesn't deserve you. Find someone who does. What did you say to me earlier – that fear of loneliness isn't enough reason to stay in a dead relationship?'

Ginnie's head jerked as if she had been hit. 'Would you like some more wine?' she asked abruptly, 'Something to eat? I'm sorry about lunch, but I've some smoked salmon. We could eat it in the lounge.' She stood up and began to collect the food together.

'That would be lovely.' Selina picked up her cue. 'This is a beautiful house,' she went on. She was making conversation again – she didn't think that at all. The place was too perfect, too contrived, over-decorated.

'Carter hates it. It was my choice. I think the house embarrasses him, like I'm always an embarrassment too, a social one. I annoy him most of the time,' Ginnie added bitterly.

'Carter's a creep. He should be supporting you, not making you feel so bad about yourself *and* screwing around. Honestly! You need to take yourself off on a nice holiday, somewhere exotic.'

'Is that what you're going to do now Geoff's gone?'

'You must be joking. I couldn't afford to do that—'

She held up her hand. 'And before you say another word the answer is no, you can't pay for a holiday for me.'

'Of course, if you went, who'd look after the shop?'

'Did you do that tapestry?'

'Don't change the subject.'

'I'm selling up.'

'Oh, Selina, no. Why?'

Selina rubbed thumb and first finger together. 'The usual. Money.'

'Why didn't you tell me? Why didn't you let me help?'

'Because you'd be throwing your money away. I couldn't let you.'

'Yours is the best bookshop around.'

'Asda selling books was the last straw – I can't compete with their prices. It isn't just that, though. The writing's been on the wall for some time – I just didn't want to face it.'

'Where will you go? What will you do? You can come here.'

'The last thing you need is a permanent house guest. I've a little put by. Maybe I can sell a lease on the shop and stay in the flat. And on my own the bills will be less.'

'Are you telling me Geoff didn't contribute?'

'He paid if we went out.'

'How often was that? And you think I'm soft! Honestly, Selina, it looks to me as if it was *him* who manipulated you into wanting him out. He's in the same trade – he must have known business was dodgy. He was probably frightened you were going to ask him to help you financially and wanted to escape! Don't you see?'

'Heavens. I didn't think. But it explains ... I'm sure he got worse recently – he wasn't like he is now when we first met. I'm not being very clear, am I?'

'Yes, you are.' Ginnie was smiling.

'You look better all of a sudden.'

'It's talking it over – it *has* helped.' She sounded quite surprised.

3

Selina's idea of selling a lease on her shop while she remained in the flat was, she soon realised, only a dream. So many shops in the town were for sale and two others in the Close weren't encumbered with a resident. When she had bought the property, shops there rarely came up for sale; she had been in a contract race and had had to pay well over the odds to secure it. At least, she had reasoned, there would never be any problem if she should wish to sell. But times had changed. The shop had been on the market a month now and no one had even been to view it.

'What if I sold it freehold – moved out?' she asked Paul Evans, her estate agent.

'It would help, of course. But even then …' He sucked in his lower lip as if about to eat it, and she longed to tell him to stop.

'Even then – what?'

'It'll be difficult, unless you're willing to take a cut in the price. It's a buyer's market.'

'I can't afford that. You know I'm not alone in owning the property – the Abbey National and Barclays want most of it.' She tried to smile, but it was hard.

If she was depressed by this interview, she felt worse after a talk with the manager of her building society who, in the past year or two, had learnt to steel his heart when interviewing people like Selina. 'At least you're fortunate in that you're not in a negative equity position as so many are.'

'Bully for me,' she said sarcastically.

'That's the spirit,' he replied, and she couldn't be bothered to explain.

Her third trip was to the bank where she was told the manager was out. She felt relieved that he was – she'd had enough for one day.

She stopped for a coffee and while she drank it worked out a few figures on paper. They were not happy reading. If she took the estate agent's advice and lowered the price she would be lucky to come out with the deposit on a terraced house, let alone a thatched cottage in one of the outlying villages, which was what she wanted. And even if she scraped together the deposit, she'd have no money to pay the mortgage instalments. Finding a job was likely to be a problem too: she'd taken her expertise to the local Waterstones where her name was put on a list in case a vacancy should occur, but she doubted it was a short list.

As she had been self-employed there was no dole to collect so she would have to rely on her savings. It sounded grand, *my savings*. If she was lucky they'd see her through the next three months and then – there was nothing.

She returned to the shop, aware of the crowds bustling through the Christmas-decorated streets. A mere month away, Christmas was too depressing to contemplate. An old schoolfriend and her husband had invited her, but she'd turned them down. How could she go when she'd no spare money to buy presents? Selina knew *they* wouldn't mind, it was she who cared. She had already made her plans for Christmas Day. She'd get a roast turkey sandwich from M & S. She had one bottle of decent claret left and she'd splash out on a half-bottle of whisky. Then she'd be able to get drunk and spend the day in bed with Sabbie wallowing in self-pity, something she normally kept sternly at bay.

No sooner had she let herself into the shop than there was a tapping on the glass of the door. She peered out to see three young men, two smartly suited, peering in at her. She pointed to the closed sign but they persisted.

'Can we talk to you?' one mimed through the glass.

She unlocked the door. 'Can I help you?'

'We wondered if you had a moment. There's something we'd like to discuss.'

Immediately she looked cautiously at their hands to see what they were selling, but they held nothing. The smartness and trim haircuts on two of the young men made her suspicious. 'Are you Jehovah's Witnesses?' she demanded.

This amused them, for they both laughed loudly. 'No, nothing like that.' The third was not so amused. Nor was he as young as the others – mid-thirties, she assessed. He was dressed in a Barbour and cords and had the look of an outdoor type. He wasn't good-looking, but he had a pleasant face with eyes of the clearest grey, his best feature. His hair looked as if it had once been blond but had now faded. He was of medium height but quite muscular. Not the type to make her stare, normally, but she was suddenly aware that she was looking at him with a bit too much interest. She opened the door wide to allow them in.

'You're closing down?' one asked.

'Obviously,' she said, a mite curtly for they could see the shelves were almost empty.

'What a shame. It was a good bookshop.'

'I'm sorry, I don't recognise you.'

'No, I've changed a bit since I used to come in here. In those days I was heavily into the tarot.' He smiled broadly. 'My name is Colley.'

'And you're no longer interested in it?'

'No, not now, it's not necessary, you see.' His tone was serious. She would have liked to find out what had made it unnecessary, but didn't like to ask. 'This is my friend

Aelins.' She shook hands. 'And this is Matt,' he said, almost as an afterthought.

'What can I do for you? As you see, I've a few books left, and I've some postcards over here, and some crystals.' She wondered if it was her imagination that Matt had held her hand longer than necessary – she found she hoped he had.

'We're aware the shop is for sale. We'd like to talk to you about it.' Aelins spoke for the first time.

'You'd better come this way,' she said, immediately regretting her former suspicions and leading them into her sitting room.

'Can I get you anything? I've a drop of whisky, wine – or tea or coffee?' she asked.

'A glass of water, perhaps?' asked Colley.

She looked quizzically at Matt.

'Nothing, thanks.' He had a pleasant voice.

She returned with the water to find Colley and Aelins sitting upright on chairs, their hands folded in their laps, feet placed precisely side by side, neither moving, and, in their neat buttoned suits, looking as if they were posing for a portrait by Gilbert and George. Matt was leaning against the wall, arms folded, apart from them. His pose should have been menacing, but instead she felt oddly safe with him standing there. She smiled tentatively at him and was rewarded with a wide smile in response.

'Did you see the estate agent?'

'No, we don't deal with agents.'

'Then you saw their sign outside?' she asked.

'No. A friend told us,' Colley explained.

If the miracle happened and they did buy, she wondered where she would stand with the agent. Would she have to pay him? Still, she was jumping the gun thinking this way; they probably wouldn't buy and were just time-wasters. 'This room was used for storage before – I made it into a sitting room. In the agent's details there are two bedrooms. I think I should point out that one room is too small – it's a box room.'

'It's the shop we're most interested in,' Aelins said.

'Really?' She tried to sound merely curious and not to show her excitement. 'If there's anything you need to know, just ask. Would you like to go round on your own? It's easier.' She congratulated herself on how unconcerned she sounded.

'You're very kind. That won't be necessary.'

'Oh, I see.' She felt disappointment rush in, booting hope and excitement out of the way.

'We have to go back and say what we've seen. Then we'll be in touch. If not us, then someone else.' This was the longest sentence either man had spoken.

'Then you're not buying for yourselves.'

'No, no. For Fohpal,' Aelins said.

'For our books,' Colley added.

'I see. Well ...' She was not sure how to continue, but the problem was solved for her when the two men got to their feet, thanked her politely for her time and the water, and shook her hand in a way that was too firm to be genuine. Matt pushed himself from the wall.

'Nice meeting you.' He shook her hand again, smiled and followed the others. Ah, well, she thought, maybe he wasn't her type. She liked men who were a bit more assertive than he appeared to be.

Fopal? The name rang a bell. Where had she heard of them, she wondered, as she returned to the sitting room after seeing the trio out. Should she know about them? 'Certainly now I should,' she told Sabbie who, once the visitors had gone, had deemed it safe to slink down from the top of the cupboard where he had been lurking, monitoring the meeting going on below.

She picked up the dirty glasses. They might only want water but she fancied a real drink. On the table she saw a leaflet they must have left since it hadn't been there before.

She settled in her favourite chair with a glass of wine and a cigarette before beginning to read.

It was 'Fohpal', with an H, she read on the cover, 'Everything You Want to Know'. Did she want to know? It was the sort of marketing phrase that always raised her hackles.

For Our Hope Peace And Love, she read. Nothing wrong with that. She read about the organisation and its leader, *H.G.* It was all coming back now. H.G. No one knew his name. He was one of those celebrities who had been around for so long that one didn't think about him. He had always been known by his initials so that no one even queried them now. Like the Archbishop and like the Pope, they were just there and always had been. He was not as famous as the Maharishi had been and no scandal adhered to him as it had to the Bhagwan. He was not as philosophical as Krishnamurti but, of them all, he was more like him than any other guru she had read about.

Was Fohpal a religion? She didn't have much time for religion, not the way the world was. Still, if she was to keep in with these people maybe she should read the leaflet. And she'd go to the library tomorrow and see if they had any of H.G.'s books. If it led to a sale she might even go to one of their meetings, which were listed on a card inserted in the booklet. What had she got to lose?

EXTRACT FROM THE
DIARY OF H.G. – THE MASTER

Yesterday I stopped writing, abruptly, since I find it painful to recall the sight of my murdered father – something no child should see.

It amuses me when I hear the experts relate a delinquent's behaviour to childhood trauma. If that is so, then I should have become a serial killer, at least. As it is, I seem to be fairly 'normal' ... even if I might be regarded as a con-man. I shudder at that notion.

Why, if I'm not an Indian, does everyone think I am?

A reasonable question. It all goes back to the simple rule that any confidence trickster knows – if you say it enough times then the punters will believe it.

When I first arrived in Britain, nut-coloured from the sun and with the same black hair as my father, I was simply accepted as such. Tanned skin is easy to keep if, like me, one is already blessed with the dark tones of the Latins. Also I loved to be outdoors and at every opportunity turned my face to the sun. Nor is it unknown for people of coloured skin to fade slightly in northern climes – my lighter skin was easily and quickly accepted.

And then I had the papers.

Ah, the papers.

Amazing things, papers: if they say it is so, then it is accepted that it is so.

I have Bay Tarbart to thank for my passport, my birth certificate. She bought them for me – she bought a whole background for me and no one, ever, questioned it.

So here I was, the impostor, and I studied and was prepared for the future. Such a future! Bay had already set up the foundation and almost immediately bought

*this house, Porthwood, in the West Country. My excite-
ment when she told me was immense. I'd never forgotten
the British consul reminding me of the Woolstons of
Porthwood and I felt an immediate affinity with the
place. I had returned, by accident, to the house of my
ancestors. This was where my mother had been born,
where she had met my father and from which she had
eloped. Inadvertently, I had come home. I was a
Woolston of Porthwood, after all. I told no one.*

*Money was pouring in from many quarters. Why? you
might reasonably ask. The thirties, you must understand,
was a strange time. The Great War and its carnage was
still a fresh memory and, with the possibility of a new
war, hedonism was, for many, the only way to block out
the fears. Wherever hedonism exists, following invariably
in its tracks comes self-analysis, discontent and a search
for something meaningful – which, of course, is where
people like me step forward.*

*All I did was to say what I thought. I was, and am, a
simple soul and so I said simple things such as:*

'The solution lies within oneself.'

'Don't look to me for help – help yourself.'

'I have nothing to teach you, only words.'

*Well, the result, you know, was formidable. Over-
night, despite my youth, I had become a sage, one whose
every word must be listened to. It was heady stuff.*

*In my defence you must look at how my life had
turned out. From being a poverty-stricken orphan,
unsure where the next meal was coming from, I had been
translated to a life of unmitigated luxury to which I had
quickly adjusted, and liked. I did not have the strength of
character to say, 'Look, I'm sorry, but there's been a
dreadful mistake. I'm just an ordinary chap.'*

*In my defence, I did once try to tell Bay Tarbart the
truth. I can see her now, sitting at the breakfast table, as*

she explained a meeting we were to attend that week in London where I was to meet an army of dignitaries.

'I'm not what you think,' I began.

'I do not wish to hear,' she replied. So that was that.

Then there is the matter of the healing. It all started by accident. At a meeting an elderly lady approached me and grabbed at my hands with a strange desperation. She stood a moment, eyes closed, swaying back and forth – I thought she was about to faint. Instead she cried out, 'I can see! I can see!' Thus my healing began.

To this day I do not know if she was a plant, a liar or an hysteric, but after that people poured in to be healed. In my defence, once again, I always say I do nothing, that they heal themselves. I believe that. I may be a form of conduit for energy, but I believe it comes from within them, not me. But I can't help it if everyone believes it's me, can I?

Similarly, since so many people appear to have been helped, I've never felt I've had the right to stop doing it. I could wish it had never begun but, then, that is something else.

And then there's my famed celibacy. How strong I am when, over the years, so many young women would have given anything to share my bed. There is no mystery. I've never felt the need, that's all. We live in a world so obsessed with sex that to be a man who has no interest in it is beyond most people's comprehension. Rather, since I've never touched a woman, they would presume I have homosexual tendencies. But neither have I touched a man – not in that way and I've never wanted to. I love many people, but their souls, not their bodies. Long ago I decided it was easier to allow the followers to be amazed and admire my celibacy, thinking it enforced, rather than to tell them the truth – far more mundane as it is.

So, there you have it. My confession. I am not who I

appear to be. But, then, who is? Once a philosopher always a philosopher ...

chapter **five**

1

Jessica Lawley stood at her bedroom window. She glanced at her watch before she looked at the view. She smiled a small, triumphant smile. She had showered and dressed in forty-five minutes.

'Come in, Bun,' she called out to the knock at the door. And Bun, her housekeeper and friend of twenty-five years, entered, preceded by two exuberant pugs, with a breakfast tray. She put it on a small side table and moved a high-backed chair of a French style into position.

'I did it, Bun! Three-quarters of an hour, how about that?' Jessica said, as she bent to pat the dogs – Romeo and Juliet.

'Don't let those wretched dogs rush around you like that! They'll have you over again and then where will we be?' Bun moved to give Jessica a helping arm.

'No thank you, I can manage.' Jessica pushed away the arm with an irritated expression.

'Where's your stick?'

'You know I don't use it in my bedroom.' She was beginning to sound petulant but either Bun did not hear or chose to ignore it. 'You might say something – about the time.'

'My dear Jessica, I don't understand the excitement. I remember when it could take you three hours to get yourself tarted up.'

'That was then, when time didn't matter because I could do it in ten minutes if I wanted – I had the choice.

Now I've no choice. I just creak towards my goal of half an hour.'

'Did you have a good night?'

'No!'

'Why don't you get some sleeping pills from the doctor?'

'I'm not going to start taking the damn things now.'

'You're pig-headed, Jessica. I suppose you're going to refuse to look at this brochure.'

'If it's another of your goddamned gadgets – yes.'

'It's a stair-lift.'

'No.'

'Why not?'

Jessica laid down the knife with which she had begun to butter her toast. 'Because I'd be giving in, that's why. Any post?'

Bun fumbled in the capacious pocket of her apron and produced a pile of letters. She pulled a wastepaper basket towards the breakfast table. 'Got everything? Then I'll get on.' She placed a bell on the table. 'Ring it if you want me,' she said, as she did every morning. She tried, unsuccessfully, to persuade the dogs to follow her, as she also did every morning, but they had other ideas and settled pointedly at their owner's feet. 'Damn dangerous, those dogs,' she was muttering as she closed the door.

Jessica cut two small squares of toast and added a dollop of the strawberry jam before feeding them to her pets. The mail was boring, circulars and bills mainly, and a letter from the bank, which she would open later.

She stacked the mail on one side of the table and sighed: the contents of her post were a reflection of the state of her life. Once the scripts and fan letters came in sack loads and two secretaries were needed to deal with them. In the past she'd rarely bothered to read her fan mail but now, on the rare days that such a letter appeared she almost devoured it with pleasure.

Still, she consoled herself, she hadn't starred in a feature film for years, and her last TV work was over two years ago, so it was hardly surprising – memories were short in this business. If her surgeon was right it would be a long time before she worked again, unless someone wrote a part for a *cripple* in a wheelchair.

She winced at that word, the C-word she called it, which she hated almost as much as *handicapped*.

She poured herself some more coffee and her hand wavered over the sugar bowl. 'One lump,' she said decisively, and the hand reacted.

The biggest problem of waking up in the middle of the night was the ease with which unwelcome thoughts wormed their way into her mind. Last night had been an orgy of self-loathing. She was too fat, she drank and ate too much, she was getting old and she would never walk properly again. Most mornings they disappeared, but today they remained lodged. Perhaps it was because Simon was coming back this evening, and she would have to tell him the latest bad news, or because she had planned to phone her agent, whose recent neglect had lessened her self-confidence. After all the percentages she'd paid him over the years his lack of calls, now that she was not earning, irked her. When she did phone him, she was usually told he was in meetings and unobtainable, which rankled even more. What did he take her for – a fool?

She'd a mind to write a book, that's what she wanted to discuss with him. Not the autobiography that publishers craved – not yet, it was too soon. She felt that writing it now would be like ringing her death knell, like those special-achievement awards given out to actors only when they were tottering towards their graves. She was determined that at fifty-four her life was not over. She'd still a lot of living to do – and maybe a novel to write.

She looked up and glanced at herself in the Chippendale mirror that hung over her white and gold Louis XIV dressing table, which had once been an escritoire. Only a glance because she didn't like what she saw and a closer study of her face would have depressed her deeply. Before the accident she had boasted that she didn't mind growing old. As her fifties approached she had been active, slim, and her beauty was such that magazines clamoured for interviews to tell the secrets of her looks.

She laughed as she remembered the shocked look on the pert, eager faces of the young interviewers when she'd boasted that her looks came from drinking too much, eating whatever she fancied and getting to bed too late each night.

How witless she'd been, how careless of her looks and youth. Such hubris!

Then, one day, she'd tripped over a pug on the stone hall floor and had smashed first onto her right knee and then her hip. She had lain breathless, and fearful she had broken something. She hadn't. Bun had pulled her to her feet, she'd had a stiff brandy and had gone to the studio where she was making a TV mini-series, feeling a slight soreness, nothing else.

She'd forgotten the incident until a couple of weeks later when the pains had begun. Minor at first, a mere irritation, but building rapidly until it was hard to sleep and walking any distance was soon out of the question.

Consultations were made, X-rays taken, a part cancelled. She had arthritis in her knee. Jessica Lawley, sex symbol for over thirty years, had an old woman's complaint. She was furious.

'But I'm only fifty-one,' she told the consultant who, alarmingly, looked young enough to be her son.

'Children can suffer from arthritis, Miss Lawley,' he said, kindly enough. 'But it was undoubtedly the fall which triggered a pre-disposition in the joint. For now, though, don't worry, keep your weight down, and it'll be a good ten years before we need to operate.'

The pain increased, as if, like a car, it had changed gear. When she walked her knee felt as if a furnace burned inside it. The joint swelled. She fired jets of cold water at it, packed it in ice, and downed Nurofen, evening primrose oil, cod liver oil. Her bathroom resembled a pharmacy as she tried one sure-fire cure after another. Aromatherapy, reflexology, acupuncture. Eventually she relied on brandy. All failed to drown the pain, and work was out of the question.

At first people were solicitous, and phoned and wrote and invited her. It was she who had begun to refuse the invitations, not wishing to be seen like this – with a stick. She'd tried a wheelchair once, but the humiliation of being talked across, as if she did not exist, had made it intolerable.

As her immobility increased her body ballooned, aided by the pain-deadening brandy and the food she ate to comfort herself. The full-busted figure with its tiny waist had soon gone. And then the face began to alter. Her nose, with its impertinent tip tilt, was still there, as were the fine brown eyes, but of her famous cheekbones, now hidden under duvets of fat, there was no sign. She'd never before had any grey in her hair, but a fair sprinkling had appeared and she'd had to resort to the bottle.

Simon had been a brick. Her adjustment to her disability had not been easy for either of them. At first she hated his reasonableness, wishing he'd shout back at the bitch she was fast becoming. She was jealous of his youth, his fitness, his ability to move without giving joints a second thought. She wanted him to hate her – if he did then she could let him go, for she knew it was unfair to allow him to stay. But she needed him. When he visited his parents she missed him achingly.

Eventually she began to accept her lot and they moved

into a calmer friendship and, she hoped, a far more stable one.

They had only been together for two carefree, sex-crazed months when the accident had happened. She was fifty-one to his thirty-one. He was not the first younger man in her life and when she had chosen him she had every intention that he would not be the last. Her lovers were actors, wannabes who needed her to enhance their careers. She used them for sex and tired of them quickly. Simon had broken the mould.

He had been a model, not in any super league, but with constant work in catalogues and knitting patterns. Approaching thirty, he had decided to try his luck with acting but had had little success. She had arranged a small speaking part for him in the TV mini-series in which she was the star and then she'd become incapacitated. He'd put his career on hold to be with her – that was where he was so different from the others.

'Darling, you should be out and about, not stuck here with crippled old me!' she said to him, using the C-word – then she had still believed she would get better.

'Don't say crippled – I hate it. You'll be as right as rain once you've had the op. And I like being with you.'

It had crossed her mind that maybe he wanted to marry her, in which case, fond of him though she was, she would have to end their relationship. She'd been married three times and only Humphrey, her first, had not required any large settlement from her. The expense of extricating herself from the other two had put her off marriage for life.

Simon had been wrong about the operation. They all had.

Even as she was returned from the operating theatre she knew instinctively that nothing was ever going to be the same again.

How right she had been. In the ten months since the

operation on her knee the realisation had dawned slowly that she would always walk with a limp. The famously subtle, sexy walk, where she swung her hips just enough to excite but not to excess, was to be no more.

Still, things could be worse, she had told herself.

They could.

The hip began to play up.

The mornings were the worst, when it seemed to take an age to crank herself up and get going. Each week the pain worsened and she became slower.

'It's arthritis again. I'm so sorry,' her doctor had said last week, when she'd finally consulted him, unable any longer to cope with the pain. 'But don't worry, it'll be several years before we need to operate.'

'That's what you said last time!' She was terrified. It wasn't the operation so much as having to acknowledge yet again that youth was gone and old age beckoned – too damned early by far.

It was fortunate that Simon had accepted the part which, unknown to him, she'd arranged, and was away on location. She had needed to be alone to come to terms with this latest diagnosis. The news would be a blow to him.

The phone rang. It was Simon.

'Simon, I was just thinking about you,' she purred into the receiver.

'Jessica, I'm stuck here for another week.'

'It's a good part. You might get noticed.'

'I love your faith in me. Are you all right?'

'I'm fine. Really,' she lied.

'Then you don't mind?'

'Of course I mind, but work comes first,' she said, and meant it. That's how she'd built her own career. No matter how she'd felt, she'd never missed a day's shooting, a curtain call. Never been late.

'I knew you'd say that ...'

They chatted for another ten minutes. He said he'd fallen in love and paused. Her heart missed a beat and she laughed with relief when he added, 'With Morocco.' Reluctantly she replaced the receiver. How she missed that world, how talking to him conjured it up. Still, a week wasn't *that* long. She picked up the letter from the bank. Odd that they were writing to her since they had been instructed that all correspondence should be handled by her accountant. She ripped it open, read the letter and wished she'd continued to ignore it. She slipped it back into its envelope and, using her stick, dragged a large basket towards her. She pulled out a stack of pre-cut hexagonal patches and began methodically to hand-sew her patchwork – it always helped to calm her.

2

'You look nice. Where're you going?' Bun asked the following day, as Jessica progressed across the stone flooring of the hall.

'London. Is the car ready?' She spoke shortly, annoyed. *Nice*, she thought. *Nice!* The adjective ricocheted inside her head. No one had ever used such a word to describe her appearance in the past, no one would have dared. To get her own back, pettily, she decided not to tell Bun where she was going.

'You back for dinner?'

'I don't know,' she said airily, as they reached the front door. 'I might be.'

'That hardly helps me. I'd like to know, to tell the cook.'

'I thought this house was run for my convenience, not yours.' Dramatically she swirled her red cape over her shoulder and stepped out of the house. 'Good morning,

Martin.' She bestowed a wide and charming smile on her young chauffeur, more to get back at Bun than in genuine greeting.

Martin held open the car door wide for her. She allowed him to take her arm, looking triumphantly at Bun, then turned and slid uncomfortably, bottom first, across the back seat, which enabled her to rest her stiff knee on the leather upholstery. She needed a Rolls or Bentley, something with real room in the back – this wriggling in was so undignified, she thought. And, even as the car moved down the drive of Shipleys, and with thirty miles of motorway still ahead, she was working out how to get out at the other end with the minimum of fuss and awkwardness.

She had dressed in a flowing black silk kaftan. She blessed whoever had invented such a cover-all garment, but at the same time wondered if its fullness did not make her look even larger than she was. Her boots were of black leather and, of necessity, flat. The scarlet cape further camouflaged her size, and a black felt hat with a large brim covered her curly hair. She wore dark glasses, even though it was pouring with rain. For all this, she feared she still looked like Jessica Lawley.

Many, many years ago she would have given anything to be noticed; then, fame had made her want to be seen when it suited her. Now, with her limp and full figure, she'd have paid for no one to see her.

The rain had turned into a blessed storm by the time they reached Fleet Street and her bank. Blessed because the cloudburst in progress made those still hardy enough to be on the street run, heads down, too intent on reaching their own destinations to warrant a second glance as the plump woman manoeuvred herself from her car and limped across the pavement under the um-brella held open for her by a doorman, who doffed his top hat and said, 'Good morning, Miss Lawley.' So much for being incognito, but she smiled in response anyway.

In a panelled, leather-furnished room she faced one of the partners, a man she had known ever since she had begun to bank here.

'I very much regret the necessity of this meeting, Miss Lawley, but we have matters to discuss.'

Five minutes later she sat, white-faced, looking incredulously at the man. 'But this can't be. How can I be broke? I've always put money aside – in case I couldn't work again. I've pension funds and then there are my investments, I've income from them.'

'Have you always dealt with Mr Greenborne?'

'He's been my accountant since I landed my first part – another actor put me in touch with him.'

'And you left all your financial affairs to him?'

'Well, yes, I'm not good with figures. They bore me,' she said. 'I appreciate you calling me, but it's Cy Greenborne you should be talking to.' She bent down to pick up her handbag as if preparing to leave.

'I would if I could, Miss Lawley. Unfortunately your accountant is dead so it makes it somewhat difficult to contact him. I presumed you knew.'

'Cy, dead? How? When?'

'He jumped off Beachy Head last week. The facts are not fully verified, but it would seem there's a discrepancy in his clients' funds.'

'You mean he's been nicking from us? *Cy?*'

'I gather he had expensive tastes.'

'He lived well, certainly. But then the fees he charged—'

'Were not, it would appear, entirely sufficient for his needs. A client, a –' he looked down at some papers on his desk and peered at them over his half-spectacles '– a Mr Rick Mainstream,' he said, as if unsure he had read the name correctly.

'He's a pop star turned actor.'

'This gentleman was on the point of suing him in the courts. Apparently your Mr Greenborne ...' He gesticulated with his hands, palms up, and coughed discreetly.

'The bloody creep. So I have no pension fund? No investments?'

'I don't know as yet. What I do know is, you have no income coming in and have not had for a good two years.'

'My knee.' She tapped it in explanation. 'I haven't worked, you see. But I thought ...'

'Miss Lawley, I'm so sorry.'

'But surely he must have belonged to some organisation of chartered accountants? Like solicitors do – you know, so that if one of them does a bunk with clients' funds, they pay up.'

'Unfortunately your Mr Greenborne was not what he claimed to be. He was not a chartered or certified accountant and he belonged to no professional organisation which might help now.'

'But his letterheads looked official enough and with letters after his name ...' She shook her head in disbelief. 'God, what a fool I've been.'

'If it's any consolation you're not alone. What we have to do now is work out what you have and how best we can utilise your remaining funds.'

An hour later Jessica left the bank, feeling like a rag doll with the stuffing falling out. She had no strength, no substance.

'You all right, Miss Lawley? You look a bit peaky,' Martin asked solicitously, as he helped her pack herself back into the car.

'Call my agent, Martin. Tell him I'm cancelling lunch. Then drive me round to the flat.'

'You want me to call Bun?'

'No. On no account. I'm all right, Martin, I just want to be quiet for an hour or two.'

'Shall I get you a take-away or some sandwiches?'

'You're worse than Bun, Martin. There's probably something I can eat at the flat.' Though it was drink she wanted, not food. 'When you speak to my agent don't let on I'm with you.' She sank back onto the soft leather upholstery and closed her eyes. She felt sick. She was half aware of Martin's voice as he spoke to her agent's secretary. 'Martin, stop at the next newsagent's,' she said when he disconnected the call. 'Get me twenty Silk Cut.'

'But, Miss Lawley, you don't smoke.'

'Oh, yes, I do. As from now.'

3

When they arrived at the block of mansion flats off the Fulham Road, she not only felt sick but dizzy, too. Her first cigarette in ten years had made her woozy. She had hoped it would help her think straight. It hadn't. If anything, the panic inside her head was worse, a screeching cacophony of anger and fear.

'I'll come up with you.'

'No, I can manage,' she said firmly. 'Call for me at three.' She felt that if Martin or anyone else was kind to her now she would burst into tears. She leant on her stick with the silver leopard-shaped handle and tapped her way across the pavement. She had no need to use her key to open the outer door for Charlie, the porter, had flung it wide as she mounted the last of the steps.

'Nice to see you, Miss Lawley. It's been a long time. How's the poor old knee?'

'Mending fast, Charlie, and less of the old, if you don't mind,' she joked gamely, as he snapped open the metal gates of the old-fashioned lift, bowing low as he did so. She smiled for the first time that day, fully aware that the depth of Charlie's bow was in direct ratio to the size of the Christmas box he expected. He was in for a shock from her this year.

'Want me to ride up with you?'

'No. I'm quite capable.' She slammed the inner door smartly shut and stabbed at the number seven on the highly polished brass plate. Once the lift had carried her out of sight of Charlie she slumped against the shiny mahogany wall.

On the landing she struggled with the gates and her stick. It frequently amazed her these days how many of the tasks which had once been so simple and which she had performed without a second's thought had become logistical problems to surmount.

She opened the door of her flat and stepped into the hall, dimly lit by the light that filtered in through the part stained-glass window. She sniffed at the stale air, switched on the light and began to walk down the long corridor with doors on either side that bisected the flat.

She had passed the two guest rooms, the door to the kitchen and the maid's room when she paused and glanced into the drawing room. Two lamps were on, which was odd. She hadn't been here for three months at least. She felt annoyed at the waste of electricity, something to which ordinarily she wouldn't have given a thought had not this morning's interview changed everything. And then she froze. She could hear voices. Someone was in her bedroom! Panic rose, and fear. She should get Charlie – quickly. She turned to enter the kitchen where there was a service phone. A man laughed and she felt the blood drain from her face. She knew that laugh!

She went into the drawing room, crossed to the drinks trolley and poured herself a large Scotch. She sat in a wing chair facing the door. From her handbag she took her newly purchased cigarettes, shook one out, lit it and waited.

About ten minutes later she heard the bedroom door open. He streaked, naked, past the open doorway to the kitchen. She heard the fridge door slam, heard the clatter of a silver salver, imagined him reaching into the frosted-glass cupboard for two flutes.

'Hello, Simon,' she said, loudly and clearly, as his form passed the open door again.

'Shit!' The tray, champagne and glasses clattered to the floor. The bottle burst, its contents spraying the walls and carpet in bubbled trails.

'Entertaining?' she asked, icily calm.

'Jessica! How long have you been here?' He bent to pick up the salver which he held modestly in front of himself.

'It hardly matters, does it? I thought you were in Morocco – on the dreary set, you said.'

He had the grace to look sheepish, taking an evident interest in his bare toes. 'I lied.' At least he had the decency to be honest, she thought. 'I'm sorry.'

'You might have put the chain on the door.'

'I didn't think.'

'Evidently.' She was calm now. Reason had taken over. She must not be too hard on him. After all, he was young. Sex had been impossible for so long because of the pain, what could she expect? This little escapade did not alter his kindness and patience with her. She would surprise him with her understanding. 'It's all right, Simon. I'm not cross. Do you want a lift back with me? Martin's calling in a couple of hours.'

'I don't think—' he began, but did not finish.

'Simon, what's keeping you?' a woman's voice called from the region of the bedroom. A moment later she was in the room. 'Darling, what – oh, hello,' she said, upon seeing Jessica. She was slim, not beautiful but pretty in a doll-like way. She glowed with health and youth, showing no embarrassment as she stepped forward, smiling in greeting. 'You must be Miss Lawley – Simon's told me so much about you.' She played with her long, bleached hair, as if to draw attention to it.

Jessica looked up questioningly at Simon. She felt her heart begin to beat faster. It was one thing to deal with Simon, but to be understanding when the object of his lust was standing in front of her was harder.

'Oh, yes, sorry. This is Sam – Samantha.'

'How do you do?' Sam held out her hand. Jessica would have preferred not to shake it, but ingrained courtesy forced her. 'It's so kind of you to let us use your flat.'

'Isn't it?' Jessica smiled grimly.

'I was saying to Simon, what I wouldn't give to own a superb flat like this. And Simon said—'

'*Lending* you my flat is one thing. My bathrobe is another,' Jessica said cuttingly.

'Oh, I'm sorry, Miss Lawley.' Sam held the towelling robe, with the large looping JL monogram on the pocket, closer to her. 'I thought – Simon said you wouldn't mind, that you had said it was miles too small for you now.'

Jessica felt as if she had been slapped. 'I don't recall – oh, for goodness sake, Simon, go and put something on. You look ridiculous standing there with that tray.' And so beautiful too, she thought, with longing. Simon laughed nervously and backed out of the room.

Sam sat down on the slubbed-silk-covered sofa, crossed her legs elegantly, patted the pockets of the robe and then said, 'May I?' gesturing to the packet of Silk Cut on the marble table. Jessica waved her hand in silent permission.

'You've been so kind to Simon, I can't thank you enough. The money has helped enormously. You must come and see the house we've been able to buy – so much nicer for Petal.'

'Petal?' Jessica asked cautiously.

'Our little girl. She loves the garden to play in. Come the summer I'll have a paddling pool for her. And Simon getting this new part we'll be able to have an au pair and I'll be able to go on location with him. Everything's working out so fabulously and it's all thanks to you.'

'How wonderful of me,' she said, with heavy irony that appeared to be lost on Sam who, with the subtlety of the thick-skinned, continued to prattle on about her house – in Woking, Jessica learnt, close to her mum, who, of course, was looking after Petal for the week so that Sam and Simon could spend some time alone. 'Like a second honeymoon.' She giggled.

'How cosy.'

'And when Simon phoned to say we could borrow your flat, I was jumping with excitement. We see so little of each other. But I'm sorry about the robe, I really am.'

'Keep it.'

'Oh, that's too much,' Sam gushed. Jessica would like to have told her she didn't want it back, ever, that she could never touch it now – even if it didn't fit. Christ, that hurt! The sheets, she never wanted to see them, either. Or the bed. Or this flat ... Despair, anger, puzzlement were all bubbling up inside her. Pride prevented her asking this empty-headed female anything. She sat, large, clothed in black, and felt like a malevolent spider.

'I think we should talk, Simon,' she said, the moment he reappeared. 'Alone,' she added, to a blithely unaware Sam.

'Sure. Sam – if you could make some tea or something?'

'Or have a bath. It will take longer. Use my bath oil. Do feel free.'

'Miss Lawley, may I call you Jessica?' Sam smiled sweetly, blue-eyed innocent.

'No, I don't think so. Miss Lawley will do.' Jessica had the satisfaction of seeing the girl finally look embarrassed and, better still, crestfallen. She left the room with speed.

'She doesn't know anything.'

'So I gathered. But, then, neither do I, Simon.'

'I'm sorry.'

'So you keep saying. I could understand your need for someone – in the circumstances. But did you have to bring such a totally vacuous young woman to my apartment?' She did not know what made her say that but she felt spiteful, she wanted to lash out, she wanted him to see Sam as she really was.

'She's very sweet.'

'Professionally so.' Jessica snorted and felt for her cigarettes.

'You're smoking!' He sounded shocked.

'Is it any wonder?' She laughed, but it was a small, mirthless noise.

'But why are you here? You never go anywhere these days.'

'Unfortunately for you I had to come up to town on business. I came here for some peace and quiet to think and make some phone calls. I didn't realise I was going to walk into this sordid love nest.'

'It's not sordid. She's my wife.'

Jessica's hand, cigarette between two fingers, was poised almost at her mouth, as if it, too, had been caught by surprise. 'Your wife! Oh, Simon. There is much I can forgive – even a wife, but not one you've never admitted to.'

'I should have told you, but one thing led to another and the longer I left it the harder it became.'

'You told me you loved me.'

'I did. I do.' He shook his head in confusion.

'Oh, really, Simon. Give me a break!'

'Well, perhaps I don't love you like that – but I'm very fond of you. I care about you.'

'I don't need your crumbs of affection,' she said. 'You were at pains to convince me you weren't a gigolo. Did you ever explain to half-witted Sam what the terms of your contract of employment were? Did you tell her about the screwing before ...' She tapped her knee angrily.

'Please, Jessica. Don't tell her.'

'What's this part your wife says you've landed?'

'It's the new Izzard film – I've been offered the second lead.'

'How nice for you,' she said coldly, so coldly that he looked at her in alarm.

'You wouldn't – oh God, Jessica, please don't stop me getting it. I need it so desperately – you know how much.'

'I don't. You told me caring for me was more important than any part.'

'That was before this one came along and I'm so right for it – everyone says so.'

'And when you'd got this part and a name and fame and money, where would I have fitted in?'

He looked everywhere but at her, and that was her answer.

'I gather I helped buy you a house. Odd I didn't know. Did you know Cy Greenborne, by any chance?' she asked suspiciously.

'Your accountant? I met him a couple of times.'

'I don't recall giving you the money to buy a house, with a garden for dear Petal. So did he, for some reason?'

'No – why should he?' He looked trapped.

'Cy's dead – killed himself after putting his sticky paws on his clients' bank accounts, mine included.'

'No!' He had the grace to look aghast.

'So it would seem. Since I didn't give you the money,

he did, for whatever reason. Did you find out what he was up to? Were you blackmailing him? I'm sure the police would be interested in this.'

'The police? What are you talking about? I didn't take a penny from him.' He looked frightened now, really so, which gave her a small measure of satisfaction.

'Then who did you get it from?'

'Humph.'

'I beg your pardon?'

'Oh, I suppose I've got to tell you. There's not much point in keeping it secret. But please explain to him that you wheedled it out of me. After the accident, he paid me.'

'Paid you? What for?'

'To stay with you.'

'You stayed with me the last year because *my ex-husband paid you to*? Like a servant?'

'Well, yes. Better paid than a servant.' He cleared his throat nervously.

'Enough to buy you a house.'

'Well, the deposit. And what he gives me monthly covers the mortgage and a bit over.'

'Why, for God's sake?'

'He felt sorry for you. He could see you'd be knocked up for some time and unable to work. He'd heard knee replacements were a bit dodgy – I guess he worried you'd never work again and wanted you looked after.'

'And the beginning? I hadn't had the accident then.'

'No. I liked you enormously. It just happened.'

'And Sam and sweet Petal? Weren't you risking a lot?' she asked sarcastically. 'Or was it worth it? Because you hoped I'd further your career? You used me – just like the rest.'

'Please don't be hurt, Jessica. I feel bad enough as it is.'

'Hurt? I'm not hurt. I'm just angry that you duped me. That I actually thought you were different.' And that you cared and that you loved me, she thought, but did not say it. 'It's a pity for you, really. I had some news last week. This pain in my hip – it's arthritis too. I'm looking at a hip replacement and, with my track record, fairly soon. You could have asked Humphrey for double, bought yourself a sodding mansion on my pain and disability.'

'Oh, Jessica, I'm so sorry.'

'Are you? What for? My hip or the loss of your revenue?' She felt in her handbag and pulled out her mobile phone. She punched in a number. 'Martin? Come and collect me now. I'll be in the hall.' She replaced the telephone and levered herself with difficulty from the chair. Simon was immediately at her side to help her. 'Don't touch me,' she hissed. Despite the pain, she walked tall, her cane idling in her hand, as if walking unaided gave her back some dignity.

'Jessica, please don't go like this,' he said, as she reached the door and turned to face him. He looked so scared and not nearly as handsome. He even seemed to have shrunk in stature. 'We can talk about this. If Izzard—'

'If Izzard finds out you've done this to me you'd be finished, yes. He's a good friend of mine and, a rare one, he sets great store on loyalty and honesty. But don't worry. I won't say a word to him. Enjoy your stab at stardom.' She saw him relax. 'I'll bide my time. I'll wait until you're a big Hollywood star making millions. Then I might drop a word in an ear or two – that is, unless *you* pay *me* off.' She laughed, almost gaily, as she left him standing in the middle of her drawing room, his mouth agape.

4

'How dare you humiliate me in this way, Humph? Just keep your prying nose out of my affairs.' Jessica, home at Shipleys, was speaking on the telephone to her ex-husband, her face distorted with fury.

'Jessica, love, calm down. What on earth am I supposed to have done?' Humphrey asked, in his pleasant, deep voice with its mid-Atlantic accent which he'd acquired thirty years before when it was fashionable to have one.

'There's no *supposed* about it. Simon has told me everything.' She tossed her head defiantly as she spoke, even though there was no one in the room to see.

'The little bastard, I swore him to secrecy.'

'I don't know what you were thinking of. How you had the audacity. Why you thought you had the right. Why you even thought it was necessary. I've never had to pay for sex in my life. Why should you think I would have to now? Because I'm in my fifties? Because I'm fat and ugly – is that what you think? That I'm so gross no one will want me? You shit, Humph!' Her pretty voice was a screech.

'I only wanted to help.'

'Why should I need your help? We're divorced, Humph. I've had two husbands since you – far more competent in the bed stakes, I can tell you.'

'Jessica, there's no need to be like this.'

'There's every need. I hate you, Humph. I fucking hate you!' And with that she flung the receiver towards its cradle, but it bounced back on the floor. From it she could hear Humphrey's disembodied voice calling her name. 'Oh, shit!' Wishing it was him, she kicked the phone, which skidded across the floor.

Jessica hauled herself to her feet and, holding onto

furniture with one hand and her cane with the other, hobbled across the thick carpeting to the door. She wrenched it open to find Bun on the other side.

'Heard all you want?' she spat angrily. 'Snoop! You're dismissed as from *now*.'

'That's not fair. I'd come to ask if you wanted any supper.'

'Stuff supper.' And Jessica climbed as noisily as she could up the stairs, anger seething through her. But she was unaware of how sad she looked to Bun, who watched her anxiously from the hall as she went, a small huddled figure in black, more like a rotund peasant than the star she truly was.

She slammed her bedroom door with such force that a water-colour painting crashed to the floor, its glass splintering. But Jessica did not notice as she threw herself on her bed and finally allowed herself to sob her despair.

The storm of emotion lasted a good half-hour until Jessica felt like a dried-out shell. She sat up on the fine blue silk counterpane, now a creased mess and damp where her tears had fallen. She fumbled on the bedside table for a Kleenex, blew her nose, longed for a gin and decided she had never felt so betrayed, lost and lonely in her entire life.

There was a tentative tap at the bedroom door.

'Go away!'

'I can't. I'm worried about you.' And Bun's head appeared round the edge of the door.

'I told you, go away. I don't need you. I don't need anyone.' She felt in danger of crying again and promptly fought the tears, determined no one should see her like this.

'Everyone needs someone, especially at a time like this.'

'Trot out any more platitudes and by God, I'll clock you one.'

The door opened fully and Bun, her face crinkled with concern, stepped into the room carrying a tray. 'I've brought the gin,' she said cautiously. Despite everything, Jessica smiled.

'You're a witch,' she chuckled unwillingly.

'It sounded like you needed one.' Bun crossed the room.

'An extraordinarily large one, since you offer.'

Bun poured gin into two glasses, topped them up with tonic, ice and lemon, all the while saying nothing. She handed a tumbler to Jessica.

'I suppose you expect me to tell you everything,' Jessica said, after one large and satisfying gulp.

'No, I don't. You can tell me what you want. I just don't think you should be alone in this state.' Bun sat down firmly on the blue and white upholstered chair that, with two others and a chaise-longue, made Jessica's bedroom more like a sitting-room.

'I'm sorry I spoke to you as I did.'

'Water off my back.' Bun shrugged her shoulders. 'So, I'm not sacked?'

Jessica waved a hand in the air with frustration, not at Bun but at her own loss of control. 'Of course not. I'm sorry. But for all that ...' And she told Bun of her visit to the bank. Bun's expression changed quickly from interest, to shock then horror. 'The man at the bank told me I was going to have to cut back on staff. As he so kindly put it, "You're in no position, Miss Lawley, to afford such a large household."'

'Well, there's only me and Mrs Dorking, young Tracey and Martin. It's not as if you've got a butler, is it?' Bun scoffed at the foolishness of the man.

'You don't understand, Bun. Shipleys has got to go.'

'Oh, Jessica, *no*. You love this house – and what will people say?'

'I'm not too concerned about that. Losing Shipleys is

something else.' She pushed her hair back from her face and played with a strand, as if twirling it helped her think. She had moved to this graceful Georgian house, set in twenty acres, at the beginning of her marriage to Humphrey. The building had been sadly neglected and it had been her joy to restore it. Between films she was more likely to be found up a ladder brushing the pediments clean of old paint, or deciding on curtains and wallpapers, than at a social event. It wasn't just a house to her, it was like a living thing. When divorce between her and Humphrey became inevitable – she no longer able to withstand the enforced loneliness of his endless business trips abroad – he declared it only fair that she keep Shipleys, for it was far more hers than his. The house had been the only constant thing in her adult life.

'But Humph gave you this house outright.'

'I know, but apparently I mortgaged it up to the hilt.'

'What do you mean? You either did or you didn't.' Bun's voice betrayed her mounting anxiety. At sixty what on earth was to become of her if Jessica had nothing?

'Cy Greenborne mortgaged it for me.'

'But you must have known?'

'No, I didn't. You know me, no time for business. I trusted Cy – if he gave me a pile of papers to sign I just signed them. Anything to do with accounts and taxes was too boring.'

'You never read anything you signed?' Bun could hardly believe her ears.

'No, never. Oh, I read my will when I made it – that I *had* to check, and a more morbid task I can't imagine. I got rip-roaring drunk, I can tell you.' She laughed at the memory of rushing from her lawyer's office to the Ritz and ordering a bottle of champagne to blot out the thought that she might, one day, die. She shuddered and brushed back her hair again. 'So, there it is.' She was silent for a few moments.

'We're going to have to find somewhere small to live – a bungalow in Hastings?' she suggested, almost gleefully, but feeling guilty at the anxiety on Bun's face.

'You might get work. Phone everyone you know.'

'There's something else I haven't told you, Bun. My hip – it's going to have to be replaced eventually. It's not just my knee that's turning me into a cripple.'

'Don't use that word, I hate it. I thought you did too.'

'Just facing facts, for once.'

'What about Simon? You said yourself his career looks as if it might be lifting off.'

'Ah, well, Simon? There's another saga for you ...' And she launched into it.

'After all you've done for him!' Bun said indignantly. 'I never liked him. I'd get on that blower and phone everyone you know in the business and ditch him.'

'That's what I first thought of doing, but what would be the point? I'd feel lousy if I did that – especially to a fellow actor.'

The two women sat late into the night drinking, trying to solve the impossible, getting nowhere. Just as they were parting Jessica suddenly remembered her Christmas present to Bun. 'That Christmas cruise, Bun. You're not to think of cancelling it. That, at least, is paid for.'

'Oh, I couldn't leave you in this mess.'

'Please, Bun. Go. I'll be fine. I've got dozens of people I can ask to have me – you know that.'

'Well, if you're sure?' Bun said, somewhat wistfully.

Jessica knew how excited she was at the prospect of her cruise to the Canaries. 'Positive', she replied. The last thing she wanted, though, was to face people. She'd hole up here alone – no one need know she was at home. After all, she'd have sacked the rest of the staff by then. She sighed at that thought. How on earth was she to tell them?

In the morning the easiest task was sacking Martin. Plastered over one of the tabloids were photographs of her hobbling across the pavement from her flat to the car, helped by him. She looked ghastly, her face ravaged by the scene with Simon. If she hadn't known better she'd have said she was drunk.

'You were the only person who knew I was in Drayton Gardens. Only you could have tipped off the paparazzi.'

'It had nothing to do with me. Honest.'

'Unfortunately, Martin, I don't believe you. The terms of your employment were, as you well know, that you had no dealings with the press. You remember? And if you did it was to be immediate dismissal, which is what I am doing. You will vacate your flat forthwith and I'll have the car keys now.'

'But it's the weekend.'

'You should have thought of that.'

'You miserable old bitch.'

'Thank you, Martin. You may go now.'

She turned her back on him and shut her ears to the abuse he hurled. How wrong one could be about people, she thought.

The dismissal of her staff emphasised the situation she was in and Jessica had never felt so afraid in her entire life. A future alone and with no money was not an idea that had ever before entered her head.

That night she and Bun ate in the kitchen.

'I've been thinking, Jessica. Your hip. Have you thought about faith healing?'

'Oh, Bun, please ...'

'I'm being serious. My aunt, she was crippled with her back and she went to see this bloke and she was racing around like a two-year-old in no time. You ought to go.'

'Who is he?' she asked, interested now since Bun was

not the sort of person to be impressed by anything alternative.

'Heard of Fohpal and H.G.?'

'The guru?'

'The very one. Just go along and see what you think. I made a call. They've a big meeting next week in London. I'll take you.'

'It might be worth a shot. If I could get moving I could work again.'

'Exactly!'

'Mind you, I'm not setting much store by it.'

'No, of course not. But nothing ventured …' Bun grinned at her. 'To Fohpal,' she toasted with her glass of wine.

EXTRACT FROM THE
DIARY OF H.G. – THE MASTER

I must explain how I have lost control.

I've always had an idle streak in me, and consequently I've never had a problem in delegation. So when he joined us and was so eager to help, so understanding and in tune with my philosophy I welcomed him. It wasn't just his flattery – I'm too used to that – I believed in his sincerity. At first, he wrote down my lectures, then helped me compose them. He suggested improvements in my writing then made them himself. How many deadlines I'd have missed but for his invaluable assistance. When I was tired it was so much easier to let him stand in for me at meetings and gatherings. I've always hated the nuts and bolts of life – making decisions, paying bills. Such mundane matters got in the way of my spirituality, I told myself, as I handed the checking accounts, the financial matters of the house over to him. Ah, so easy.

As I'd been the son Bay had never had, so he became mine. He became my confidant, I put my trust in him, but only to a point, of course, since he knows nothing of these secrets that I've told you.

He is motivated by greed. How it hurts me to write that. It is something I cannot understand. We have everything we could possibly need here. A life of such pleasantness. But he wants more and I fear it is for himself. I begin to suspect he has a bank account somewhere, Switzerland maybe. I've never asked for anything from the followers, it has always been given me, and I've been grateful. But now he demands money, I'm sure. And, worse, he is doing it in my name.

And he is lustful. I feel my position is like that of a

doctor or a priest: young women come to me, they must feel safe. But he, I fear, uses them.

Why don't I do something? I have no proof – and, of course, it is not in my nature to accuse without full knowledge. Everything I say is based on instinct and odd remarks. Together, one by one, they become a jigsaw, whose picture I do not care for.

The danger I sense is because I think he has guessed my suspicions. He cannot afford to let me uncover him.

I don't know what to do.

I am surrounded by people who all revere me and no one is my friend.

Something is afoot. Two months ago, after I started confiding in you, after my suspicions arose, he introduced Dominic to us and suggested we have a resident doctor.

I could have said no. But the doctor himself looked ill and in far more need of help than us, and how could I possibly turn away one who had such an air of desperation? Of course, now I know why. Dominic drinks to excess. Coming here was his saving. I sense he was on the edge of an abyss, probably had lost his job. No doubt, he would not have been able to carry on much longer out there in the real world.

Dominic is as interested in self-discovery and fulfilment as a deaf man is interested in Mozart. He has an easy life here: most of us use homeopathy so he can hardly be overworked. He is an ideal candidate for him to manipulate – get him dependent, supply him with what he wants and then he'll do anything. If he talks, threaten him with withholding what he needs – so blissfully simple.

But what does he want him to do? That's my problem. If Dominic was injecting me with something – vitamins, let's say – then I'd have reason to be afraid. He does nothing, though. I sit and wait for him, for something to happen, fearing I know not what.

It's a dreadful way to live ...

chapter six

1

'So what happened? Did Carter come back from Munich?' Selina asked, as Ginnie drove them along the motorway towards London. She'd tried several topics of conversation since they'd left Finchester and so far all she'd had were monosyllabic answers.

'Of course he came back,' Ginnie replied sharply, and unnecessarily overtook another car to cover her embarrassment. Selina looked at her from the corner of her eye and saw the set expression on her face. Oops! she thought. Confidence time over. Obviously Ginnie had decided to forgive Carter so she in turn had better forget that their conversation that Sunday had ever taken place.

There was a hope, Selina supposed, that Ginnie had forgotten what she'd said about Carter. Calling him a creep was bad enough, but it was a pity she'd also said that Ginnie would be better off without him. She'd been right all along: one should never get involved in others' relationships and say things one might regret when, as they invariably did, they kissed and made up. Fool! She looked out of the window as they shot past Bristol. She wished Ginnie would slow down; she liked speed but only when she was behind the wheel and in control.

Ginnie knew she was driving too fast but it felt as if, by putting her foot down, she could speed away from her disloyalty to Carter in confiding to Selina. If he ever found out, his anger would be justifiable, she thought. All her threats had disappeared the minute he'd returned, late at night, excited at having the Munich gallery agree to an exhibition of his work and holding, of all things, a monstrous cuckoo clock, a peace-offering for her. She had laughed at the huge carved contraption, complete with its wooden oom-pah band. But she was touched that he'd remembered how, years ago, she'd confessed she'd love to own one. The clock made it easy for her to welcome him as if nothing had happened. They'd gone to bed and made love. It had all been so perfect.

In the morning she'd heard him on the phone to Anna. He'd made no attempt to hide who it was he was talking to, even waving to her as she'd entered the room. The next day he said he had an urgent appointment in London. Ginnie had suggested she went too, that they make a treat out of it with a show, a good dinner and a night at the Cadogan, her favourite hotel. But he'd fobbed her off with a story that he'd made plans to meet business associates. She'd appeared to accept his explanation – but what sort of idiot did he take her for?

Knowing she was weak and a fool, Ginnie despised herself. As she drove she felt as if she was disintegrating inside. That the screaming of her soul must be audible to anyone. She didn't want to live like this …

People were exasperating, thought Selina, longing for a cigarette but not liking to light up. After all, *she* had told Ginnie things she hadn't meant, too – two glasses of wine on an empty tum was the probable cause, she had decided. She did not regret it – it had been a relief to get things out in the open. And she was sure that if she had had second thoughts about it she wouldn't have taken it out on Ginnie …

'When I told Carter I was coming with you to the Fohpal meeting and to listen to H.G. speak, he laughed,' Ginnie said, easing off the accelerator.

'Why?' Selina asked, jolted out of her thoughts.

'He said hadn't I left it a bit late in the day to find or need self-fulfilment. I thought that was funny too!' She hadn't, she'd thought it unkind and just another way for Carter to put her down.

'Is he self-fulfilled?' More than likely he was afraid that Ginnie might come back a different person, thought Selina.

'He also said H.G.'s probably a charlatan.'

Takes one to know one, thought Selina. 'I expect some gurus are, but not H.G., not from what I've read. He just talks to people and heals them. I read that if you have a healing session with him you don't even have to pay, you just give what you can.'

'That's what I said. Carter suggested I left my cheque book at home.' She had relaxed a little. Talking was helping her again.

'God, how patronising.' It was out before Selina could stop it.

'Exactly. I said there wasn't a hint of scandal about H.G. He wasn't a cult thing. I don't think it did any good.'

'If someone's made their mind up about something like this, it's impossible to get them to budge,' Selina said sagely, remembering how adamant Chris could be. 'Is Tessa home? Hasn't the university term ended?'

'Yes, just for a week and then she's off to France with friends. They rented a chalet in the Alps for Christmas. At least I'm spared her constant nagging – all she does is tell me to get an interest. I've loads of interests. And, in any case, it'll just be Carter and me on our trip to New York.'

'That still on?'

'Of course. What made you think it wasn't?' she asked tersely.

'Nothing,' Selina replied unconvincingly. 'I always think Christmas is overrated, don't you? All that excitement and build-up and it's always a big let-down. My dad hated it so – he even died on Christmas Eve to really ruin it.'

'Selina! What a dreadful thing to say! First you were going on about your mother, now it's your father. Whatever next?' Ginnie's voice was full of disapproval.

'At least they can't hear me.' She noticed Ginnie make a prissy shape of her mouth and the car moved faster again. 'And, in any case, I thought you didn't go much on your mum either.'

'I never said any such thing! Really, Selina, you are impossible!' She overtook, speeding along the fast lane again. Ginnie need never take a lie detector test, Selina thought. Just put her in a car and note her speed at each question asked.

'Do you mind if I smoke?' Selina asked finally.

'If you must.' Rather pointedly, Ginnie pressed the central control button, which opened the window.

'I won't bother,' Selina said, and pressed the window shut again resignedly. Friendship was an odd thing. She and Ginnie had known each other for five years, yet now all manner of cracks were beginning to appear. Ginnie had once tolerated her smoking, now she didn't. On the other hand, Selina had used to accept it when Ginnie was sharp with her – usually, she'd been certain, when things weren't working out with Carter – had made allowances, even felt sympathy. But today she felt affronted.

It had been confiding in each other, she thought. She was sure her initial feeling about best friends had been right, that the more one told the more vulnerable one became. There was no difference, really, between sharing secrets and lending money. How often did borrowers cut a lender dead because they didn't like the feeling of obligation? Perhaps it was the same with secrets shared. She doubted that she and Ginnie were unique. It probably happened sooner or later to most friendships. She wished now that she had come alone.

'Which hotel did you say we're going to? Only we're just approaching the Chiswick flyover. I like to know which way I'm going in London otherwise I get in a flap,' Ginnie said, pleasantly, and Selina felt she must have imagined everything. Maybe it had been the stress of driving on the busy motorway.

'This is the stupidest thing I've ever allowed you to talk me into,' Jessica fretted in the back seat of the car. 'Watch that lorry. Mind!'

'Who's driving? Shut up or you can walk to London,' Bun snapped back. 'And I wish you'd stop twittering. You're going. What have you got to lose? You'll meet some interesting people and, who knows, you might get your hip sorted out and your knee as well.'

'A likely story! My surgeon's the best in London.'

'Oh, yes, and what did he say when you told him you were coming?'

'He said he never shut his mind to anything.'

'There you are, then. If he can say that, why can't you have a bit more open-mindedness and faith?'

'I think it's pointless to raise my hopes. And I don't want to meet people.'

'Sometimes, Jessica, you're a real pain.'

'As you are, dear Bun – frequently! But I love you, for all that.'

At this exchange they both grinned. During the past month Bun had been a tower of strength and Jessica was sure that without her to confide in as each of her plans foundered, she'd have been in a psychiatric institution by now.

Despite a reportedly stagnating property market, Shipleys was no sooner on the market than she had three buyers champing at the bit. The young man from Knight Frank explained that such compact estates with a beautiful house and so close to London were highly sought after.

'I'll be homeless by February,' Jessica had complained.

'Don't ham it up, Jessica. With all the moolah you'll get for this, there'll surely be enough over to buy a dear little cottage somewhere.'

'Can you honestly see *me* in a *dear little cottage*? Oh really, Bun, you do talk a load of crap at times. I'd rather have a flat in London.'

'The pugs would be happier in a cottage with a garden,' Bun had replied slyly.

And Jessica's novel writing had not progressed. Publishers were interested, certainly – but only in an autobiography, provided she spilled the beans. 'The trouble is, Bun, do I really want to? I mean, how can I ditch my friends? Some of the living are married, happily. And those loves who are dead – I don't want to be the one to damage the myth.'

Bun felt such anger for Jessica and the predicament she was in. Famous and adored for so many years, it was hard for her to find herself out on the rubbish dump. The book was only one of the plans to which Bun had been privy: she had tried to launch a perfume, then costume jewellery, and finally a range of clothes, all using her name. Bun had heard Jessica put the concept to agents and manufacturers, and she'd listened to the rejections. Everyone had been polite, but the bottom line was that she was a plump, crippled has-been, and which was the worst crime, being overweight or limping? Neither knew for sure.

Now, as they drew up outside the hotel where the conference – or *gathering*, as Fohpal called it – was to be held, Bun took hold of Jessica's hand and squeezed it. 'You look lovely,' she said softly.

'Oh, Bun, I don't.'

'You do, Jessica. Oh, you're a bit on the heavy side—'

'A bit!' Jessica snorted derisively.

'Shut up. Let me finish. Nothing can take that face away from you. You're beautiful – and don't you forget it. You're beautiful because of the person you are inside. It shines out.'

'My face has gone and I'm a crabby old bitch.'

'It hasn't and you're no such thing. You go in there and you sock it to them.'

'I wish you were coming. You'll be all right, at your sister's?'

'We'll have a lovely time hating each other.'

'I'm scared.'

'You? Ridiculous, after all you've done. Go on. Out with you. Put this show on the road!' She smiled at Jessica as they stood on the pavement. Bun suddenly hugged her and shuddered.

'You cold?'

'No. Someone walked over my grave.'

2

The foyer of the large London hotel was a seething mass of people. Tourists, Christmas shoppers and the followers of Fohpal all mingled noisily together. It was impossible to tell which category was which since everyone milling about was dressed conventionally and the meeting was not restricted to those of British nationality.

Jessica stood slightly apart from the crowd by a window, fearing she might be recognized, gawped at and asked for autographs. She scanned the large hallway for reporters – the last thing she needed was anything in the papers about her being here and the conjecture *that* might lead to. She was not aware of how incongruous she looked in the artificial light of the hotel: her huge dark glasses with her scarlet cloak made her look like a giant ladybird.

Finally, reassured that the coast was clear, she joined the crowd, feeling, to her surprise, a comforting anonymity. A huge gilt-framed, black-lined board told her that the Fohpal meeting was in the conference centre on the lower ground floor. She waited with a sizeable group for a lift and when it arrived was swept into it by the sheer press of people. The lift descended, stopped and decanted them into another packed foyer.

'If you could pick up your identity tags over here,' a tall young man was shouting over the heads of the throng. 'Identity tags and registration here.' He sounded like an old-fashioned street-seller.

Seeing a chair set against the wall Jessica lowered herself on to it to allow the crowd to clear slightly so that fewer people would be around when she had to give her name. Beside her was a large floor-length glass showcase, artfully lit, inside which were displayed two exquisite, highly complicated patchwork quilts. She bent forward admiring the work, knowing from her own efforts that these quilts were in a class of their own. A card stood in front of them and she peered closer to read it. 'The Master's work,' she read. That was interesting. At least she had one thing in common with H.G. Were they for sale? She would like one – and then, with a jolt, she remembered her present financial state.

She had an overwhelming longing for a cigarette. She could kick herself now for smoking that awful day. Since she had not smoked for so long she had thought she could stop again easily. Not so. Her body, as if reminded of the nicotine of which it had been deprived, had acquired a greater craving for it than ever before. Looking around, she saw no one else smoking and decided she had better wait for a coffee break. This thought took her by surprise; Jessica normally did what Jessica wanted and a No Smoking sign would not have stopped her in the past.

The lift arrived again, disgorging another group, including Ginnie and Selina, who hurtled out looking flustered.

'We made it!' Selina gave a sigh of relief.

'I never thought we would, not with that last traffic hold-up. Have you bought tickets?'

'No, it's first come, first served. I hope we're not too late and we can still get in.' They joined the slowly shuffling queue.

Ginnie was excited: she so rarely left home and Finchester that this was quite an adventure. The buzz of anticipation in the air was catching. She felt all the anger and frustration of the morning dissipate, leaving her intrigued.

At the desk four young women were calmly and efficiently processing the crowd. 'Name?' they were asked.

'I'm Selina Horner and this is Virginia Mulholland.'

A young, very slim woman, who, according to the label pinned to her sky-blue robe was called Abigail, began to write their Christian names on white discs. As she did so, she pushed back a strand of straight, fine blonde hair, looked up at them and smiled. It was a smile like none other they'd ever seen: it was calm, almost madonna-like and seemed to drench them with a feeling of well-being.

'I'm so sorry, I didn't hear your name?' asked another woman, who was sitting beside Abigail. She was middle-aged, rotund, grey-haired and wore spectacles that slid constantly down her nose. She was dressed in a navy robe, and although she smiled she was too thin-lipped for it to have the galvanizing effect of Abigail's. Her name tag proclaimed her to be Mathie and she was talking to a woman in a scarlet cloak standing beside Ginnie, leaning heavily on a stick, who leant forward, almost conspiratorially, as she spoke her name.

'Jessica, did you say?' Mathie said, loudly enough for all to hear. 'If you don't speak up, how am I expected to know what to write?'

'J – E – S – S – I – C – A. Loud enough for you?'

'Some people!' muttered Mathie, and her smile disappeared. Abigail dug her in the ribs and Mathie's smile promptly returned.

'You poor dear! Do you need assistance, a wheelchair?' Abigail, still smiling, stepped forward.

'That won't be necessary! I'm not a total cripple, I can walk,' Jessica said firmly.

'Of course you can,' Abigail cooed. 'But can someone show you the way?'

'Just point. I think I've enough grey matter to work it out. Thank you for your charming welcome,' said Jessica, flashing a sardonic smile at Mathie, who looked down at the baize-covered table.

It was Selina's turn to dig Ginnie sharply in the ribs. 'It's Jessica Lawley,' she mouthed.

'Who?' Ginnie mouthed back. Both stood aside to let Jessica by as she limped towards the doors to the auditorium, which were being held open by two young men with equally broad, calm smiles.

'You know, the actress,' Selina risked speaking now that Jessica had moved on.

'It never is. Mind you, now I can see her properly, you're right.'

'Lovely face, hasn't she?'

'I'd no idea she was that old.'

'Age gets us all in the end.' Selina smiled at Ginnie's ill-concealed excitement.

'Let's hurry. Maybe we'll sit close to her and goggle a bit.' The change in Ginnie's mood was dramatic, thought

Selina, as they hurried in pursuit of Jessica, Ginnie dragging Selina along by the hand.

It was bedlam in the auditorium as people greeted each other like long-lost friends and others introduced themselves to their near neighbours. The excitement they had felt in the vestibule was as nothing to the atmosphere here.

'How many of us are there, do you think?' Selina asked Ginnie.

'A thousand? I'm not too good on numbers.' They took their places, settling into the comfortably upholstered blue velvet armchair-like seats, arranged on mounting tiers like a theatre so that they looked down onto a blond-wood stage, bare but for a large, throne-like chair in the centre.

'Not as many as that. Four, five hundred, perhaps. Just think, twenty pounds each – that's a lot of money for a day.' Selina was watching the crowd, hoping to see the young man who'd come to the shop, Matt. 'There's money to be made in the guru business,' she added, a mite too loudly, and then wished she hadn't since a woman sitting in front of them turned majestically in her seat and gave her a filthy look. 'I'd expected a crowd of the sandals and homespun tunic brigade, dun coloured clothes right for eating lentils in, a lot like my customers,' she whispered.

'Too right, but they're in the minority. Everyone looks very respectable.'

'And middle class. And professional.'

'And smart.' Selina smiled at Jessica, who was sitting beside her on the outside of the row, her right leg stretched rigidly in the aisle. 'It's like waiting for the curtain to go up on a play, isn't it?' she said, but at the look of alarm on the older woman's face – as if she knew she'd been recognized and didn't want to be – she wished she hadn't spoken.

'Selina, this lady says that H.G. won't be here.'

'Oh, no! Really?' Selina leant forward to see a black-suited, pearl-earringed woman, smartly made-up with immaculately groomed hair, sitting beside Ginnie.

'He's not well,' she said, in the clipped tones of a Knightsbridge matron.

'What's wrong with him?' Ginnie asked, disappointed that they were not to see and hear the man she'd been reading about ever since Selina had suggested she come with her to the meeting.

'His age, no doubt. They don't say, of course, everyone's so discreet. But a friend of mine went to visit Porthwood last summer and she said she saw H.G. being wheeled into the garden so that the group could acknowledge him, but he didn't say anything and my friend said she doubted he could.' The woman leant forward, glanced left to right, then cupped her hand around her mouth so as not to be overheard. 'A stroke, probably.' She nodded wisely, enjoying her role as provider of information.

'Oh, what a disappointment. They didn't say at the door,' Selina said, hoping the old boy wasn't too ill. If he croaked it, she assumed that it would be the end of Fohpal and they'd never buy her shop.

'It is and it isn't. It gives us a chance to listen to Xavier, his disciple. He's a wonderful man, so inspirational. I promise you both, you're in for a treat,' she said.

All this time music had been playing in the background, not that anyone had been listening, but when it stopped the talking began to subside. Quickly the hall fell silent as the lights were slowly doused. Vivaldi was replaced by the sound of a single sitar. The audience listened quietly. There was the odd rustling, a sneeze, a cough or two. The stirring ceased. The people sat silent and then even the plaintive notes of the sitar faded. The low lights were dimmed further until there was nothing but blackness.

Ginnie felt for Selina's hand and squeezed it. Sitting quietly in the darkness she realised that the excitement she had been feeling was evaporating, to be replaced by a strange calm.

'Remember this,' a melodic, disembodied, but beautiful, male voice intoned, 'remember this. You are no longer alone.'

From the packed audience a collective sigh rose to the rafters.

3

'It would appear you can have Malvern, Highland Spring or the Porthwood special,' Selina announced, pointing across at a table laden with mineral-water bottles, glasses and ice buckets.

'I'm spoilt for choice!' Ginnie laughed. 'I suppose loyalty wins. I'll have the Porthwood.'

'Can I get something for you?' Selina asked Jessica shyly. After her initial failure at friendliness she didn't want to rush the woman, or to have her think she was muscling in on her because of who she was.

'I'd kill for a gin!' Jessica's beautiful husky voice replied, and Selina and Ginnie laughed. The ice was broken. 'Bit of a nerve isn't it, inflicting their rules on us? Oh, I don't know – Malvern, I suppose. But thanks,' she added hurriedly, as if suddenly aware of how ungracious she sounded.

'Don't they even drink coffee or tea?' Ginnie said, wistfully when they returned to Jessica with their glasses.

'Apparently not. Presumably no stimulants are allowed. But most of them don't appear to need anything – they look as high as kites to me,' Jessica said amicably.

'If it's just from spirituality then it's cheap enough, isn't it?' Selina said.

'They all look so happy. They smile with such contentment, as if they know something we don't.' Ginnie looked around at them.

'As if they had a secret,' Selina agreed.

'As if they're half-witted, more like,' Jessica ventured. 'You know what they remind me of? Evangelical, born-again Christians. They have that same idiotic smile. Indicative of a blank mind.'

Even while laughing at Jessica's joke, Ginnie felt she shouldn't be since, secretly, she rather envied the followers. She doubted that, with her problems, she could ever look as serene, ever feel their calm. She'd like to be like them, but she wasn't about to say so and have Jessica mock her.

They were sitting in a large lounge in comfortable deep armchairs in what, at a normal conference, would have been a mid-morning coffee break. To Ginnie it seemed wrong to be sitting in ordinary surroundings when they had spent the last hour and a half listening to talk of the spiritual self.

H.G. might not have been there in the flesh but his spirit had been present for, one by one, the speakers had paid tribute to his ideas and philosophies. They told of how finding the Inner Way, as H.G. described it, had changed their lives. How happiness was within everyone's grasp – all they had to do was seek and find it. Reach out and take it. *Join with us* was the rallying cry.

After such a talk, Ginnie wanted to be in the open air, preferably in a garden in the country, with only beauty and serenity around her. For, laugh as the others might, she had been listening to beautiful ideas and concepts, all of which made stunning sense to her.

'Have you everything you need?' A woman in her thirties, dressed in a dark blue robe, bent down in front of the three women. 'I'm Hesta.' She tapped her name tag. She was quite small but large-breasted with a mass of reddish curly hair which framed her fair-skinned face. She was rather plain, not helped by her pale eyelashes and brows, but it was a strong face, that of a person with purpose.

'I'd like a gin and tonic,' Jessica replied, with an almost defiant toss of her head.

Hesta smiled beatifically at her. 'But of course – whatever you want … Jessica,' she said, leaning forward to peer at her name. 'I forgot my specs. I'm sorry you weren't offered a drink, but most of our followers don't partake and, well …' She looked at her watch rather pointedly.

'Make it a double,' Jessica said belligerently.

'And you two?' Hesta asked.

'I'm perfectly happy,' said Ginnie.

'A coffee would be wonderful,' added Selina, and Ginnie wished she'd had the courage to be honest too.

Selina was surprised that Hesta had not recognised Jessica, whose face she'd have thought everyone knew.

Hesta flicked her fingers somewhat arrogantly and two young women, in paler blue, came running as if in competition to see who could get there first.

'Is that a uniform you're wearing?' Ginnie asked, hoping to make amends for what she saw as Jessica's gross rudeness.

'It makes it easier for friends to identify us, of course. Each colour has a significance – it shows what level we have reached along the Inner Way. The paler the colour, the longer the road.'

'Then you must be very senior.' Ginnie put out her hand almost as if she intended to touch the dark blue silk of Hesta's robe.

'How sweet you are ... Ginnie.' Again she had to peer at the name tag. 'I could not agree with such words as junior, senior. We are, of course, all equal ... It's just that some of us have been working on our Inner Self a little bit longer.'

Hesta's accent was hard to place, Jessica thought. One moment she thought she detected a hint of Scottish – soft, from the Western Isles perhaps – and then she'd heard a shade of Canadian, a touch of Essex ... It annoyed her. Jessica prided herself on her ability to place people and this was a hard one to crack.

'At home, we can wear whatever we want, but most stick to the robe.'

'Where's home?' Selina asked.

'Porthwood, of course. It's lovely there, so calm and peaceful. We've wonderful gardens – they're famous, you know. The countryside, the sea. It gives our minds the right atmosphere to think straight. Coming to London is a real shock to the system – all the noise.' She shuddered.

'I like it. It makes me feel alive,' Jessica said.

'There are different ways of being alive,' Hesta said.

'How many of you live at Porthwood?'

'It varies, Selina. Sometimes fifty. Sometimes a hundred, and in summer, at the meeting, we become thousands.'

'So you come and go as you like?'

'Of course. What a funny question.'

'You know, you read these things ...' Selina felt herself colouring with confusion, fearing she sounded rude and suspicious.

'You mean these cults that imprison people? Oh, we're not like that. People come to us because they want to, they need what we have to offer. What would be the point in making people stay where they didn't want to be?' Hesta laughed at such a notion.

'And what do you have to offer?' Jessica asked, in a voice that, to Ginnie, sounded almost aggressive.

'Did you not listen to the seminar, Jessica?' Hesta asked patiently.

'I listened,' Jessica said enigmatically.

'We offer whatever it is you want to receive.'

Hesta smiled with such tenderness, Ginnie thought.

'I hate riddles. And if you look at that sentence you'll see how crass it is. It means that if I'm a cannibal you'll make sure I'm supplied with human flesh, I suppose?'

'Oh, what a funny idea, Jessica! I can't say we've met many cannibals, but if you were then I'm sure we would talk to you and find out why it is you wanted to be a cannibal and help you stop wanting to be one,' Hesta replied.

'I'm a cannibal because I like it and don't want to stop.' Jessica stood firm.

'You know, Jessica, in all my experience I've never met anyone who didn't want to rid themselves of the bad and negative things in their life and to let in the good and the hopeful.'

'So, you're a religious sect?' It was Jessica again, and Ginnie wondered what the woman's problem was, why she had to be sharp with Hesta, who was being so sweet and kind.

'Heavens, no! How H.G. would laugh if you said that. Your spirituality lies in you. If you need God, then believe in him, if it helps you. Or nature, or the wind, or the sun. H.G. wants people's minds to be free. It's up to you, that's what he says,' Hesta explained.

'Why isn't H.G. here? Is he seriously ill?' Ginnie asked, not quite liking to ask if the stroke rumour was true.

'He's been a bit poorly. Nothing serious. He works too hard, you know, travelling the world giving the message.'

'So what is this message?' Jessica asked, leaning forward. 'As far as I can make out from my reading,

H.G. is telling us to go do our own thing – hardly an original idea, not if one was around in the sixties and seventies.'

'What H.G. is telling us is to free our minds. To reject everything that is negative and thus harmful to us. If you think bad things you'll become bad. He takes our hand and leads us down a spiritual path and restores the equilibrium of our minds. Love and hope transcend and we become much better people. It's all a matter of balance.'

'It means nothing.'

'To you, Jessica, but to me it makes total sense. We're not asking you to join us, you do what you want. You find your way. But if our way isn't yours then I don't quite understand why you have to sound quite as harsh as you do. Have we hurt you?' Hesta asked gently, and Ginnie was pleased to see that suddenly Jessica looked embarrassed.

'No, of course not.'

'Do we hurt anyone?'

'I've never heard that you do.'

'So. If it works for some, then what is wrong?'

'Why give hope? Hope is often an illusion,' said Jessica, who knew the truth of that better than most.

'We don't. We say try to allow hope to enter your soul. We can't promise that you'll find it – that would be a complete misrepresentation.'

'Certainly you only have to look around to see how happy your followers are,' Ginnie added helpfully, wishing Jessica would stop.

'But it can't be that simple. It can't just be a matter of joining Fohpal and everything is solved,' said Jessica.

'But of course not. We have to work at it. We have to find this inner place, which is inside all of us. Now that I *can* promise you.'

'Then how?' asked Selina, knowing she could do with a good dollop of inner peace herself.

'Meditation. Reading. Listening. Purging the bad, nourishing the good.'

'How do we find these things?'

'We'll help you all we can, Selina. We have weekend retreats at Porthwood and you're welcome.'

'Is it expensive?' was Selina's next question.

'We ask for a basic contribution of fifty pounds, after that you give what you want and what you can afford. I have no money – nothing. But I offered the one skill I have. I can organise things, and I was welcomed. You met Mathie? She's in charge of the cooking.'

'I can't think of anything I could offer.' Selina grinned. 'I'm a lousy cook. I hate housework. I'm no good at managing and I've no money. I'd be a total loss to you.'

'No one is ever that,' Hesta said.

A gong sounded. 'There. That's time for group discussion, though you three seem to have done that already. Are you together?'

'No. We're split up. I'm with …' Selina checked the dossier she'd been given '… Berihert.' She wished it had read Matt, and then she chided herself for her foolishness, he'd probably forgotten her already.

'Ah, the gardener. There, maybe you can come and help with the weeding.' Hesta smiled.

'You wouldn't know if Matt were here?' Selina asked shyly.

'Matt? I'm afraid I don't know,' Hesta replied, and Selina hoped she hid her disappointment.

'I'm with Ancilla,' Ginnie said.

'She's quite a philosopher. American.' Ginnie pulled the slightest of faces at the thought of philosophy.

'And you, Jessica, who have you drawn? Bethina? That's perfect. She's into herbal medicine – she'll sort that knee out in no time.'

After the group discussions Jessica was thoughtful. It had been interesting and everyone was kind, but in a way that had not annoyed her. They had a peacefulness that she envied. The followers talked to them on any level: the philosophy of H.G. which, although she still found it a shade woolly, seemed to work for them. They talked about the day-to-day organisation of their lives. They talked about their pasts; some had had unhappy lives, and yet had managed to find peace. Equilibrium and balance were the buzz words, and Jessica was the first to admit she was sorely lacking in both.

Lunch was vegetarian but although everyone seemed so fired up they showed little interest in food. It was just as the meal ended that Selina saw Colley, one of the young men who had visited her shop. She had a sinking feeling when, obviously, he did not recognise her.

'Of course, the shop in Finchester! Forgive me, I've so much on my mind. Did you hear from us?'

'Well, no.'

'That's odd, we told them it was ideal. It's H.G's illness, it's made everything chaos. No one likes to make decisions.'

'Of course. I'm sorry ... at a time like this ... the last thing ...' Disjointedly she trotted out a list of platitudes, thinking, Just my luck! 'It doesn't matter,' she lied courageously.

'Look, when you get home, telephone. Ask to speak to Bethina.' Colley looked as if he felt sorry for her.

'I could, I suppose ...'

'Or, better still, come to one of the retreats. It would do you a power of good.'

'Would it?'

'No doubt about it. Shall I put your name down? The next one is over Christmas but, of course, you probably won't want to come to that.'

'No, you're wrong, Colley. That would be perfect. I'm not doing anything—'

'Great. Leave it to me. See you then!'

He'd gone back into the crowd when she realised she'd forgotten to ask him if Matt was here, but decided she'd probably forgotten on purpose.

'What was all that about?' Ginnie asked.

'It looks as if I've signed up to go on a retreat.'

'You're joking! When?'

'Christmas.'

'Not Christmas? Still, you don't enjoy it, do you, because of your father? Well, come back from it, won't you?' Ginnie joked.

The afternoon session was to be the high point. Although Xavier rather than H.G. was talking to them, there was such excitement among the followers at the mention of his name that the guests forgot their initial disappointment. It was even rumoured that he was to give a healing session.

'Which one is Xavier?' Ginnie asked Hesta, who had rejoined them as if they were her special responsibility.

'He hasn't attended. He prefers to conserve his energies for his lectures. He'll be meditating now. Shall we go back into the auditorium? You should sit as close to the front as you can, then you can see everything.'

The three sat four rows back, with Jessica again on the outside. There was a hum of anticipation in the hall, but not the rowdiness of the beginning: it was as if everyone had calmed down. 'Or is tired out,' Jessica commented acidly.

There was no darkness this time, no music. Instead a tall, well-muscled, black-haired man, with fine features and large dark eyes, slipped quietly onto the stage. He was dressed from head to toe in a blue so dark it could have been black. He sat down on the throne-like chair, which was so large that it made him appear strangely vulnerable. He bowed his head, studying his hands as if in prayer.

'Clock those cheekbones,' Ginnie whispered to Selina.

'He's quite good-looking, isn't he?' Selina said, although he was definitely not her type.

'To die for!' Ginnie sighed exaggeratedly. 'Don't you think he looks a bit like my Carter?'

'Does he?' Selina asked. She couldn't see it herself.

There was total silence in the hall as he got to his feet.

'Hello, everyone. My name is Xavier,' he said modestly. 'Welcome, all of you.' Jessica approved of his well-modulated, attractive voice, and from his delivery presumed he must have been an actor or had at least trained as one, and from the West Country, probably Dorset, she'd lay money on it.

'If H.G. were here he would say to you, "The Inner Way is open to you, come take my hand, let us go together." ' He held up his hand beckoningly as if willing them to join him. Ginnie leant forward and half lifted her own hands in acknowledgement, and she was not alone in the gesture.

An hour later Ginnie and Selina sat mesmerized. Neither spoke as Xavier's words still sounded in their heads. He had ended by saying, 'Let me give you hope. Let me give you happiness. Let me show you the way to peace.' Ginnie felt elated, over half-way there already. Jessica wanted to believe it was possible, but was not as sure. Selina wondered if there was a road map – while listening to him, she had felt a peacefulness she had never experienced before. She had never spoken to him and yet, oddly, she felt he was her friend. With him in the world she was not alone.

To Jessica it was still all too simple. If she'd learnt one thing in life it was that nothing came easy. And yet ...

Ginnie sat overwhelmed with emotion – love. She

wanted to hold this man, she wanted to be his, his alone. It was as if she had no past, as if she'd been waiting for this moment all her life.

Xavier was on his feet again and, in answer to a shouted request from the audience, was talking quietly. 'I can't promise you anything. I'm tired, you understand. I don't know if I can help but I'll try, if you'll all assist me with your love, with your strength ...'

A small queue had formed at the side of the platform. Several young women in pale robes fluttered helpfully around them. First to be helped across the stage was a man with a white stick. He was gently seated on a chair and Xavier placed his hands either side of the old man's head and bowed his own, as if in deep thought. He remained so for minutes while the audience collectively held its breath. Xavier leant across and kissed the top of the old man's head. 'Peace,' he said quietly, and the man was led away, his stick still tip-tapping.

A woman in a wheelchair, with hennaed hair and a heavily wrinkled face, was next. Xavier knelt before her. His hands placed on her knees. His head bowed. For minutes the ritual was repeated.

'Now, give me your hand. Now stand.'

'I can't,' the woman said.

'You can, you know. Trust me.' He took both of her hands in his and slowly pulled her forward in the chair. The woman protested, her fear almost palpable. 'You will walk. You can. I know you can.' He pulled harder. The woman stood, swaying slightly, supported by Xavier.

'I'm standing!' she cried out in disbelief.

'Now walk. Come with me – just a little walk.'

The woman lifted one foot tentatively and then, as if finding it working, lifted it higher then forward and placed it gingerly on the ground. Her left leg followed and then she took another step.

'I can walk!' she called. 'I'm walking!' Tears were tumbling down her cheeks and the crowd stood and cheered and applauded, and many were crying with her as, jubilantly, she crossed the whole stage.

Welsh, thought Jessica, but has lived in London most of her life.

EXTRACT FROM THE
DIARY OF H.G. – THE MASTER

I fear his patience is running out. He lost his temper with me the other day. It was over something minor but I did not react quickly enough and he did not like my response. I fear him. No one would have known he was angry with me – he appeared the same. But I know. I saw him clench his fist. I saw the flash of fury in his eyes. The hatred, too.

How it pains me to write that!

I'd hoped that sufficient fondness and respect for me remained to stay his hand. But now I see how that respect has faded. It can only be a matter of time; I have become an impediment ...

chapter **seven**

1

'Humph! What the hell are you doing here?' Jessica asked
at the sight of her ex-husband on the steps of Shipleys on
a raw December day.

'You always were such a gracious welcomer, Jessica,'
he answered, with good-natured irony, as he entered the
house that had once been his home too. 'Unusual for you
to be opening your own door. Where's Bun?' he asked, as
he unbuttoned his overcoat.

'On a cruise to the Canaries. My Christmas present to
her.'

'A bit generous, in the circumstances, isn't it?'

'How I spend my money is my own affair,' she said
sharply, and walked across the hall, pugs skittering about
at her feet. With superhuman effort and a measure of
pain she managed almost not to limp.

'You're walking well,' he said.

'One of my many accomplishments,' she flashed back.
'So, why are you here? What do you want? And I trust
you're not staying long.'

'Dear Jessica, you're so funny.' He laughed.

'As a matter of fact I'm not even trying to be funny.'

'I was just passing and thought I'd pop in and wish you
a merry Christmas.'

'Humph, you never *just* pass anywhere. As you never
do anything without a motive.'

'I'd heard about Cy Greenborne. I was worried and
wondered if you were all right. If I could help.'

'Oh, that. Stupid little man.' She waved her hands

dismissively at Cy's crooked dealings. 'Don't worry. I was luckier than most. I didn't trust him entirely – I'm not *that* stupid,' she lied.

'So, why is the house for sale? I saw it advertised in *Country Life*.'

'Because it's too big for just me. It's silly to keep it up.' The lie compounded.

'Where are you going?'

'I haven't decided. To the sun, perhaps.'

'Better for the arthritis,' he said kindly.

'No, because I've always preferred the sun.' She bridled.

'Jessica, you never have. You've always fussed about your complexion. You'd die away from England and all your friends.'

'Which shows, Humph, how little you know me.' What friends? she thought dismally. There hadn't been many who'd bothered with her since she had to drop out of the social scene.

'Mind if I pour myself a drink?'

'Help yourself. A bit early, isn't it?' she couldn't resist adding – just like a watchful wife, she thought. He ignored the remark as he clattered among the bottles on the tray, searching for his favourite malt.

'Nice that you still keep a bottle of Laphroaig for me.'

'I don't buy it for you. You're not the only person in the world who drinks it,' she said. It was not the truth. She always had kept a supply of it in case he called.

'Look, Jessica, don't keep carping at me. I've said I'm sorry about setting up Simon. It was wrong of me, I shouldn't have interfered.'

'Too right.'

'I didn't want you to be alone.'

'I wouldn't have been. I'm not *so* decrepit.'

'I didn't say you were. It's just – I care about you, you know I do. I wanted to ensure you were all right.'

'A weird way of showing it, haven't you? Making sure I was tucked up in bed with a young stud. Quite perverted, if you think about it. Or was that it, Humph? You hoped one day to be invited to watch?'

'Jess, don't say these things. You don't mean them. You've always known how I feel.'

'Oh, yes! You *really* cared about me – so much that you were never at home. And God knows what you got up to and who you screwed on your "business" trips.' She lifted both hands and sketched inverted commas in the air as she spoke the word business. 'Don't give me that crap, Humph.'

'Won't you ever believe me? I never slept around. I was wrong to leave you alone as much as I did. But good God, Jess, that was years ago. Can't we ever be friends?'

'It's all irrelevant to me now. I was just pointing out a fact to you, since you appeared to have forgotten.' Her memory had not let a minute of that lonely time escape. She had only to ponder a moment to recapture the humiliation and sadness she had felt during those years. She, the supposed Love Goddess, with a husband who was never at home so that she always slept alone. She'd convinced herself he was unfaithful – there had to be an explanation for why he left her for such long periods. It was he who had changed her from a sweet, trusting person to one with a carapace of hardness. 'And while we're about it, I've told you before, don't call me Jess. I don't like it.'

'I always called you Jess.'

'That was then. I'm talking about now.'

'Sorry. I'll try to remember – *Jessica*.' He emphasized the syllables of her name, grinning sheepishly as he did so.

She wished now she had asked for a drink, but since she'd been so snide about his she felt that she couldn't. Seeing him always upset her. She could never be in a room with him without being physically conscious of him. In his late fifties he was still attractive to her, and she couldn't say that of many of her contemporaries. She acknowledged that he was probably not as handsome as he had been; that his face was more lined, his jowls heavier, his hair greyer, his eyes duller – but to her he was perfect, for love truly was blind. Abruptly she looked away from him. Thinking like that – she must be mad.

'So, how is the arthritis?'

'Fine.'

'Whoever thought a day would dawn when swinging young chicks like us would be discussing such a thing?' He laughed. 'I've a bit of a twinge myself.'

'Really?' She sounded bored at this, and was. She had little time for those people who complained to her that they had arthritis when all it was was a creaking joint or two, just like those neurotic women who complained they suffered from migraine when all they had was a headache.

'I wondered whether I should go and see your chappie, see if I need a joint replaced too.'

'It doesn't look as if it's that bad. You only go and see my surgeon if things are serious.' She sounded cool, but that was down to the hurt he was still capable of inflicting on her. She had hoped he had spoken the truth and really *had* come to see her for herself. But it looked as though it had been only to get the address of her surgeon and cadge a little sympathy. He wasn't going to have any of *that*, she resolved.

'I'd like to help out – money.' He looked embarrassed, as if *he* was asking *her* for help, which struck her as so silly that she had the grace to smile. 'You'll let me?' he said eagerly.

'I explained, I thought. I'm fine. I don't need your help.'

'Why are you so prickly, Jess? Why won't you accept my help? Stop being so bloody proud.'

'I'm not prickly. I just don't need you,' she said, with the pride he complained of but over which she had never had any control.

He looked about the room, discomfited, as if he wasn't sure what to say next. She could almost feel sorry for him.

'Would you care to join me for Christmas? I'm off to the Caribbean, if that'll tempt you.'

'No, thank you, I've made my arrangements,' she replied, and cursed the pig-headedness that prevented her accepting. But still, she told herself, it was for the best. No doubt he'd have some vacuous blonde in tow and she would hate her, be jealous of her and the holiday would end up as a rowing mess.

'Oh, I see.' Again he looked about him as if the room would reveal the next topic of conversation.

'What have we here?' He bent towards the coffee table on which lay the books Jessica had been reading. 'Fohpal.' He read the title of one. 'Don't tell me you're getting involved with a bunch of weirdos? Oh, Jess!'

'I'm interested in many philosophies. They're not a bunch of weirdos and it's none of your business what I do.'

'So you keep telling me. Sorry again.' He stood to go. 'If you go, take my advice and leave your cheque book behind.'

She chose to ignore his remarks. 'Have a nice Christmas, then. What's her name this year? Romeo, Juliet, stop that!' The pugs were doing nothing, but it was a ruse she often used: Humphrey turned to look at the dogs and therefore did not see her hauling herself with difficulty from the chair.

'Jess, I wish—'

'Jessica!'

'Oh, what's the use? I'll be in touch.' And before she could reach the door to show him out he was gone.

She wanted to cry – she longed to – but although her throat felt constricted, no tears fell. It was as if she had none left in her, as if she had shed them all those years ago.

Still, he'd decided one thing for her. She looked in her Filofax for the number of that nice young woman she'd met at the Fohpal meeting.

'Selina? It's Jessica here.'

2

Since Ginnie had returned from the meeting in London she had changed. She had difficulty sleeping and found it hard to concentrate on anything except Fohpal. Her mind brimmed with images, hopes and dreams. Her thoughts were full of the words and philosophies she'd heard. It had taken only one day of her life for everything to be made clear, for everything to be turned joyously topsy-turvy. She felt she had travelled her own personal road to Damascus. Best of all, there was Xavier.

'Xavier,' she said to the empty room, enjoying speaking his name; it made him seem nearer to her. She sighed with longing, then hugged herself with an odd happiness.

It was all very strange, she decided, and laughed. She did not know the man, had not actually met him. Until that day she had not even known he existed and then it had been like being hit by a truck, a car or a train. She had been stunned by the physical impact of his presence. She had never longed for anyone as she longed for him. She loved him, she knew she would die for him. She had thought she loved Carter – maybe she did – but that emotion was nothing compared to this. The nearest comparison she could find was that she felt much as she had when she first met Carter except that this was an even more intense passion than she had experienced then. The last thing she had ever expected was to know anything like this. Just thinking about him swamped her with sexual longing. She knew that if he came through the door this minute she would be moist and ready for him.

Instead, though, all she had were her books. She had scoured the shops and when Finchester could only come up with one small book on Fohpal, now that Selina's shop was closed, she had gone to London, to Hatchards, had opened an account and bought every book they had on it. She had asked them to find everything H.G. had ever published and send it to her.

As each new book arrived the first thing she did was search the index for Xavier's name. He was not mentioned in any of the earlier books but popped up in something published six years ago. Luckily for her, H.G. liked to chat to his followers, to hold discussions. Some of these had been published and Xavier appeared in them. Whenever she spotted his name she kissed the page. With a magnifying glass she combed the illustrations, the group meetings, the followers sitting at H.G.'s feet until she found two pictures with Xavier in. She'd taken them the next morning to Finchester, to the local branch of Prontaprint, and had had them blown up and copied, a dozen times each.

She knew she looked different. She glowed with the excitement of her secret, the plotting and planning she must do. She could almost hate Selina, who had signed up to go for a Christmas retreat. The thought that Selina might see him, touch him, even, made her flesh crawl. What if he fell for Selina? What would she do? Still, best not to think of such things.

If she was to impress Xavier she had to know her

subject so she'd bought exercise books and had studied harder than she ever had before. She knew everything that had been written by and about H.G. How he'd been found on a beach in Sri Lanka. How he'd been civilized and educated, but had refused to be regarded as the new messiah. How he'd stormed out of a meeting and only returned when they'd promised they would never worship him again.

There was a lot she would have to learn, like how to meditate, how to clear her mind of everyday rubbish. How to release her inner self, for H.G. said the goodness was inside us and it was up to us to release it. Lovely, she thought.

She hadn't touched meat in the two weeks she'd been back. She'd given up alcohol and coffee and was working on tea. At least she didn't have to give up cigarettes since she'd never smoked.

Best of all, Xavier and Fohpal had sorted out the debris in her mind: she did not torture herself any more over Carter or where he was and what he was up to. After all these years she had finally learnt there was nothing she could do about him. It wasn't her problem. It was his. He was at fault, she'd done all she could. She didn't want to try any longer. She felt a freedom that had never existed for her before.

Tessa had been shocked when Ginnie had told her to do her own washing and ironing for her trip to France – her mother had always done it before. But no longer: Tessa should be looking after herself, Ginnie had said, and not depending on her to fetch and carry. She hadn't the time, she'd important things to attend to, to learn, to dream about.

The longed-for Christmas trip to New York, alone with Carter, had now become a nuisance, something to be endured until she could be free to see Xavier again. She had thought of telling Carter she did not want to go ...

But when they got back she would go for a weekend to Porthwood and if Xavier wanted her she'd be his for the asking—

'What's for supper?'

She jumped at the sound of Carter's voice breaking in on her happy dreams.

'I've made a ratatouille.'

'Not bloody vegetarian again!' Carter grumbled as he poured himself a drink. 'You want one?'

'No, thank you. I've given it up,' she said primly.

'It's Christmas, not Lent.' He laughed.

She watched him and thought how wrong she'd been when she thought Xavier looked like him. He didn't. Xavier had a far finer face, not damaged by self-indulgence. Xavier's eyes were clear and full of excitement and emotion while Carter's were bored, dead. There was no comparison.

'Penny for them?' he said.

'Nothing,' she lied in response, and felt almost gleeful that she had a secret of which he knew nothing.

'I hope you're not going to have nut cutlets on Christmas Day?'

'*You* can eat what you want. I don't insist you become a vegetarian, do I?' she asked with spirit.

'You'd better not,' he said, but he looked at her in surprise. 'Ginnie, what's got into you?'

'Nothing has got into me. I just don't wish to eat meat. How can we release the goodness, the conscious stream of what is right, if we pollute our bodies with dead and rotting flesh?'

'Put like that!' He laughed again and she found she could not remember if he had always laughed so much. If he had, she was surprised it hadn't annoyed her as it did now. 'Still, I wish you'd shut up. I like my meat.' He settled himself in the chair she'd been sitting on and flicked open the newspaper. Then, feeling uncomfortable, he felt under himself and produced a book. 'Ah, that's better,' he said, and then looked at the cover. *Answering the Impossible* by H.G, aloud. 'H.G.? Who's he? Oh, yes, of course. What was that joke I heard?' He thought a moment. 'What's a guru? Gee Are You? Get it?' He found this funny.

'That's a joke?'

'Maybe I said it wrong.'

'Are you in or out?' she asked coldly.

'I'm here, aren't I? So *in*. What *has* got into you?'

'Nothing.'

'I wish to Christ you'd stop saying *nothing*.' He mimicked her. 'When you say that it means all PMT hell is about to break loose.'

'And I wish you'd stop asking what's got into me. It's so boring! How's the painting gone today?' she asked suddenly, conscious of her inner self and her need to guard it.

'Fine. Since when have you been interested?'

'That's not fair, Carter.' She felt a twinge of resentment and fought it. She would not let him rile her. 'I've always been interested in your work, you know I have.'

'Oh, you say, "That's *nice*. I like the colours" – asinine remarks like that – but you don't really *see* them. You don't understand them. You never have, you never will.' He was goading her, she knew. He wanted a row so that he could storm out to meet his mistress and say it was her fault.

'Probably not. I'm sorry if I don't. I would like to have understood. I can see now how hurtful and frustrating that must have been for you.' She was collecting her precious books together, she did not want him touching them.

'You what? What did you say?' His mouth hung open in amazement.

'I think you heard me, Carter. I realise now how

difficult these years must have been – living with me. You really would be better off with Anna. I see that now. I've been grossly selfish.' She felt so much better, saying that. And it was the truth. She'd seen it in a blinding flash. She'd only ever thought of her own unhappiness, never his – and these years trapped with her must have been hell for him too.

'I think I'm in the wrong play. What do you mean, with Anna? You still think I'm having an affair with her? Don't be ridiculous. Any dealings with Anna are strictly business.'

'You don't have to pretend any more, Carter. I really do understand, this isn't a bluff.'

'I think you've gone mad.' He stood up but sat down with a bump at her next sentence.

'I believe a divorce is the best answer. I've given it a lot of thought. You can stay here – or if you want we can sell this and buy something else. You never really liked this house, did you? You can keep the car, of course, and I'll make an adequate allowance for you. I'll buy Tessa a flat, you needn't worry about that. I think we'll both be a lot happier, don't you?' She smiled sweetly, thinking how easy it all was suddenly.

'Have you gone mad or something?'

'I don't think so.'

'Then you're menopausal?'

'Oh, Carter. Why do you men always blame everything on female hormones?' She smiled gently, almost indulgently at him. She'd been practising her smile in front of the mirror, and hoped it was becoming worthy of one who loved Xavier and all that he stood for.

'I know. You've got another fellow,' he said suspiciously.

She had a fleeting feeling of satisfaction as she realised he might be jealous. 'Don't be silly,' she answered, though he was close to the truth. She knew that although she hadn't been physically unfaithful, she certainly had mentally.

'I'll kill him!' He was on his feet again. Oh, bliss, she thought, he really is jealous, then caught her thoughts and reined them in – this was no way to be.

'Sit down, Carter, please. There is no one else – not in that sense.'

'Then in what sense?'

'I've met some people. Their ideas interest me. They've changed me.'

'Who? What?'

'Just after you came back from your trip to Munich – with Anna,' she could not resist adding, 'I went to a meeting in London with Selina. I found it very interesting.'

'Oh, not one of Selina's New Age groups or something. Her ex-husband told me if anything new came along she jumped on the bandwagon.'

'He would. I don't expect you to understand, Carter, I'm just telling you how it is. I'd have thought you'd be pleased – it's made it easier for you. I think I'm being very reasonable.'

'What's reasonable about it? I don't want a divorce. I'm happy married to you. Why should I want to change anything? What about our trip on Concorde?'

'Take Anna.'

He looked at her, horrified, as the penny dropped. 'Ginnie, it's not one of those cults? You're not involved with one of those – you know, they alienate you from your family. Oh, Ginnie, no!'

'Don't be silly, Carter. It's Fohpal. They're a highly respectable fellowship of people. Since I met them, they've touched my life, they've changed me. The only way I can describe it is that I feel as if I've been blinkered and the blinkers have been removed.'

'Don't talk such unmitigated rubbish. You're to stop seeing them. You hear?'

'I can't.'

'You bloody well can. I'll make sure of that. Is this their rubbish?' He picked up the books and, one by one, hurled them onto the fire. She stepped forward, her hand outstretched, too late. She saw her picture of Xavier fall from one of them and the flames eat into his beautiful face.

'You shouldn't have done that,' she said, so calmly that he thought he had won.

'I don't want your pretty head clogged up with evil rubbish like this. I admit I've not been as attentive as I should have been but it'll change, I promise you. I'll look after you, you won't need half-baked gurus to make you happy.' She let him put his arm around her shoulder. He was afraid, she thought, but sadly it was probably at the prospect of losing her money rather than her. 'You're wrong about Anna. It's purely business.'

She didn't believe him, not for one moment.

'Fancy some ratatouille, then? And I'll grill you a steak if that will make you happier.' She smiled at him. She felt quite sorry for him, now that she knew what she must do.

'That's my good girl.' He patted her rump. Once upon a time she had liked him to do that.

3

With an early start in the morning Selina decided to go to bed at nine. She unplugged the telephone extension in her room – no one but Ginnie would call at this time and if she did she would have to try again in the morning. Then she looked at the jack-point and wondered if she shouldn't reconnect it. Ginnie had been behaving differently since their return from London. What if she called, needing to talk?

On the drive back from the meeting Ginnie had been almost monosyllabic. At first Selina had put this down to fatigue, until they'd stopped at the Granada service station. Then she saw Ginnie full face, as she sat opposite drinking an orange juice. There was an aura of suppressed excitement about her which, if Selina had not known her better, she'd have thought was due to some stimulant. And, oddly, she wore a strange smile that seemed to flirt with her lips, as if she was suppressing a secret. It was not unlike a less pronounced version of the beatific smiles of the followers.

Ginnie talked rather more on the second leg of the journey but, alarmingly, on only one topic. Xavier. Selina judged it unsafe to criticise the man. Not that she'd have said anything about him as a person – how could she since she did not know him? But caution told her it would be unwise for anyone to be attracted to someone such as he, a guru in the making, a man already being placed on a pedestal by devoted followers. Selina had enjoyed the meeting and had gained from it, but there was a degree of theatricality about Xavier that would make her think twice about him as a romantic interest – if that was how Ginnie now viewed him.

Still, she told herself, she was probably worrying unduly. Ginnie was too involved with Carter for there to be room for anyone else. Probably it was euphoria from the meeting, so different from anything else they'd ever experienced, which was making Ginnie talk about him incessantly.

Two weeks later, though, Ginnie had called only once, which was strange. And that was only to ask if she'd any books left on H.G. She had sounded quite ratty when Selina said she hadn't.

Why she worried she didn't know, she thought as she brushed her hair. Ginnie was ten years older than her, for goodness' sake, and was quite capable of looking after herself. And as she climbed into bed she left the telephone jack-point as it was.

The early night was pointless. She couldn't sleep. She missed Sabbie for a start – he always slept with her and his warm lump was a comfort, like a living hot-water bottle. But she'd taken him to Joyce, three shops down, who always looked after him if she went away. The cat flap meant he could always get back here for security if he wanted.

Sabbie must have been glad when Geoff left, for when he'd been here she had had to ban him from the bed – Geoff thought it unhygienic to sleep with a cat.

There were days when she still missed Geoff. They'd had some good times, it hadn't always been bad. She missed having someone to talk to, chew over problems with. It was worse in bed; there was comfort in lying beside someone in the empty hours of the night. She didn't miss him physically, which surprised her because as they'd enjoyed good sex she had thought she would.

She had telephoned Fohpal to speak to Bethina, but she was never there, and away from Colley's enthusiasm, she began to wonder if she was doing the right thing in attending the retreat. It was easy enough to get caught up in the excitement at the meeting, but back in her empty shop it all seemed pointless. When she couldn't contact Bethina, though, she realised that attending the retreat was the only way of finding out if they were still interested in buying the shop. It would be fifty pounds she could ill afford and she wondered if that was all there was to pay. Heavens, what a mess she was in that fifty pounds should be such a significant sum.

She moved restlessly in her bed. The Fohpal people wanting the shop was her only hope of survival. It was bloody inconsiderate of Bethina not to return her calls. She sat up and thumped her pillows into a different shape.

She'd enjoyed that day in London. She'd felt oddly safe – what a strange word for an independent young woman to use. She smiled into the darkness. She was excited to be seeing them all again – especially now that Jessica was coming. Imagine her giving a lift to a famous person like Jessica! And it had solved the problem of her solitary Christmas.

An hour later she had given up hope of sleep, and, as was her habit, was making herself tea when the telephone rang in the sitting room. Sighing she picked it up. The last person she wanted to speak to was Ginnie with her matrimonial problems.

'No, it's not your mate, it's me, Geoff.'

'I recognised your voice.' She felt happy at hearing it again.

'I miss you, Selina. More than I can explain. Are you missing me too?'

'Yes, I do. And I don't.'

'You always were a bit potty.' He sounded pleased with her honesty. 'Bet I know which bits you're missing!'

She frowned. He'd spoilt it.

'Can I come over?'

'I'm going away tomorrow for Christmas.'

'I meant now.'

'I don't think so, Geoff.'

'Please! I want to see you. To say I'm sorry. I want to make amends, I want to try again,' he pleaded.

She looked at the phone, puzzled, as if she hadn't heard right. 'It's not that simple, Geoff.'

'Course it is! Nothing to it. Kiss and make up, admit what berks we've been—'

'No, Geoff. I don't think so. We were beginning to

annoy each other and we'd have ended up loathing one another.'

'I doubt it. Where are you going? Got a new feller?'

'No, of course not. I'm going on a retreat.' She felt embarrassed as she said it – it did sound odd to be using that word.

'A what? You? What, with nuns and things?'

'No. Heard of Fohpal?'

'No. Is it a religion?'

'No, nothing like that. It's a fellowship of people.'

'Sounds dodgy to me. Sure it's not one of those cults? All sex and black magic?' He laughed. 'Come to think of it, can I come?' He laughed even louder. 'Watch your back, Selina, you never know what you're letting yourself in for.' He was suddenly serious. 'And you know how gullible you can be.'

'Well, thank you, Geoff. I was certainly that over you!' And before he could answer she had replaced the receiver sharply.

4

Having packed the previous evening, Selina now unpacked. She had never been on a retreat before so had no idea what clothes to take with her. Yesterday she had decided jeans and leggings were out. Now she put them in her bag – after all, she was to be a guest, not a follower. Then she added a skirt and her favourite shawl. She repacked the carton of cigarettes somewhat forlornly, convinced that smoking would be banned. She tucked several bars of chocolate down the side of the bag, not relying on the food to be sufficient. Last night she'd had a huge steak, stocking her body with protein just in case. And, wrapped in pyjamas, she had surreptitiously put in the bottle of vodka she'd found at the back of a cupboard. She'd swooped on it: it was ideal to have with her since it wouldn't smell on her breath. She felt gleeful as she packed it, as if she was packing her independence with it. She reassured herself that she had the estate agent's details on the shop, then checked the window catches, and that the gas and the water stopcock were turned off. Totally unnecessary, since she had already checked them twice. She had the door open when the telephone rang; she was in two minds whether to ignore it, but decided she'd better answer it.

'I tried calling you last night several times,' she heard Ginnie say, almost accusingly.

'I disconnected my bedroom phone and went to bed early.'

'It was engaged at one point.'

'Well, I'm here now, so what is it you want?' she said patiently, not feeling up to talking about Geoff.

'Can I come?'

'To Fohpal? I thought you said you were going to New York for Christmas.' Oh, hell, she thought, not more trouble with Carter.

'I changed my mind. Carter can go to hell. I've called Porthwood and they say there's room for me too. I thought if we went in my car there was more chance of us getting there.'

'You never said a truer word!' Selina said wryly. 'But you must get a move on. I'm meeting Jessica at the station in half an hour.'

'Why's she coming?'

'I didn't ask.'

'She frightens me – I don't think I like her. She's too hard.'

'Or hurting.'

'What does that mean?'

'Look, Ginnie, if I'm to get a cab I must ring off.'

'All right, don't flap!'

The knowledge that Ginnie was coming with her BMW relieved Selina of her worries about the reliability of her Mini. The state of the car, let alone its size, was far from ideal for a world-famous star to travel in. She had warned Jessica, who had said that she couldn't care less about its condition provided it got her from A to B, but Selina was not convinced. Jessica hadn't seen the car, which was held together more with prayer than engineering, so she had had no idea what she was letting herself in for.

She looked out of the taxi window at the raindrenched street, crammed with shoppers on the last Saturday before Christmas, and wondered what had made Ginnie decide to come. It must have been something cataclysmic for her to cancel her holiday.

Selina glanced at her watch, worried that she would be late at the station, and certain that Jessica was the sort of person who would not tolerate waiting for others. It was strange, she thought, how two people could see the same person so differently. She had only spent those few hours with her in London but she had liked Jessica and found her amusing and feisty. Though she was obviously the type who did not suffer fools, Selina hadn't felt intimidated by her – in awe of her fame, yes, but not of the woman. She had been puzzled when Jessica had telephoned asking if she could travel with her to Fohpal. She had assumed that someone as rich as Jessica would have arrived in chauffeur-driven style. It was also strange that she should choose to go to a retreat at Christmas. Surely she would have had hundreds of invitations. How odd, too, that she had excused Jessica to Ginnie by saying she might be hurting inside, she hadn't thought about it and yet the word had popped out. But now, when she considered it, there *was* something vulnerable about Jessica, almost as if she was afraid of something. If it was her instinct making her think that then she was probably wrong. She had discovered that her instinct was a totally unreliable faculty in deciding anything!

It was likely to be an odd Christmas, for only the lonely and the misfits would want to spend it on a retreat. Her own mother had been fond of saying that if someone was alone for Christmas it was probably for a good reason. She smiled at this – how easy her mother's life had been made from seeing everything in black and white.

Once she had paid off the taxi she glanced about the station forecourt. Ginnie had not yet arrived but when she reached the platform Jessica was already out of the train, standing surrounded by her baggage. She was wearing a large-brimmed black hat, her dark glasses and today an emerald green swirling cloak. If they were meant as a form of disguise they had failed, for Selina saw people glancing curiously at her and a couple of times she heard Jessica's name whispered. As she approached the actress, she looked at her admiringly and thought how marvellous it must be to get to her age and still look as stunning as she did.

'Sorry I'm late – change of plans.'

'Selina, this is so kind of you, and you've found a trolley too.' Jessica spoke quickly, breathlessly, as if she was nervous.

Selina began to pile the expensive luggage on the trolley. 'When was the last time you travelled on a train, Jessica?'

'I worked it out coming here that the last time I travelled by train must have been a good twenty years ago – other than the Orient Express, of course – and I assure you, this is the last train journey I shall take. It was abominable. A girl with a Walkman thump-thumping away sat opposite me, some lager louts were swearing and shouting and there wasn't a guard to be seen.'

'That's the real world for you, Jessica. I'd stick to cars and planes, if I were you,' Selina said, not unkindly, as she pushed the laden trolley towards the exit, Jessica beside her, leaning on her stick.

'It's just, well – it must sound stupid – but I didn't feel safe. I don't often travel alone.'

'Then it must have been difficult for you,' Selina said gently, realising now that this journey had been something of an ordeal for Jessica. 'One's so used to all the unpleasantness that one doesn't think about it. It's just life. Still, it'll be nice and peaceful at Porthwood, I expect. You've brought enough gear.'

'I didn't know what to bring – I mean, what does one wear to a retreat? – so I packed for every eventuality.'

'We won't be dressing for dinner, that's for sure. Ginnie!' she called and waved at the same time, as she spotted Ginnie standing by her car.

'You didn't say your friend was coming.' Jessica paused, one hand on the trolley for support.

'She only let me know this morning. It's better, though. Her car is guaranteed to get us there. Is it a problem that she's here?' she asked defensively, hearing annoyance in Jessica's voice, and began to make for the parked car.

'No, of course not. She's very sweet.' And somewhat boring, she thought. 'There's a vulnerability about her, don't you think?'

'She's got husband troubles – I think she might have had a row with him. Maybe the meeting helped her make up her mind,' said Selina, thinking how coincidental it was that she had seen a vulnerability in Jessica too. She wondered if anyone said it of her. Probably not.

'In what way?

'You know, finding inner peace.'

'And all that crap!' Jessica snorted.

Oh dear, thought Selina, in the back of the car as it sped

down the motorway towards Cornwall. Ginnie really doesn't like Jessica. She had welcomed her amicably enough, but had barely concealed her irritation with the time it took Jessica to settle into the front seat. Ginnie was normally kind and patient, but today there was an urgency and tension about her that such minor delays appeared to exacerbate.

'You ought to get Xavier to do something about that knee,' she said.

'I doubt if he could help.'

'Well, you won't know unless you try,' Ginnie almost snapped.

'I wouldn't like to ask – I don't want to let him down,' Jessica explained.

'How could you do that?' Ginnie asked, as if the idea amused her.

'If it didn't work. I don't want to embarrass him.'

'You wouldn't do that, Jessica,' Selina said. 'Didn't you hear what he said? You heal yourself. So it would be you who didn't pull it off.'

'Of course it's Xavier – he just said that because he's modest. He has the power, it's obvious,' Ginnie announced confidently.

'What power?'

'A cosmic one. He's blessed.'

'Or just lucky.'

'What does that mean? You were deeply impressed when he healed that woman at the meeting.' Ginnie turned in the driving seat and Selina saw she was really angry.

'Maybe the woman had a good day,' Selina said, as lightly as she could.

'She'd been in the wheelchair for two years – they told us.' Ginnie turned round again.

'Fine, fine. I wish you'd concentrate on the road and not on me.' Selina made herself laugh.

'You're changing the subject. You always do that when you're losing an argument.'

'Or not wanting to pursue it further,' Selina said, under her breath. 'What do you think, Jessica?'

Jessica looked out at the passing scenery. 'I would need a bit more evidence, I think,' she said guardedly. 'Is it much further?' she asked, side-stepping the debate. She did not want anyone to know how she felt, or put herself in a situation where she could be laughed at. She didn't know how she would approach it, but she had already decided she would ask Xavier if he could help her – not in public, like in London, she could not bear that, everyone gawping at her. No, she would ask him if he could do it in private. That was her dream, but it was one she did not like to face in daylight. It seemed so silly then, an impossible hope. At night it was different: then she allowed herself to imagine Xavier making her leg straight and true, taking the pain from her hip. Some nights just thinking about it made her weep with longing to be whole again.

'I bet this cost a pretty penny,' Selina said, as the car reached the end of a chestnut lined, mile-long drive, turned a corner and Porthwood, despite the gathering dusk, came into view. 'That hill behind looks as if it's protecting the house, doesn't it? Oh, do stop, Ginnie. Let's take it in.'

The large house, nestling at the base of a steep hill, was built like a giant U, so that the two protruding wings looked as if they were protecting the rest of it. Welcoming lights shone from many of its long, mullioned windows.

'Just think of the electricity bill,' Selina said admiringly.

'You're always going on about money. Don't spoil it!' said Ginnie accusingly.

'That's because I haven't got any.'

'As you keep telling us.'

Selina put her hand out and touched Ginnie's shoulder. 'Ginnie, love, what's the matter? You're so edgy.'

'I'm fine. I just get fed up with the money talk, that's all.'

'Sorry. I won't say another word.' Selina sat back, hurt.

'It is lovely, though, isn't it?' Ginnie said quickly, and smiled to make amends. She stretched contentedly. And he's there, inside that house, and I'll be seeing him any minute now, she thought. Just thinking it made her feel warm inside and all the irritation she had felt with the others disappeared. 'I have been a bear – I'm sorry.' She flashed another smile at both of them apologetically. 'Shall we press on?'

The car had only moved a few feet when suddenly floodlights came on and they could see the house clearly. It was Jacobean, built of soft grey stone, battlemented, ivy-clad, and if it was possible to fall in love with a house, Selina felt she just had. 'It's perfect, like a model.'

As the car came to a halt on the gravel semi-circle, the huge oak door swung open. Hesta and two young men appeared on the steps.

'Oh, welcome, dear Jessica, Ginnie and Selina!' Hesta's arms spread wide. 'Welcome to your future happiness,' she said expansively.

'We're already so happy just to be here,' Ginnie said politely, like a young girl, but feeling a warm glow of contentment; and she hadn't even stepped over the threshold, she thought.

'Bit OTT, don't you think?' Jessica said quietly behind her, and Selina just managed to keep a straight face.

But as she stepped into the brightly lit hall Jessica felt suddenly apprehensive and could not imagine why.

chapter **eight**

1

The routine to which they were expected to conform was soothing, Jessica discovered to her surprise.

'I've always avoided routine like the plague,' she said to Selina, as they began to wash the breakfast dishes on their second day at Porthwood.

'Most of us can't avoid it.' Selina began to load the dishwasher. 'Kids have to be got to school, buses and trains caught, shops opened on time, houses cleaned.'

'I suppose I've been lucky but, then, there are lots of people who don't have a strict routine to keep to, aren't there?' Jessica asked, from her perch on a high stool at the sink.

'Like who?' Selina added the dishwasher powder, slammed the door of the machine and looked at Jessica who, with large yellow gloves on her hands, was cleaning the frying pans in the awkward way of one who was not sure how best to do it.

'Well, a heart surgeon, say. You couldn't call a brilliant surgeon's life routine.'

'Oh, no? What about him looking at his list and sighing, "Oh, not another transplant." Surely if you do something often enough it becomes routine, doesn't it?'

'I can't believe that.'

'But didn't you sometimes think not *another* film, not *another* session in Make-up, not *another* ...'

'Costume fitting?' Jessica offered, as Selina paused. 'I never looked at it in that way. To me routine was cleaning the house. I remember my mother – washing on

154

Monday, ironing on Tuesday. We even knew what we'd be eating every day of the year.' She leant her hands against the rim of the deep stainless-steel sink. 'That's what I meant by routine. But, you know, you're probably right. My life just had another sort of routine.'

'And imagine Michelangelo! Hell, not another bit of the Sistine to paint today – will it never end?' Selina grinned.

'You're depressing me.' Jessica threw a Brillo pad at her.

'Sorry!' She laughed as she ducked.

'What's funny?' Ginnie asked, hauling a large sack of potatoes into the kitchen.

'Nothing really, just having a minor discussion about life,' Selina said airily.

'And the reality of routine,' Jessica added.

'We've got to peel these when you've stopped being so clever,' Ginnie said shortly, as she heaved the heavy sack onto the scrubbed pine table.

'Hang on, I've just scrubbed that,' Selina remonstrated.

'Then you're going to have to do it again.' Ginnie gave her a rigid smile.

'Do you know, you haven't stopped carping since we set out?'

'I'm doing no such thing. I'm happy – happier than I've been in years. All right?' She tugged drawers open and shut noisily as she looked for a potato peeler.

'You could have fooled me.' Selina slashed open the sack and decanted some potatoes into a saucepan. 'How many?'

'The lot.'

'The what? Heavens, we'll be here all day!'

'We're supposed to be at meditation in half an hour. Have you finished those frying pans, Jessica? We're going to have to peel like demons.' Ginnie looked at her watch.

'One more, then I'm through. Do you think we're

going to have to get up at six every day? I don't think my system can cope with it.' She inspected her last pan for grease. 'It was so dark this morning.'

'I didn't realise we were shelling out fifty quid to work like this, did you?' Selina asked, as she began to peel. Ginnie scowled and Selina mouthed, *Sorry*. She was talking money again.

'I suppose we're cheaper than servants – mind you, they're not aware how useless I am yet.' Jessica chuckled, but she stopped as she discovered the impossibility of peeling the potatoes with washing-up gloves on. She took them off and looked sorrowfully at her nails.

'Hesta says it's to make us feel we belong and that everyone here is the same,' Ginnie offered.

'So, where are they?' Jessica snorted.

Selina liked her snort, though perhaps that was the wrong word to describe it. It was more a soft, snuffly noise, not unattractive as a snort could be.

'They're having a meeting. They do each morning at seven thirty. They discuss the day and any problems.'

'At seven thirty. Good God!'

'All right, Jessica. We're fully aware that you're not used to being up at this time. You've made your point,' Ginnie said cuttingly.

'Sorry.' Jessica pulled a face at Ginnie's back. 'Anything wrong, Ginnie? You homesick or something?'

'Of course I'm not. It's just – if we're going to live together for the next week then I think we should be a little more considerate to each other, not annoy one another, and then maybe we'll get this work done on time.' She looked flustered as she peeled potatoes quickly.

'How can we when we don't know what annoys you until you tell us?' Selina smiled as she spoke.

'I'll tell you one thing that's getting me down and that's your bad temper, Ginnie. Maybe you could spare us that,' Jessica said, concentrating on her potato as she spoke.

'I'm not bad-tempered. It's you who don't like to be criticised, Jessica. Please, get a move on!'

Selina laid her potato peeler down on the table. 'Ginnie, love. Come on now. Relax. So what if we're late for meditation? It won't be our fault. If they want the potatoes peeled then they'll have to wait.'

'I can't peel faster than this anyway. And I'm not very good at it – just look at this one.' Jessica held up a potato, more holes than flesh.

Ginnie looked anxious. 'I think this is some sort of test. If we do these chores without complaint I'm sure it's noted.'

'By whom? The beatific Bethina? The angelic Abigail? The holy Hesta? So what? Come on, Ginnie, it's not as if we're making a career here, or staying permanently.' Selina patted her hand and noticed that Ginnie glanced quickly away. 'You're not thinking along those lines, are you? Say you're not, Ginnie, please.' She play-acted, putting her hands together in supplication.

'Don't be silly. Of course not. It's just that I like to do things properly, you know I do. And, well, it's—' She couldn't quite bring herself to say it.

'It's all a bit of a disappointment. You thought it would be talks and learning and sitting at the feet of whoever – I can never remember his name,' Jessica said, but not unkindly.

'Xavier,' Ginnie volunteered.

'Yes, him. Me, too, if it's any consolation. But I'm getting over it and, you know, I quite enjoyed this morning – even the ungodly hour!'

'Well, yes, you're right,' Ginnie admitted, reluctantly. 'I could peel potatoes at home. I did think it would be, well, more spiritual.'

'I'm sure you're right, Ginnie. They're testing us – so

we'll show them what we're made of. Give me more tatties, do!'

Selina was concerned. She'd never seen Ginnie quite so on edge and irritable as this before. It was unsettling.

Half an hour later she felt even more unsettled when Bethina took her to one side as they were about to enter the meditation room. 'Selina, just one thing. The Master doesn't like his women to wear trousers, he likes us to look feminine at all times.' Bethina smiled her all-encompassing sweet smile.

'And if I refuse to change?'

'That's entirely up to you, dear. I'm just telling you so that you'll feel more comfortable.'

'I'll change later,' Selina said, feeling a surge of defiance and resolving not to. This was ridiculous. She looked down at her leggings. She was here as a guest and if they'd wanted to tell her what to wear then they should have done it at the beginning.

Ten minutes later, as she sat on the floor of the meditation room, she felt out of place as she looked about her at the other women in long, flowing skirts.

Jessica was in a kaftan and Ginnie had had the sense to pack a Laura Ashley. Maybe she was wrong. Maybe she'd think of it like a hotel with a 'no shorts' rule in the dining room. She felt better with that decision. She stood up and tiptoed between people sitting cross-legged, with eyes closed; she opened and closed the door quietly, sped up the stairs to her room and changed.

Xavier had given the first of his seminars later that day. Ginnie had sat in the semi-circle of chairs arranged around the large fireplace in which burned a log fire. It must be applewood, she thought, registering the sweet smell. Xavier sat on the long club fender or stood, his arm resting on the shelf of the ornately carved mantelpiece. He was so beautiful, she thought. Today he was dressed in a long midnight-blue tunic with a wide leather belt, which had an intricate silver buckle. The sleeves were full, pinched in at the wrists so that they ballooned out when he gestured. His tight trousers were tucked into shiny black leather boots. He looked like a Cossack, Ginnie thought.

Like a Shakespearian ham, Jessica decided.

Like a throwback to the sixties, Selina reflected.

'So, how did you find your meditation this morning?' He was talking to the three women, who were the only guests this Christmas and were sitting in the front row. The rest of the followers, thirty in number, sat in similar armchairs – blue-upholstered and with wooden arms.

'It was fine, so relaxing and really enjoyable. I hadn't expected it to be so easy.' Ginnie was the first to speak.

'Impossible!' That was Jessica.

'I ended up not knowing what I was doing,' Selina confessed.

Ginnie glowed with pleasure that she alone had spoken for the meditation.

'It *is* hard to empty your mind completely of all the rubbish we allow in. But it will come, don't fear. Were you aware of your tummies muttering?' He smiled his half-crooked smile, which made Ginnie long to put out her hand and outline his mouth gently with a finger.

'Yes. I'm going to make myself have breakfast tomorrow!' Jessica volunteered.

'And did Berihert's farting upset you?' Everyone laughed loudly at this.

'Berihert – with the long blond hair? Well, I wasn't going to mention it but – yes!' Selina joined in the laughing.

'A regular bag of methane is Berihert. I've warned him it's the minstrel's gallery or banishment to the potting shed for him at this rate.'

'It's the lentils!' Berihert complained, red to the roots of his blond hair.

Ginnie laughed because everyone else did, but she did not like this sort of talk. And she felt angry with herself for not being honest and admitting she, too, had found meditating impossible. The other two were getting all the attention while she longed for Xavier to notice her.

'And Ginnie enjoyed it. How advanced of you, Ginnie. Have you meditated before, then, that you can just do it?' Xavier asked her, and she looked up sharply to see if he was mocking her.

'Well, no. It just happened – I felt so at peace with myself,' she answered, confident that he was being kind.

'Well done, then. Now, Selina and Jessica, come to my room after lunch and we'll talk about this. I can't teach you how to meditate, you have to do that for yourselves, but there is the odd trick or two I can tell you.'

Why, oh why hadn't she said it was hard? She never lied – well, hardly ever – and now she'd spoilt it all. Unless –

'I could do with some tips too.' She smiled up at him, willing him to see her longing for him in her eyes.

'No, Ginnie, you're obviously so good at it that that won't be necessary. You can be of more use to Mathie in the kitchen, I'm sure. And what I want you all to do is write down a list of your talents for me.'

Ginnie thought she'd never felt so downcast in all her life.

'That won't take me long!' Selina said, self-deprecatingly.

'You'll be surprised once you start. Now,' he looked at his watch, 'there's an hour of quiet time. We like you to read or write during this period. May I suggest you read some of H.G.'s work? It will help you understand more of what our aims are here, the goals we seek.'

'How is H.G.?' Selina asked, disappointed that evidently they were not to meet him.

'Poorly, I'm afraid. It's a tragedy to see such a mind trapped in his body, unable to communicate. Dreadful! Still, Bethina's nursing is of the best. We care for him deeply.'

'Of course.' Selina looked down. She felt as if by asking about him she was intruding on their sorrow.

'And I tell you another thing you can do – when you list your talents list your aspirations too.'

2

Despite her tiredness Selina attempted to write her list of talents and aspirations. She had already torn up several efforts. In the spiritual atmosphere of Fohpal she had felt that 'to make myself debt free ...' and 'to be financially independent ...' and 'to cock a snook at the bank manager ...' were not exactly apt, even if true, and were unlikely to win her any Brownie points.

But it wasn't just that. The truth was that she did not want to offend anyone, even in the smallest way. She had been overwhelmed by the kindness with which they had been treated the past two days. At the large meeting in London everyone had been considerate and attentive, but it had not prepared her for the intensity of care here.

Apart from the time in the kitchen or when in their rooms, they were never left alone for one minute: someone was always with them, entertaining them, ensuring they were happy. She did wonder if in time such attention might become irksome but decided that was an uncharitable thought. Perhaps she had become unaccustomed to such thoughtfulness.

She attacked her list again, ruling the paper neatly

down the centre. She scribbled and then pondered before writing again. She read the result. *Talents: Getting on with people. Good colour sense. Ability to catalogue books. Able to keep a financial ledger.* She winced at that one and her pen hovered over it, as if unsure whether to delete it or not. *Speed reading. Good at history and Jane Austen* was the final entry.

'Pathetic,' she said aloud. It was very little to show for thirty-four years of living and, supposedly, learning.

Aspirations was not much better. *To read* War and Peace. *Not to worry so much and find inner peace.* That should please them she thought. *Learn to cook properly. Be able to identify wild flowers.* She'd almost written she'd like to fall in love for keeps but had decided that was too flippant. She picked up her pen and quickly, before she could change her mind, added *loyalty* to talents. Well, it was true, she felt she was a good friend, and with an even more rapid flourish, before she could chicken out, she scribbled *To sell my shop* under *Aspirations*.

She placed pen and paper firmly on the desk. It would have to do. She couldn't keep changing the lists, she'd be at it all night. In any case, did it matter what they thought of her? She was only here to sell her shop and that done she'd be on her way and probably never see any of them again.

Except Matt, she found herself thinking. She didn't like to consider the idea of not seeing *him* again. And yet, what a stupid concept *that* was. Love at first sight was not a theory she'd ever had any truck with. Love, real love, she'd long ago decided, was built on knowledge of each other and respect – not that she'd ever scaled such lofty heights. So, since love was out, what was it that made her keep thinking about him? She rested her chin on her hands, deep in thought, conjuring up his image. She fancied him like hell, that's what! But also, and here was the odd thing, she knew, she simply knew, they were to be important to each other. So maybe it was love, after all. She yawned. Not possible. Not in this day and age.

Still, she wished he was here. She acknowledged what a disappointment it had been when she'd asked Colley if he was around to be told he was in France and wouldn't be back until the New Year, by which time she'd be gone.

Ah, well. That's life, she told herself, as she padded to the *en suite* bathroom for a shower. She brushed her hair, not that that ever achieved much, with her curls, put on her nightie and climbed into bed. She looked about the large room before turning off the light: all the furniture was antique, the curtains high-quality chintz, expensively made, the lamp bases crystal. Certainly they didn't stint themselves and at fifty pounds for almost a week's stay this place had to be the best bargain around! She could do with a bit less of the regimentation – they always seemed to be rushing from one meeting to the next – but she quite enjoyed listening to Xavier talking, he made everything sound so easy. And today she'd felt that with a few more tries she might get the hang of meditating – using a candle and concentrating on the centre of the light, as Xavier had suggested, had helped. And to be able to empty her mind of all the rubbish chattering about in it was an enjoyable prospect, to say the least, was her final thought as she clicked off the light.

In the room next door Ginnie was gazing up in the darkness to the ceiling, half smiling to herself. She felt – how *did* she feel? she asked herself. Content was not a good enough word: old men felt content; she felt content when a sponge cake turned out well risen; people felt content sitting by a fire after a huge meal. The word did not convey the joy she felt inside her, which could soon, she knew, become an inner glow. She could imagine it, could almost sense how she would feel then – as if she was full of molten gold. She hugged herself in the bed, her hands gliding over her body. She'd felt almost like that once or twice in her life when she'd been in bed with Carter and everything had been perfect and they had melted together, climaxing in unison. She shook her head. How could anything with someone like Carter be on a similar plane to what lay ahead of her when she and Xavier were one, as she was convinced they would be – soon.

He'd touched her today. That, she knew, was why she felt like this. He'd put his long elegant hands either side of her head and had looked into her eyes, even into her soul. Her legs had weakened at his touch, her genitalia had moistened, her eyes had spoken to him of this great longing and this great need. He'd touched the centre of her forehead gently; it felt almost like the caress of a butterfly's wing. 'Remember you have the power,' he'd whispered conspiratorially. 'Remember only a few of us have the third eye.' And, although she was not sure what he meant, she knew instinctively that whatever it was set her apart; that she was different and he had recognised it in her. She knew tonight that she was chosen, it was only a matter of time. She was glad now that she'd lied about her skill at meditation. If she'd told the truth he would never have spoken to her like that. Never!

Her lists had been easy to do since she did them for *him*. She could use them to tell him about herself and so bypass the need for trivial conversation and finding out about each other. She'd been quite proud of the length of her list of talents – good feminine ones that would make her even more attractive to him. *Cooking, dress-making, home-making, gardening, painting, piano playing, singing, interior design, reading, philosophy and religion, caring for children.* She went over the list in her mind. Well, maybe she'd exaggerated a bit about philosophy – she didn't know that much about it, but she had once read the first book of Bertrand Russell's autobiography, even if she couldn't get on with the second. And she'd always been interested in Buddhism: she always felt guilty if she squashed a fly. In fact, her reading tended towards the bestseller list. What if Xavier asked her what she'd last read? Well, she'd tell him, she'd be up-front about it. 'The Cobweb Cage', she'd say, 'by Marina Oliver.' By being honest she'd be showing him that she had a lighter side, a relaxed, fun side.

She was confident he'd approve of her aspirations too. She'd written a long list of them. *To learn more. To improve my mind. To seek and find. To find inner peace. To help those who have no inner peace. To be at one. To love.* And she'd underlined the last one and hoped he'd see the message she was giving him.

It was all such a whirl, such a surprise. Less than a month ago she would never have believed this could happen to her of all people. Selina had always been the fey one whereas she'd always been practical and of the world.

It was as if when she'd got out of the lift and entered that first Fohpal meeting she had put her foot on a path from which already she knew she would never deviate. The path would be long and hard and, yet, what had happened so far? It had all been so easy. She felt almost as if it was what she had been waiting for all her life. This – and him!

Quickly she got out of bed. She'd try again for him. She lit the candle he'd given her and sat cross-legged in front of it, concentrating on the centre. 'No, no-ing. No, no-ing. Nonoing, nonoing, nonoing, nonoing,' she said softly, as they'd taught her this afternoon, rhythmically, rocking back and forth, emptying her mind, leaving it void, leaving it blank, velvet black, ready ...

Carter, she suddenly thought.

'Oh, hell!' she said loudly. Trust him! Exasperated, she

blew out the candle and hopped back into bed. Tomorrow, she promised herself fervently.

Jessica could not sleep. She sat in the comfortable wing chair wrapped in a soft blanket and gave up on her attempt at reading the thoughts of H.G. from a calf-bound book, inscribed by him. Even the knowledge that he'd touched it was of no help or inspiration.

It was madness being here, really. Gobbledegook, all of it. She was the last person likely to be influenced by an Eastern mystic or whatever the man called himself. Yet for all that she was content here. The comfort was exemplary – just look at this room. She'd been housed thoughtfully on the ground floor, so she had no stairs to bother with. She was in H.G.'s guest suite, she'd been told, and obviously the old boy didn't stint himself, judging from the quality of furnishing, curtains, the fine linen sheets, the silver tray, crystal lamps and good paintings. If this was for his guests she could imagine what his own quarters were like. No one had said where they were, but presumably further along the corridor in this wing of the old house. She had this room, a bathroom even she couldn't fault and a small sitting-room overlooking a knot garden of such intricate design that even in winter it was a pleasure to look at.

She was tired out so sleep should have been easy, not impossible. She couldn't remember when she had last been so active, both physically and mentally. There'd been the kitchen work, then she'd helped lay tables. She'd attended several lectures, tried the meditation, walked in the grounds – her knee not excuse enough to get her out of it. Tonight they'd had communal singing, which had been pleasant. Certainly a surprise, since she could not remember enjoying anything done in a group since she'd left school ... perhaps she couldn't sleep because she had no alcohol inside her – that was a first for a good many years. More likely it was excitement. Late that afternoon she'd been to see Bethina, the herbalist. It had been a long session at which, initially, Jessica had had difficulty keeping her patience: she could not see the relevance of her diet as a child to her condition now. But out of politeness – another new experience for her, being patient and not wanting to offend – she'd sat and answered the endless questions. At the end Bethina had measured out some liquids and mixed them in a bottle. 'It might be a long job, your arthritis is well established. But I'm sure we can improve it and Xavier will, no doubt, want to heal you himself. But let's hurl everything at it, shall we? I'll analyse these answers and come up with a treatment for you, but until then, try this. A teaspoon every three hours until bedtime. I don't promise anything but it might help a little. It's a stop-gap until we can try the proper treatment.'

'What is it?' Jessica asked, suspiciously eyeing the small bottle of topaz-coloured clear liquid.

'Just a distillation of various herbs. Nothing harmful.'

She'd only taken three teaspoons and already she was feeling better. The rats that since her operation had vacated her knee but taken up new lodgings in her hip seemed to have lost their teeth.

Still she mustn't let herself get carried away, there had been other times when the pain had eased up a little. Maybe being more active had helped – loosened her up a bit. Bun was always nagging her that she didn't exercise enough. No, she'd keep quiet about this, she didn't want to appear a complete fool.

Idly she picked up her lists. Under *Talents* she'd put *To amuse. Patchwork quilt making. Ability to hold my liquor.* She'd put that in out of mischief and rereading it she still laughed. *Aspirations* was short and to the point: *To be healed and to act again.* Dare she even begin to allow herself to hope and dream?

She looked up sharply on hearing a noise. She held her breath listening. She could not be sure what it was – possibly a dog far away in the valley. Or just an old house creaking in the night. She unwound the blanket. Best to try again, she told herself, as she climbed into bed – fairly easily for her.

She lay awhile, going over the events of the day again. Without doubt Bethina was one of the most beautiful women she'd ever met, and Jessica had a professional's ability to assess the looks of other women. She was tall and willowy and moved gracefully. The dark blue of her robe was ideal for her pale-skinned beauty. Her bone structure was fine, her eyes luminously grey. Her hair was silver which, since she was young – in her thirties, perhaps early forties, Jessica guessed – and her face unlined, gave a stunning effect. She was intelligent and it showed in her expression, for the smile on her full red lips was the only one here that didn't drive Jessica demented. Bethina must have a good soul to look like that was her last thought as sleep finally welcomed her.

3

'I feel he betrayed me. And I'd been a good wife to him.' Ginnie was crying as she spoke, the tears rolling down her cheeks and plopping unheeded on to her immobile, folded hands. 'I'm so unloved.'

Jessica looked down at her own hands and wished Ginnie would stop. She saw no point in this public airing of her problems, she found it self-indulgent. But she also looked at them because it helped concentrate her mind. Bethina's medicine, while helping her was also, she was aware, making her feel slightly detached, as if she was moving in a fog she could not, as yet, see.

'Was this the first time your husband – how shall I put it? – strayed?' It was Hesta who asked, in a gentle tone, like a nurse speaking to one with a terminal illness.

'Oh, no. He did it often. But you see the awful thing is it's my fault. All my fault.'

'If it's your fault how come you feel betrayed?' Ancilla asked, in her staccato New-Yorker-in-a-hurry voice.

'You're taking on too much, there's no balance here,' Berihert, the gardener, said kindly, and the others leaned forward in their seats concentrating their energies on her. Briefly Ginnie glanced wildly around her as if finding herself trapped.

'Tell us everything, Ginnie, it'll help – release that tension you're feeling. Purge yourself of this pain. We'll help you.' Hesta's voice was relentless, even in its softness.

'We love you, Ginnie,' the others, sitting in a ring on the floor around her, said in unison.

Only Jessica was sitting apart, on a chair. She and Selina did not join in the chorus, but looked at each other, embarrassed.

'She's upset, leave her alone,' Selina protested.

'It hurts to let the pain out, like a rebirthing,' Hesta explained patiently.

'But this isn't like Ginnie.'

'Fohpal changes us all.'

'It's not fair. Stop it, do!'

'What's not fair, Selina? You make it sound as if it's not fair to you. You can have your turn next.' Hesta smiled sweetly at her.

'I didn't mean that. You know I didn't.' She allowed the irritation she was feeling to seep into her voice. 'I know Ginnie. I know she'll regret telling you these things. She's a private person, she always has been—'

'Why don't you mind your own business, Selina?' Ginnie glared at her friend.

'But I – I was only trying to help.'

'Then don't!'

'I'm sorry. I didn't realise—'

'Didn't realise what?' Ginnie interrupted.

'That you'd changed so dramatically. That you'd suddenly enjoy letting everything hang out in this way.'

'Maybe I never wanted to tell you because I never felt you were sympathetic to me and my problems.'

'Ginnie, that's not fair.'

'Gracious me, nothing's fair for you, is it? You sound like a spoilt brat, honestly you do.' Ginnie was laughing now, but it was not a laugh of joy or happiness, rather a sardonic, bitter one.

'What you say, it's not strictly true.'

'You accusing me of lying, Selina?' Ginnie leant forward aggressively.

'No, exaggerating.'

'Oh, what?'

'You're not sure Carter had an affair.'

'I am! You're not in my marriage, how can you possibly know what goes on?'

'What about Tessa? She loves you.'

A frown flickered over Ginnie's face, but she tossed her head. 'Not any more, she's on her own now. She doesn't need me.' Hurriedly Ginnie wiped her eyes.

'Not needing isn't not loving,' Selina said with exasperation.

'What the hell do *you* know about being a parent? You're *childless*.' She spat out the word, as if it was a communicable disease. 'I told you nothing. How could I explain myself, relive my pain to someone as cool and detached as you?'

'You did. We both did. That Sunday lunch at your place.'

'Rubbish. You were drunk!'

'Great! Thanks. And bless you too.' Selina clambered

to her feet. 'If you'll excuse me,' she said, with as much dignity as she could muster and left the room. Hesta looked at Berihert and Jessica saw her nod so slightly that she might have thought she had imagined it, had Berihert not got to his feet also and silently followed Selina.

Hesta put out her hands and grasped those of the two women sitting either side of her. Everyone else took their prompt from her and the circle was quickly linked.

'No, no-ing. No no-ing ...' Hesta began to chant, and the group followed her, rocking back and forth in rhythm to the sound. Jessica watched from her position outside the ring, and saw Ginnie, who had been flustered and tearful, begin to calm as the chanting persisted. It was hypnotic and, although not part of it, she felt almost drowsy. There was no sign from Hesta, but the chanting began to slow and fade, and the group sat still and calm, the only sound their measured breathing.

Jessica's eyes were on a young woman who had said nothing all through the meeting. She was plain-faced, slightly overweight, and her appearance was not helped by her mousy, lank hair, which looked as if it could do with a brush. Although with the group she was not part of it. Jessica felt a sudden surge of sympathy for the girl, wanting to make her look happier, less a victim.

'Now, where were we?' Hesta said, rather like a primary-school teacher coddling her young. 'Ginnie, do you want to continue? You need not say another word. We're not prying, as your friend seemed to imply. We're not snoopers – gracious me, no. We're here to help you, Ginnie. We want you to find your inner peace. Only then can your mind expand and be liberated, and you will be rooted.'

Hesta had a good voice, with a subtle range, Jessica noted, and she knew how to use it, too. It would be difficult to resist such blandishments.

'I know, Hesta. I understand. Don't take any notice of

Selina. She thinks she knows everything, and she doesn't.'
She laughed, but uneasily, and Jessica wondered if she
laughed like that because, in a way, she was betraying
Selina.

Ginnie folded her hands neatly and took a deep breath.
'You see, Ancilla, it *was* my fault. I was pregnant. Carter
would never have married me but for that. He's a
gentleman, you see,' she said, with a proud lift of her
head, as if there had been no interruption.

'But it takes two to screw,' Ancilla replied.

'I know, but then ... well, I lied.' Ginnie flushed bright
red at the memory as well as at Ancilla's language – she
and Carter *made love* they didn't do anything so vulgar
as *screw*. 'I've never told anyone this, ever – but I told
him I was on the pill and it would be all right. And I
wasn't. I just hoped, you see.'

'You mean you wanted to get pregnant?' Hesta asked
gently.

'No, not really. It was just – I didn't like to ask my
doctor, he'd have told my mother. You don't know my
mother!' She managed a genuine enough laugh at that.
'The truth is, I was afraid Carter would drop me if I
didn't sleep with him. There were plenty who'd have had
him, quick as a flash. He was – is – so handsome. I
couldn't believe my luck that he wanted me. It was like a
fairy story unfolding, only I spoilt it, and the dream got
all unravelled, and I was pregnant.'

'What did he say when you told him?'

'He was wonderful, then. He said he'd had a good run
for his money – almost as if he wasn't even surprised. He
didn't accuse me of lying – not then. That came later. He
wasn't even cross with me. Only ...' She twisted her
fingers together and looked at them rather than at the
others. 'I wished he'd said he loved me, only he never
did.' The misery of the years when she had longed for
him to say those special words flooded her voice.

Oh, Lor', she's going to cry again, thought Jessica, and wondered if she should follow Selina. She'd quite like to curl up on her bed, but on the other hand – and to her shame – she was hooked on Ginnie's story.

'Some people find it difficult to say those words. Maybe he did love you, but could not verbalise it.' Bethina spoke for the first time.

'No, it was duty. The Mulhollands are strong on duty. Otherwise his mother would have stopped him marrying me. She'd never approved of me, not from the first day I met her. She'd rather an impoverished doctor or solicitor's daughter for her son, not her local greengrocer's. It must have shamed her so.

'His father wasn't too bad. He was a barrister. Portly, and pompous, but quite kind. But his mother was something else. You know the type. Always looking as though she's got a bad smell under her nose.' The others giggled at this. Not, it seemed to Jessica, because they found it funny, but more as if they were encouraging her by doing so. And they did – all the hurts and rejection that Ginnie had kept bottled up inside her came pouring out.

'She was so rude to me, without appearing to be. And it was only later you realised just how awful she'd been. It was like the first time I met her. "So you live over the shop?"' Ginnie acted her mother-in-law's speech, with its strangled vowels. '"How nice, how convenient. And you say your mother works. How very supportive of her. Carter tells me you work as a temp. I'm not sure what that implies. Oh, a typist. Now I understand."' She aped the woman well, and the laughter of the group was genuine now. 'You see what I mean? Nothing you could pin down. Nothing I could complain about to Carter. But, oh, she hated me. I knew it. I knew it *here*.' She tapped her chest.

'My dad had tried to talk me out of it. He felt Carter

173

wasn't good enough for me, you see. He thought being an artist wasn't a proper job, and marrying because a baby was on the way was not reason enough. I didn't listen to him. What girl does? I loved Carter, that's all I could think of – I loved him, and I was going to spend the rest of my life with him. The fairy story had the perfect ending, as fairy stories should! Only it didn't.' She hung her head. Ancilla, who was sitting beside her, put an arm round her shoulder and patted her comfortingly.

'And then what happened?'

'Oh, yes.' Ginnie looked up, with a rather dazed expression, as if in those few moments she had been somewhere else. 'I lost the baby. On our honeymoon. I had bad food poisoning. I was really ill,' she said bleakly. 'And to this day Carter thinks I lied, and that I wasn't pregnant at all, and I trapped him. And he's used it. Every row we've ever had, he's at pains to tell me he never wanted to marry me. I worked and worked to make life comfortable for him, and to allow him freedom to paint, but it was never enough. The guilt got in the way and ruined everything.' A tear escaped and trickled down her cheek.

'Poor, poor Ginnie. But you're holding back. I can sense it. You must be free. Let the anger out. No negative feelings. No no-ing ...' Hesta began.

'It's not *fair*! I *was* pregnant. It wasn't my fault I lost the baby! But they've been punishing me ever since – I sense the hate, the loathing. And these affairs, endless affairs – why? I've tried, God, I've tried. Why should I be abused in this way? Tell me.' Ginnie was shouting now, standing, fists clenched, her face distorted with fury and pain.

'Abused? You call that abuse? My uncle abused me when I was nine. You hear me? Nine! Can you imagine the terror I felt as he groped me?' Carmel, a young woman who until now had not spoken, was also on her feet, hands on hips, leaning forward towards Ginnie. 'You're a spoilt middle-class cow. You know nothing. My mother was an alcoholic bitch. I never knew my dad. First my uncle had me, then I was gang-raped as a teenager. My husband beat me, and my boyfriend put me in hospital. What d'you think of that?'

'I'm sorry,' said Ginnie, taken aback.

'I'd begin to wonder what was wrong with me,' Jessica said, under her breath.

Carmel swung round. *'What did you say?'* she yelled.

'Nothing.'

'You lying cow. You said something. You smug bitch, sitting there like a malevolent toad.'

'Fine. OK. I'll tell you. I just thought it was about time you questioned why you're constantly a victim.'

'You bitch!' Carmel screamed. 'I hate you! I hate, hate, hate you!' She was jumping up and down. 'No no-ing! No no-ing!' she screeched.

'Oh, please stop this,' the defeated-looking girl said.

'You keep your fucking nose out of this, Esmeralda!' Carmel said spitefully, which made the girl look even sadder – not sad, Jessica realised, frightened.

'I'm sorry about that,' she said laconically, which only made Carmel jump higher and faster, with frustrated, inarticulate anger.

'And who are you to stand in judgement, Jessica?' Ancilla asked, and there was an aggressive mumbling from the others. 'You're not making a valid judgement, just a smart-arsed one.'

'Not necessarily. I believe someone like Carmel is often a victim from choice, that's all.'

'I want to kill!' Carmel shrieked, but made no attempt to approach Jessica or to lunge at her.

'I'm not saying you are, Carmel. I just think perhaps you should question your life a bit more.'

'And what about your life, Jessica? Maybe it's time for

you to assess yourself.' Bethina was speaking, not angrily like the others but with a compassion that made Jessica look up at her with surprise.

'There's nothing to assess. I take full responsibility for my past and my future. I don't go around blaming others if anything's gone wrong,' Jessica said with conviction.

'So you accept your health is your fault. Oh, Jessica, that's good. That's very advanced on the Inner Way.'

'I didn't say that. Of course that's not my fault.'

'Oh, but it is, Jessica. Of course it is. You've created the imbalance in your body, and that has caused you all this pain. Don't you understand?' Bethina's face was creased with earnestness.

Ancilla and Ginnie swivelled round to face her, and Jessica felt as if they were gawping at her. 'No, I don't. Why should I? There's nothing to understand – I've never heard such stupid twaddle in my life. Ask any rheumatologist.' She felt angry, yet vulnerable too.

'If it's stupid, why are you feeling so much better? Whose medicine has helped you? Theirs or mine?' Bethina smiled her gentle, beautiful smile.

'Yours. I'm grateful. But I can't accept that this is my fault.' She tapped her hip. 'I find that insulting in the extreme.'

'I'm sorry you do, Jessica. We don't mean to offend, only to get you to look at the truth.'

'I can't.'

'The truth is frequently hard.'

'It's not that!' Jessica said in frustration. 'It's not the truth, that's why!'

'And you're an expert on truth and *karma*, are you?' Ancilla asked. 'Since when? You're being so arrogant.'

'You can keep your insults to yourself, Ancilla.'

'I'm not insulting you. I'm speaking the truth, the one you don't want to hear.'

'Hell! You're all mad!' Jessica stood up. 'I don't have

to listen to this crap. How dare *you* stand in judgement on *me*? None of you understands what has happened to me, what a tragedy this is, what adjustments I've had to make.' She was having to control herself, aware how close she was to losing her temper.

'Come on, Jessie, admit it. Look at all the attention you're getting as you hobble along. With a fading career, it must be a godsend. Face it, you want to be a cripple.' Morveen's gentle, lilting Summer Isles accent seemed to mask the content of what she was saying, so there was a pause of several seconds before Jessica reacted.

'How dare you! How can anyone say such cruel things?' She slumped back into her chair, shaking, about to cry. 'And don't call me Jessie. No one calls me that.' And Jessica saw that Esmeralda was crying, as if for her.

'What about me? Why is no one listening to me?' Carmel shrieked, and then began to scream heartrending, blood-curdling screams. One by one the others jumped up and joined in, shrieking, ranting, jumping, leaping, bellowing. Jessica sat rigid, pushing herself back in her chair as if she was trying to escape the wall of noise. Her cheek was damp now from the first tears she had shed in ages.

Ginnie stood in front of her, white-faced, rigid. Suddenly she began to beat her chest with pummelling fists. Then she opened her mouth and her scream was louder than any of the others.

4

Jessica was still shaking as she climbed the wide oak staircase. Behind her, despite the thickness of the draw-ing-room door, she could still hear the wailing and bansheeing of the others. She was muttering to herself as she moved along the thickly carpeted corridor. She stopped in front of a door on which was pinned a card with Selina's name printed neatly on it, and knocked sharply, urgently.

'Jessica! You climbed the stairs! That's marvellous,' Selina said with pleasure.

'So I did.' Jessica was astounded. 'Do you realise, I did it without even thinking. I was in such a bloody hurry to see you. And, oh, my mind's in such a muddle.'

'Come in. What's happened?'

'It's a bloody madhouse down there. They've gone barmy. Screaming and shouting at each other. And, you'll be interested to know, my arthritis is all my own fault. There was a bitch down there called Morveen who implied I was an attention-seeker. I'm poleaxed!'

'Jessica, I'm so sorry. What things to say!'

'What's so stupid is they've got to me and I feel so hurt.'

'Have a drink. It'll make you feel better.'

'I wish I could.'

'Then you shall.' Selina opened her wardrobe, and from the back produced the untouched bottle of vodka and waved it triumphantly in the air.

'That's not a mirage, is it? Please say it isn't!' Jessica clapped her hands with pleasure.

'I thought supplies might be necessary if things got too heavy. Please don't let on I've got it, especially to Ginnie. She'd tell in her present mood. You'll have to put up with a tooth mug. I didn't think to pack glasses.'

'What about you?'

'I've got a cup. Berihert brought me some tea to help calm *me* down. Only it was camomile, which I can't stand, so I poured it down the sink. And he did go on, you know, wanting me to open up my inner self.'

'That's a stupid name – Berihert – who ever heard of

it? D'you think it's really his name?' Jessica accepted her tooth mug.

'I doubt it. All the names sound a bit dubious to me. Don't they to you? Ancilla, Bethina?'

'Xavier.' Jessica drained the glass. 'Ooh, that feels better.' She smiled, and Selina poured her some more.

'Perhaps they sat down with the *Oxford Book of Names*. Perhaps they just change their names for change's sake.' Selina sipped her vodka.

'Or to hide behind,' Jessica added, a shade darkly.

'That's an interesting idea. I hadn't thought of that. What made you say it?'

'Maybe I'm being a touch melodramatic – you know, the actress in me. It's just – I like it here and then suddenly I notice something and I feel uneasy.'

'Like what?'

'Have you noticed that girl called Esmeralda?'

'Rather dowdy – specs – one of the pale blue, lowest of the low? I saw her in the kitchen and I swear she was crying. She always looks so sad.'

'I thought that, but then there was something about her expression and I knew I was looking at fear. It's probably my overactive imagination ...' Jessica said.

'I hope you're wrong.' Selina frowned. 'Do you remember at the meeting we were told that everyone was equal, the colours just denoted how long people had been here? Well, that's not true for a start. Do you ever see those in dark blue doing kitchen duties or cleaning up?'

'You're right. And I'll tell you another thing that bothers me. It's so easy to get lulled by them, to want to be like them. But, then, *who are they*? Everyone's very kind and sweet and everything, but ... we don't really know them, Selina, do we? But they know about us. And it's thanks to us that they do. Those lists of talents and aspirations they asked us to make – they said quite a bit about us, but we didn't learn anything of them. Xavier yesterday, when he led us through our lives, very nicely, I admit, he's very charming. But no one else was saying anything, just us. And then just now, they were digging information out of Ginnie I'm sure she'll regret telling them, probably stuff she's never ever divulged at all. Why do they need to know? Still, that's not strictly true – admittedly after you left, Carmel had her say and told us all, and how!'

'Where's Ginnie now?'

'Exercising her lungs – last time I saw her – or should I say heard her.' Jessica pulled a face at the memory. 'They're mad. What a racket!'

'Well, I suppose we'd get confrontation sessions like that in a drugs rehab unit or a psychiatric hospital, wouldn't we? And we wouldn't think twice about it.'

'True. I'm probably being paranoid – take no notice of me.'

'Did the session make you feel better?'

'Hardly. I've got a headache I didn't have before and I just find all this baring of the soul distasteful. Maybe I'm too old for it. Maybe you youngsters enjoy it. But I don't see how letting a load of strangers know your most sensitive secrets is going to help. You can talk to yourself and be honest with yourself, that helps. But not an exhibition like that.' Jessica shuddered.

'Berihert said they had the most incredible results. He said Carmel was virtually catatonic when she came here.'

'Pity she didn't stay that way.'

'Do you want to leave? I mean earlier than planned. Once I've got somewhere with the shop I don't mind going home.'

Jessica's shoulders slumped. 'Yes, I do, and no, I don't. I can't think of anything more blissful than to escape to a large steak, a bottle of good claret, and my own bed. But – don't laugh at me – I'm hoping Xavier is going to do a healing session on me sometime before we go. I don't want to leave until he has.'

'I wouldn't laugh at that. Strange things can happen. Remember that old red-haired woman at the meeting in London. Go for it, Jessica. What have you got to lose? In a way, I suppose it's part and parcel of what they were going on about earlier. If you think it will help you, undoubtedly it will.'

'You don't mind waiting, then? You looked really upset when you stormed out, as if you wanted to leave there and then.'

'I've calmed down. And in any case, I'm to talk to their treasurer tomorrow about my shop.'

'Who's that?'

'Oh, some bloke called Caleb. He was an accountant in the outside world. And, according to our friend Berihert, there's a crowd coming tomorrow earlier than expected. They've been to France, H.G.'s got another place there.' And Matt too, she thought, but refrained from saying so.

'Look, this is none of my business, but ... I wonder if you shouldn't be beginning to worry about Ginnie. I think she's taking this all a bit too seriously. Women who think their husbands are unfaithful are vulnerable at any time. And at her age – probably early menopausal – even more so.'

'Oh, it won't last. Ginnie's like that. She gets crazes for things – she's had a go at spiritualism, ouija boards, the lot. She's been into crystals, shamanism. This'll be the same. She throws herself in, buys all the books and equipment and then gets bored with it. She likes to think she's matter-of-fact and I'm the fey one, when actually it's the other way around. She's a sucker for most things, even those travelling fish men, with their over-priced fish. In any case, she'll soon be champing at the bit to get back to her beloved Carter.'

'Why, if he's as grim as she claims? Sounds to me as if she's better off without the bastard.'

Selina laughed. 'He is a bit of a smoothie, and flirts like mad, and he oozes with charm. I find that type gross. But I've always thought that he loves himself most of all – the rest of it's fake. If he had affairs like she says, he'd be putting too much at risk because he needs her money. I can't see him risking it all for a bit of bonking on the side.'

'Have you known Ginnie long?'

'A few years. She likes to think we're best friends, but I don't see it like that. To be honest, I don't need that sort of friendship – I never have.' Selina was surprised at how easy Jessica was to talk to. She was a good listener – maybe that was the key.

'Friendships can be a dead dodgy thing, if you ask me, and female best friends can be a disaster.' She paused as if thinking of something long ago. 'Ginnie strikes me as a very prickly person. And she certainly doesn't like me, I don't know what I've done,' she suddenly added.

'It's not that she dislikes you, it's that she's frightened by someone like you. You're confident and successful, you're your own woman.'

'I've never understood what that phrase means.'

'You know who you are, and she doesn't. I guess you don't give a stuff what other people think of you but she does. Her mother-in-law has made her life hell. I know Joan, she'd be impossible to please. But it's sad, because Ginnie's much better than they are, in so many ways.'

'Isn't it odd, in this day and age, that someone should be made to feel "not good enough"?'

'You don't live in Finchester – it's so snobbish, it would make the Indian caste system look quite liberal!'

'Remind me not to buy my dream cottage there, then.'

'Are you moving? I saw your house once in *Hello!*. It

looked wonderful. I don't think I could give that up easily.'

'Neither can I. But the bank and I have a different philosophical approach to my domestic arrangements.' And as she told Selina about her financial catastrophe, Jessica discovered she was able to make the odd joke about something that, before, had virtually reduced her to tears. 'How odd,' she said. 'I've been telling you about myself when all along I said how unnecessary it was. Still, I must go.' She stood up. 'My hip's beginning to twinge. I'm late with my medicine.' She wasn't, she was using it as an excuse to leave, but she was rather shocked at how much she had told Selina, and thought it best to leave before she said too much. After all, she barely knew the woman and although she seemed nice enough she had known others she had thought nice but who, for all that, had shopped her to the tabloids.

5

Ginnie moved swiftly along the corridor towards the office. She'd been summoned to take a telephone call, and was puzzled as to who it could be since she had made sure no one knew where she was. Her letter to Carter had been ambiguous; it had merely told him she was going away for a few days to think, and she had left *The Good Hotel Guide* on her bedside table so that he would assume she was safely holed up in a country-house hotel somewhere.

By the time she reached the office her imagination was working overtime. She had begun by imagining, with barely any concern, the house burning down or her mother-in-law terminally ill, but the idea of Carter in a car crash had bothered her more than she could admit.

Tessa in an avalanche was her latest preoccupation as she rapped on the door and skidded into the room without waiting for a response.

Bethina was at the desk writing calmly. Xavier stood by a cabinet, a file in his hand but staring dreamily into space.

'Ah, Ginnie, how pretty you look, but how flustered!' He smiled warmly at her and she saw just the tip of his tongue wet his lips, slowly but so sexily that she thought her knees would buckle.

'There's a call for me?' she said, her anxiety still rooted but eased by the excitement of seeing him, being complimented by him and the pleasure of his suggestive smile.

Bethina pointed to a phone and, pressing a button on her console, connected Ginnie as she picked up the receiver.

'Hello?' she said tentatively.

'Mum? Is that you?'

'Tessa! I've been so worried. I thought something had happened to you.'

Ginnie sat down sharply feeling weak with relief. 'I'd got you under an avalanche and dead.'

'Had you got round to planning my funeral? I hope you chose "All Things Bright and Beautiful",' Tessa said, with the confidence of youth.

'Tessa! Don't even think such things.' Ginnie touched the solid wood of the desk for luck. 'Are you still in France? How did you find me?'

'Deduction. I phoned Gran's to wish her a merry Christmas and Dad answered the phone. He said you'd done a bunk.'

'I needed some peace and quiet to think. I told him in my letter.'

'Yes, but he was upset that you hadn't said where you were going.'

'I didn't want him following me. That's why.' She had lowered her voice not wanting Xavier and Bethina to hear her problems, but they appeared be engrossed in their work.

'I wish you'd speak up. This line is so echoey.'

'It's difficult.'

'So, you're not alone? What's the secret?'

'Nothing.' She felt on edge, as if Tessa could read her thoughts. 'You haven't told your father where I am?'

'What's it worth?' Tessa laughed.

'Anything you want.'

'Heavens, Mum, I was only joking. What's up?'

'Nothing.'

'So you keep saying. Look, I haven't said a word to him – for starters, I wasn't sure you were there. When you weren't at Selina's I remembered how you'd got interested in Fohpal and so I took a shot at it and called International Enquiries and hey presto! Haven't you got a clever daughter?'

'Brilliant. Look—' Ginnie half turned her body in the chair so that she faced the wall, her back to Bethina and Xavier, and hoped they weren't offended. 'Tessa, please, do me a favour, don't tell your father I'm here. I don't want him barging in making a fuss – you know what he's like.'

'If that's what you want. Are you all right?'

'Tessa, I've never been happier.' She could turn back now and she smiled at them as she spoke. 'Everyone here is wonderful. I'm learning so much about myself. You've no need to be concerned. I've never felt so contented, so sure of anything.' She looked meaningfully at Xavier.

'You sound as if you're talking about a fellow, not a following,' Tessa teased.

'Don't be so silly. What ideas you do have.' Ginnie laughed even as her heart sang her secret.

'You'll be home in the New Year?'

'I haven't fixed on my dates yet.'

'But you will be back?'

'Of course. Why are you worried?'

'Me? I'm not worried. I just don't want you doing anything daft. Mum, I've met this wonderful bloke ...'

They chatted for a few minutes about Tessa's holiday and the new man in her life until Ginnie noticed Bethina glance at her watch. Immediately she tried to close the call.

'All right, then, if you don't want to hear my news?' Tessa sounded petulant.

'It's not that – of course I do. But it's difficult at the moment. We're bus—'

'Suit yourself!' Tessa snapped, and the line went dead, or she thought it had, but then she heard a clicking noise.

'Tessa? Are you there? Tessa?' But there was no reply. 'Daughters!' She shrugged her shoulders. 'They're all the same.'

'You should invite her to join us,' Xavier said.

'I don't think that's a good idea.' She looked straight at him again and smiled a small, secret smile. 'Thank you, Bethina.'

She was half-way along the corridor when she heard Xavier calling her name. She paused to allow him to catch up. She wondered what he wanted to say to her.

As he reached her he put up his arm and caught hold of her. He pressed her hard against the wall, his leg prising both hers open. His lips crashed down on hers. His tongue shot into her mouth. His right hand groped at her crotch, his fingers searching her through the folds of her skirt. Abruptly he let go, laughed and continued his walk along the corridor.

Ginnie stood, her hand to her mouth, the other straightening her skirt, her heart racing. It had all happened so quickly that it was as if it hadn't happened at all.

She had to rest awhile, breathing deeply, clutching at her equilibrium, all thought of Tessa and Carter totally replaced.

'I gather you were upset this afternoon. Do you want to tell me about it?' Xavier leant back in his chair, one dark-blue-velvet-clad leg elegantly crossed over the other.

'I probably overreacted.' Jessica sat opposite him in a worn leather wing chair, which she found so comfortable she wondered if she could dare ask if she might buy it.

The small room they were in was off the main hall: in its previous life it had been a morning room, but was now Xavier's sitting room. It led off his study, which in turn led off the administration offices, and the whole was in the wing of the house opposite the one in which Jessica slept. A fire burned in the grate, the lighting was subdued, the storm outside was muted by the heavy claret-red damask curtains, which were closed against the night. With red walls, red curtains and red carpet, the room was comforting, womb-like, and Jessica felt relaxed. Though whether it was the medicine, the vodka she had had with Selina, or the warm room making her feel so woolly and detached, she was not sure.

'A sherry? Or something stronger? It's gin you like, isn't it?' Xavier asked.

'You're offering me a drink?' she said, astonished, not even registering he knew what her tipple was.

'Don't look so startled.' Xavier grinned. 'What's wrong with a drink? Surely you're not TT?'

'No, it just took me by surprise. I presumed you didn't drink. But since you've asked, I'd love a gin.'

'Why should we not drink? Drink can be good for one, liberating, relaxing.' He was standing at a side table, pouring as he spoke. Jessica watched him with a practised eye. He really was extraordinarily handsome, and she liked them tall and lean, as he was. Another woman of her age might have longed to be younger, but Jessica wished she was two stone lighter. She willed him not to say 'Drink in moderation' and was overjoyed when he didn't as he gave her a glass. He gently touched her hand as she took it. She did not look up for she knew what games he played.

'Bethina is mortified that she upset you. She misunderstood. She thought you were further along the Inner Way than obviously you are. But you will be, dear Jessica, I promise you.' He sat down in his chair with one fluid and elegant movement, crossed his legs and raised his glass to his lips.

'Were you an actor?'

'What makes you ask?'

'Your voice for one thing, and the way you move. Most people just sit down but an actor can't do that. An actor makes a production out of everything.'

'Do you?'

'I wasn't that sort of actor.'

'You use the past tense. Why?'

'Well, there aren't many roles for actresses with obvious limps, or maybe in a wheelchair.'

'If you hadn't the limp, then would there be many parts to play?'

'Markedly more.'

'Are you sure?'

'Of course.'

'Many actresses complain that not enough parts are written for older women.' Xavier smiled at her. Jessica did not reply, but thought, Ouch. 'I don't want to upset you further, but had you thought that maybe you use the limp as an excuse against reality, which is that your career would, in any case, be coming to its natural end?'

Jessica laughed. 'Well, that's a nice way to put it. You mean middle-aged, over the hill, redundant. Maybe you're right.' She was surprised that she was not upset, as

188

she had been earlier. But somehow, sipping this drink, in this room, opposite this delicious man ...

'That's good. You begin to accept.'

'I'm not sure what it is I'm supposed to be accepting.'

'The inevitable. If you fight it, then you create a thousand imbalances in your body. Everything is dependent upon balance.'

'You mean, *karma*?'

'Yin, yang, *karma*. It's all balance.'

'You really think I created this arthritis?' She managed, even through the fog of drowsiness, to sound indignant.

'No, nothing as simple as that. Bethina over-simplified earlier – I don't blame you for being upset. No, I believe you can exacerbate it by being tense, angry, afraid. Everything gets worse.'

'I have noticed, if I'm upset, yes, the pain worsens.'

'Exactly. So we work on that. We calm your spirit, we make you grasp an inner happiness. It's there for you to take. We operate on the inner you – not the outer. We leave that to the butchers who call themselves surgeons.' He laughed contemptuously.

'And you?' She paused, feeling awkward. 'Your faith healing?' she said, in a rush.

'And that, of course, in time. But first things first.'

'But I thought ...'

'That I'd lay my hands on you now, tonight? Of course I could, and it *might* work – it sometimes does, you saw it yourself in London, but such subjects are exceptional. To be sure, to assure you of a total cure, then we have to work on your mentality, and then the physical part will be easy.'

'Oh, I see.'

'You sound disappointed.'

Jessica laughed. 'It's nothing. It's just me. I've always been the same. I want everything to happen immediately. Geminis aren't famed for their patience, are they? So.'

She sat up straight in the chair, decision made. 'How long will it take?'

'That's up to you, of course. But you must give us at least a month.'

'Just my mind, no healing?' Her voice was filled with disappointment.

'You are too persuasive. For you I'll make an exception. We will work the two in tandem and I shall commence the healing – but you must be patient.'

'I will, I promise. Then I'll book in immediately.'

'No need to do that. We'll start the day after tomorrow.'

'But we leave tomorrow.'

'Not necessarily. Do you have to go? Anyone expecting you? Waiting longingly for you?'

She looked up sharply at him. What did he know, to be so ironic? All she saw was his gentle smile, and she was annoyed with herself for being so cynical. 'No, of course I can stay. How much, is the important question?'

'I do so hate discussing money. I've no idea. But Caleb will. You can discuss it with him when he returns tomorrow. Not much. About ten, I should think.'

'Ten pounds?' she said, amazed.

'Oh, dear Jessica, like so many wealthy people you've no idea about money, have you? No, thousands, of course.'

'Problem is, Xavier, I'm not wealthy.'

'No, of course not. I understand.' She knew he didn't, that he thought she was joking. Well, she'd just have to find the money from somewhere, Humph if necessary. Sensing that the interview was over, she stood up. It would be worth it. Look at her already. She thanked him, and moved towards the door.

'Just one thing, Jessica. No more medicine or vodka. You want your mind totally clear. Good night. Sleep well.' He put his hand on the doorknob ready to open it.

'And if you can't – sleep, I mean – you know where I am.' He bent down and kissed her full on the mouth and, as quick as a lizard's, she felt his tongue slip easily in and out of her mouth.

In the hall, Jessica leant against the door. She felt so happy, so relieved he'd treat her. She knew deep down she'd be all right now. If he was wrong and they asked double, somehow she'd raise it. But she didn't want to pursue that kiss, she didn't want any complications. Odd that he should mention vodka, especially since she normally drank gin.

chapter nine

1

'How much?' His voice rose in astonishment.

'You heard, Humph. Please don't say no. You said you'd be pleased to help.'

'Jessica, my darling, of course I am. But are you sure it will work?'

'Don't be such a Jeremiah. Of course it may not work. It's a gamble. My knee op was a gamble too, that didn't work. But I've got to try this.'

'Have you seen any results by this man Xavier?'

'Yes, wonderful, miraculous healings, Humph. I know it's a huge sum of money, but please don't let me down.' Used to doing and having whatever she wanted, Jessica hated having to plead for this money.

'It's not the amount. It's nothing. No, I'm afraid for you. I don't want you getting your hopes up, only to be let down again.'

'I can deal with that, Humph. But it won't happen. I'll make it work, I know I can. It's within me, you see. I can make myself better.'

'Curiouser and curiouser!' Humphrey laughed. 'You're still with the same bank? I'll transfer money this morning. Have you had a nice Christmas?'

'You know, I never gave it a thought. It's been different.' She was happy now. 'Could you do me a favour, Humph? Phone Bun and let her know I'm staying here longer than I planned. I'll always be grateful for the money, and I'll pay you back.'

'No need. When will you be home?' But the money on

Jessica's BT card ran out before she could answer, so she hung up and limped out of the red telephone kiosk which stood incongruously in the ancient hall.

She was in pain. She still had her bottle of medicine from Bethina, with a good inch of liquid left in it. This morning, she had looked at it with longing, wanting the drowsy, almost pain-free effect it could give her, but resisting, determined to follow Xavier's instructions to the letter.

As she turned to go back to her room, Ginnie appeared on the stairs, lugging her case behind her, banging noisily on each tread. Jessica was surprised by her appearance. She had become used to seeing Ginnie looking neat and trim but this morning she was dishevelled, plainly dressed, her hair awry and wearing no make-up.

'Ginnie, how are you?' She was keen to make it up with her. She might have pooh-poohed the idea of *karma* last week but now she would not allow anything negative to stand in the way of her cure.

'Fine, of course,' Ginnie replied, but she was white-faced, and the dark smudges under her eyes indicated a sleepless night. 'You'll have to make your own way back. I'm staying.'

'That's great, so am I.'

'Why? What's here for you?' Ginnie asked suspiciously.

Jessica took a deep breath. Maintaining her balance was obviously going to be hard, she thought, especially with Ginnie. 'Xavier hopes to cure my hip, and then he might do something with my knee, too.' She forced a brightness into her voice.

'Xavier? When? Where?' she asked with urgency.

'I don't know. Sometime. I'm here for a month at least,' Jessica replied, wondering why Ginnie should be taking the news with quite this amount of concern. 'Have you seen Selina?'

'No, I haven't had time. I'm moving rooms, you see. I'm being given a permanent one. I'm staying here for ever!'

'Are you? Ginnie, it's none of my business, but have you thought this through?'

'You're right. It isn't any of your business.' And, dragging her case behind her, she disappeared along the side corridor. Jessica watched her go. So much for trying to be pleasant and concerned.

The corridor led to the back of the house. Ginnie passed the kitchen, abuzz with members preparing lunch. Ancilla bustled out, and Ginnie smiled a greeting. She hauled her heavy case up the back stairs to the upper level of the house, and along a corridor under the eaves, until she found the door to number ten, and pushed it open.

The room was small, painted white, with gingham curtains and a candlewick counterpart on the plain pine bed. On one side was a chest of drawers, and in the corner a curtain covered a hanging rail. Ginnie looked about her with a small smile of satisfaction. It was perfect. It was like a cell. It contained the bare essentials, nothing else. This room would be her model, she would make her mind like this, uncluttered, the rubbish rejected.

She opened her case and saw where she must begin. She did not need all these clothes and toiletries. She'd get a box, put all the extra things in it and give them away. The few clothes she decided to keep she stowed away, then lay full length on her bed.

She lay quietly, her eyes closed, her hands folded on her chest, and allowed herself to savour this moment. 'I have found such happiness,' she said, almost as a sigh, to her empty room. And then she laughed, a low, happy sound, and she hugged herself tight. She still couldn't believe it had happened. She had dreamt of it happening, but had not dared to think it would. And yet it had, and she felt so young, so free, so deliciously whole. She was truly in love but, more miraculously, she was loved!

Late last night Ancilla had come to tell her that Xavier wanted to see her. She was already in bed, but had dressed in double quick time, had made up her face, sprayed herself with Ma Griffe – even, she giggled at this memory, her thighs and stomach, not something she'd normally do, but after Xavier's kiss …

'Did the session this evening help you?' Xavier asked, as she entered his sitting room.

'Oh, yes, my throat's sore from all that shouting. But everyone was right. I feel purged of all my anger now,' she announced proudly.

'That's good. I knew it would happen for you. I wanted so much to be there as you became one of us – but duties, you understand.'

'Of course. But just knowing you intended to be there, well …' She giggled, and felt ridiculously like a schoolgirl yet again. She lowered her head, shy with the intensity of her emotions.

'What is it, little one?' He put his hand under her chin, and gently lifted it. 'Look at me. Don't be afraid. I won't hurt you. I want to care for you, take away all the misery and pain you've suffered at the hands of others. But it's over now, for ever.'

'Oh, Xavier.' She sighed, and melting into his arms seemed the most natural thing to be doing.

He had taken her there and then, with an urgency that proved to her that his feelings for her were strong. He had ripped the clothes from her and had quickly mounted her, and was tearing into her. The roughness of the carpet hurt her back. The heat from the fire was too hot, and his member felt too large for her. Everything was painful, but it was not like any other pain she had felt. Rather, it was pleasure, and she cried out her joy and clung to him as he battered into her body.

'I didn't mean it to be like that, I'm sorry,' he said as they lay in each other's arms exhausted, and, she thought, satiated.

'It was wonderful.' She smiled up at him.

'I wanted to woo you properly, seduce you, not virtually rape you – forgive me, but I wanted you so desperately.'

She pulled herself up, leant on her elbow and looked down at him, one bare breast grazing his chest. She bent forward and kissed his face, small, sweet, urgent kisses. 'No apology, it was perfect. No one ever made love to me like that.'

'Me neither. We were good together. So good.' And he put up his hand and stroked her breast, and held it, and guided it to his mouth, and was sucking her, pulling at her. She could not believe this was happening to her, as she felt herself aroused, and saw that he was too. She climbed on top of him, impaling herself on him, and, feeling an alien wantonness, she flung back her head, her hands playing with her breasts as she brought him to his climax.

The whole night passed in love-making, and in between they talked. She told him of her life, her fears, her unhappiness. He told her of his dreams and plans.

'I want the world to join us, to know the happiness that being part of Fohpal can bring into their lives. Imagine a world where we all love one another, are at peace with one another.'

'You sound just like John Lennon.' She began to hum 'Imagine' but stopped when he frowned as if he did not enjoy the comparison. 'When H.G. is better, you must organize him to talk to larger groups, spread the message further.'

'None of this can happen while H.G. lives,' he said.

'Why ever not?'

'Oh, he drives me mad sometimes. Don't get me wrong, I'm in awe of him, he's a great man,' he added hurriedly. 'But he doesn't seem to realise the potential we have here. We could do so much more, if only he'd ask for help from his followers.'

'What sort of help?'

'Money,' he said simply.

'How much money?'

'Whatever it takes. Look at some of the movements. Look at the way some of the gurus attract money. He could do that, but he won't. The fifty pounds you paid for your five days here, he set that rate years ago.'

'But you could charge ten, a hundred times more, and people would still come. I'd have come.'

'Exactly. But he won't.'

'This house, though, he bought that, so he must have got money from somewhere.'

'No. It was left to him by Bay Tarbart, lock, stock and barrel. The trouble with H.G. is, he's never had to work for anything in his life. It's all come so easily to him. He doesn't understand the value of money.' He sighed, deeply and sadly as if burdened with all the cares of the world.

'I could give you money – I've masses my father left me. Everyone thought he was a poor struggling greengrocer but he played the stock market, and he made a fortune and he left it all to me. I hoped it would make my in-laws feel differently towards me, but it didn't. They took it when they needed it but didn't respect me any the more.'

'My poor darling. People can be so cruel and so grasping. Thank you for your sweet offer but I wouldn't even dream of asking you for a penny. I'll find a way, one day, to realise my dreams.'

'If you ever do need some, promise to let me know, won't you?'

'Only if I was desperate. Then I'll turn to you.' And he kissed her so gently on her nose.

'If H.G. dies, what happens?'

He held up his hand. 'Don't even think such a catastrophe, let alone say it. Fohpal would fold – it's H.G. everyone comes to see, and believes in.'

'I don't,' she said quietly. 'I believe in you,' she whispered, and was rewarded ...

She sighed loudly at the memory of their intense conversation, their even more intense love-making. Sometimes, in the past, she had wondered if she would feel wicked or different, somehow, if she was ever unfaithful to Carter. She felt different all right, but wicked – no way. Making love to Xavier had been the most natural thing she had ever done in her life; they had been destined for each other, of that she was sure.

She looked about her new room. Her old one had been a guest room. Now that she had decided to become a member of Fohpal, she was honoured as the others were. It was an honour to be housed like this, she was certain. Idly she picked up her hand mirror. Heavens! She'd no idea she looked such a mess. Dark rings under her eyes, washed out. Still, what a wonderful way to have acquired them. God, she was sure she would burst from the happiness! She was full of it, like a pregnant woman come to term. She felt like a novitiate, as if she was at her own rebirth. A whole new world lay before her.

Selina's bags were packed, and stood on the rug in her room. She was watching out of the window for the expected arrival of the members who had been to France, including the treasurer, Caleb.

'Come in,' she called, to a knocking on her door.

'Would you mind? I'm sorry ...' A wan-faced Esmeralda stood there, clenching and clenching her hands.

'Come in, do. You needn't look so scared – I've had breakfast!' Selina laughed, but Esmeralda merely looked puzzled. 'What can I do for you?'

'Are you leaving today?'

'I hope so, if your treasurer gets here. Otherwise I don't know what I'll do. You all right?' Esmeralda's face was covered with sweat and her breathing rapid. 'What's up?' she asked, more kindly.

Esmeralda looked wildly about her and kept glancing over her shoulder as if she expected to see someone behind her. 'I didn't know who else to ask. Would you take this for me?' she said urgently, as though she was afraid that if she did not say the words quickly she would lose her courage and not say them at all. She held out an envelope, which shook violently in her hand. 'Post it outside.'

'I'm not the best person to ask, Esmeralda. I forget everything. You're better off posting it here.'

'I can't. It's private. It'd be read. Everything's read.'

'Oh, surely not.' What a dramatic lot they were, Selina thought.

'It is. I'm sorry. Please. I can't take the risk. I'd be punished or worse.' She looked on the point of tears.

Selina frowned. Esmeralda's fear was genuine, there was no doubt about that.

'I'll take it, but you'd be better off giving it to Jessica or Ginnie. They're more likely to remember it than me.'

'They're not leaving.'

'Not leaving? What do you mean? We're all going today.'

'No. Jessica and Ginnie, they're staying on. Didn't you know?'

'They haven't said so to me. But I didn't see them at breakfast and I skipped meditation this morning – I had some papers to check out.' In fact she'd spent the early part of the morning studying her figures on the shop, terrified she might have got them wrong. 'Isn't that bloody marvellous, though? How considerate of them both!' she said. How would she get away, if Ginnie and her car were staying? Porthwood was so isolated that a taxi would be expensive. 'Do you think someone would run me to the station?'

'Maybe. I don't know. But *please* could you take this?'

Esmeralda held out the white envelope, which was still in her trembling hand. 'It's to my parents. I want them to ... Can I trust you not to tell a soul? Oh, Christ!' Esmeralda jumped, and stuffed her fist into her mouth as she heard the sound of voices outside in the corridor. 'Please!' she begged.

'Fine, keep your hair on, you needn't make such a song and dance about it.' Selina took the envelope from her and threw it on the bed with her own papers. There was a knock on the door, which burst open.

'Selina, there's—' Ancilla stopped and looked from Esmeralda to Selina and back. Esmeralda seemed drained of blood. She rocked on her heels, as if about to faint. 'The others have arrived. I thought you'd like to know. Sorry, am I interrupting?' Ancilla asked.

'No, Esmeralda just came to say goodbye, didn't you?' Selina smiled warmly at the terrified-looking woman.

'Yes, yes, that's right.'

'I didn't know you'd made friends.' Ancilla sounded suspicious.

'Aren't we all friends here? Thanks for letting me know, Ancilla. I'll be down in two ticks,' said Selina, who for some inexplicable reason had plopped herself down on her bed and spread out her skirt so that Esmeralda's letter was hidden.

2

'What I don't understand is the suddenness of your decision. Don't you think it would be wiser if you left today, went home, distanced yourself for a while, and then decided what you're going to do?' Selina was sitting in the empty dining room opposite Ginnie, whose face was sulky and defiant, reminding Selina of a rebellious teenager. So unlike the normally controlled, polite Ginnie.

'You can nag me until the cows come home. I'm staying so you might just as well save your breath.'

'But what about Carter? He's sure to get in touch with me. What am I supposed to say to him?'

'The truth, of course. That I've found myself and I don't need or want him. I don't expect you to lie for me.'

'And Tessa?'

'She doesn't mind. I spoke to her yesterday and explained everything.'

'I hope you know what you're doing. But if you're not coming, then could I possibly borrow your car? It's miles to the station.'

'No can do,' Ginnie said bluntly.

'I'm sorry.' Selina looked puzzled. Ginnie had often let her use her cars. 'I'll drive carefully and take great care of it, I promise. I could come and collect you when you decide to leave, if that's what's bothering you.'

'I shan't be leaving. Haven't you heard what I've been saying? And I don't own a car any more.' Ginnie shrugged her shoulders. 'It's a good feeling.'

'But ... Oh, I see ... Well, who does own it, then?'

'Xavier. I gave it to him,' Ginnie announced, and she flicked her hair back as she did so, a sure sign that she was expecting an argument.

'But it's a BMW!' Selina couldn't hide her astonishment.

'So? I don't think Xavier cares about the make. I doubt if he even knows what sort of car it is. He's too spiritual to care. I don't need one. I need nothing. I have everything I could possibly require here. So no lecturing, all right?' she said firmly.

'Why should I? I think you're mad, but it's your car, you can do what you want with it.'

'Exactly.' Ginnie pushed back her chair, stood up and prepared to leave but then swung round, put out her hand and touched Selina's. 'I'm sorry, Selina, I've let you down, not giving you a lift back. Will it be too awful?' For a moment it was the old Ginnie speaking.

'No, of course not. Did you know Jessica's staying too?'

'I heard. Xavier said he's going to cure her, and then they hope she'll stay permanently too – he told me,' she added, unnecessarily but proudly.

'Jessica! I doubt that. She's far too worldly for this place.'

'But if she stays, she won't be, will she? She'll change, like a chameleon, as I have. Then she'll be all the better for it.' Ginnie looked smug, in an emphatic way, and Selina decided there was little point in arguing further with her.

Both women turned as the door of the dining room opened.

'Excuse me, it's Selina, isn't it?'

Selina stood up as if, like a puppet, she was being pulled by invisible strings. Immediately she needed to sit down again. It was Matt. He stood in the doorway smiling, and she felt as if her heart had turned turtle and her solar plexus had been punched. 'Hello,' she said, somewhat inanely.

'You probably don't remember me, I'm Matt Ripley.'

'Of course I do. You came to my shop. And you're someone with a normal name,' she said, and grinned broadly, finding that talking made her feel more in control. Common sense was already warning her not to be so silly.

'You're waiting to consult Caleb. I've a message. He's been delayed, and won't be here until this evening. Would you mind spending an extra night?' He was grinning too, as if inordinately pleased to be asking her.

'Of course,' she said. 'No problem,' she added, and it was, without doubt, the truth.

That evening after supper the dining room was crowded and there was a babble of excited noise, as those who had been to the house in France swapped news with those who had been left behind in Porthwood.

Ginnie felt shy of the new people, and threatened too. Her glance never moved from where Xavier stood. She watched him hungrily, warily, as other women greeted him effusively. Xavier looked across at her, as if her relentless stare had finally attracted his attention. He smiled, and for Ginnie it was as if everyone else in the room had disappeared, and she was looking down a narrow tunnel at the only other person there, Xavier. She felt as if her body was dissolving with excitement, and longed for his touch again.

Selina was looking for Matt, and was annoyed with herself at the disappointment she felt when she could not see him. She looked about for the frightened Esmeralda too, but there was no sign of her. She felt she knew one young dark-haired woman, small and bird-like, but for the life of her did not know from where.

A few minutes later, when Matt entered the room and gave her a small wave, Selina's heart began to pound again. Of course she'd heard and read about such instant reactions to men, and had never believed them possible, but now she wasn't so sure. Still, someone belonging to this group was hardly what she'd had in mind when at night, sometimes, she allowed herself to fantasise about Mr Right. She mentally shook herself and was puzzled at the way her mind could jump from just fancying someone to imagining wedding bells. She'd despise a reaction like that in any of her friends, so she was no more lenient with herself. She fancied him, that was all. How could it be anything else when she didn't even know him? Leave it at that, she told herself, and felt a lot better.

All this noise reminded Jessica of a cocktail party, not her favourite pastime. She would prefer to spend her time being healed rather than 'energised'. What silly words they used! She'd looked the new people over but could not find one she thought would be remotely interesting – all of them had the same vacant, asinine expression as the others. She did hope she wasn't wasting a month of her time here and wondered how best to get out of meetings like this without offending Xavier.

'Jessica, if I could have a word.' Ancilla smiled at her, and Jessica wondered if the smile was so permanently welded to their faces that it continued in their sleep. Even if it did, it would not make it any more genuine, she thought.

'Sure.'

Ancilla crouched in front of her. 'How's the poor old hip and knee?'

'Fine, thanks. Bethina's medicine helped.'

'Not too painful now you're no longer on it?'

'No, I'm fine,' Jessica answered, but not before thinking that she'd feel more comfortable if the details of her medication were not common knowledge.

'That's great. I wanted to talk to you because we saw that in your talents list you mentioned you enjoyed patchworking.' Ancilla put her head on one side, the smile still in place.

'It's only a hobby,' Jessica said, sensing she was expected to say something.

'H.G. makes wonderful quilts.' She put her hand on Jessica's knee.

'I saw some in London. But I'm not in his league.' Jessica moved her leg to escape Ancilla's touch. There was too much touching here, she thought, and although she was not averse to physical contact – she'd had plenty of it in her life – she preferred to decide who would and who wouldn't touch or caress her. It was debased here with these strangers forever putting hands on one, arms about one and kissing incessantly.

'But do you think you could finish an incomplete one for us? It's promised as a present to a very important person, and poor H.G. didn't have time to finish it before he became so ill.'

'It depends what's needed. The ones I've made are fairly basic. I couldn't do some of the intricate patterns he does. He's an expert, I'm just an amateur.'

'He's done the hard bit. This is finishing off the border. Esmeralda ... He used to have a follower who helped him with the more mundane bits. She's not here any more,' and Ancilla looked shifty as if she might have said too much. 'Perhaps you could have a look tomorrow morning?'

'Why not now?'

'There's the energising meeting. You don't want to be bothered tonight.'

'It wouldn't be a bother. After all, I've nothing else to do.'

'But after this evening's energising you'll be too tired.'

Jessica forbore to point out that if the meeting was to energise her, then why should she be tired? Instead, she asked politely when the meeting would take place.

'Now, of course. Didn't you read the schedule I took the trouble to have printed out for you?' Ancilla sounded annoyed and used the American pronunciation, 'skedule', which always put Jessica's teeth on edge. She was not sure whether it was the woman's audacity in speaking to her as if she was an errant child or her accent that enraged her most.

Ancilla jumped up. 'Everyone's coming. It's so spiritual, so rewarding, when we're all together on the Inner Way,' she trilled. The tone of her voice upset Jessica too: she preferred melodious voices to the harsh screech which was Ancilla's.

3

Ginnie was one of the first on her feet, and quickly joined the others who had begun to leave the dining room. She pushed through the crowd, endeavouring to get close to Xavier. If she couldn't manage that, then she'd get as close to the front as possible.

Selina and Jessica were at the rear of the throng, which, chattering noisily, was moving up the oak stairs and through double doors on to a small mezzanine that looked down into a long gallery. From ceiling almost to floor, tall casement windows marched along one side, and two massive stone fireplaces, ornately carved, stood on the other. Between them was a marble table, behind it an alcove with concealed lighting in which stood a large, beautifully carved box of what looked like sandalwood. In front of this was a Persian rug in pinks and blues on a small dais, but on which no one stood. Selina, looking up, saw an intricately plastered ceiling stretching the length of the long room.

The furniture had been pushed back against the walls, and in the empty centre the group were taking their places. The first half in had turned, and were now facing back the way they had come, and Ginnie, to her frustration, having pushed her way to the front now found herself at the back.

'Sorry, I must be near the centre,' she said urgently, and unceremoniously proceeded to thread her way back to the middle of the room, close to where Xavier stood.

'I think I'll stay here and watch,' said Jessica, easing herself into a conveniently placed high-backed Jacobean chair, in shadow on the mezzanine. From her high vantage point, she could look down into the room, and watch the two groups now facing each other. She estimated that there must be about forty people, but such was the size of the room that everyone had plenty of space around them.

'I'll sit on these stairs.' Selina lowered herself onto the top step – she'd never been good in crowds. From here she could see Matt standing to one side, leaning against the wall. He looked like an observer, as she supposed she was too. She was surprised at how pleased she felt, if this was the case.

The curtains at the windows were already closed, the light coming from huge cream candles, more normally seen in a church, which were placed at intervals in large wrought-iron candlesticks, modern in design and looking a little incongruous in this beautiful old room.

Jessica jumped when a drumming noise issued from a speaker standing close to her chair, which, in the dark, she had not noticed. The sound was not loud, but soft and persistent and stopped the chattering from the group below. Everyone sat cross-legged on the floor, folded their hands in their laps, their backs ramrod straight.

'Won't you join in too, Selina?' Xavier's voice rang out from his position in the centre of the room.

'I thought I'd watch,' she called back, colouring slightly as she was aware that everyone had turned and was staring at her.

'And how often have you set yourself aside, Selina? How often have you avoided confrontation, contact, love maybe, by sitting aside and being an observer?'

'I beg your pardon?' Her blush deepened, and at the same time she felt indignant, even though he asked gently enough, and smiled at her as he spoke.

'Come with us. Free yourself from your constraints. You're creating barriers in your mind, you know. Liberate yourself, soar with us, and become whole. Live life totally.'

A united roar of 'Yes!' came from the group and several punched the air with their fists. Mob hysteria, thought Jessica, willing Selina to find the strength to resist.

'Come, little one, escape the prison of your mind. You think you're secure in your narrow little world – but that's not living ... Join us.' Xavier held up his hand dramatically and, painfully aware of everyone watching her, Selina tiptoed through the seated group towards him. She was unsure of what he meant, but knew, although she did not understand why, that she'd no wish to offend him. He put his hands either side of her face, held her, and looked intently at her. 'I'll take care of you. You've nothing to fear,' he whispered. Ginnie, sitting at his feet, observed how tenderly he held Selina, the secret whispering, and was consumed with anger and jealousy. She felt an almost overwhelming desire to jump up and demand he held her like that, too. Then Selina felt herself being pushed down on to the carpet. Oh, well, she thought, I'd better see this through, whatever it is.

As if on cue, the soft drumbeat became louder, its rhythm regular, persistent, like a heartbeat, Selina thought. A different noise began, soft, as the followers began to breathe in and out through their noses. As the drumbeat quickened, so did the breathing.

On the tiny mezzanine, in the shadows, Jessica began

to feel distinctly dizzy, until she realised that she, too, was breathing in unison with the drum and the others. She made herself hold her breath then force herself out of synch with them.

Selina's pulse began to race. Her head ached, as if it was about to explode. She looked at her hands, and in the candlelight she could see that small crescents had appeared in her palms, where she had dug in her nails, so as not to fall into a trance as the others around her had. She tried to fight the drumbeat, but it was as if it had entered her body, delved into her soul ... She felt afraid.

Ginnie felt she was floating, detached from herself. And the faster she breathed the more removed she became. The room faded and she was running in a field of corn, the scarlet red of poppies scattered among the bright yellow sheaves, as if it had been raining blood, and she could see her father in the far corner, and she was running towards him, calling his name, but he ran away in the opposite direction ... Such sadness she experienced. 'Daddy!' she screamed, tears gushing down her cheeks. 'I want my daddy.' And she was standing and crying and screaming and ranting and hitting herself, as she allowed her inner anguish free. No one noticed her, for everyone else was on their feet, arms flailing, mouths open, noises of horror, of anguish, of fear, and of sheer joy issuing out, in a vast cacophony of sound. And the drum beat on relentlessly, louder and louder, until the very walls appeared to be vibrating in time.

Selina sat rigid and silent among the hysterical throng. She put her hands over her ears as if to shut out the racket. 'Baked beans on toast, Welsh rarebit, sausage and mash ...' she muttered to herself, visualising each meal, the ketchup, the mustard, anything not to become like the others. Think anything to stop this contagious madness from claiming her. She looked up, sensing she was being stared at. At the far side Matt winked at her. She smiled with relief. When she looked away from him, she took the image of his wink with her, knowing that if she held on to that, she'd be all right.

Ginnie, still crying hysterically, fell to the floor, and began to writhe and flail about, looking like a fish that has just been landed, fighting for breath. Xavier stood over her, as her blood-curdling screams became louder, until they dominated all sound. Then, as abruptly as she had fallen, she stopped screeching and began to make a strange mewing noise, pulled her legs up to her chest and put her thumb in her mouth.

From her position on the mezzanine, Jessica watched the scene below with mounting horror and distaste. She was so appalled by what she saw that she even wondered whether to put on the light and stop it there and then, but she was afraid to do it – not afraid of Xavier's wrath, but that the light might be too much of a shock for the participants, some of whom appeared to be regressing to such a degree that the shock of sudden light might even, she supposed, kill them. If this was how they liberated their minds, she'd rather keep hers constrained, she thought, matter-of-factly. Getting her hip seen to was one thing but she had had no idea she would have to sit through a sinister ritual such as this. She stood up, craning forward, looking for Selina, wondering if she should venture down to find her, and then she saw her, sitting quietly but with her eyes opened, a look of bemused horror on her face.

Jessica, reassured, had had enough. Quietly, though given the noise level she was not sure why she bothered, she got to her feet. She opened the door and escaped from a scene she thought worthy of Hieronymus Bosch.

4

Jessica sat alone in her room, writing a letter to Bun. She had tried phoning this evening, but the pay-phone was on the blink. She had asked Mathie if she could use another phone, but Mathie, in her thin-lipped manner, told her it was not possible, that all the lines were down.

'I just heard a phone,' Jessica said.

'I don't think you did, my dear. Perhaps all the noise at the meeting has given you noises in your head.'

'No, it was a telephone I'm sure,' Jessica argued. She did not trust Mathie, she had always found that thin-lipped people who used endearments were invariably false – the two were incompatible.

'I can assure you it wasn't, love. It was probably the television. You could try again tomorrow. Though I wouldn't hold out much hope. With the New Year bank holiday, it'll be ages before anyone comes to fix it.'

'I'll write a letter, then.'

'What a good idea. You do that. Leave it on the desk here and I'll see it catches the next post.' Mathie turned her back and concentrated on the pile of recipes she'd been sorting, and Jessica felt herself dismissed. 'Oh, Jessie dear, by the way, we were wondering earlier, your cheque, when can we expect it?'

'I haven't even been told how much the course will cost. And, if you don't mind, it's Jessica. No one, but no one, calls me Jessie.'

'All right, don't get your knickers in a twist,' said Mathie, a child of the seventies if ever she'd heard one.

So Jessica was writing to Bun, asking her to call Humphrey to check if the money was in her account – she didn't dare write a cheque until she was certain it was. My, how she'd changed. Such caution was totally out of character – lack of cash had once been no reason for her not to spend. 'Come in,' she called, at a knock on the door.

'Mind if we talk?' It was Selina, holding a small bucket bag aloft as she entered the room. 'Vodka?' She grinned.

'Still got some left? I'm surprised after the way we hit it the other night.' Jessica cleared some space on her desk for glasses. 'This reminds me of a health farm I went to with a friend, and she smuggled booze in, too.'

'Did you lose weight?'

'No! Oh, those were the days.' She sighed deeply: the reason for the visit had been to get in trim for an important film, funded by American money, which had led to greater things. 'I had work then. Fat chance of any now. Cruel world, show-biz.'

'But you're still as lovely, you know, in a different way.'

'Old, you mean?' Jessica laughed at the horrified expression on Selina's face.

'No, I don't mean that. You were stunning when you were young, yes, but I think you're really beautiful now.'

'Nice try, Selina.'

'It's the truth,' she said staunchly.

'Pity producers don't see it the same way. Still, where's that drink?' Jessica asked.

'What did you make of this evening's shenanigans?' Selina asked.

'I thought the whole exhibition was gross. What happened in the end? I left early – I couldn't stomach any more.'

'Well, Ginnie flopped about like a cod for about five minutes, then she's up on her feet, laughing fit to bust, and they're all hugging and congratulating her. And then they all went deathly quiet, silent for five minutes, till Xavier started that "no no-ing" business, and they picked up on that. It would have been too easy to give in to it, but I thought of bacon sarnies, and I was saved.' She grinned.

'That must be an original way of dealing with it. How's Ginnie now?'

'I left her looking all dreamy. It would be funny if it wasn't so scary.'

'At least we don't have to join in unless we want to. I've heard of some communities where you're forced to do things you don't want to. I suppose I was a bit wary of that at first, weren't you?'

'I'm getting a bit edgy about Ginnie, though. I thought she'd be bored with it all by now. But I think she's fallen in love with Xavier.'

'He's a very attractive man.'

'I'm worried, she's a bit naïve where men are concerned.'

'And just separated. The worst time to start an affair.'

'She's vulnerable, no doubt about it. And, Jessica, don't laugh, but I think there's something going on here. I asked to use the phone, and was told it was broken, and then I heard it ring,' said Selina.

'That happened to me. But Mathie explained it must have been the sound of a phone on the television – it happens.'

'That's what she said to me, too. D'you think that's all it is?'

'Well, nothing much else has happened, has it? Just rather bizarre behaviour.'

'Yes, I suppose you're right.' Selina felt better at Jessica's ready acceptance of the explanation. But something stopped her telling her friend about the frightened Esmeralda and the letter, and she wasn't quite sure why she kept that to herself but the atmosphere of this place was conducive to secrecy.

'Have you noticed there are no children here?' Jessica asked.

'They're in France. Years ago H.G. decided that the children would be healthier in the Alps. He set up a school there for them. Matt told me that the parents go too, until their children reach thirteen, then they're like boarders. Quite an incentive to have a kid, isn't it? Thirteen years in the Alps, all the ski-ing you could want. Matt's to die for, isn't he?' she said. 'Do you believe in love at first sight, Jessica?' She spoke abruptly as if embarrassed by her own question.

'Lust at first sight I know about. I'm not too good on love. My track record.' She raised an eyebrow self-deprecatingly.

'Maybe it is lust. But if it is, then I've never felt that either. I know that ever since I met Matt I can't stop thinking about him. It might sound daft, but I have been wondering if, by coming here, I haven't removed some mental block or something.' Saying it made it sound sillier than when she'd only been thinking it.

'I wouldn't have thought so, Selina. You're far too sensible to need any help to sort yourself out.'

'Am I? I'm not so sure.'

'Maybe you just needed to get away so that you could see yourself. Maybe you *have* just fallen in love. Don't worry about it. Loosen up. Life isn't that complicated, you know. What was it H.G. wrote? "The complications in your life are your own creation," ' Jessica said encouragingly.

'Well, that's daft, for a start. I hardly created the crisis in the book trade.' Selina chortled at the very idea. 'All the same,' she became serious again, 'did you hear Xavier tonight, when he accused me of standing back and being an observer of life? He came uncomfortably close to the truth. I've never had the guts to really let myself go. I've always put up barriers, kept some of me back, if you know what I mean.'

'Very sensible of you, too, if you're talking about

relationships with men. They're such unreliable creatures, so if you do keep a bit of you detached and they hurt you, you can always scuttle there. A friend of mine calls it her hurricane room, a place detached from everyone else in her mind. I've been striving to build mine for years.'

'But do you think they're on to something here? OK, I laughed about the meeting, it was a bit OTT, and Ginnie, well ...' She shrugged. 'But for all that, they do seem so happy and content. And they smile so much and are so gentle with each other.'

'You weren't at that slanging match the other day, when Ginnie did her first little cabaret act. I'd hardly call that being kind.'

'No, but it's not meant evilly, is it? It's meant to help you release all your pent-up anger and repression. Get those out of the way and then you can move on, become a whole person, the person you want to be – I mean they're not saying it's all spirituality, are they? They're saying, follow us and anything you want can be yours. Success, fame, money, anything you want.'

'I think it takes a lot more than that to become famous or successful. It wouldn't have helped me in my career – the opposite in fact. It's much more professional to repress anger and irritation than let it all hang out – people who do that are a pain in the arse.'

Selina laughed. It always surprised her when the beautiful Jessica was vulgar – like a crack in a lovely piece of porcelain. 'Xavier said five followers had become millionaires since joining Fohpal.'

'No doubt they'd have done the same even if they hadn't. And that sounds a long way from H.G. I haven't read anywhere that he said, "Follow me, and I'll make you a millionaire." The place would be bursting at the seams if he had.'

'You've really read up on him, haven't you?'

'It's interesting. And a lot of what the old boy says is just simple logic – very much after my own heart. I wish he wasn't so ill and we could have met him. But you're not alone, I'm finding it confusing too – it's like Xavier is using H.G.'s philosophies but then adding a bit of his own. I find myself swinging back and forth – half the time I think it's all a load of cobblers, and then that I could believe anything Xavier said!' Jessica drained her glass. 'Come in,' she called, to a rap on the door, and Ginnie entered, smiling broadly.

'I thought I should tell you myself that I shan't be seeing you for a couple of days, so don't get into a flap.' Ginnie was so excited, she couldn't stand still and prowled round the room, glancing at pictures, picking up ornaments, putting them down.

'Going away?' Jessica asked, thinking that Ginnie, with her glittering eyes, looked as if she was high on something.

'No, nothing like that. Oh, I'm so thrilled, I've simply got to share it with you! Xavier and Bethina couldn't believe I had become awakened so quickly. They said it normally took weeks or months, and that some people never achieve it. And little old me did it in a matter of days.'

'Did what?'

'Oh, Jessica, you try to annoy me on purpose, don't you? Well, it won't work. I'm too happy to let you bother me. I've purged myself. I'm awake.'

'Did it hurt?'

'I don't know why you're here, Jessica. You sneer at everything,' Ginnie flashed back, momentarily her old self. And then she seemed to put a brake on herself, and smiled beatifically instead. 'They're both so pleased with me. And guess what? Xavier says there's no doubt that I have the power – he's sure of it. He knows I could become a mystic, a healer. Me! Imagine!' She was babbling with excitement now. 'That second stage, just now when I was, oh, possessed is the only word to use – possessed with sheer joy, well, they say that can take for ever. And I did it in one. Did you see me? Releasing my repressions?'

'One could hardly miss you,' Jessica said laconically, even though Selina had pulled a face at her to keep quiet.

'Oh, my poor, dear Jessica, you're so deeply repressed. You've buttoned up all your emotions. It's so restricting for you, you know. You need to release all that bitterness you hold inside you.'

'Thanks, but no thanks, Ginnie.'

'But, Jessie, you must. You must have a free mind, or how can Xavier help you?'

'I've got an open mind, Ginnie. I'm convinced Xavier will help my aches and pains but I don't need to make an exhibition of myself for him to do that.'

'So where are you going?' Selina asked, to relieve the pressure that was obviously building between the other two, and before Jessica had time to bawl out Ginnie for calling her Jessie.

'Xavier's allowing me to go on to the next stage immediately. He says I'm so advanced there's no point in waiting.'

'What's involved?'

'I go into isolation for a few days, so that I can delve into myself further, know myself, get into every recess of my mind. That's how he put it. Clear the debris once and for all, and I'll emerge a better person. I can meditate, study in silence. It will be so ...' she paused '... cleansing.' She clapped her hands together with excitement. 'I thought I'd better let you know.'

'Thanks. I'll probably be gone when you come out,' Selina said.

'Selina, if you see Carter would you give him a message? Tell him I've found true happiness. Tell him that he's free now to do whatever he wants. Be with whoever he wants. I give him his liberation with tender love, and my blessings,' she said, with the expression of a wise saint, or so she hoped.

'What did you make of that?' Selina asked Jessica, when Ginnie had left them alone again.

'If it's what she wants. But I hope she'll be all right.'

'What makes you say that?'

'I don't know. After all, she's a grown woman, isn't she? And—'

'What was that?' Selina looked around the small sitting room. 'That noise. Did you hear it?'

'Yes, I often do late at night, like now. I think it must be the pipes.'

'Sounded like a cat wailing. Perhaps it's a ghost.'

'Don't say such things! I'm pretty isolated in this wing.'

'You haven't seen Ginnie's new room, have you? It's ghastly. A bit like a monk's cell, or a Victorian house-maid's bedroom. It's rather barren, for thirty thousand quid.'

'Part of the purging, perhaps. Well, that's decided me, if I needed persuading – I like my creature comforts too much.' Jessica gestured at the comfortably furnished sitting room. Then she registered what Selina had said. 'Thirty *what*?'

'Haven't they asked you? Me neither. But they have Ginnie. She told me, pleased as Punch, when she showed me her new quarters. It's probably because she's so much further along the Inner Way than us.' Selina giggled. 'It's like a time-share, she explained to me. It ensures her a room here for life. They guarantee her occupancy – all she has to do is telephone to say she's coming, and it's hers.'

'And she's already paid them?'

'Oh, yes. Gave them a cheque this afternoon, said she'd

put a little bit on top too, to help out. And she's given Xavier her car, and that's brand new too.'

'Well, I trust she can afford all this generosity.'

'She's loaded. But all the same ... it *is* a lot.' Selina frowned. 'She's a bit silly with money. Too generous by far. I could imagine her giving it all to them if they asked for it.'

'Then let's hope they never do. Carter might have something to say about that.'

'When I get back, I've been wondering if I shouldn't tell him what's going on. I know it's none of my business, but all the same ...'

'I think I would, if I were you. It's for her own protection. Did you see the accountant?'

'No. It's such a bore. He hasn't arrived. Tomorrow, they say now.' She grimaced. 'I must let you get to bed.' She stood up.

'Sleep well,' Jessica called.

Later, Jessica could not sleep. She'd told the truth when she said she wavered in her feelings towards Xavier and the others. She was normally a cynic, she knew that, but being so, she realised, and as Ginnie had pointed out, was likely to obstruct the thing she wanted most, to be cured. She must be on guard against herself.

Selina could not sleep either. She'd never seen Ginnie like this, so hysterically excited, so unguarded. Normally she'd say that she was more open than Ginnie, but now the roles were reversed. Ginnie had too much money, it made her too vulnerable, too susceptible, and yet ... If she was happy, then who was she, Selina, to criticise her? And then there was Esmeralda's letter. She leant over the side of the bed to check that it was still where she'd put it, under the mattress.

Ginnie couldn't sleep but, then, she hadn't expected to. She sat on a hard bed, in a cold room, deep down in the cellar of the great old house. It was pitch dark, and all around her was sound, like a thick wall, sound that was high-pitched, unidentifiable, and never-ending. She was frightened, and felt her sweat trickling down her skin. She clenched her fists to control the shaking of her body, which would not stop. She was frightened, and tried to prepare herself to be terrified.

chapter **ten**

1

'I wondered what was along here,' Jessica said, the following morning, as Ancilla led her from her room, and they turned along the corridor, going further into the West Wing past several closed doors similar to Jessica's.

'There's one other guest room for VIPs and these others are empty,' Ancilla explained. 'H.G. always had this wing to himself, even back in Bay Tarbart's time. He liked to be isolated from the crowd.'

'Necessary for his work, I'd have thought,' Jessica said, noting how Ancilla spoke of him in the past tense.

'Oh, yes, totally. He needed peace and quiet. It's through here.' Ancilla led her into a small, stone-flagged hall. A massive oak door gave to the outside but it was securely locked and bolted. She tapped at another linenfold door, then opened it. They entered a large drawing room, flooded with light from long mullioned windows, which looked out on the same knot garden as Jessica's did.

'What a beautiful place. Such wonderful furniture,' Jessica said with pleasure, looking around the immaculately tidy, beautifully decorated room. The chairs and sofas were upholstered in the palest cream slubbed silks. The curtains were full, and in silk also. Their paleness made the rugs on the oak-planked floor predominate, with their wonderful reds and blues. On one wall was displayed a vast selection of elephants, in ivory, stone, quartz, jade, wood and crystal. There were tiny elephants, large ones, and on the floor, studded with jewels, stood one that was a good three feet tall.

'So many elephants.'

'Oh, H.G. loved them. He was brought up with them as a child, you know, in Sri Lanka.'

'Why do you speak of him as if he was dead?'

'Do I? How silly of me. Perhaps because he's not been active within the community for so long.'

'What's wrong with him?'

'His age, probably. Bethina can find nothing specific. As she puts it, it's as if he's become too tired for his burden.'

'Hasn't he been to a hospital, seen a doctor, a specialist?' Jessica asked disapproving.

'You have to be kidding. H.G. would never countenance that. He's only ever been treated in the old ways. He wouldn't want to change now.'

'But surely the thinking these days is that there's room for both conventional and alternative medicines, so that they complement each other, and the experts in both fields are no longer warring against each other.'

'That sort of thing might be all right for London, but here?' she scoffed. 'And in any case, if you really knew H.G., as we do, you'd never believe that.'

'Did he tell you himself?'

'Not me personally, but it's well known. Oh, shit, Bethina said she'd leave the quilts out. She must have forgotten. Wait here a moment.'

While she was gone, Jessica wandered around the room. The furniture was a hotch-potch of styles – one massive wing chair had to be Georgian and the coffee table was lacquered and Japanese – but the mélange worked. It was a room planned for comfort, and everything the man required was here. There was a large Empire desk, with paper and pens lying ready and waiting, as if H.G. had just slipped out of the room. There was writing on the paper, and she glanced quickly at it, ashamed at her own nosiness. But she laughed when she read it: instead of deep, wise thoughts, as she had expected, it was an unfinished shopping list – an endearing list, Penhaligon shampoo, shaving foam, black silk socks and Bath Oliver biscuits.

Photographs in silver frames were scattered about the room, H.G. with Elvis, H.G. with President Reagan, the Queen, Charlie Chaplin. These were endearing too, that after all these years he should be proud to know so many famous people. And there were others, of a younger H.G. with followers in the dress of the thirties. One indomitable-looking woman was, undoubtedly, Bay Tarbart.

She was surprised to see a Georgian silver tray with several heavy and full crystal decanters. She had assumed someone like H.G. would be teetotal. Perhaps he was, and these were just for guests.

The books lying about were interesting. There were two by Richard Dawkins, a couple of heavy philosophical tomes, but then a pile of thrillers, Ruth Rendell, Patricia Cornwell, Minette Walters. The light reading outnumbered the weightier stuff by a good three to one.

By the television, which was the largest obtainable, she also saw a stack of video games. She liked that. He looked after himself well, there was no doubt of it. A box of Belgian chocolates was just one small indicator. And he had an ego – not only the photos, but the number of times his initials appeared, entwined and wrought in silk and gold thread, on cushions, his spectacle case. It was the room of a person confident in himself and in what he liked.

'The quilts are in here. I think it's okay for you to come in. Perhaps you'd just sort out what you need.' Ancilla had reappeared at the door, and frowned to see Jessica with a book in her hand, studying H.G.'s book-plate.

'Hope you don't mind, I've been snooping at H.G.'s reading matter. Surprisingly light, isn't it?'

'What's surprising about it? The greatest minds have to relax sometimes.'

'Of course,' Jessica said, knowing she had been told off.

The bedroom was as large and luxurious as the drawing room had been, but this room was decorated in a lovely pale blue, with darker blue cream-lined curtains and bedspread on the huge oak four-poster.

From a large oak chest Ancilla had already unpacked a double patchwork quilt, and had draped it over a chair. The centre was worked in tiny squares, in graduated, jewel-like colours, in an abstract, almost 3-D design.

Jessica swooped on it. 'This is wonderful. I could never do something as intricate as that. And just look at the neatness of the work, the confident use of colour, and all done by hand, too.'

'He found it relaxing. He hadn't started the surround before he was taken ill, but we found this box. It's full of patchwork pieces already cut out and lined with paper – see, they're all tacked in. We've presumed these are what he wanted for the border, since they're bigger.' She delved into the box, and held up a pile of hexagonal patches. 'Can you do it? If so you'd better take the ones you think are for this quilt.'

'Yes, no problem. This is about my level,' Jessica said. 'Who's it for?'

'None of your concern.'

'I was only asking.' She turned to inspect the box, and jumped with surprise. 'Oh, I'm so sorry, I didn't see you,' she apologised.

'He can't answer.'

'Poor soul.' Sitting in the corner of the room, propped in a large wing chair, his feet up on a tapestry stool, a blanket around him, but fully dressed in white, sat a man, shrunken, thinner, smaller than she had expected, but undoubtedly H.G. His skin was pale, far paler than the photographs she had seen implied.

Jessica approached him tentatively. 'I'm so sorry you're unwell. I hope you get better soon. Are you comfortable?' she heard herself saying, unsure if he could even hear her.

'He's probably deaf, you know. You might as well save your breath,' said Ancilla.

Jessica felt annoyance at the glibness in the American's voice, and an impatience with illness, a sorry fault in some of the young, which she had sadly identified for herself. 'If you don't know that for sure, then don't say it. The hearing is the last faculty to go.'

'Really?' Ancilla brightened somewhat at this snippet of information – she reminded Jessica of a magpie, but collecting facts instead of shiny things. 'He never reacts, so he's probably dead in his head,' she said coldly, quite spoiling the idea.

'Don't listen to her, H.G.,' Jessica said kindly, and took hold of his claw-like hands. She looked into his eyes, expecting to see no emotion, then caught her breath. In them she saw an expression of unadulterated fear.

'What's up? Why did you gasp like that?' Ancilla asked.

'His hand, I – I didn't expect it to feel so cold.' And she squeezed H.G.'s warm hand, hoping he would understand that she had seen and recognised his expression, but there was no response. 'If you don't know whether he can hear or not, why not put some music on – just in case?' She nodded at the tall, expensive stack of Bang and Olufsen music equipment.

'Why not, indeed?' Ancilla began to look through the library of CDs. 'What do you think, Mozart, Beethoven?'

'Either.'

'This'll do. Beethoven's Mass in D, just right for the brain-dead.'

'You bitch,' Jessica said, under her breath. The music began to soar into the room. She looked down at H.G.'s face, with its sculpted cheekbones, and to her sorrow, saw the glisten of a tear. She was on the point of telling Ancilla, to prove that he was not deaf, but something stopped her. While the woman was packing the quilt into the box, her back turned, Jessica surreptitiously wiped away the tear.

'Who put that music on?' Bethina stood in the doorway, hands on hips, annoyance marring her beautiful face. 'Turn it off this instant. He shouldn't have too much stimulus, it agitates him.'

'Jessica here thought H.G. might like some music.'

'It's none of Jessica's business. Switch it off, Ancilla. Leave him alone, Jessica. He doesn't know you. You'll disturb him. In any case, what are you doing here? This is out of bounds to everyone – H.G. is a very private person, he'd hate strangers staring at him, especially in his condition.'

'I brought Jessica in to collect the quilt, as you told me to. When it wasn't next door in the drawing room, Jessica suggested we looked in here and we found it,' Ancilla lied smoothly.

'Snooping, were you?' Bethina asked, and Jessica was astonished to hear the suppressed anger in her voice, Bethina was normally so placid.

'No, just collecting the quilt. I'm sorry, I didn't realise. I haven't harmed him in any way,' Jessica said sharply.

'Get out,' Bethina snapped back, no pretence at sweet calm now. 'And don't ever come in here again, understood?'

'Fine.' Jessica held up her hand, palm outwards, and backed to the door, aware with mounting horror that H.G. was watching her, terror evident in his eyes.

2

'How long have you been here?' Selina was asking Matt, as they sat together sipping mint tea. What she wouldn't give for a cup of strong espresso, she thought. What she wouldn't give to be curled up in bed with him.

'Nearly a year.'

'Hell, a year with no coffee, cigs or booze. Grim.'

Matt laughed. 'I'm a lot healthier than when I came here, that's for sure.'

'What do you do mostly?' she asked politely, longing for his hands to be touching her.

'I work outside, growing veg and things. There's not much to do at the moment. And I seem to have become a sort of handyman where machinery's concerned – I mend stuff, though I knew nothing about boilers and washing machines and suchlike when I came. Still, I quite enjoy the gardening and the tinkering. It's a change.'

'What did you do before?' She loved his lips, full and sensuous.

'I'm an architect.'

'I'm glad to hear you use the present tense. Everyone else always talks in the past, as if that was them in another life, one that they're not going back to. So you intend to leave one day?' Maybe they could meet then: with no restraints, anything could happen, she thought.

'I didn't mean you to interpret it that way, it was just a way of speaking. I'm happy – why shouldn't I be? Why should I go?'

'Because you don't seem to belong here, not like the others.'

'That's because it's harder for me to find the Inner Way, I suppose. One day.' He looked about him at the others scattered around the room. She sensed he was on edge.

'Have I said something to offend you?'

'No,' he replied shortly.

They sat in silence, Selina kicking herself for being so inquisitive, so rude. She hadn't meant to be, she'd just wanted to find out more about him. She couldn't help her mounting curiosity: her attraction towards him was intensifying. She imagined the scenario if she should suddenly tear off her clothes and jump on the table shouting, 'Take me!' She smiled at the very idea.

'What's funny?'

'Nothing,' she replied, but she could feel herself colouring slightly. How intensely she wanted him.

'Were we your first contact with Fohpal?' he suddenly enquired.

'Oh, I'd read about it, always been interested,' she said politely, and then thought, What the hell. 'Quite honestly I knew nothing about it. And, in any case, I didn't think you'd remember me, not when you weren't at the London meeting. Someone left the details of it on my coffee table. Was it you?' she asked, hoping he'd say yes.

'It's policy, when we make a possibly fruitful contact, to leave the details of the next meeting,' he explained. He spoke slowly, deliberately, but her disappointment that he'd not left them specially for her made her deaf to what he was saying.

'Oh, I see.' She looked dejected.

'I hoped we'd meet again, somehow. And be able to talk to each other, get to know each other, but this isn't the best place, Selina. You do realise? I wish we were elsewhere.' He leant forward and looked at her so intently that she felt her heart lift with joy.

'Me too.' And this time she really blushed, but she didn't mind. 'I was so disappointed when you weren't here over Christmas.'

'I was sent to France. I drove one of the minibuses. I was pleased to go. I wanted to see my sister. But, of course, when I heard you were coming I wished I could be in two places.' She felt herself glow with pleasure at this information.

'Has your sister lived in France long?'

'She teaches at the Fohpal school.'

'Did she join the movement before you?'

'Long before.' He began to look uneasy again.

'Do you know Esmeralda well?' She decided to risk asking him, certain he was the one person she could trust. It also changed the subject and she did not like to see him uncomfortable.

'Why do you ask?' he queried guardedly.

'Do you like her?'

'Of course, but she's not got many friends.'

'She seems to be in a bit of a state.' Selina fished for information.

'Don't tell her I told you but she's pregnant and pretty devastated about it.'

'Who's the father?' In answer he shrugged his shoulders. Not you, I hope, she thought, but refrained from saying it. 'That explains it. She gave me a letter for her parents. She's—'

'She what? What did you do with it?' He looked up, alarmed.

'I hid it. Don't worry, it's safe in my room. What's the hassle?'

'Selina, destroy it. Don't get involved.' He spoke urgently.

'I can't let her down.'

'You must. Promise me. Destroy it.'

'I promise,' she said, with her fingers crossed under the table. What *had* got into him? 'Don't look so worried.'

'Why are you here?' he asked suddenly, as if purposely changing the subject. He looked about him again, as if checking that he was not being overheard.

'You know the reason. I want to sell them my shop.

Only I can't pin anyone down to discuss it with me.' And she explained how Colley had spoken to her at the meeting in London and had set everything in motion. 'I wouldn't have come otherwise. None of this sort of thing is my bag. I mean, I used to sell books on cults and mysticism, and crystals and suchlike, and I've dabbled a bit in alternative New Age stuff. But I don't really go for this. It's all a bit heavy – well, not all of it,' she added, afraid she must be sounding rude about something in which he believed, and which was important to him.

He put out his hand and took hold of hers. She felt a pleasurable jolt soar through her body at his touch.

'Selina, be careful. Get sound advice before you do anything,' he whispered urgently and, to her regret, removed his hand.

'I liked you touching me,' she felt bold enough to say. 'I'd like to be alone with you.' She sat back astonished at her own temerity – this wasn't like her at all.

'Look Selina, I can't. It won't work. It would mean trouble.'

'What would?' She felt downcast but blamed herself for being too forward, scaring him off probably.

'You and me together.'

'How?'

'It just would.'

'I'm sorry if I spoke out of turn just then. I don't normally.'

'It isn't that. I like you being so up-front. It's just not possible.'

'Don't you fancy me?' she asked miserably.

At that he groaned. 'Of course I do, like crazy.'

'Then what's stopping us? Are you married?' She forced herself to ask the dreaded question.

'No, it's just that it's the rule.'

'What rule?'

'Xavier decides who goes with whom.'

Selina sat bolt upright. 'You have to be joking.' Matt shook his head sadly. 'I've never heard anything so ridiculous.'

'It's how it is,' he said, resignedly.

'Then leave.'

'Easier said than done. There's my sister to think about.'

'But she's in France.'

'I know. It doesn't make any difference.' He looked long and hard at his hands, work-worn from his gardening. 'Has Xavier tried ... You know.' He looked bashful.

'Has he tried to seduce me? No. He'd better not try. I don't like the thought.'

'That doesn't hinder him. If he wants you, he'll have you.'

'Not me. I do what I want, go with whom I want. I'm not going to be ordered about by someone like him – he gives me the creeps.' Defiantly she half stood, leant across the table and kissed Matt full on the mouth. 'So there.' She sat back triumphantly.

'That was nice.' Matt put his hand up and touched his lips, as if he hadn't believed what she had done. 'But look, Selina, not here. It's too ... difficult.' She was aware that he chose the word deliberately, but she was certain it was not the word he really wanted to use.

'But when?'

'I don't know, but some day. I've got work to do still, you see.'

She nodded, but she didn't understand. She wished he'd explain what work could be so important that it could come between them. And he was afraid, she was certain he was. She wished she knew of what or whom.

3

'Love will only survive if there is no possessiveness, Selina. Jealousy is fatal to a relationship.'

'That's your opinion, Xavier.'

'Not just mine. We all believe that here at Porthwood.'

'Well, I don't,' Selina said defiantly. 'If there's no jealousy, it means you don't care enough. It's as simple as that.' She was already suffering this emotion cruelly, loathing to see Matt even talk to someone else.

'Then I would guess you've never been in love. You would understand if you had.'

'I have,' she blustered, riled. She knew she protested too much, that in doing so she had revealed more of herself than she had intended.

'Love, in its purest state, is proven by giving that person their liberty to do as they will, screw where they want. You need to purge yourself, Selina. Enough of us have told you. You can't hope to experience peace and love until you do. You're withdrawing, fighting, all the time. You're a mess inside, Selina. I feel such pity for you.' Xavier stroked her hair. She shook away his hand. 'You see? Look at the resistance then, how afraid you are to loosen up.'

'I'm no such thing. I just don't like being pawed by people I don't know, and who I haven't invited to touch me.'

'Did your parents reject you? Did your mother say kissing's dirty? Did she wipe her mouth if you kissed her?'

'What a daft load of questions you do ask,' she said forcefully, hoping she was covering up her shock at how close he was to the truth. How many times had her mother turned away her face, when as a child Selina had eagerly tried to kiss her hello or goodbye? How easily she could remember the bleak feeling of rejection at the seemingly innocent movement of her mother's head. How could he possibly know that?

'But it's a pertinent query. Admit it. Tell me, Selina, you've been wanting to be loved since you were a child. You're desperate for it.' His hand caressed her shoulder, sliding almost imperceptibly down to the swell of her breast.

Selina knocked away his hand and jumped to her feet. 'Xavier, I came to enquire about the state of play regarding my shop. I didn't expect this. How dare you?'

'I dare because I love you, Selina. I've so much love to give you.' He stood, arms open wide, as if in invitation to her.

'Well, try someone who'd appreciate it, not me. My shop.' She stood defiant, determined not to leave his room until she had an answer.

'What a persistent little one you are.' He laughed, but to her it sounded false. It was as if he switched it on and off when needed, like a light, not because he was amused. She wondered who he thought he fooled. 'Very well, if that's what you want, we'll take over your shop. I'll get the papers drawn up, and you can sign them tonight. But you needn't think you can resist me for ever. You will succumb.'

'But what about a survey, the searches?' She decided to ignore his boast – bloody nerve! Still, if thinking that way induced him into sorting out the shop, let him dream on, it didn't bother her – well, not much.

'Oh, they'll have been done, no doubt,' he said airily. 'Happy now?'

'Xavier, I don't know how to thank you. You've no idea what a relief this is to me.' In a trice she changed towards him, smiling, her face open with her happiness, feeling she could hug him from sheer relief if he hadn't been such an oily so-and-so. And then she asked herself, Who was being false now?

'I do know how important this is to you. And *you* know how you can thank me.' He took a step towards her, his hand outstretched, an expectant look on his face. He'd misread her reaction, but this time she couldn't blame him.

'You've got the wrong person, Xavier. Look, I'm sorry. I've met someone else already,' she said with pride, but fully aware that she must not betray Matt by mentioning his name – not yet.

'You mean Matt. Not a good idea, Selina. I couldn't honestly approve of such a match.'

'No one's asking for your approval,' she retorted cheekily. 'Thanks then. Until this evening.'

Selina was searching for Matt. If Xavier knew of their attraction to each other, and disapproved, perhaps he would be sent away again, and then she'd never find him. Leaving tomorrow, she needed to search him out, arrange when and how they could meet. And, most of all, she felt she had to warn him that Xavier knew about their feelings for each other.

It was strange, but she noticed that people avoided her eyes when she asked if they'd seen Matt, and when they said they'd no idea where he was, she thought they were lying. Then she chided herself for her mounting paranoia. She must guard against becoming like the others, which included Matt, jumping at Xavier's command. She and Matt were adult people, they could do as they wished. There was nothing Xavier could do to stop them being together. One minute she had thought him nice and caring, and now she was behaving as if she was scared witless of him. One thing she was sure of now, Matt had been here too long. He needed to get away and see things as they really were.

She tramped around the grounds, searching the various out-houses and sheds. It was raining, she was cold, and her shoes were soon ruined as she squelched through the mud. He was nowhere. She returned despondently to the house where she bumped into Colley.

'Have you seen Matt anywhere?'

'He's up in his room. He said he thought he'd caught a cold.'

'Where's that?'

'Right up at the top – West Wing. Room five. And don't tell anyone I told you.' He grinned at her.

As Selina climbed the back stairs and tiptoed along the upper corridor, high under the eaves of the old house, her heart was beating so loudly she feared it would alert everyone.

It beat so violently not because she was nervous at being here – she didn't give a monkey's who saw her – but because she knew what she was going to do and never in her whole life had she behaved in such a way.

'Nothing ventured …' she whispered to herself as, jaw set, she rapped smartly on the door of number five before she could change her mind and run downstairs.

'For Christ's sake, I said I'd be down in a minute,' an exasperated-sounding Matt called.

'Matt, it's me,' she said, not so sure of herself now.

The door swung open. 'What are you doing here?' Matt asked, peering furtively out of the door and looking up and down the corridor.

' "What a nice surprise" was more what I had in mind,' she said sassily, to cover her hurt at his reaction.

'I'm sorry. You'd better come in.'

She stepped into the room and knocked against him as she did so. The room, like Ginnie's, was bare of furniture and small so that physical contact was inevitable.

'I'm sorry,' he said, as he brushed past her to close the window.

'Don't shut it for me.'

'It gets stuffy even in winter.'

'Then leave it open.' With two steps she was beside him, looking out of the window across the leads and through the battlements to the park far below them. 'Lovely view.'

'I like to sit here and watch it.'

'Understandable.' She turned to face him just as he swung round to look at her. 'We're like those Swiss weather dolls.'

'Not quite. Isn't one always in the house when the other's out?'

'No, my grandma had one. Sometimes they were both out together, but I can't remember why – I think I'm in love with you, Matt,' she blurted out, and felt herself redden and her stomach somersault.

He looked at her wide-eyed, as if with astonishment – Or was it apprehension? she found herself thinking. 'You needn't look so scared.' She practised a laugh that wobbled alarmingly. 'I mean, I won't – you know ... I wanted you to know ...'

She did not finish the last disjointed sentence for his arms were about her and his mouth was on hers and she just knew everything was going to be perfect in a way it had never been before. Their longing and need for each other were so strong that they rapidly undressed themselves. Holding on to her as if to stop her running from him, Matt led her to the narrow bed and lowered her onto it. He eased himself beside her so that her whole naked body was touched by his skin. She seemed to melt into his arms, eager for his kisses. As their passion mounted and the kissing became a nipping and then a sucking, a pulling, a devouring, they began to cry out their pleasure in each other's bodies, not caring if anyone heard, as they made each other blissfully happy, completely released.

*

They drifted into sleep and it was only the chill that woke them a couple of hours later.

'My darling, you've made me so happy.' He spoke softly into her hair. 'I love your hair. It's like you – free, uninhibited.'

'I'd like …' She began to tell him she didn't normally do this sort of thing, coming on so strong, and she hoped he respected her still. But it all sounded so clichéd that she didn't bother and hoped he didn't mind. She smiled – it didn't matter how independent she liked to think she was, her mother's morality had a nasty way of popping up when she least wanted it to.

'What's funny?'

'I was wondering what my mother would say.'

'Bizarre! Does it matter what she says?'

'No, of course not. But …' She paused again, unsure whether to tell him, knowing if she did that this contented mood would evaporate but feeling, in fairness, that she should. She put out her hand and gently stroked his hair – needing to touch him.

'Xavier's guessed about us, Matt. I can't imagine how.'

'That kiss in the dining room. Someone was sure to tell him about it, earn themselves Brownie points.' He sounded bitter. 'But I already knew. He spoke to me earlier too.'

'He warned me off. What did he say to you?'

'That I'm not to have anything to do with you,' he said baldly. And then he laughed, a short laugh that was no laugh. 'Didn't work though, did it?' She snuggled up closer to him, convinced that nothing and no one would separate them now. 'But we must be careful, Selina. We can't do this again, that's for sure.'

She sat up on the bed. 'I'm sorry?' She looked down at him, puzzled, as if unsure she had heard correctly, but the sinking feeling in the pit of her stomach told her she had.

'It's not a good idea, Selina. You must realise that. Xavier could make things difficult.'

'You agreed with him, is that it? You promised to lay off me.' Still he was silent. 'So I'm sufficiently unimportant to you that you do just as he wishes. I don't believe this! Was I just an easy lay? Is it sod-Selina time?' She knew she sounded shrewish, she couldn't help it. 'That was pretty wimpish of you, wasn't it?' She wanted to hurt him too. She was off the bed now, scrabbling on the floor for her discarded clothes. She'd been a fool yet again, allowing herself to be swept along on a tide of stupid emotion. Throwing herself at someone who obviously did not feel the same about her. So much for listening to Xavier and trying to knock down her barriers. Her tights were on. Roughly she pulled her shirt over her head.

'Selina, you don't understand.'

'Oh, I do. I thought we had something. Forgive me for being so stupid.' She didn't bother with her bra but shoved it in the pocket of her skirt. Her jumper was inside out and back to front, but she didn't even notice.

'I wish I could explain to you but I can't.'

'No, you can't do anything you want, can you? You're just a glorified anorak, and I thought you were my Mr Right. There's a laugh. Don't worry, I'm leaving anyway. We've only got the rest of today to get through, then you're safe from my unwanted attentions.'

He grabbed her by the upper arm.

'Do you mind!' She glared at him but the effect was somewhat spoilt when she could not keep it up, for her body was betraying her, pleased that he should be touching her.

'You're leaving? Has something happened about the shop?'

'They're buying it. We're signing the papers tonight. I'll be off tomorrow.'

'Selina, be careful. You shouldn't sign anything without a lawyer. Please listen to me. If I could tell you
everything I would, but there are other people involved.
It's impossible. Give me a week – stay another week,
please, then maybe I can explain everything to you.'

'Not bloody likely. I'm off! The sooner I'm away from
a creep like you the better! And you can forget trying to
find me in a week, a month, or a year. I won't be around
for you. Understood? You mean absolutely nothing to
me.'

She turned on her heel and stalked out of the room,
slamming the door noisily behind her. Outside she put
her hand over her mouth to stifle a cry. She'd been so
sure, so confident. She ran along the upper corridor and
skidded down the steps blindly, tears filling her eyes. She
raced to her room and only when she was safely inside
did she allow herself to cry. Another dream biting the
dust. What a prat she was, she told herself, as she
wallowed in her misery.

4

Jessica felt good. She had had her first healing session
with Xavier. She'd been nervous as she sat outside his
office waiting to be called, because she knew that, despite
her stern lectures to herself, she had been setting too
much store by Xavier's ability to heal her. But if it only
half worked, how much easier everything would be. Just
a little more mobility, a little less pain. She'd gladly
accept any change, so long as it was the smallest bit for
the better.

She looked up as the door opened and a young woman
with dark hair emerged. One of the contingent from
France, whom Jessica had not met.

'Now, remember what I say, Clarissa,' Xavier said.

'Am I likely to forget? That was a wonderful session.' And she laughed a low husky laugh. Jessica smiled up at her and her obvious happiness. That was strange, she thought, she recognised the voice – Welsh, she thought, with a touch of London – yet not the face. Jessica had a good memory for both. Odd. She frowned.

'Right, Jessica. You ready?' Xavier was smiling down at her, his hand out ready to help her stand. She did not mind *him* helping her and all thought of the other woman disappeared. 'Here, drink this tincture of Bethina's, it'll help you relax.'

Lying on the couch in Xavier's room, the lights low, with soft music – Indian, she had thought, but it was so low it was difficult to tell – and the warmth from the fire, she had immediately relaxed. So much so that when their session was interrupted by the telephone ringing she wasn't even annoyed, as normally she would have been.

'I'm sorry about that, I've disconnected it now so it won't ring again,' Xavier said, after he had returned to her side. 'That was Hesta, from France. She sends her best love and she says she just knows this session will go well.'

'How kind.' Jessica smiled up at him.

'Now, where were we … ?'

Xavier had not touched her, but had ordered her to close her eyes, to relax, and she had sensed, rather than seen, his hands sweeping up and down her body, hovering for a slightly longer moment over her hips. She could not see, but she knew – she could feel him.

'You can open your eyes now. See what I have got for you.' In his hand he held a large crystal pendant on a chain. It was swinging back and forth in front of her face, like a pendulum. 'See the pretty lights, Jessica, see the pretty lights. You're so relaxed, aren't you, Jessica?

240

Follow the lights, follow the lights. Go to sleep. There's a good girl ...'

Now she was in her room, resting as she had been ordered to do, and she knew she felt easier and more free of tension than she had for a long time. She decided not to question him as to how this state had been achieved but just to accept. She sat up, slid off the bed gingerly and stood a moment before crossing the room to the low table where the box of patchwork stood. She carried it back to the bed. She had moved more easily. It had hurt less. She dared to hope.

She took the quilt off the top of the box and, folding it in half, laid it on the bed. She took out the prepared pieces and sorted them into their various colours, working out which colours H.G. had intended for the border. Evidently he'd meant to have a row of dark blue shading into paler, for there were larger numbers of the hexagonals in the paler shades. It shouldn't take too long: the pieces were prepared ready to sew. Each fabric piece was lined with paper cut from a template, which kept the fabric the right shape. The narrow seams were neatly tacked in place, all she had to do was join them together.

For an hour she worked methodically, happily relaxed, enjoying the task. With a long strip ready, she then began to attach it to the main section. Half a row completed, she turned it over, and with her nail scissors cut the tacking that held the paper in place. One by one she removed the papers – crisp, good-quality notepaper, she noticed, she mostly cut up magazines to line hers – and, with her fingers, flattened the seams.

Admiring the quilt, she decided the effect was good – the old boy had excellent colour sense. She paused. Just remembering that expression of fear in his eyes made the hairs on her arms stand up. It wasn't surprising that he was experiencing such fear: she could barely begin to imagine what it must be like to have one's mind trapped in a useless body, unable to communicate, dependent on others for everything. She shuddered. Such thoughts were too close to her fears for her own future.

Idly she picked up one of the paper squares and smoothed it with her finger. There was beautiful writing on it, italic like H. G.'s. One didn't often see that, these days. It must have been written by someone fairly old – the young had no patience with such a hand.

64
The fear
is mounting. Yet I'm
to blame. If only I'd taken notice of
so many discrepancies. The
noises in the night.
The vacant

The writing was small, but distinct. She picked up another paper on which the script was minute.

136
then I'd
have reason to
be afraid. He does nothing,
though. I sit and wait for him, for
something to happen, fearing
I know not what. It's a
dreadful way to
live

Jessica frowned. How strange. She wondered who the writer was and what was to be feared. She was certain that these hexagonals had not been cut from a larger sheet of paper already written on. Each had been written on separately: there was no punctuation at the beginning or at the end, as if the next part was somewhere else. She had once seen an antique quilt where the lining papers had been cut from letters: there the writing went right to the end with no margins. It had belonged to a friend, who on deciding to wash it and hearing rustling, had realised the guiding papers were still in position, and that she would have to remove them. She had discovered the quilt was lined with love letters from a soldier, in the trenches in the First World War, to his girl, neatly cut up and secreted away for ever. To find out what they'd said, her friend had fitted them all together, like a giant jigsaw. It had taken months, but once she had read them she had sewn them back, feeling they should be back where they had come from.

These pieces, though, were numbered. Who had written them? She began to study the others. Some of the templates were written on, some not. She began to unpick them all, putting them in number order.

5

Selina was ready to leave first thing in the morning. She wanted to get away as quickly as possible. She felt such a fool. She coloured now and touched her flaming cheek as she thought of her humiliation with Matt.

She wondered if Ginnie had twigged how she felt. And, of course, Jessica knew because Selina had taken the unprecedented step of discussing Matt and love with her. Oh, God, how embarrassed she'd feel when she faced her again. But it mattered less that Jessica knew everything: once they were back in the real world it was unlikely they'd ever meet again. Jessica wouldn't be interested in her world, and she doubted if she'd ever be invited into

Jessica's more exciting one. Ginnie was another matter altogether. She'd hate her to know what a fool she'd been.

'That's odd.' She paused in her task. She was searching in the back of her wardrobe for the remains of the bottle of vodka. She needed a good slug of it, but it wasn't there. She scrabbled further into the wardrobe. It had been nicked! Bloody cheek! And then she smiled. This Matt business had certainly made her neurotic – good job she hadn't gone screaming and yelling, 'Thief!' She had felt the bottle's familiar shape, lying to the side of the cupboard. She must have knocked it over while she was packing.

She sat at the small desk, a tooth mug beside her with the last of the vodka in it. She began to pile her books together. She mustn't forget the letter she'd promised to post for Esmeralda. She got up and felt under her mattress. It had gone! She knew she'd put it there. It was where she used to hide love letters from boys, when she was a kid still at school, so that her mother wouldn't find them. Still, with all the Matt business, maybe she'd moved it and forgotten she had. She opened the top drawer of the desk. Nothing. She sat down again. She could have put it somewhere else, she supposed. She'd been pickled enough last night after her session with Jessica – now there was a woman with a tough head. She opened the lower drawers of the desk. No. She got to the bottom one—

Someone had been searching through her things. There was no doubt. She hadn't bothered to unpack most of her stuff and she could remember clearly where she had put the little she had taken out of her bags. She'd left her cigarettes on the right; now they were on the left. The diary she'd meant to write, but had got bored with, was the wrong way round. And, if she had needed further proof, her small envelope handbag, in which she kept her pens and address book, was clipped shut – and she never bothered to do that.

Systematically she went through everything again, searching for the letter. She shook every book, but nothing fell out. They could not have known about the letter – or could they? Matt! She'd told him and only him. No, he wouldn't! He couldn't. She mustn't think that of him, not without checking with him. He'd seemed to be her friend – but then he wasn't that much of a friend, he'd not even stood up to Xavier for her. Then, all the shame she felt because of him swept over her and she felt like crying again, but she didn't. Instead she threw her cardigan around her shoulders, pulled her hairbrush through her tangled, curly hair, and swept from her room.

Quickly she climbed the stairs to the top floor, where she knew Esmeralda's room was – just three doors along from Ginnie's. She tapped on the door. All the way up she'd been worrying what she was to say to the woman; she'd been so scared when she left the letter with Selina. This was going to be awfully difficult to explain. She tapped again, a little louder. When no one answered, she pushed open the door. The room was empty – really empty. There was not one possession to be seen, just a neatly made-up bed. Nothing on the chest of drawers. She opened the small wardrobe: it was bare.

Along the corridor, she knocked on Ginnie's door. She might be wanting solitude, but this was serious. Again, there was no reply.

'Ginnie, I'm sorry—' Selina said, as she walked in but stopped dead. The room looked just like Esmeralda's, empty, deserted, not one of Ginnie's things anywhere.

Selina hurtled down the narrow stairs, pounded along the richly carpeted corridors of her own floor, and then rushed down the main staircase, as if pursued by all the furies. She must find Jessica.

'Where's the fire?' In the hall Bethina stepped forward. Selina screeched to a halt like a cartoon character.

'I need to speak to Ginnie and Esmeralda,' she said, trying to control her voice.

'Have you forgotten? Ginnie's in retreat and must not be disturbed. And didn't anyone tell you that Esmeralda left this afternoon?'

'Where's she gone?'

'To France. Her little girl is poorly. She needed to be with her. Can I help you?'

'My room's been searched.'

'Are you sure?' Bethina looked appalled.

'Of course I'm sure. I won't have it. How dare someone do that?' she ranted.

'No wonder you're upset. How awful for you! We had a sneak thief here a couple of years ago. We got rid of him, of course. I suppose we've become too relaxed again. I can't apologise enough. Was anything taken?'

'No, nothing. But just the idea of someone snooping ...' Selina's voice trailed away. She felt rather stupid now. After all, she hadn't lost anything, except, of course, the worrying letter – and the memory of Esmeralda's fear was still too clear for her even to think of mentioning it.

'Well, that *is* a blessing. You're to sign the papers tonight, aren't you? You'd better come with me. Have a drink to calm you down. We don't want Xavier to see you upset, do we? He needs to keep his equilibrium – he has such important work to do.'

'Of course. I'd love a drink.' She was feeling better already, but she was not about to turn down the offer of a drink.

She hadn't been in Bethina's room before and it was how she imagined a prioress's would be. Everything was white, and neat, and calm prevailed. Selina sat on the edge of a large white upholstered armchair, and felt a little as she had when in her headmistress's study: Bethina's aura of perfection was a little unnerving.

'There you are.' Bethina handed her a glass, clinking with ice in a clear liquid.

'What is it?' Selina was off-hand, but she didn't want Bethina to think everything was fine now. It was not all right if her room had been searched.

'Vodka. That's your favourite drink, isn't it?' Bethina laughed. Selina had never heard her laugh before and it was a delightful sound, gentle, bubbling, but it didn't defuse her anger, or her rekindling suspicions.

'How do you know that?'

'Oh dear, you're still upset, aren't you? It was just a lucky guess. And, in any case, it's the only drink I have here.' She laughed again. 'You look like someone who'd like vodka, and this is a special one. One of H.G.'s followers is Russian. He brings us this when he comes. Cheers.' Bethina raised her own glass. This did surprise Selina: Bethina was the last person she'd imagined she would ever see with a tumbler of alcohol in her hand.

'It's good,' she said, after the first sip. 'Excellent. It's got a taste, though. Most vodka is tasteless.'

'Yes, it's nice, isn't it. Just a hint of, what do you think, coriander?'

Selina took another, larger sip, savouring it. 'I think you're right.' They drank in silence for a moment. 'How long have you been at Porthwood?' Selina asked politely, feeling she should make conversation.

'All my life. I spent my childhood here. This room was my grandmother's, my mother's and now mine.'

'Then you've always known H.G.?'

'He's like a very special honorary grandfather to me – for a long time I thought he was. You see, my grand-mother was Hyacinth Boothly. She was with Bay Tarbart on the day he was found. She loved H.G. and, I suppose, since I loved him too, I longed for him to be a blood relation. My real grandfather was so understanding when I explained.'

'And you never married?'

'No. I never met anyone I loved enough and eventually there was no need.' She laughed her delicious laugh, a hint of suggestiveness in it this time, which hadn't been there before. Selina wondered why.

'Jessica had her first session with Xavier tonight. It was successful. She's a very good patient.' Bethina changed the subject.

'It would be wonderful if he could help her. She's so frightened of the future.'

'Poor woman. It must be hard to age in her profession. I'd love to have seen her when she was younger. She's so beautiful still.'

'She doesn't think she is. She thinks she's ugly. I can't get her to understand she's still lovely.'

'Maybe someone has hurt her deeply, said something cruel to her about her appearance.'

'Perhaps. She's a very private person. She'd never say.'

'I wish she'd purge herself, come to a counselling session.'

'She won't do that. She'd be too scared someone would sell what she'd said to one of the tabloids. It's under-standable, isn't it, with someone like her?'

'Quite. But you haven't either, have you? And, forgive me saying so, but you're not famous.' She laughed again, it really was a lovely sound, the sort that made one want to laugh oneself.

'Quite honestly, I didn't feel I needed to. In any case I've nothing to say. Dead boring, I am.'

'Everyone has something they need to release. Often an incident buried deep in the past that they're afraid to let free.'

'I did a regression once. Scared myself witless.' Selina drained her glass.

'Another one?' Bethina suggested. 'And what about Matt?' she asked, as she gave Selina a fresh drink.

'Matt? Oh, the blond bloke. Xavier spoke to me about him. He seemed to have some odd idea that I was interested in him. I'm not.'

'Very wise.'

Selina took off her cardigan. She was suddenly feeling very hot, but didn't know whether it was from the heat of the room or from her embarrassment that everyone seemed to be aware that something had happened between her and Matt. 'It's hot in here, isn't it?'

'Not particularly. Would you like me to open a window? It's beginning to snow, and it's blowing everywhere. I didn't want to get the carpet wet.'

'No, it's me. I must be getting menopausal.' She giggled, then felt rather stupid.

'Xavier will be here in a minute. To sign your papers.'

'Oh, good. Can I read them?'

'Let's wait until he comes, shall we? He can explain all the tedious legal jargon. The bits and bobs we wouldn't understand.'

That was out of character, Selina thought. Bethina had a razor-sharp mind. Then she found she couldn't remember what she'd said that had made her think that, nor why she was here. Something had happened. 'If you could open that window, I—'

'Ah, Selina. Waiting to sign, are we? Fantastic. You understand everything? Good. I'm in a bit of a rush – I've a healing, some people have travelled all the way from Newcastle. Imagine that, it's so humbling. Jessica's well – did Bethina tell you? Now the pen. Where's your pen, Bethina?'

Selina watched him as he fussed about the desk. His tall, dark blue figure against the whiteness of the room looked like an animated silhouette. She had questions to ask, a lot of questions ... Odd that she couldn't remember them ... Odd how far away their voices seemed.

'Here we are. If you sign here, here and here.' Xavier stabbed at the papers with his forefinger, holding the pen towards her. 'Sign what?' she wondered, as she took it from him and pulled the paper towards her. She uncapped the fountain pen, and became fixated with it. It had such a lush green barrel, grass green, moss green, and it was prettily speckled with gold, which sparkled as she moved it in the light. She didn't know if the giggling she could hear was her or not – she had an idea it was.

'Here,' Xavier said, and pointed at the paper again. She felt he was angry with her. Why?

'Sorry, it's the pen ... Such a pretty pen ...' She was slurring her words, but she couldn't help it – her tongue felt as if it didn't fit her mouth. Selina tried to read the print, but the words were blurred. There was no way she could decipher them.

'For Christ's sake, woman. Here!' Xavier prodded the paper again.

'I don't want to stab your finger. Would you please move your digit?' This made her giggle again, and she just couldn't stop, but with exaggerated care she lifted the pen over the paper, aimed at it, and with a flourish signed her name.

chapter **eleven**

1

Ginnie was cold. She huddled on the end of the bed, her knees pulled up close to her chest, hugging herself for warmth. She sat slightly forward, so that her back did not touch the chill, slightly damp stone wall. She was in darkness, a darkness so profound she felt that if she put out her hand she could touch it, tear it apart. How she longed for it to be so, to remove it in chunks, to burrow to the other side and see daylight again, and feel the sun and hear the birds.

She had no idea how long she'd been here, if it was night or day. She had thought it would be the easiest thing to measure out the passing hours, but had soon lost track. She was hungry, desperately so, and yet she felt as if the gnawing hunger pangs in her stomach had lessened, as if her stomach had contracted because it knew no food was coming its way.

Ginnie looked up, suddenly attracted by a light. Across the tiny room she saw the glow of a pyramid of oranges, fruit that shimmered and shone as if made of gold.

'Dad.' She spoke aloud. 'Are you there? Please speak to me.' She held out her hands, aware of her voice swelling and echoing in the emptiness. She *knew* he was there, knew she had only to concentrate hard enough and he'd appear. She wanted him more than anything in the world. He'd hold her tight, he'd take away the hunger that gripped her entrails. He'd tell her this was the Inner Way. He'd be proud of her. If only he'd come to her and reassure her.

She watched as the light of the oranges surged like coals on a fire. Then the pyramid collapsed, and the oranges scattered, bouncing on the floor soundlessly, and as they bounced they began to fade away, softly glimmering until the darkness returned, enfolding her.

'Oh, no,' she cried out.

Then she began to weep, large gulping sobs that tore through her body. The darkness pressed down upon her, making her isolation total, as if she were the only person left alive on the planet. Or was she dead and buried? Was that what the darkness was?

Cold fear clutched at her, made her insides churn, made her sweat when it was icy cold.

'Please, someone, come to me,' she cried into the all-pervading darkness, a sad wailing cry, the sound of a woman keening for life, for love.

'He'll come, I know he'll come. He'll come. He'll come,' she began to repeat, over and over again, certain that if she said it enough times then he would, although this time it was not her father she was thinking of.

She tried to remember when he'd last come, how wonderful it had been, as she'd first heard him enter the room, and approach her, softly and with a stealth that added to her excitement and made her feel as if the blanket of darkness was about to be lifted. But she could not remember, try as she might, when that had been.

'Why is it so cold and dark?' she had asked him, as he took her in his arms.

'To test you, my darling. To ensure you are one of us, that you are truly "rooted". You do want to be, don't you? You need not stay here if you don't want.'

'No, I'm sorry, I didn't mean that. I long to join you, to be totally rooted with you, to belong. The outside holds nothing for me now.' She was proud at how easy it was to use their words.

'Then not much longer, my sweetheart. You'll be out

of here soon. We all understand, we've all been here, in the Reclamation Room. It is the only way to the Inner Way.' And in the darkness, on the hard bed, he had taken her. He had taken away the chill, as he warmed her with his body, and as their passion increased she glowed with heat and happiness.

'Such happiness,' she sighed. When? When had that been? If only she could remember how long she'd been here ...

'Ginnie. Are you asleep?' His voice made her jolt upright.

'No, I'm here,' she said eagerly.

'What are you doing?'

'Waiting for you,' she said, her voice brimming with joy that he had come to her.

'My sweet one,' he said. She moved on the bed to make room for him, and then with despair she realised that no one had climbed on it beside her.

2

Her watch said twenty to two. Jessica was amazed at how quickly the time had flown. There was nothing like a complicated puzzle to make the hours pass, and what a puzzle! Her bed was covered with the pieces of paper, which she had collected into numerical order. On some the writing was so small that she almost needed a magnifying glass to read them, and on others the writing was large and scrawled, as if the writer had been in a hurry. Some pieces were completely covered, others had only a word or two. It had taken her nearly an hour to stack the papers and to divide them into neat bundles.

Readjusting her spectacles on her nose – no member of

her public had ever seen her wear them – she repositioned the lamp and began to read.

An hour later she sat back, clutching at her neck with one hand, a gesture she recognised as one she had often employed when a character she was playing had been shocked or frightened. Now, however, it had been for real. If these papers were not a joke or a forgery, this was serious. If what they said was true, she understood the look of terror in H.G.'s eyes. If he had written this, the man was convinced he was about to die.

She leant back against her pillows and wondered what she should do. Who was the best person to show these entries to? Bethina was too ice-cold and close to Xavier – for Jessica presumed he must be the unnamed protagonist. Ancilla would rush around in a panic, but achieve nothing. Hesta? She'd have trusted her but she was away. And, of course, there was always the possibility that they were all part and parcel of it. And Xavier. How could a man so gentle be involved in this? It just didn't make sense. Better not to speak to any of them.

Perhaps she could talk to Ginnie and Selina. But Ginnie had already joined them, and was almost 'rooted' as they so quaintly put it – really, some of their expressions were *so* ridiculous – but that being so, there was no way she should be told anything.

What about Selina? She hadn't been seduced like Ginnie: she laughed at a lot of the nonsense going on here and there was no way she'd ever become a permanent member. But, still, she was taken with that young man, Matt. Maybe he'd been planted to get at her. Women were such strange creatures and, in love, could so easily absorb the attitudes and interests of their lovers.

She shook her head as if to clear it of such over-dramatic thoughts. It must be the hour, the atmosphere. She was getting spooked from reading such a dramatic litany. He was an old man, she'd seen him, and old men sometimes had strange fancies. Why, after a stroke her own father had ended up convinced his wife was poisoning him. This could be the same thing. And, if that was so, it would explain the look of terror she thought she'd seen on H.G.'s face. Although undecided what to do, of one thing she was sure; that she was better acting alone, at least for the time being.

Kicking off her shoes and turning off the light, Jessica tiptoed across the room. She opened the door gingerly, and peered out into the empty corridor. Moving as swiftly and silently as her handicap allowed, she walked towards H.G.'s apartment.

When the door into the little hallway squeaked her heart felt as if it was about to stop. She stood as still as a statue, not daring to breathe, as she waited to see if anyone had heard her. Like a ghost – a cumbersome one, she thought wryly – she crossed the hall and opened the door into the drawing room. Half-way across it she stopped again, as she heard a man's voice. She couldn't hear what was being said, so went softly to the door and listened. Someone was singing, out of tune but singing all the same. 'Tiptoe Through the Tulips.' The door was ajar; she closed one eye and peered through, her heart beating so loudly now that she was convinced it must be audible.

H.G. was sitting upright in bed, singing softly to himself. 'Tiptoe' finished, he began 'Daisy, Daisy'. There did not appear to be anyone else in the room. She wondered what to do, feeling foolish now, seeing him awake and singing, and reverting to her theory that what she'd read must be part of some complicated joke, or maybe H.G. had begun to write a novel.

Suddenly he stopped singing, and looked directly at the door. He must have heard her, though she was sure she had made no sound. Maybe he could sense someone looking at him, as people do. Abruptly he lay back on his pillows and closed his eyes. His hands, which had been drumming out a tattoo on his bedspread, in time to his off-key singing, lay still and lifeless at his sides. He seemed hardly to be breathing, as if he'd slipped into a coma. What on earth should she do if he had?

She was being useless, she told herself. If he had fainted or something, he would need help. She could easily say to the others that she had heard a noise and had come to investigate – better than appearing a nosy snoop, which in reality she supposed she was. Squaring her shoulders, and with a purposefulness she was far from feeling, she pushed open the door and entered his room. She crossed to his bedside and looked down anxiously at him.

'H.G., can you hear me?' she whispered. 'Only I've found what I think is some writing of yours. In the quilt. I need to talk to you.'

His eyes opened smartly as she spoke, and she found herself looking down into two of the bluest eyes she had ever seen.

'Ah, it is you. I felt certain the other day, when you looked at me, you understood and would come. At last you have.' His voice was husky, and he had to cough slightly before he could continue. 'You heard my singing? I practise at night sometimes, since I found I was losing my voice from not using it. And then I hoped it could be a signal, and someone might hear me – not *them*, of course, or I'd have been in trouble. And now you're here. Someone has finally come to help me, and I find I can't stop speaking. I can't explain how excited I feel, how elated that you've come.' All the time he talked he was pulling at the hem of the sheet. It reminded her of her father – he'd done that when death was near. H.G.'s tugging became desperate, and his face suddenly crumpled with anxiety. He sat up. 'But I don't know you – I know your face, and who you are, but how can I be sure of you? What if you're with them? You're not, are

256

you? But if you were, would you tell me? Oh, my God, I just don't know what to do. What if I've made a mistake? What if you tell them?' His voice was growing in volume as he spoke, as if his fears were giving him added strength until finally he was almost shouting at her.

'Sh, calm yourself.' She grasped at one of his relentlessly moving hands, and held it firm in her grasp. 'Please, H.G., relax,' she said. How thin his hand was, how dry the skin, as if it was covered with tissue paper, and how prominent the blue-grey veins. 'It's all right,' she continued, 'I promise I won't say anything to anyone. We'll resolve this somehow,' she said, with false confidence.

'I've been so afraid,' the old man said, and to her horror he began to weep. She let him, and patted his hand ineffectually. Jessica had never been any good with people racked by emotional storms but it did not stop her feeling sorry for him. She hoped her silence would comfort and calm him. When she was upset, the last thing she wanted was gratuitous advice.

'What's the time?' asked H.G., a good ten minutes later, some degree of equilibrium restored.

Jessica looked at her watch. 'Nearly twenty past four,' she replied. The night had flown.

'We're safe for an hour at least. Bethina or one of the others usually comes at six to give me my injection and bathe me, but to be on the safe side ...'

'How are you?'

He sighed. 'I'm weak from lack of exercise, and sore from sitting and lying here day in, day out. But I'm not ill. They keep me here like this.'

'But why? And how, if you're not ill?'

'When we have visitors they keep me sedated, using some drug that paralyses me. Then I can't get out of bed and run away.' He snickered at the improbable notion. 'That's why no one is here – they think I'm out for the count. Otherwise I'm watched constantly, twenty-four hours a day. It makes me feel like an animal in a zoo. I don't know which is worse, the helplessness of being drugged or the lack of privacy. When I'm not sedated I can read, but they won't let me write. And, oh, the knowing that one is watched even when asleep.' He shivered.

'But no one is here with you now,' she pointed out kindly.

'That's because they don't know the drugs wear off.' He giggled. 'I'm becoming immune to them. For the past two weeks I've woken at midnight. Then, when they come at six, I pretend to be asleep. I'm very good at that.' He laughed then and, having started, seemed unable to stop.

Jessica waited for the hysteria to abate. 'I've been here two weeks, so you've built up your immunity quickly,' she said eventually.

'What does that mean? That you don't believe me? You think I'm lying?' he said sharply, staring at her with those improbably blue eyes.

'No, of course not. I was just wondering ...' She paused, unsure what she was thinking.

'You're wondering whether I'm not imagining it all.'

'Of course I believe you.' But she could not banish the memory of her own father and his paranoia. She took a deep breath. 'Why on earth should they be doing this to you? For what reason?'

H.G. sighed deeply and looked at the ceiling. 'Power, and money. It's as simple as that. I am, of course, uninterested in money – it is not necessary to me, you understand,' he said airily.

'Yes,' said Jessica, suppressing a smile; he lived in rather grand style for one to whom money meant so little.

'He knows there's a lot of money to be made. He thinks I should ask for more from my followers but I'm content that people should give only what they want and they think they can afford. How much are you being charged?' he demanded.

'Ten thousand pounds for a series of healings.'

He thumped his fist ineffectually on the bedclothes. 'You see, I'm right. It should be free, of course it should.'

'I quite agree. When we've resolved this muddle, you can give me a rebate.' She allowed herself a chuckle at this exchange.

His fingers began again to pluck at the sheet. 'Have they got you to buy a room here? It's the latest scam. Like a time-share, he calls it.'

'One of the women I came with gave thirty thousand pounds.'

'There, you see?' he said triumphantly. 'I didn't make that up, did I?' He looked at her with the cunning of the aged.

'They haven't approached me.'

'They will,' he said ominously. He sighed again, wearily. 'When I wouldn't agree to his ideas they put in the newsletter that I was ill. Have you met a Dr Dominic?' She shook her head. 'Pity. I'd hoped you had. I didn't ask to see him. I didn't need him. I wasn't ill. Vitamins, that's what Dominic said the injection was. When I felt the paralysis creep through my body it was, I think, the most appalling day of my life. Dominic was a drunkard. Maybe he'd been struck off, I don't know for sure. More than likely they were blackmailing him, for he was a sad man. He did not like what was going on – he had compassion, you see. He always apologised to me before the needle went in. I overheard him one night. "It's not ethical," he said. "The overlong use could easily kill him. You can't make me." He was shouting but the others only mumbled in return. When he came into my room he said how sorry he was, and that he was leaving. I never saw him again. I think they must have killed him.'

'*What?*' Jessica sat bolt upright.

'These people are ruthless, my dear. I feared for you and your friends. I heard them discussing what they hoped to get from you. Your friend Ginnie, she's very rich, is she not? And Selina – such a pretty name – has a shop to give them.'

'I don't think she'd do that. She's too bright to be conned and she needs the money desperately.'

'She won't have any choice in it. They will acquire it, mark my words.'

'They won't have much luck with me. I'm poorer than a church mouse.'

'But it's your fame they want. Even I have heard of the famous Jessica Lawley, though I regret I've never seen any of your films. If you join, then you will be bait, to encourage others to come. Once they're sure of you, they'll send you out to recruit your rich friends.'

'But I've no intention of joining. This organisation is not for me.'

'Then take my advice and leave while you can.'

'But I don't think I can go. It's working, you see – my hip's so much better, and I've another three weeks of treatment.'

'I could heal you too. I can, you know. I've never known how, just that it works if you want it badly enough. You see, as I've always said, everything is up to you. I can open the door for you, take your hand, be there for you, but in the end you find peace yourself, you heal yourself.'

As he spoke, she became aware of what a beautiful voice he had, what a tender expression – but so did Xavier, and she knew he could make her better. And, really, what madness all this was. It was almost morning and she'd spent the night feeling threatened by a sick old man's ramblings.

'Look, I don't want to undermine what you're saying,

but I have to say that I've found everyone to be very pleasant here. Some of their meetings are bizarre, not my bag – screaming your head off, emoting. But harmless. These cults go in for that sort of thing, don't they?'

'This isn't a cult. That's the difference. It's becoming a cult. There were none of these energisings, self-searchings, when I was in control,' he said, with quiet dignity.

'No, well, that was your way, and this is Xavier's. You see, no one's being made to do anything – I don't. I sit at the back and watch. No one's nagging me to join in, and I'm happy to pay for my treatment. I haven't had a gun at my head to make me.'

'Have you seen their eyes? Most of them are drugged.'

'I admit they look a bit imbecilic but, then, born-again Christians have the same spaced-out look about them, and the same idiotic grins, as if the smiles are prosthetic, as if they've a secret you don't know about.'

'Then how do you explain my not knowing most of them? My followers aren't here any more. I don't know where they are. These are all new people to me. Wrong people.' He spoke urgently.

'You know none of them?'

'Well, a few.'

'Who?'

'Xavier, of course. He's been here for six years now. He was like a son to me.'

'When you referred to *them*, is it he you speak of? Or is it someone else, Bethina perhaps?'

'What silliness you do talk.' He sounded angry. 'Of course it's not Bethina. She loves me. She takes care of me.'

'But you said it was Bethina who injects you.' She thought she'd caught him out.

'Because she thinks it's good for me. She thinks she's helping me because he's told her to,' he said, frustrated.

'And I can't speak to her, she's never alone. I don't want to put her in danger. You're so silly!'

'But if what you say is true, she must be very thick.'

'How dare you speak of one of mine like that? No, it's the others, all new.' He looked so sad that she felt ashamed of herself.

'People do move on,' she said hopefully.

'Why do they drug me? Why do they keep me locked in here?'

'I walked in. It was no trouble.'

He clenched his fists again. 'Haven't you listened to *anything* I've said?'

'Please don't upset yourself. Of course I'm listening.' Poor old man, she thought. She knew better than most how easy it was to deny illness, the onset of old age, that things were no longer as they used to be. She had, for far too long. She must humour him gently, she told herself. 'I believe everything you've told me. But I do wonder if, since you've been alone so much, you haven't worried unnecessarily.'

'Imagined everything, you mean.'

'No. But you say yourself they look after you well. If they wanted you out of the way, wouldn't it be the simplest thing, well, to bump you off?'

'You understand nothing. Don't you see? I'm the honey-pot. All the time they can wheel me out at a meeting, pretend what they write is my writing, then people will come. Where H.G. goes they will follow. But once Xavier is fully established as the leader and wise man – thanks to people like you – when that happens, oh, yes, then they will kill me.'

3

Moving was never easy, but this morning, after a night sitting up, sorting the papers, talking to the old man, she felt as if every part of her body needed a good dose of Three-In-One. And she was annoyed by her own stupidity – she had felt so good after her session with Xavier. She must get the old man out of her mind and concentrate on herself. That, after all, was what she was here for.

'Dear Jessica, you *are* stiff this morning, aren't you? What have you been up to? Here, give me your arm.' Bethina teased her gently.

'Don't even talk about last night ...' she began to say, and decided not to continue. She'd give H.G. the benefit of the doubt for a little longer. 'I couldn't sleep. Don't ask me why. Excitement at the success of Xavier's treatment, probably.' Smooth one, Jessica, she thought. 'So I sat up most of the night reading. Now I'm suffering.'

'Dear me. It looks to me as if you need a good massage and an extra treatment. I'll ask Ancilla if she'll see you. She's a trained aromatherapist, you know.'

'Sounds brilliant—' Jessica got no further for they were interrupted by a banging and clattering on the oak front door.

'Someone's in a hurry. What a dreadful noise!' Bethina crossed to the door and opened it. A tall man burst into the hall, a flurry of snow following him like ectoplasm.

'I want to see my wife,' he demanded, without preamble.

'Good morning, Mr ...?' Bethina said questioningly, looking pointedly in a school-marmish way at the spreading pool of water that dripped from his clothes onto the polished woodblock floor.

'Mulholland. Carter Mulholland. You have my wife, Ginnie, here. I'm not leaving until I see her.' Either he had not noticed Bethina's displeasure at the water or he had chosen to ignore it.

'Of course, Mr Mulholland. There's no need to be so agitated.'

'No need! I've phoned time without number, and you never let me speak to her. You're always fobbing me off with some lame excuse.'

'No doubt she was occupied. She's been working very hard, you know. One of our most enthusiastic guests in a long time.' Bethina smiled serenely.

'Well, then, why was I refused entry at the gate? Some goon stopped me,' he bellowed.

'We're in a deep contemplation session of the Inner Way and no one wants the outside world to intrude. We told the gateman. I'm sorry if he was rude to you. I'll speak to him. But that's the reason why. Still, you're here now.'

'Only because I stomped through the bloody snow, through the sodding park – that's how I got here.' Still he shouted.

A knot of people had gathered, attracted by the commotion.

'Please, Mr Mulholland, you need not shout at me. I'm not deaf,' Bethina said. 'Morveen, could you find Ginnie for me? Tell her she has a visitor. And inform Xavier we have a guest. Now, if you'll give me your wet coat, I'll have it dried for you. There's a fire in the sitting-room here. Would you like some tea, or a whisky to warm you?' Bethina fussed about him, in a normal, solicitous-hostess manner.

Carter began to look somewhat sheepish. 'I'm sorry about the floor,' he mumbled.

Jessica looked at him with interest. So this was Carter. As was her way, she inspected him from head to toe. He might have been good-looking when younger, she decided, but not so much now: too paunchy, and a little thin on top. And he had the face of a bully, she thought. Ginnie must have loved him deeply to find him as handsome as she claimed.

'Jessica, would you care to join us?' Bethina asked. 'Of course you know Jessica Lawley, Mr Mulholland.'

'No, we've never met.' They shook hands formally, and she saw the spark of interest in his eyes. Once she could have been confident it was because she was desirable but, sadly, now it must be because she was famous.

'I'm sorry. I presumed because your wife and Jessica came together ...' Bethina's voice trailed off.

'I didn't know my wife knew you, Miss Lawley. But, then, there's a lot I find I don't know about my wife.' He sounded bitter.

'We met in London, at a Fohpal meeting. Just a chance encounter,' Jessica explained, suddenly feeling sorry for the man. He looked so confused and worried.

They were in the small sitting-room, off the main hall. Jessica sat on the window-seat, framed by the opulent chintz curtains, not sure if she wanted to be involved. But if she sat aside from them, distancing herself physically, she would be telling them she was distancing herself mentally too. Bethina was pouring the scotch, which Carter had decided he wanted and looked as if he needed.

'Is my wife being kept prisoner here against her wishes, Miss Lawley?' he suddenly asked her.

'Why, no, of course not,' she replied, with a little laugh to show how silly the notion was.

'I suppose you're one of them too,' he said angrily.

'I'm not sure what you mean by "one of them". I'm a guest here. But whatever my function, I don't see what concern it is of yours.'

'Then why won't they let me speak to her?'

'Perhaps she didn't want to speak to you,' Jessica said reasonably, and was rewarded with an extra special smile from Bethina.

'And why shouldn't she want to speak to me, for heaven's sake?'

'I don't know. I don't wish to get involved with your marital problems.'

'Is that what she's told you? That I was having an affair? It's all in her head, you know. She imagines everything.' He looked at her intently.

'Please, Mr Mulholland, I really did mean it. This is none of my business, and certainly none of my concern.'

'Well, could somebody explain to me why there's over a hundred thousand pounds missing from her deposit account? What about that?'

'In my book, you do what you like with your own money,' Jessica said shortly, feeling sucked into the situation, whether she liked it or not. 'Still, she's probably spent some of that buying ...' She trailed off, having remembered with a start that it hadn't only been Selina who had told her about the time-share type rooms. H.G. had too, and she didn't want to get him involved.

'Probably buying what?' Carter demanded.

'It's gone – I can't remember what I was about to say,' she said, unconvincingly to her own ears.

'I can explain that. I didn't know, but, oh, how exciting. Obviously Ginnie's bought a room here.' Bethina clasped her hands together.

'What the hell for? Why would she need to do that? She's got a huge bloody house of her own, full of rooms. You coerced her.' He stood tall and threatening. 'Where the hell is she?'

'I'm here, Carter. I wish you wouldn't shout. I heard you right down the hallway.' Ginnie stood in the door, dressed in a long pale blue robe, white-faced and tired-looking, but with the requisite smile of the true follower. Oh, Lord, thought Jessica, she's caught it too.

'Ginnie, thank God. I've been worried sick.' He moved quickly across the room, his hands held out to her. She placed hers behind her back, and when he tried to kiss her, she moved her head adroitly to one side, so that he missed contact by a good four inches. She glided into the room. 'Hello, Bethina, Jessica. How's your poor hip?'

'Much better, thank you.'

'Xavier told me how well the healing was working.' She spoke in a proprietorial way, Jessica realised. 'Camomile tea! I love it!' she exclaimed, as Ancilla carried in a tray. Ancilla didn't leave the room, but joined Jessica on the window-seat just as Xavier entered.

'Welcome, Carter,' he said, his arms held wide in an expansive gesture.

'Mulholland to you,' Carter snapped.

'We don't go in for such formalities here. We like to think we're all equal friends.'

'You can think what you want, but I'm not.'

'Carter, please don't be so aggressive. These are my true friends. I'm so happy here,' Ginnie interrupted.

'Why didn't you tell me where you were? I've been out of my mind with worry.'

'I left you a note.'

'Yes, one that said you'd be away for Christmas. Not where. And it's now January. Or hadn't you noticed?'

'But you found me. I wasn't far, was I?'

'Only because I tried to find Selina, and the woman looking after her cat told me where she was. And she's not too happy either – left with someone else's cat and no phone call, nothing to say when she'd be back. Have you both gone mad – lost all your senses?'

'Don't be so abusive, Carter, please. It's not necessary, and it's damaging for you,' Ginnie said calmly.

'Where is Selina? I want to talk to her too.'

'She's in bed, poorly. An upset stomach.' Bethina jumped in quickly. A shade too quickly? Jessica found herself wondering. Then she put a brake on that train of thought. She was still influenced by last night.

'I know about the money, Ginnie.'

'What money?'

'The wad you've given these crooks here. The money they coerced from you.' At this, the others laughed, gently, musically, as if enjoying a joke at a dinner party. 'And you can wipe those bloody smirks off your faces. I'm on to my lawyer. You'll be hearing about this.'

'Oh dear, I am sorry. Ginnie, you told us it was your money. You naughty little one. Look at the trouble you might get us into.' Xavier spoke to her with an indulgent expression on his face. 'I'm so sorry, *Mr Mulholland*, if we're taking what is rightfully yours. Of course we shall pay you back in full,' he said smoothly.

'It *is* my money. I do what I want with what's mine,' Ginnie said indignantly.

'Let's get this straight. It is truly yours, not his?'

'Yes.'

'Not a penny of it is his?'

'Only what I choose to give him, and the little he earns from his paintings.'

'And did we make you sign the cheque, Ginnie?'

'No, I wanted to. You tried to persuade me not to. To wait a while, to make sure I still wanted to live here permanently.'

'You can't do this, Ginnie. Please.' Carter was looking at her imploringly.

'Oh yes I can. I can give them everything if I want. And I probably shall.' She flicked her hair back defiantly.

'But, Ginnie, what about us? What about Tessa and me?'

'What about you? You don't need me. You never have. And Tessa's grown up. She doesn't need me either.'

'Ginnie, this just isn't true. Of course you're needed. You always have been. You always will be. I can't function without you.'

'Without my money, you mean,' she said coldly. 'It's not stopped you having your grubby little affairs, has it? How's Anna, by the way? See how I can ask? It doesn't matter to me any more. You can do what you like. You're free as a bird to sleep with whomever you want.' Ginnie's voice was rising dangerously.

'There were no affairs, Ginnie. You imagined it all,' Carter said wearily. And Jessica again found herself feeling sorry for him, at the awful humiliation he was being put through. She looked away, wishing she was anywhere but here, having to listen to this. What if she slipped out? She got to her feet, meaning to leave quietly.

'Jessica, I'd rather you stayed.' She sat down again at Xavier's request.

'Don't worry, Carter. I'll make a generous allowance for you. You won't starve.' Ginnie's voice rang out.

'But, Ginnie, this isn't fair.'

'Oh yes it is, Carter. When I lived with you, what was mine was yours. Remember? One honey-pot, that's what we used to say. Now I'm here, and I intend to share what's mine with these new, loving friends of mine. But there's ...' She held up her hand to stop her husband interrupting. 'But there's a big difference, Carter. With you I shared and found no happiness. Now I can share and I know I will find only joyous happiness. There's no contest, Carter. You might just as well go. I'm staying here, and of my own free will. Got it?'

Carter stood. 'I'm still going to see my lawyer.'

'You do that, Carter.'

'I might even go to the police,' he added.

'What? And give them a good laugh?' Xavier chuckled. 'Look, I'm sorry if your wife prefers it here, but there it is. She wants us, not you. She needs us, not you. We love her and will care for her. You need not worry about her. I think you'll find there's nothing you can do about it. She's an adult, and she has declared her intentions in front of an independent witness. Quite honestly, I think it's better you go now. You're upsetting everyone, especially dear Ginnie.'

Carter moved to leave the room. At the door he turned. 'OK, you've beaten me today. But I'll be back, I promise. I'm not alone, you know. I've been investigating you lot. There's a mass of people out there who don't like what's happened to their friends and relations. How they can't contact them, no longer know if they're dead or alive. You won't get away with it much longer. We'll smash you. That's a promise.'

'See me quaking.' Xavier smirked. Ginnie poked out her tongue at the closing door. But Jessica did not like the way she'd been manoeuvred into being an 'independent witness'. She had not enjoyed being party to the scene, and she found the image of worried relations upsetting.

4

Somehow Selina eased herself out of bed. As her feet touched the floor, the red-patterned Turkey carpet lifted up and aimed for her face with such speed that she flinched away from it and sat down again on the bed, only to see that the carpet was where it should be, firmly held in place by furniture. She shook her head. What on earth had happened to her? She felt clammy, and her nightdress was sticking to her like a second skin. One minute she was hot, and then, like now, she was shivering with cold. Her head was pounding relentlessly and painfully as she struggled to get some order into her teeming brain. Steeling herself against the dizziness, she shuffled across her room to the bathroom, splashed her face with cold water, and drank from her tooth-mug with the desperation of the seriously parched. But it didn't remove the odd taste in her mouth, like the one she had had after a general anaesthetic when her appendix had been taken out.

'Am I hung over?' she asked aloud, hearing a clogged huskiness in her voice. She undressed and stood in the forceful spray from the water jet. There was a bar to hang on to, otherwise she was certain she'd have fallen. 'Bookshop Owner Drowned in Shower'. She smiled at the headline she'd composed for the local rag. At that thought, however, her head jerked up, and she winced from the pain of moving it. Was she still a bookshop owner?

She couldn't remember anything. Inside her head memories lurked, appearing suddenly with a snippet of clarity. But, a second later, they were swathed by foggy tendrils of forgetfulness, as they slipped away from her grasp.

Hell, this was what old age must be like, or a brain trauma. Perhaps she had fallen and banged her head. She felt her skull but found no bumps, no points of tenderness.

Out of the shower she wrapped herself in a bath sheet and returned to her room. She sat in a chair. Now think, she ordered herself, think!

Last night she'd been in a room ... but was it last night, or another ...? It had been white and cell-like but she'd felt contented there, not afraid ... And someone had been with her. There'd been papers and she'd been writing ... A finger had been pointing – a man's finger ... on the white paper ... a pen. Someone was angry with her ... writing, writing her name ... She sat bolt upright. Not writing but signing. Had she sold them her shop?

This was ridiculous, she told herself. She stood up,

opened her window and stood for a while breathing deeply, but the air was damp and misty when what she needed was a good dose of cold, bracing oxygen. Maybe she'd got drunk. It had been known. She could remember a drink, and Bethina ... Then it all faded again. Yes, yes, she remembered a drink, and dizziness. She'd felt dizziness then, but she could not remember if it was before or after the drink. It was so frustrating, not being able to remember. Of course, there was always the possibility that they had drugged her.

She shook her head. Christ, that hurt. Oh, come on Selina, pull yourself together. Stupid. Drugged! She'd read too many books, that was her problem.

Still, she did feel so odd. She must get moving and sort things out. She'd find Xavier and ask him what had happened. From somewhere she must dredge up the energy to search out Matt. A letter – she wanted to know something about a letter. But she was also going to ask him to leave with her. She'd forget the hassle in the past. Maybe she'd overreacted ... But there was another problem: she did not know what the hassle had been about, only that it had been with him, and that she'd been angry ... She'd try to think about that later. Meanwhile, maybe Jessica and Ginnie would want to go with her too ... She frowned. There was another problem, but for the life of her she couldn't think what it was. But she thought it had something to do with a car ...

In that precious moment between sleep and wakefulness, Ginnie stretched and knew she had never felt such inner happiness, such contentment. She offered a silent prayer that she should be privileged to be receiving such joy.

Everything had happened so quickly, she still felt she was reeling from the sheer speed of her ... It was difficult to put her feelings and emotions into words. She could call it her conversion, but that wasn't quite right. That word smacked of parish churches, collection plates, 'Jerusalem', and Joan, her mother-in-law. Oh, she didn't want to think of her, not now. That would spoil everything. Joan belonged in the past, a past that she had jettisoned and from which she had been released. Xavier had put it so beautifully: 'The past is a land you visited, the future is where you might travel next, the now is here, real, of this moment, and all that matters ...' Well, something like that. She couldn't remember it exactly, word for word. She'd ask him again what he'd said, and write it down so that she'd never forget it.

To find such love – now when she had least expected to. She smiled at her awareness of the present. How proud Xavier would be of her. She hugged herself tight, allowing her hands to roam over her body. How glad she was that she'd taken such care of herself – all those hours in the gym, all the meals she'd missed, the cakes and chocolate she'd never eaten, the drinks she'd refused. All those little sacrifices had finally paid off and she had a body to be proud of. She felt no shame at Xavier seeing her naked. Even thinking of how he'd looked at her, the longing in his eyes, made her excited, made her body ready for him. She moved sensuously in the bed, wishing he was here with her now, this moment, feeling his hardness, his charismatic aura. She wished she had the confidence to go to his room, slip into his bed beside him and wake him with her kisses, with her touch. Bliss!

Still, not long, and no doubt they'd be sharing a room. Not long, and they'd be married. She was sure he'd be asking her soon. Then, together, standing side by side, with his healing ability joined by hers ... She could barely control her longing to try her power – maybe she'd ask Jessica if she could test it on her. Imagine if she succeeded on someone as world famous as she. Yes. That's what she'd do – the world would be theirs to conquer. She'd be famous. She'd be important, one day soon!

No, she mustn't do this. She mustn't think of the future, Xavier didn't like it. Now. Think of now. Still, this particular now was boring, alone in her bed, filling up with lust like a cup filling up with tea. She giggled at such a notion. Not very romantic, tea. Champagne, perhaps, that would be better. Still, no one would know she was breaking the rules and allowing herself to daydream about her glorious, happiness-filled tomorrows.

Better than the dreary past. Carter never looked at her like Xavier did. He'd never touched her constantly, as Xavier did, as if he *had* to feel her to reassure himself that she was real. Carter had never wanted to explore her mind and listen to her ideas. He never complimented her on her logic, intelligence and clear-sightedness, as Xavier had done. She couldn't remember him ever asking her opinion on anything.

What a shock was coming Carter's way. How she longed to see the expression on his face when he realised she'd meant what she'd said: that she was divorcing him – to marry Xavier. Maybe she'd arrange it so that she could tell him face to face. Such sweet revenge for all the slights and sneers of the past. And he needn't think he could rely on her for money either, even though she'd said he needn't worry. No. Now she might give it all to Xavier, rather than let Carter have a penny. That would be a rightful punishment for the awful way he'd behaved yesterday, demanding, ordering, shouting abuse at dear, patient Xavier, who'd smiled so sweetly through the whole tasteless onslaught.

She'd show him!

Then she frowned. For all that, for all this excitement and new-found happiness, she missed Tessa. She should have asked Carter if she was safely back from France. She must write to her and explain, tell her she'd taken her advice and had 'found herself'. Maybe she'd arrange for her to come and see for herself. Perhaps she'd join too – and wouldn't *that* annoy Carter? That really would be revenge. Still, she must be up and doing. She had chores to do, things to learn, responsibilities.

She leapt out of bed. She couldn't remember when she had last felt so excited at the start of a new day.

She smiled at her reflection in the mirror. She hadn't got it quite right yet, her smile was a little too tentative – not surprising, she hadn't had much to smile about for some time. She'd have to practise, as often as she could, to perfect it, so that her smile would match the placidness, the madonna-like quality of the others'.

So much to do. A new life, and a new world to explore – the world of her mind.

Jessica was tired again. Another night with no sleep – not because she'd visited H.G. – she'd decided not to – but she'd had other things to occupy her mind. The scene yesterday with Ginnie and her husband, and its implications, had ensured that she had spent most of the night analysing it. As she went over it, and what Carter had said, she had tried to persuade herself that she had witnessed the reaction of a jealous man about to lose his wife and her money. It was a reasonable premise: it would be a rare man who didn't raise Cain over his wife running off to join a sect.

Still, she hadn't liked the way Ginnie looked. She was so wan and so out of it, her eyes burning with an expression of unhealthy zeal. It had crossed her mind again that Ginnie might be on drugs, and if so was in no fit state to make any decisions. If Ginnie was drugged she'd like to know if she had taken whatever it was knowingly, or if it had been slipped into her food or drink.

If she was right, then H.G. was right, and he wasn't a rambling, silly old man, which was what she'd rather hoped. She was going to have to work out what she was to do or, more accurately, what she could do.

The idea of rescuing him when she was hardly capable of rescuing herself would be laughable, if it weren't so serious.

Last night she had been pretty sure she'd heard H.G. call out, but had chosen to ignore him and had put her pillow over her head. Why hadn't she gone to listen to him, hold his hand and reassure him?

She put her head in her hands. She knew only too well why, and she wasn't proud of herself: she had done nothing because she didn't want to leave here, not yet. She wanted Xavier to continue to work on her. She knew he was making her better. She didn't want to risk offending him in any way, by word or deed. She was being selfish, but knowing that didn't make her feel better about it. Something had happened to her here. In the past she would have done exactly what she wanted, and to hell with anybody else, now she was ashamed of that too.

5

'Xavier, might I have a word?'

'Selina! Are you better? Oh, dear me, no, you're not, are you? Poor little one, you should be in bed.' He put out his hand and touched her face gently. 'Such a sad, worried face, and fevered too, if I'm not mistaken.'

'Xavier, I know this sounds silly, but the other night, did I sign some papers?' She was fully aware of how odd her question sounded, how stupid it made her look.

'What papers would they be, Selina?'

'You know, for my shop.'

'Your shop? What about your shop?'

'That you're buying it. Well, not you, but Fohpal were thinking of buying it from me. Don't you remember?'

'I can't say I remember anything about buying. Are you sure you shouldn't be in bed, Selina? You look really rotten. Shall I call Bethina to give you some of her medicine?'

'So I didn't sign a conveyance, anything like that—'

'A conveyance? Hardly, my dear, not when we aren't buying. What use would a conveyance be?'

The room spun and Selina rocked on her feet. She couldn't believe what she had heard. The memory of that night might be vague, but not the other conversations she'd had about the shop. He was lying, she knew he was. And if he was lying about that, he could just as easily be lying about what had happened on that night too.

'Jessica, come in, you're early.' Xavier smiled expansively at her as she stood tentatively in the open doorway. 'I *am* proud of you. You really are walking so much better, aren't you?' he said kindly, shutting the door behind her.

'You know, Xavier, I think I am.'

'You must stay here for ever, then. We'll have you entering the Olympics before you know where you are. The hurdles, maybe.'

'Anything's possible. Hello, Selina. My God, you look rough. Shouldn't you be in bed?'

'No. I've got to get going. Have you forgotten I'm leaving today? You've decided to stay, then?'

'Yes. I can't go now, Xavier is helping me so much. But it was yesterday we were supposed to leave, don't you remember?' Jessica was puzzled. 'And, in any case, how will you get away with no car?'

Selina opened her mouth to say she was borrowing Ginnie's, and then shut it sharply, as, in one of the flashes of memory that were plaguing her, it came to her that

Ginnie had given her car to Xavier. 'Oh, I don't know. I'll cadge a lift from someone. Or get a taxi.'

'The telephone's on the blink again so you can't call a cab. And no one's going anywhere today, Selina. So that could be a problem. No cars, you see.'

'Can I borrow Ginnie's BMW to get me to the station? Matt will drive me.' She decided to ask boldly. Once she and Matt were far away she'd work out some way of getting the car back to them.

'No.'

'I beg your pardon?'

'I said, no one is going anywhere.' He spoke in a reasonable tone of voice with no hint of an admonishment.

'But – I – you know I want to leave today. You can't keep me here against my wishes. Jessica, please.'

'Quite honestly, Selina, you don't look fit to drive anywhere,' Jessica said.

'I'm leaving,' she said, sounding braver than she felt.

'You're too ill.'

'I'm not ill, Jessica. There's something very wrong – I think I've been drugged.'

'You what?' Jessica snorted with amusement, preferring not to remember her worries over H.G., Ginnie and drugs.

Xavier was in fits of laughter. 'Oh, poor dear Selina, you must be burning up with fever. Where on earth did you get such an idea? Drugged? By whom, pray? You've been hallucinating. You need bed—'

'Then why can't I think straight? Why am I woozy? Why can't I remember things?' Selina felt a surge of panic. She looked pleadingly at Jessica who, embarrassed, looked away. Suddenly Selina felt alone and afraid. She turned on her heel and left the room, banging the door behind her.

'Poor soul, she really is ill. It looks like the flu to me,'

Xavier said, full of concern. 'Saying she's drugged. Whatever next?'

'Is the telephone really out of order?'

'Of course, Jessica. What a strange question. We're always having problems with it.'

The door opened, and Ginnie's head appeared around it, smiling sweetly. 'Hello, everyone,' she simpered.

'Were you not taught to knock?' Xavier said coldly.

'I'm sorry. I heard voices, I didn't think you'd mind. What's up with Selina? She steamed up the corridor – she didn't even see me.' Ginnie was fully in the room now, and to Jessica, seemed oblivious of the stormy looks Xavier was giving her. Instead she crossed to him, stood on tiptoe, and kissed him on the cheek, whispering huskily, 'Good morning.'

Xavier could not have acted more quickly if he had been stung by a wasp. His hand leapt to his face and wiped the spot she had kissed. At the same time he stepped back smartly so that she could not touch him again.

'Xavier,' Ginnie whined.

'If you wouldn't mind, Virginia, I'm in conference here. Have you no duties to attend to?'

Ginnie seemed to shrink before his gaze. He had used her full name just as her mother had when angry with her and just as Carter did when he wanted to put her down. Dejected, she left the room.

'Stupid woman,' Xavier spat.

'She was only being friendly,' Jessica said, feeling she should defend Ginnie, 'She's very sweet,' she added, unsure why. 'Sweet' was not normally the first word to jump to her mind when describing Ginnie. But she could make an educated guess at the game Xavier was playing with her. She, too, had had experience of the type of man who enjoyed playing cat and mouse with a woman, blowing hot one day, cold the next. She might not be close to Ginnie but she did not like to see her humiliated in this way. 'I feel sorry for her. She needs to be able to show her feelings – she's had a rough ride with one particular man, I'm told.'

'Of course, you're right, Jessica. It was thoughtless of me. Will you ever forgive me?' He smiled at her in a boyish, apologetic way, confident she would.

'It's not up to me to forgive you, it's Ginnie who's been upset.' But she said it good-naturedly.

'I was rude. But she should not have walked in on us like that. What if we had been in the middle of a session? That wouldn't have been nice for such a private person as you are.' And she saw that he had neatly turned everything round so that he was in the right again. 'Now, where were we? You've come to arrange your next session, I presume. When would you like?' He flicked open the large appointment diary on his desk, which she could see was almost full. 'This evening, latish? Or now?' He smiled up at her as he bent over the book, a lock of dark hair flopping forward as if by chance – but Jessica knew otherwise.

'It's good of you to make time for me, I can see how busy you are. Now would be wonderful.' It couldn't be better, she thought. These sessions were like a drug to her: afterwards she felt so elated, so energised and yet so calm. God, she was beginning to use their words, to think like them.

'Fine, then. You'd better sit in the armchair, hadn't you?' He came round from his side of the desk.

'This is for you. Don't forget it when you leave.' He held up a small bottle.

'What is it?'

'A medicine to help relieve the inflammation and to give you sleep. Take one teaspoon half an hour before bed and you'll sleep like a baby. Now, are you comfortable?' He was holding, as he always did, a large crystal on a gold chain, which he began to swing from left to right. It always reminded Jessica of a Greek with his worry-beads. She did not hold the thought for long, for unknown to her, she had slipped into an hypnotic state as she always did in these sessions. She would never remember it. How could she? After telling her that the pain would be one degree better today, he would also tell her that she would have no memory of being hypnotised – and she didn't.

6

'Have you seen Matt?' Selina asked everyone she could find, but the answer was always the same: 'No, not since breakfast.' The snow had become rain, which was teeming down. It was unlikely that he was in the garden in that, unless, of course, he was in the potting shed or down by the swimming pool.

She felt dreadful. Worse now than when she had first woken. Her head was pounding agonisingly, and her physical misery was compounded by an increasing tide of fear.

Rain or not, she was going to have to go in search of him. In a porch at the back of the house she had seen a collection of coats, macs and wellies, which appeared to be for general use. Dressed in an oversized trench coat, wellingtons two sizes too big for her small feet, and an old, sludge-green canvas fisherman's trilby, she set off. She carried her small leather grip, but left her case in the hallway. It was too heavy.

The bitter cold rain lashed at her cheeks, and her hair, unruly at the best of times, was pushing its way free of the hat. As it dampened, so her curls tightened, as if she'd had a home perm that hadn't worked. Despite her fear and fever, she had enough humour left to know she must look a fright, like a New York bag lady, undoubtedly. And she expected Matt to fancy her! Or did she? Why was she searching for him? She had a vague idea that he'd let her down ... She was angry with him – but the fog would not clear enough to let her grasp what he'd done.

He wasn't in the potting shed or the greenhouse. The walled kitchen garden was empty, as was the pump room of the swimming pool. She wandered back through the copse, and sat down on a stone bench to rest, unaware of the damp beneath her. Her breath was hard and rasping, and it hurt to breathe. It was cold, icy cold, and yet she was bathed in sweat.

A shard of memory came back to her. Clearly and painfully she recalled the last time she'd been with him. He had made it abundantly obvious that he didn't want to be involved with her.

'Oh, no,' she groaned, and put her hands up to her face as if she could blot out her humiliation. But she couldn't. However, she could suddenly recall their conversation. And yet ... yet she felt she didn't quite believe him, and hadn't, even as he had spoken. It was strange and contrary of her to think that he was pretending but it was a feeling that refused to go away. And, she was the first to admit, her instincts, where men were concerned, were not reliable – she had only to look at her track record in the romance stakes to be dismally aware of that.

'Take stock, Selina,' she said aloud, her breath making steamy tendrils in the cold – she'd never seen that before, steamy breath in the rain. Perhaps it was about to snow again, which was all she needed. 'Right, make a list of what's bothering you,' she ordered herself. If only she could marshal her thoughts into some sort of order maybe she would hold onto them longer.

To start with, Ginnie was a prime worry. She had gone completely off her head and Selina had no idea how she was to get her away from here – but she would have to try.

Then there was the idea that she'd been drugged. She had no proof, just this awful feeling of wooziness and the strange taste in the back of her mouth.

Esmeralda! She sat up with a start. Of course! The terrified Esmeralda had given her a letter but it had disappeared.

The letter ... The vodka ... Her room had been searched ... And how could there be no cars to drive when she'd seen loads of cars here, in the great giant double garages? And telephones that never worked ... And people looking like zombies ... And Matt, not allowed to love her ...

She wished she'd got a cigarette. Hell, she'd sell her soul for one right now.

So what? Her practical side logged in. Ginnie often took up causes with zeal. And it was a bit OTT to think that, just because of a taste in her mouth, she'd been drugged. It was more logical that she was ill. Perhaps she had flu. Esmeralda's daughter might be ill in France, she had changed her mind about the letter being posted and had taken it herself. She could not be certain they'd searched her room. Maybe the cars were all in use; it was typical of her to expect one now, this minute, ready and waiting for her. And in exposed rural areas power and telephone lines were often down. Zombies was a fanciful word for her to choose: at first she'd thought their expressions beautiful. Which left Matt.

At the thought of him she dug her fingers deep into her pockets. He'd used her. He was like so many men ... He didn't fancy her. She'd imagined he loved her. He was hiding behind Fohpal so as not to get too involved. Still, perhaps that showed he was a nice chap and was blaming them to avoid hurting her feelings.

And then a truly unpleasant thought hit her. Esmeralda's letter: What if she was wrong and Esmeralda hadn't taken it back, who else knew of its existence? Matt! She'd told him about it, only him. And then it had disappeared, so who had known to tell on her? Matt! He'd betrayed her. That was what had been bothering her about him. How could she, even for one moment, have forgotten he was a traitor?

'Oh, hell,' she muttered, and got to her feet. It all looked pretty stupid when she analysed it. But she'd shown herself one good thing: she was beginning to think straighter. She picked up her bag wearily and left the garden to make her way back through the copse towards where she presumed the main gate to be.

She stared at a fallen log, covered with a mat of green moss. Drops of rain sparkled on it as if it was scattered with silver. Such a pretty colour, just like the pen but silver, not gold. She stopped dead in her tracks. There had been a pen! She remembered she had admired the light playing on its barrel. She could see it now, and her hand holding it ... Xavier getting angry with her, ordering her to sign. And she *had* signed something. Oh, my God. Oh, my dear God.

The doubts and fears swooped back into her mind, clattering in her head like a flock of birds. She began to run or, rather, tried to – her legs felt as if weights were tied to them, and that she was running through thick, sticky treacle. Her heart was pounding and as she gasped for breath the pain in her chest was sharper, crueller. Still she pressed on – she could see the large wrought-iron gate now. A red car paused the other side of it on the road. She'd thumb a lift.

'And where do you think you're going, Miss?'

She looked up, her way barred by two burly men she did not recognise.

'I'm going home.'

'Oh no you're not, Miss. You're not leaving here, that's for sure.' One took hold of her right arm and the other her left. She winced at the roughness of their grasp.

'You're hurting me. Let me go,' she objected, but even as she spoke she knew it was pointless and that she might as well save her painful breath.

The car's engine revved and she turned her head. It was Ginnie's BMW. She stepped towards it, breaking into a smile of relief, then wavered, remembering through the fog of fever that it wasn't Ginnie's car any more.

The tinted driver's window made a sibilant swishing noise as it opened smoothly.

'Going without saying goodbye? Now is that polite, Selina?' Xavier asked with a smile, cruel and mocking, before she collapsed like a rag doll between the men, who were still grimly holding her arms.

7

Matt was working in the cellar. He had just finished tinkering with the central-heating boiler, which, in his opinion, was on its last legs. He'd have to tell Xavier again that it needed replacing. He wiped his hands on an oily rag. It was odd how Xavier was resistant to buying a new one when there was no shortage of money. He thought he knew the reason: Xavier didn't want to lay out money since he considered it his. If so, was he thinking of doing a bunk with Fohpal's funds? In which case …

From the corridor Matt heard a loud commotion and dropped the rag. Curious, he approached the slightly open door and peered out of the crack. Two large men, whom he recognised as security guards, were gripping

Selina by the arms and dragging her along the passage-way, her feet trailing lifelessly on the rough stone floor.

Instinctively he raised his hand to open the door and rush out to rescue her, but caution stayed him. There were three of them, for now he could see Xavier walking behind the group, hands held behind his back, his normal asinine smile in place. At the sight of it Matt's hand twitched with longing to wipe it off.

He crouched behind the door and waited. His heart was thudding and his stomach churned with a mixture of anger and fear for Selina. He eased his weight and put up his hand to switch off the light. His foot brushed against a spade leaning against the wall, which began to slide noisily against the cement. His heart leapt into his mouth and he grabbed it before it crashed to the floor.

A door further along the corridor opened and shut with a noisy bang, the sound echoing off the stone walls. He inhaled deeply, stocking his muscles with oxygen. At the first sound of those bastards hurting or touching Selina, he'd have to take them on even if he was outnumbered.

He held his breath as the three men appeared again and walked out, laughing at something Xavier had said. He felt a surge of hatred towards him. But he must be patient, must be controlled, he told himself. He could mess up everything for both of them if he rushed in.

He waited a good five minutes after the men had passed him by and he had heard their footfalls fading as they ran up the cellar stairs. They had turned off the light, so he had to feel his way along the wall to the third door on the right-hand side.

They were confident that no one would interfere for they had left the key in the door. His hand wavered at the memory of the awfulness of this room. Everyone eventually entered the Reclamation Room voluntarily and he had, too. But he'd been prepared for it and trained in how to prevent himself being taken over by it, how not to be brainwashed. Yet for all that it had been an experience he never wanted to repeat. But Selina had no way of protecting her mind. He forced himself to turn the key and entered the pitch-black room. He heard the sound – that awful, relentless, all-encompassing hissing. It could drive you mad. But madness wasn't their aim: they wanted to reduce Selina to a trembling, susceptible jelly.

At most he had forty-eight hours, not long in the circumstances.

'Selina,' he said gently, and was rewarded by a heartrending groan. 'My darling, it's me, Matt,' he said, feeling her flinch from his touch in the darkness.

'Matt – thank God,' she mumbled. Her speech was indistinct, as if she spoke through swollen lips. He feared the bastards had beaten her. He ran his hands over her face. She was so hot she felt as if she was on fire, but he was as certain as he could be that they had not hit her.

'Darling, you've got such a temperature. Oh, my God,' he said, worried, and wondering what to do.

'You called me darling,' she said with difficulty, but he heard a faint note of happiness in her voice.

'You are my darling, Selina. I love you. We'll say all these things when we get out of here. Please, can you concentrate? Just for a minute.'

'I'll try.' She sounded drunk.

He began to take off his padded Puffa jacket. 'Put this on. You've got to keep warm.'

'I am warm.'

'I know, sweetie, but you mustn't get chilled, not with your fever. Put this on. Let me take that mac. Look, it's soaking. I'll put it here on the floor. Are you listening?' He helped her put on the quilted waistcoat.

'Mm.'

'The mac's by the bed. When you hear them coming

back, put it on. You must cover my jacket – it's obviously not yours, it's miles too big—'

'Don't leave me alone, Matt – please.'

'I'll be back. I promise. I've got to get you out of here. I've got to arrange things. Be patient, darling. I love you.'

Selina began to cry as he kissed her cheek gently. She grabbed at his hand and held on to him with a desperation that made his heart turn over.

'Matt – there's a letter – we've got to talk about a letter – but I can't remember.'

'Shush, later. Try to sleep.'

As he crept from the room, he hated himself for having to leave her, sobbing, afraid and ill, in the terrifying darkness – but he had no choice.

chapter twelve

1

Tessa Mulholland looked moodily out of the window. An air of apprehension hung in the aeroplane as the other passengers, having seen the stormy darkness they were entering, braced themselves for the inevitable turbulence.

Tessa was unaware of it for her thoughts were miles away. The small concern she had felt after she had spoken to her mother on the telephone had, in the last few days, magnified alarmingly. She had called Porthwood many times to be told again that Ginnie was 'not available', 'out', 'in retreat' or plain 'busy'. She had tired of dialling her home number only to have the answering machine respond. Neither was her grandmother at her house.

Deep inside her Tessa knew that something was terribly wrong. Logic had told her it was unlikely and reason had said not to panic. But Tessa *knew*, and sufficiently strongly for her to curtail her holiday, ditch the new man in her life and catch the first available flight out of Grenoble airport.

She had hoped that now she would calm down and begin to feel silly at acting so precipitately but she didn't. If anything she felt more agitated as the journey progressed bumpily towards England.

It was evening by the time Tessa's taxi turned into the driveway of her parents' house. Lights were streaming from the windows. So great was her relief at the sight, and the ensuing certainty that she had overreacted, that she gave the driver fifty pounds and, to his astonishment, told him to keep the change.

She bounded up the steps to the front door, pushed it open and raced into the hall, dropping her bags higgledy-piggledy onto the floor.

'Mum – Dad – it's me. Surprise!' she called, as she pushed open the drawing-room door. She stood stock still as two men she did not know got to their feet. 'Oh, hello,' she said, looking wildly about for her father. They were too respectable to be burglars, she thought – but what did a burglar look like?

'You must be Tessa.' The younger of the two approached her, hand out in greeting. 'I'm Karl Richardson.'

'And I'm Humphrey Lawley,' the second, more distinguished-looking and kinder-faced man said.

'Is my father about?' She felt dizzy with fatigue.

'He's getting some ice. Are you all right? You look a little pale,' Humphrey said solicitously.

'I didn't expect to see you. It was a pig of a journey.' As she spoke, the door opened and she hurled herself at Carter. 'Oh, Daddy, I've been so afraid!' she said, her voice muffled in his jersey as he held her tight.

It was the first time she'd called him Daddy in years, he realised, and he hugged her tightly. 'You need a drink by the look of you,' was his studied opinion once they disentangled themselves.

She laughed. 'At least something's the same. That's Dad's recipe for everything, isn't it, Dad?'

Carter agreed, while feeling a tinge of sadness that he was 'Dad' once more.

'Your wife keeps such a meagre store-cupboard, Carter my darling, that all I could find was some tuna.' Joan Mulholland swept into the room with a tray of perfectly cut sandwiches and exotically folded napkins. 'Tessa, where did you spring from? Shouldn't you have taken those dreadful shoes off? Think of the floors. And is that your luggage scattered all over the hall? So inconsiderate.'

'Yes, Grandmother.' Tessa kissed the air above Joan's shoulder and winked at her father.

'You've heard, of course. That stupid woman, your mother. She's—'

'Mum, could you leave this to me?'

'What's up? What's happened?' Tessa could feel the panic welling again as if it was bile.

'Sit down, Tessa. Nothing has happened.'

'Nothing? Nothing?' Joan said harshly. 'That worthless creature's giving her money away left, right and centre. And you call that nothing! Really, Carter.'

'Is that all?' Tessa sat down and gratefully took the glass of wine her father handed her.

'Typical! You're just like her – no idea of responsibility, loyalty *or* duty.'

'Hang on a minute, Gran. I'd rather you didn't speak about my mother in this way. I know about loyalty.'

'Virginia's never been stable, you know, Mr Lawley. Always lived off her nerves. It's all this alternative rubbish. I knew it would go to her head eventually. I just knew she'd start doing silly things with her money when she should have been thinking of her family, and especially Carter. The wrong people so often have the money. Have you not observed that, Mr Lawley?'

'I couldn't say, Mrs Mulholland. However, I've frequently noticed that others often have a certainty that they know better than I what I should be doing with mine.' He smiled kindly, immediately removing any implied criticism.

'Are you an American, Mr Lawley?' Joan asked suspiciously.

'No, Mrs Mulholland. Cockney born and bred,' he replied proudly. A shadow of disappointment, or perhaps disapproval, flitted across Joan's face and she wavered a second before she collected herself.

'How nice,' she said unconvincingly.

'If I might suggest—' Karl began.

'I have been wondering if her actions aren't certifiable, if we shouldn't call my doctor – a charming man.'

'Mum, I'd rather—' Carter began, but Joan rushed on.

'And power of attorney – that's what you need, Carter. Yes. In the morning I'll call your father's chambers and we'll set that in motion. And then—'

'Would somebody please explain to me what's happening? Where's Mum? What's going on?' Tessa stood up, drink in hand, all her agitation returning four-fold.

'Your mother's gone off with a guru. That's what's happened. She's giving him all her money and it's got to be stopped.'

'Hang on a minute. What exactly is concerning you, Gran? That she's gone or she's giving away the money?'

'Tessa – look, calm down—'

'No, Dad. I won't. Gran's always been a bitch to Mum.'

'Well, really!' Joan was astounded.

'If she's living off her nerves, a lot of it's down to you, Gran. You were always sniping and sneering at her,' Tessa continued.

'I don't think you should be talking to your grandmother like this, Tessa.'

'I do, Dad. It's gone on long enough. And how dare she speak of my mother like this in front of strangers. She lectures me about loyalty and duty – I doubt she can spell the words. My mum's been a saint with what she's had to put up with. All she wanted was for you to love and respect her.'

'How pathetic!' Joan sneered.

'*That does it!* Gran, will you please go to bed. We've

got problems that need sorting and we can't do it with your smart-arse remarks.'

'You're a foul-mouthed ingrate—'

'Ladies! Please.' Humphrey was on his feet.

'He's right. This won't get us anywhere,' Karl added.

'I'm sorry, Gran. I shouldn't have spoken like that. I'm just so on edge.' Tessa was close to tears.

'Nor you should. As to my accepting your apology – we shall have to see. But I'll say this, young woman, it would appear that, unfortunately, you seem to have inherited a lot of your mother's *common* blood.' And with that Joan swept from the room, head held high, while Carter, finger on lips, prevented his daughter answering back.

2

'I'm sorry about that, everyone,' said Carter, 'and, darling, don't let her upset you.' He put his arm around his daughter's shoulders.

'Now, perhaps we can get back to where we were before World War Three broke out!' He grinned and Tessa coloured. 'Mr Lawley is the husband of Jessica Lawley – you know, the actress?'

'Sorry, Mr Lawley, I'm afraid I don't.' Tessa smiled apologetically. She knew the likes of Demi Moore and Sharon Stone but not this Jessica woman.

Humphrey was glad that Jessica was spared this example of how transient fame could be. 'Ex-husband, actually, but that fact doesn't alter my very real concern at the situation.'

'What situation? I know Mum's at the Fohpal headquarters but she said she was happy there.'

'You knew? Then why ...?'

'Not now, Dad. Later. Is Selina back?'

'No. It looks as if her business has been sold, too.'

'Might I?' The other man stepped forward.

'Karl's a cult expert, Tessa. I contacted him to advise me how to get your mother out of their clutches. She's threatening to stay and sign everything over to them.' Carter said this with marked bitterness and Tessa felt no satisfaction at learning that her unease had been based on fact.

'Like you, Tessa, I'm in the dark too. But I thought we were better off joining forces,' Humphrey said kindly.

'You're a cult-buster?' Tessa asked Karl.

'That's what the Americans call people like me, yes. I've been on to Fohpal for some time. I'm sufficiently concerned that I've rented a cottage for a year, close to the estate.'

'Fill us in,' Humphrey ordered.

'I don't know how much you know about cults, but—'

'Just tell us how we're to get them out,' Carter interrupted. He'd been pacing the floor in his agitation.

'Dad!'

'I think we should listen to Karl,' Humphrey intervened. 'If we're to free them we have to know what we're up against.'

'Right, Fohpal – For Our Hope Peace and Love,' Karl began. 'There was nothing wrong with Fohpal until about five years ago when I began to get whispers that things were changing. The group has been in existence since one Bay Tarbart claimed she had found the guru known as H.G. – Haré Gan. Except his real name is Harry Vicente. An interesting story, but that is not what concerns us. He might not be quite what he claims, but he's always been harmless and legit. Fohpal was primarily a self-help group – you know the sort, the answer is within you, meditation, self-improvement, that sort of thing, and he was highly regarded as a healer. With reason, because he had many successes, quite a number of them medically verified.

'The group is financed principally by wealthy Americans, mainly women. The organisation – H.G. owns nothing – has property in the French Alps, where followers with children live, and an estate in America in the hills behind Santa Cruz. The main centre, Porthwood, is in Cornwall. It has a large income from a portfolio of shares and from its various books and videos.

'The membership worldwide is probably in the region of fifty to sixty thousand. The core group is about a hundred and fifty. They meet mainly in large conferences under canvas at their centres. They recruit by word of mouth and from meetings held in large cities. And they do no harm – or didn't.

'Six years ago a Xavier Melbourne joined. That's when the problems began. Insidiously he has taken control from H.G. He is rotten to the core. He's known to us as Phil Cooper, born in Gillingham, Dorset. He was a failed actor, became a used-car salesman. That also failed and he turned to small-time crime, finally becoming a con-man, with OAPs his speciality. Amazingly no police force is looking for him – a few irate fathers and husbands may be. Women adore him and that has been his strength. He subsequently became a stage hypnotist. Significant, that fact.

'He's virtually hijacked Fohpal. H.G. is rarely seen – rumour has it that he's seriously ill. It's become a closed community. Members are being alienated from their nearest and dearest, conned out of money – large sums, too. I've been retained by five separate families. Just recently a worse rumour has leaked that people who stood up to him have disappeared.

'He uses several techniques to control the followers. Hyperventilation disorientates them and makes them malleable. Sensory and sleep deprivation, starvation, drugs – all are used to control the minds of those he's got his talons into. And if all this fails he has his all-important ability as a hypnotist and, I can assure you, he is one of the best.' He paused to sip his drink.

'Get on with it, man,' Carter barked. 'How are we going to get them out? I don't give a stuff what this Xavier bloke is like.'

'The more we know the better we'll be prepared, Dad. We can't just go crashing in, alerting them.'

'I'm interested in how they were coerced into going in the first place. How normal, sane people can possibly get involved,' Humphrey said, and was rewarded with a bad-tempered scowl from Carter.

'You would be horrified at the ordinariness, but also the positions, of some of the people I've come across in the various cults I've investigated. MPs, judges, doctors, teachers, even a peer of the realm.'

'I'd have expected you to say misfits, inadequates, people searching for excitement to cheer up their hum-drum lives.' Humphrey was perplexed.

'Just because someone is a professional it doesn't mean they're not lonely. A judge could be inadequate in other ways, surely? Like personal relationships, sex?' Tessa asked.

'True!' Humphrey laughed, despite the seriousness of the situation. 'I've seen some very dodgy beaks in my time.'

'Tessa's right. There are conditions that make a person more vulnerable to these people. Often they are at a crossroads in their lives. Divorce, or a relationship ending or in difficulties makes them a good target.' Tessa looked at her father but he did not react. 'Bereaved people are vulnerable too,' Karl continued. 'Or maybe they have lost a job. In the recent recession bankrupts were particularly exposed – it's so easy to promise them renewed wealth – follow me and all will be well.'

'What use would a bankrupt be to them?'

'Even bankrupts have contacts, Carter, people who might be of use to them. And just because a man has no money it doesn't mean he has no skills. He might be sent out to recruit, or used as an unpaid servant or as a heavy. They'll find a useful role for them.'

'But, tell me, Karl, how do they find each other? I haven't seen adverts, have you?' Humphrey looked at the others.

'They've many ways. Many will have been set goals – recruit X number of people with X amount of money to contribute and get a bunk up the cult's hierarchy ladder and undoubtedly they were then rewarded with sex or more drugs. A simple way would be to watch what houses are for sale, what businesses—'

'Selina! Of course!' Carter interrupted. 'Her bookshop was for sale.' .

'Yes, and Mum told me that some young men visited Selina and showed an interest in buying it, and that was why they went to London to the Fohpal meeting.'

'Perfectly respectable, you see. Another method – works well with students – is to watch who's alone in the college cafeteria, target them, make friends, tell them where they can make a lot more friends. Don't forget such an approach would not be confrontational. They use charm to persuade them that if they follow them a wonderful new life awaits them.

'And you're wrong, Humph, they do advertise but you'd be hard pushed to know. It's even easier, these days, with the interest in New Age thinking. How innocent an advert for yoga lessons or meditation sounds. And with Fohpal they have had enormous success from aromatherapy groups they've set up. Unsuspecting people sign on to learn the craft, from which a good living can be made, and they are the sort of people who are already interested in an alternative lifestyle. They are promised the Fohpal diploma – for a fee, of course. That done they are offered an even more prestigious qualification for even more money. Ideas are introduced – Fohpal's, in particular, is that there is money to be made, and the instructor has the secret, so they innocently attend a meeting. From there it is so simple to suggest going to a retreat. Then, put quite baldly, they've invariably had it if Xavier deems them worth enough to fleece.'

'Hang on there. None of this describes Jessica. She wouldn't have been interested in any of that sort of stuff – good food and wine, possibly,' Humphrey protested.

'Something would have happened in her life to worry and destabilise her.' Karl spoke with conviction.

'She's been ill – arthritis. Nothing has helped, and she had high hopes of their treatment.' Humphrey was not about to divulge Jessica's money worries too.

'She would have been an ideal candidate.'

'Ginnie doesn't fit any of those categories.' Carter sounded almost as if he was scoring a point. 'She'd plenty of money, fit as a flea, my daughter and I aren't dead. What on earth could have attracted her?'

'Wanting to be loved,' Tessa said quietly. Humphrey smiled at the young woman, impressed again by her mature understanding.

'Do you really think that's the case, Tessa?' Karl asked.

'Yes,' she replied, almost in a whisper, looking at her father.

He shifted from foot to foot, remembering the scene on his birthday, and the one at Porthwood. He'd never taken Ginnie's accusation about his supposed affair with Anna Tylson seriously, had put it down to menopausal anxieties. 'Rubbish! She is loved.'

'Dad, I told you ages ago she thought you were having an affair with Anna Tylson.'

'It was all in her imagination. I don't know how many

times I told her my relationship with Anna was purely business.'

'That would have been irrelevant if she didn't believe you,' Humphrey said.

'Mum was convinced you only stayed with her because of her money. And hadn't you noticed how wired up she'd become? She'd have been an ideal subject for them,' Tessa added.

'I don't see how washing our dirty linen like this is going to help.'

'None of this will go further, Carter. It helps if you can understand better,' Karl said kindly.

'I know that's what she thinks but what else am I to do to persuade her it isn't true? I love my wife – Christ, I've put up with enough stick from my mother over the years for staying with her.' Carter buried his face in his hands.

You could have done more, thought Tessa, but decided that this was neither the time nor the place to discuss it.

'So, he's got them there. How is he going to keep them? After all, Jessica's a strong-willed woman – and don't I know it!' Humphrey manoeuvred the conversation back on track.

'With religious cults they use the fear of damnation, that if they leave or tell hell awaits. We're up against the fact that they really believe in their leader and don't believe you, and some are too proud to admit they've been duped. There are other fears – fear of ridicule among the group, fear of damage to family and loved ones if they report them, flattery – they might have been told they're special people, chosen ones, that they're healers and don't know it. There's debt – some have got so far into debt to them that they stay working it off, no better than the lowliest servant. And blackmail – perhaps they've compromised themselves, been indiscreet, had a sexual adventure and been filmed—' At this Carter groaned. 'Maybe they've found happiness there and are happy to stay, don't forget that. And there is, of course, another fear. Fear of being killed if they welsh.'

'We have to go to the police.' Tessa's face was marked with fear.

'Unfortunately, we've a problem there. The local police are in Xavier's pocket. One, in particular, he keeps supplied with crumpet. No doubt the bastard enjoys himself but if he decided to go straight Xavier would inform his chief constable – he'll have records, film, you can bet on that.'

'How do you know all this?' Humphrey asked.

'I've contacts,' he said enigmatically. 'On the inside,' he added, as if in response to the cynicism on Humphrey's face.

'Then why haven't you done anything about it, knowing all this?' Tessa asked, incredulous.

'It's difficult. You can't make people give up what they believe in just because you don't agree with it. Proving anything in these cases is difficult – the very nature of a cult makes it impossible for the followers to make allegations for the reasons I've just given you.'

'But you've got a mole on the inside.'

'Yes, and he's in constant danger. He's been there nearly a year now – and how he's kept sane I don't know.'

'How does he contact you?'

'I'd rather not say.'

'Why does he put himself at such risk?' asked Humph.

'He has relatives in the group. If he overtly spills the beans they could be killed. And don't think for one moment that they wouldn't be.'

'I presume all this is tied up with money?' Humph stated.

'Undoubtedly. There's a lot at stake – millions. It might be power too. I've seen cult leaders who could have retired to South America, set up for life, but the adulation gets them like a drug. And, in the end, they can't live without it. I wouldn't be surprised if Xavier won't find it difficult to give up the followers' adoration which, of course, makes H.G. even more vulnerable. With him out of the way Xavier is God.'

'What do we do? A snatch, of course! We could go in under cover of darkness and take them out. I'd go,' Carter volunteered.

'Carter, we're hardly the SAS.' Humphrey grinned broadly.

'It's been done,' Karl said. 'I've been involved. We rescued two young women from a religious cult – sexual abuse, assault of children, you know, the usual. It took us weeks of intensive work debriefing them. It's dangerous too. My phone's been tapped illegally, my life's been threatened, excreta in the post—'

'I'm not interested with what you've done in the past, or what others want to do to you. I'm only concerned with now,' Carter snapped.

'Somehow we've got to get into Porthwood, haven't we? Suss out the score. There's no point in rushing in and then finding our sweet ladies don't want to come with us. Can your contact help us here, Karl?' Humphrey asked.

'Difficult.' Karl pursed his lips, deep in thought. 'He's not contacted me for days.' He hadn't had anything in the dead letter drop, which was unusual. 'Of course, he can't get to a phone, and I guess he's constantly under surveillance.'

'I'll go,' Tessa announced. The three men looked at her, startled.

'No way.' Carter was on his feet.

'It would be too dangerous, Tessa,' Humphrey said, worriedly.

'I'm the obvious choice. What's more natural than that a daughter should go to find her mother? Once there, I can pretend to be interested and find out what's going on, how best to get them out.'

'Xavier would home in on someone as young and as pretty as you,' Karl said.

'I can look after myself. I've had enough creeps try to maul me to know what to do.'

'He wouldn't maul you, he'd be much more subtle than that. He'd seduce you without you even realising.'

'I can't allow this,' said Carter.

'You can't stop me. I'm going and that's that.' Tessa felt quite excited at the prospect.

chapter **thirteen**

1

Ginnie was hurt and confused. If she hadn't had the odd bruise on her body, she might have thought she'd dreamt Xavier in her bed and making love to her with such passion. But you didn't acquire memories like hers from dreams. She folded the linen she was pulling out of the large commercial dryer.

Why, though, was he suddenly so cold? He'd been so angry when she'd interrupted him with Jessica – which was fair enough, she should have knocked. But since then he'd ignored her. At breakfast this morning he'd looked right through her as if she didn't exist or, even worse, as if she was of no importance to him. She stuffed another load of washing into the machine, fed it soap powder, and spun the dials.

Of course he had said, right at the beginning, that they were to keep their affair secret for the time being. Others might be jealous, he'd explained. Far better to let them get used to the idea slowly of the two of them together. He was right – he was always right, wasn't he? That was probably why he was ignoring her, to put the others off the scent. The theory cheered her immeasurably. She must be patient. Difficult, when she wanted the whole world to know that she was the chosen one. She plugged in the big rotary iron.

'Ginnie, Xavier wants you in his study, pronto,' Ancilla called into the laundry room as she passed.

She could have wept with relief. At last! He wanted her again! She tore off the white apron that covered her plain pale blue robe. Once Xavier went public with their relationship she'd have her own robes made to measure. She'd already designed them in her mind's eye: she'd go for silk, dark blue, of course – the length of time she'd been here would be less important than that she was his wife – and she'd have a touch of gold braid, which would make her stand out as different from the rest.

Feeling as light-hearted as a teenager, she rushed along the maze of back passages, past the still-room, the silver vault, the butler's pantry, until she emerged through the green baize door into the front hall. She paused, caught her breath, patted her hair, straightened her robe, wiped the grin off her face and replaced it with a more celestial smile, then walked sedately along the thickly carpeted corridor towards Xavier's rooms, her heart pitter-pattering.

Xavier was waiting for her in the corridor. He beamed at her, his arm held up in welcome. She felt herself glide towards him. He was like a magnet, irresistible.

'I came as quickly as I could.'

'I wanted to have time to talk to you, explain everything, but I've been caught on the hop. You love me, yes? Totally?'

'Of course I do. With all my heart.' She felt quite dizzy at the thought of what such questions might lead to.

'And you'll do anything I ask?'

'Anything,' she said breathlessly.

'Even if it seems a bit odd to you?'

'Yes.' She was mystified now.

'And no questions asked?'

'No. Why? What do you want me to do?'

'Go to bed with a friend of mine.'

'Xavier!' Her eyes widened with shock.

'Don't let me down. You promised.' And he pushed her towards the door as if to stop her asking further questions. 'Here she is. This is Ginnie.'

'Not as young as you promised.' A grey-suited, beer-gutted man was standing with his back to the fire, a glass of Scotch in his hand, rocking slightly but pompously on his heels. He looked her up and down with such patent insolence that she had to look away.

'There's nothing like experience, though, Ken, is there?' Xavier laughed. 'Ginnie, this is ...' and he paused and laughed again. 'His name is of no importance to you. Just call him Ken.'

'How do you do, Ken?' she said obediently, holding out her hand to be shaken, but finding it ignored.

'Nothing else available?'

'You've caught us at a difficult time, Ken. The bird I had in mind for you – a new recruit – isn't too well. Flu.'

'There's a lot of it about.' Ken drained his glass. 'How about little Esmeralda?'

'She's away.'

'It'll have to be this one, then. Pity she's not as her name implies. Now that would be a treat.'

Ginnie looked at him with disgust. She had endured too many virgin jokes in her life to find them even remotely amusing. But what horrified her was that she was standing, as if paralysed, accepting them talking about her as if she was a commodity.

'Use your old room, Ginnie.'

His voice finally galvanized her to protest, even if she did so in a whisper; she had a distorted fear of seeming impolite. 'Xavier, I'm sorry, but ... I can't do this.'

'Charming,' interjected Ken.

'You can, and you will,' he hissed at her.

'Xavier!' She grabbed at his sleeve. 'Please, I love you.'

'Then if you do, you'll do as I wish, won't you?' He smiled, but his eyes did not.

Ginnie shuddered. She whispered urgently to him, 'But if you love me, how can you ask me?'

'Sorry about this, Ken. I'll just have a quiet word with Madame here. We'll only be a moment.'

'No problem. Don't calm her down too much, I quite enjoy a challenge.' Ken laughed unpleasantly. 'Makes it more interesting, bit of rough stuff, if you get my drift.'

'Outside, you!' Xavier pushed her roughly towards the door to his study. Once there he held her arm tight and twisted it. 'You promised to obey me.'

'I know.' She was fighting tears. She knew he didn't like crying women.

'You said you'd do anything I asked.'

'I know I did. But don't you understand? I love you.'

'For Christ's sake, can't you talk about anything else?'

'I can't, and that's that,' she said, with a defiance she was far from feeling. Her head rocked sharply before she felt the pain of his hand lashing across her face.

'You'll do as I say, understood?' He spoke menacingly, through his teeth. She put her own hand up to her cheek, a look of disbelief on her face.

'But not this. Not this, Xavier. He's a stranger. I don't even like him.' Her voice caught on a sob, which she hastily changed to a cough.

'Listen, you little fool, he's an important policeman. I need him on my side.'

'Your side of what? Why do you need him?'

'I do, that's all. I don't have to explain myself to you.' He bent forward suddenly and kissed her roughly, full on the mouth. 'I do love you, my little one,' he said softly. 'I couldn't say in there. He might not want you if he thought he was poaching you from me. Please, Ginnie. For me. For Fohpal.'

'For Fohpal?'

'Oh, you know how the general public are about groups like us. You've seen the witch-hunts on television, haven't you? He's a policeman. We need the police in our pocket. You'd be doing it for all of us. I'll always be grateful.'

'Well ... put like that.' Her mind was racing. She could keep her eyes shut, get it over and done with quickly. And if her reward was his gratitude, well, that put a totally different complexion on it. 'Of course, Xavier. For you and the movement,' she said bravely.

'I'm sorry I hit you.'

'It doesn't matter,' she said, reeling with confusion at his sudden change in manner.

Xavier pushed open the door again.

'Would you like to come this way, Ken?' She smiled sweetly at the man. 'I can promise you a time you'll never forget,' she said, amazed that she could even say such things – and to a stranger!

2

Selina had lost track of time. She had no idea how long she had been in this small, dank room – how many hours or, worse, days. She could not remember when she had last eaten and how she had got here. She did not know if anyone had been here to check on her. She was convinced that that dreadful noise, from which there was no escape, would eventually drive her mad.

She dug her hands deep into Matt's padded jacket – she knew it was his for his smell lingered on it and comforted her. She longed for him to come and take her away from here.

She rubbed her cheek so hard against the zip on the collar that she winced but it made her feel she existed, that she was awake and that this was not just a nightmare.

He had said he loved her! Or had he? What was real

and what was wish-fulfilment? Then she floated, trying hard to hold on, but her mind seemed packed with cotton wool, and she felt herself fading away.

There was no way of knowing how long it was before she was capable of thinking again. One moment she could grasp the awfulness of her situation, the next she was floating off and not caring about anything. And yet ... and yet she knew she should.

The noise had stopped. That must have been what had woken her. It was almost pleasurable to be in silence. Suddenly she heard a shrill noise, like the cry of a child or the scream of a rabbit. Perhaps she was not alone here – wherever 'here' was. She was not sure if such an idea made her feel better or more afraid. She listened hard but there was nothing more and then the hissing noise began again. She groaned and clapped her hands over her ears but it did no good.

She felt about in one of the jacket's pockets, concentrating on what she was doing – with something to think about she could stay aware longer – did she really want to?

There was a piece of string, easily identified by her prying fingers, and then a cold metallic ball – a ball-bearing or a marble, she had no way of telling. His hankie and, beneath it, a slim paper packet. She took it out carefully, so as not to drop the other things, and sniffed it. Chewing-gum.

These treasures made her smile: the contents of the pocket should have belonged to a little boy – all that was lacking was a conker for the string. She put a stick of the gum into her mouth. She sighed: nothing she had eaten in her whole life had tasted as sweet and nourishing as this. She sat, rhythmically chomping, savouring the taste, feeling it relieve her hunger a little. Then she sat bolt upright, ignoring the pain in her head, the dizziness. She removed the gum from her mouth and rolled it into a ball which she then wedged into her ear. She put her finger in the other ear and listened – it deadened the noise considerably.

Now she was in a quandary: should she reserve the remaining stick of gum to stave off her hunger, or chew it into a bung for her other ear? The ear won.

It was so blissfully quiet, she decided. She leant over the side of the bed and felt on the rough cement floor for her wet mackintosh, which she suddenly remembered Matt had laid there.

It was dry. Though she welcomed the extra warmth the coat would give her, its dryness depressed her for it showed too clearly that she must have been here for some time. She covered herself, lay down and curled up small to retain as much of her body heat as possible. Compared with a few minutes before she felt almost in luxury.

She had so much to think about. So many problems. Pity she didn't have the energy for them now. Later, she'd go over it all later. Her eyes felt prickly, her lids heavy. Mercifully she was quickly asleep.

Sitting in the Land Rover as Tristram drove them into town, Matt was trying to control the panic bubbling inside him. Yesterday he had emerged from the cellar, unseen by anyone he was pretty sure, but since then he had not been left alone for one minute. He was convinced he was being watched. There had been no way he could get back to comfort or rescue Selina, not without putting them both at risk.

This morning he'd been told to collect some chicken feed with Tristram, yet he was certain the supplies had come in yesterday. They probably wanted him out of the way to search through his things – at least he had the satisfaction of knowing they would find nothing incriminating. But it was odd that he'd been sent out with

Tristram. No one was allowed out alone, but Tristram normally worked on the computers.

As they drove, Matt planned – not an exact description of the chaos in his head for he grabbed at ideas and almost immediately rejected them. The scenario he was left with might succeed in a film but, in reality, it didn't seem to stand a chance. He was going to have to rescue Selina from the cellar, unseen, put her in a car he'd already have stolen and then either he or someone else would drive her to hospital. But who?

He could not trust any of the other followers, which left Selina's friends. No doubt Ginnie would go screaming to Xavier with the details of any plot. Jessica looked too crippled to drive and he was pretty sure she was one of those self-absorbed individuals who was unlikely to put herself out for anyone.

Some plan, he thought, as Tristram parked.

He looked longingly at the police station and debated whether to burst in and demand they raid Porthwood. He didn't: H.G. was revered among the local community and he doubted that anyone would listen to a word against Fohpal.

And always there remained his fear for his sister and her family if he stepped out into the open. .

'What's the attraction?' Tristram asked, sounding edgy.

'I've got a thing about Victorian architecture. Just look at those crenellations up there.' He pointed to the eaves of the police station. 'Great workmanship.'

'Of course, you were once an architect, weren't you? Then I'll take your word for it. Too old and fussy for my taste, though. Fancy a curry?'

'Why not?' he replied, although food was the last thing on his mind.

As soon as they arrived back at Porthwood Mathie bustled towards him, flapping her arms to prevent him skidding away. 'Thank heaven you're back, Matt. One of the washing machines has sprung a leak. If you could see to it immediately. We've that big party of Americans this weekend – we must have the linen.'

'I'm not an engineer. Why's it always me?' He was cross. He had intended to slip down to the boiler room where, even if he couldn't get in to see Selina, he'd be able to think in peace and quiet.

'What's the problem?' Bethina asked, as she glided towards them.

'Matt's being difficult about mending the washing machine,' Mathie complained.

'I'm not a repairman – that's all I said.' Old bitch, stirring things up, he thought.

'Dear Matt, we're sorry to bother you yet again. You must forgive us but you are so wonderfully clever with your hands, aren't you?' Bethina flashed him a flirty smile which, like most men, he found difficult to resist.

Tristram was still with him, now ordered to be his plumber's mate even though he didn't need one and protested that he was better off alone. They finished the task quite quickly.

'I need a slash,' said Matt.

'Me, too,' Tristram said at once.

'I think I'll go for a walk.'

'I'll come with you.'

'I prefer to walk alone – helps me think.'

'I understand ... but all the same.' Tristram had the grace to look shamefaced and awkward as he put on his anorak and boots.

Matt opened the door, and gestured for the other man to precede him. Tristram stepped out. 'I've changed my mind,' Matt said. 'Look at the weather – it's grim.' And he shut the door and leant against it with all his weight. He did not have time to bolt it before Tristram, a bigger fellow than he, had elbowed it open.

'Look, Tristram. Come clean. Who's told you to keep an eye on me?'

'I don't know what you mean,' he blustered.

'You sure as hell do. Out with it.'

'Don't say I said. Xavier.'

'Great!'

'I'm sorry, but you know Xavier – I didn't want to cross him.' He shrugged his rugby player's shoulders and grinned, not too successfully.

'Fair enough. Yes, we all know Xavier. Do you happen to know why?'

'They didn't tell me. But, then, they wouldn't, would they? I'm too new. There's something else. We moved a divan into your room – we're sleeping together from now on.'

'It would be nice to be told. Hope you don't snore!' Matt forced himself to be casual. 'I'm on veg duty now. I suppose you are too?'

'No. Sholta's doing that with you,' Tristram said sheepishly.

'Better let me have the rota of minders, then I can search everyone out on time.' He slapped Tristram on the back good-naturedly and had the satisfaction of seeing him relax. 'I just wish I knew what it was I'm supposed to have done.' He sighed exaggeratedly and Tristram looked sympathetic.

As they crossed the hall they were in time to see a slim, pretty, dark-haired young woman being let in by Bethina.

'Hello. My name's Tessa Mulholland and I've come to see my mother.' She smiled, despite looking nervous.

'How perfectly sweet.' Bethina beamed. 'Come in, do.'

Hell, thought Matt, not another one to rescue.

3

'Come,' a male voice barked, in response to Bethina's knock. Tessa felt her stomach lurch with nerves.

'Xavier, look who we have here,' Bethina said, as she pushed open the door to his study and gently ushered the girl into the room. 'This is Tessa, Ginnie's daughter.' Xavier stood up.

'You need not have said, Bethina. This young one is as beautiful as her mother. Indeed, dare I say, even more beautiful. Welcome. Welcome.' He came round from behind his desk, hands held out towards her and grasped hers tightly.

'I hope you don't mind me just turning up like this,' said Tessa, thinking, What an oily pluke, but managing to smile broadly despite her fear.

'Mind? How could we possibly? It's a joy to have you here.'

'I've been trying to get hold of my mother on the telephone and I never could and I thought I'd better come and see for myself that she's okay.'

'How come Tessa hasn't spoken to her?' Xavier said sternly, still holding her hand as he looked questioningly at Bethina.

'You know how hard Ginnie works, Xavier. You see, Tessa my dear, your mother is, without doubt, one of the keenest students we've ever had. She longs to find the Inner Way, and she studies so hard. I can only assume that when you called she was so involved that she probably said she didn't want to be disturbed.' Bethina smiled at her and Tessa felt herself relax and the worry peel away like an onion skin.

'Don't feel hurt, Tessa. No doubt one of our helpers followed her instructions to the letter. I can't imagine her not rushing to the phone if she'd been told you had rung,'

313

Xavier said smoothly. 'Your mother is a changed woman. You will be amazed. She's so happy. So *intensely* involved. She's truly found herself.'

'That's good. And about time too. I've told her so often she should do that.'

'Then she's succeeded beyond your dreams. Now, Tessa dear, I do hope you intend to stay with us?' Xavier finally let go of her hand.

'I'd like to, if you don't mind.' She wanted to wipe her hand on her jeans, but stopped herself. Xavier was too smooth by far, and too old. But she was fascinated by Bethina and her astounding beauty. ·

'You must stay as long as you like.'

'I was thinking of just a couple of days. I have to return to college next week.'

'Of course. Then we shall enjoy your company even, sadly, for such a short time. But never mind, next time! Now Bethina will settle you in your room and after that we can talk.'

For a moment Tessa thought he was going to kiss her and, involuntarily, she took a step back. But he was only moving to the other side of his desk. Tessa followed Bethina from the room, but she had the uncomfortable feeling that he was watching her intently as she left.

Bethina seemed to glide up the stairs and Tessa, slim and graceful herself, felt clumsy and awkward beside her.

'I think you'll be comfortable in this room. It's my favourite – just right for someone special like you.'

Tessa was aware that she was being charmed and yet, although she would have recoiled from Xavier saying such things, she accepted them willingly from Bethina.

'It's lovely.'

'Now, I expect you'd like to freshen up. I'll be downstairs in my office just off the hall. We'll meet in half an hour. I'll keep my door open so that I see you immediately. Then we'll find your mother, shall we?

You've everything you need?' And, good hostess that she was, she glanced quickly about the room as if making a speedy inventory. She went to the bed and bent down to switch on the light. 'There, that's better, isn't it?'

Alone, Tessa crossed the room. She tugged at the latch of the mullioned window. Having convinced herself it would be locked, she was surprised when it swung open easily. She leant out, noting to her right a handy, solid creeper. If necessary she had an escape route. She closed the window against the cold and couldn't help smiling at how melodramatic her thoughts were – especially when Bethina was so charming.

Her bag was on the floor. She burrowed inside and felt at the bottom for the mobile phone her father had given her. She punched in the number of Karl's cottage, where he, Humphrey and her father were holed up, about ten miles from Porthwood.

'Dad, it's me. I've arrived.'

'Have you seen your mother?'

'Not yet. They've just gone to get her.'

'You're all right?'

'I'm fine, Dad. Honestly. Xavier's a bit of a bozo – you know, fancies himself something rotten. But I'm being looked after by a woman called Bethina and she's lovely. My room's fine. Honestly, there's nothing to worry about.'

'Hang on ...' She could hear her father speaking to someone in the room with him. 'Karl says don't be lulled into a false sense of security. They're going to switch on the charm for you.'

'I know that. I promise I'll be on my guard all the time. I'm not an idiot, you know.'

'I wish I'd stopped you—'

'Dad, I'm fine. I'll call again later today, okay? Stop wittering, you sound like Mum.' Her voice bubbled with laughter. ''Bye.' She disconnected the phone. She began to replace it in her handbag but then had second thoughts. What if it rang when she was with them? Karl had said she must keep the telephone secret, that if they knew she had it they would probably take it away from her and then she'd have no way of communicating with them.

The wardrobe and drawers were the first places anyone would look. She glanced around the room, crossed to the empty fireplace and felt up the chimney. There was a ledge a little way up. It was just like the one in the bedroom she used when staying at her grandmother's house. She'd often hidden treasures there and no one had ever found them.

She unpacked the few clothes she had with her, looked at her watch and decided she had time for a quick shower.

Under the jet of water, as she soaped herself, she realised that all the nervousness she had felt when she first arrived had gone. It was thanks to Bethina, she realised. And she was beginning to wonder if Karl was as expert as he said. She'd know better when she saw her mother.

As she padded back into the bedroom she was singing, totally unaware that the bug in the bedside lamp had picked up every sound she had made.

4

'Ginnie, it's Jessica. May I talk to you?'

'What about? It's my meditation time. You know that's sacrosanct – or should be,' Ginnie said, sounding sanctimonious as she opened the door an inhospitable crack and peered out.

'It's about Selina. I'm worried, Ginnie.'

'I suppose you'd better come in, then,' Ginnie said grudgingly, and opened the door further. 'But only for a minute, I've things to do.'

'You're *too* kind.'

Ginnie smiled at the apparent appreciation of her forbearance, and Jessica wondered if she was thick-skinned or just thick.

'Do you mind?' Jessica indicated the chair and sat down before Ginnie had time to say whether she did or not.

'So, what's the problem?'

'Selina's gone and she didn't say goodbye.'

'Perhaps she was in a hurry.'

'Bethina says she's gone home but I can't believe she would go just like that. The last time I saw her she looked ill. She was almost in hysterics, claiming she'd been drugged. You saw her – you came in just after she rushed off, don't you remember?'

'No, I can't say I do,' Ginnie said vaguely, but she did, too clearly. How could she forget when she had been so humiliated in front of Jessica? 'Who does she claim is giving her drugs? And what sort – cannabis, ecstasy?'

'She didn't say. She didn't accuse anyone. The followers, I suppose.'

'What arrant nonsense! More likely she was hung over – she's been drinking, you know.'

'Who told you that?' Jessica remembered Selina saying she mustn't tell Ginnie, who might snitch on her.

'Bethina did. They were really shocked when they found the bottle in her room.'

'Why should they be shocked? They drink. And what do you mean "found"? Were they checking her out?'

'Don't be silly. Presumably they found the empty bottle after she left.' Ginnie was flustered, wishing she hadn't been so indiscreet. It had bothered her when Bethina told her, but she had preferred to concentrate on the honour of Bethina confiding in her behind Selina's back, as though Ginnie was already one of them. Now Jessica was spoiling it and making her unsure again. 'I think you're overreacting. If Bethina says she's gone home then she has. Why should she lie? It would be too silly.'

'There's something else. Selina's case is in the corner of Mathie's office. I think she's still here.'

'It's too heavy, probably. Someone said she was having to walk to the station because there were no cars.'

'There's a whole line of cars out at the back. I checked.'

'Quite the little snoop, aren't you, Jessica?'

'Must be catching,' she retorted.

'You can be so sharp, Jessica, and so distrustful – it's not very attractive.'

Jessica took a deep breath and tried to keep her temper. She would get nowhere if she lost it.

'I think we should search for her. And I think we should not tell anyone we are.'

'And where would we begin?'

'The cellars.'

'Why there? You're sure this isn't a scene from some rotten film you played in years ago?'

Jessica ignored this remark. 'Wasn't the room you went to for your "retreat" down there? Where you *found* yourself?' Jessica reined in her tongue. 'Maybe that's where she is.'

'In the Reclamation Room? Never! That place is sacred. Only those who are well along the Inner Way are allowed in it. She wouldn't be there for a start and certainly no one would keep her there if she didn't want to be. Now, Jessica, if you don't mind, I've my meditation to do and you're stopping me.' She rewarded the older woman with one of her madonna-like smiles, which she was still working on.

'Don't you care about your friend?' Jessica asked

sharply, that false smile annoying her even more than what Ginnie had said.

'She can look after herself. I wouldn't appreciate her rushing about after me and I know she feels the same. It's about giving people their space. I really can't be bothered with all this.'

'God, you're so self-obsessed. Selina's worth two of you. All you do is whine and sniffle at how unfair everything is. Quite honestly if your husband screwed every woman he met, I for one wouldn't blame him.' Oh, Lor', thought Jessica. How did we get to this?

'Jessica, if you're trying to anger me, you're failing. I'm above all this now. You can't touch me. I've released myself, I'm *rooted*!'

'Oh, for Christ's sake, Ginnie. If you could hear yourself you'd realise what a neurotic, egotistical person you are. Selina says you weren't always like this. She would, she's a nice, loyal person. I can't understand your total lack of concern for her.'

'What am I supposed to do? I don't know where she is. If I found her she wouldn't listen to me.' She was linking and unlinking her fingers in agitation. She must not lose her temper, she must stay calm. 'And, in any case, you're a fine one to talk. You're as selfish as they make them. All you ever do is think about *yourself*.'

'I agree. But at least I admit it. You refuse to face the truth. You're a fool. Why, Xavier's bonking virtually anything in a skirt.'

'How dare you say that? It's a lie,' Ginnie yelled, knowing she was about to let rip the temper she had already lost. 'You're jealous! He won't be bonking you, that's for sure. You're too fat and old.' Her voice was rising at an alarming rate and, try as she might, she couldn't get it back down into the lower register. It was as if it had taken control of her.

'Then why did I have to spurn him the other night?'

'You bitch! You filthy-mouthed old has-been!' Ginnie leant forward and scratched Jessica's face, raking her nails down one cheek. With a hefty shove, Jessica pushed her assailant away, slapping her hard across her face as she did so.

'Don't you dare touch me, you parasitical nobody!' And, mustering her dignity, Jessica swept from the room.

With all prospect of meditation ruined, Ginnie glanced in the mirror before rushing after Jessica. She passed her on the steep back stairs and had an almost uncontrollable urge to shove the fat cow down the flight and hope she broke her neck. But composure, of a sort, triumphed. Instead she sped past her, needing to get to Xavier first. Needing to tell him what was going on. That would put her back in his good books for sure.

'Mum, hi!' Tessa called. Ginnie stopped and turned to see her daughter on the landing above, just as Jessica popped into sight.

'Tessa? What the hell are you doing here?'

'I came to find you. See if you were all right.'

'Well, you've seen. This is my place, my space. You don't belong here. Get out!' Ginnie shouted, and continued her race down the stairs.

'Nice to see you too,' Tessa called after her, but it was doubtful that her mother heard.

5

In an excited babble, Ginnie had poured out Jessica's fears and accusations. She was, therefore, somewhat put out that Xavier welcomed Jessica warmly, a few minutes later, when she arrived at his study.

'But, Xavier, didn't you hear me? Jessica's against you, she's been saying awful things—'

'Nothing we don't already know. That's correct, isn't it, Jessica? You see, Ginnie, we were here together when Selina made her wild accusations. I thought I'd reassured you, Jessica. I was convinced Selina was imagining everything – high temperatures can do funny things to one's mind. Have you never had the flu, Jessica?' His voice was calm and rational, his smile in place.

'But she implied that Selina was still here because she saw her case in Mathie's office.' Ginnie was almost jumping up and down in frustration.

'Oh, that! It's too heavy. We're to send it by rail to Finchester. I took Selina to the station myself.'

'Then why didn't you take her bag too?' Jessica asked logically.

'Because, dear Jessica, I found her in a dreadful state by the main gate. She was wet, fevered, rambling. She'd left the bag since she was attempting to walk to the station.'

'If she was so ill, why did you let her go on her own?'

'Gracious, is this an inquisition?' Xavier asked. 'You both know Selina. When she decides to do something she'll do it, and heaven help anyone who stands in her way. No one could have persuaded her not to catch the eleven-thirty. There was no time to collect the bag. Simple explanation, when you know the facts.'

'All the same, I hope she's all right,' Jessica said, feeling less worried.

'Perfectly. She telephoned that she'd arrived safely. I made her promise she would. Also I made her agree to go straight to bed with a hot toddy, so all is well. Did she mention that she was also concerned about a letter Esmeralda had given her and that she thought had gone astray? Another unnecessary flap. Selina found the mysterious letter, tucked in a pocket in her handbag. Satisfied now?' he said, with studied patience. Jessica wondered if she had imagined a smidgen of irritation in his voice at having to make all these explanations.

'Thank you, Xavier, you've taken a weight off my mind.' Jessica smiled at him. She didn't often smile, but when she did, as now, her beautiful face became more animated, even more lovely. Xavier saw the transformation and Jessica chuckled inwardly at the interest in his eyes.

Ginnie saw his expression, too, and felt the jealousy that had always plagued her but which now, over Xavier, was becoming a gnawing agony.

'Jessica said we should search the cellars,' Ginnie said, still wanting to make trouble for her.

'What for?'

'Nothing, Xavier. You've put my mind at rest.'

'I'm glad to hear it. The cellar steps are steep and dangerous, and we don't want you falling, Jessica, not when you're doing so well.'

'Don't worry, Xavier. I'm not putting my hip at risk for anyone.' She bestowed another smile on him.

'Is your medicine helping you sleep?' he asked.

'Like a top,' she lied. She hadn't taken it. Despite all his reassurances, something had counselled her not to swallow anything of which she was not sure. She crossed to the door. 'If you'll excuse me, I'm going to sit and sew, good as gold. 'Bye, then,' she said, as she let herself out.

'You fancy her, don't you?' Ginnie swung round to face Xavier, the accusing words out of her mouth before she could stop them.

'Perhaps.'

'You wouldn't sleep with her? She's old and fat.'

'I don't agree with that assessment. Some women are sexy whatever their age – and she's one of them. I'd call her Rubenesque.'

'Only another word for fat!' Ginnie said, unaware how spiteful she looked, but panicked at his appreciation of

Jessica. 'Sleep with her? You couldn't! It would be disgusting.' She shuddered. 'I bet she's got cellulite,' she added, desperately.

'Are you jealous?'

'Of course not!'

'I think you are. Come here.'

'No. Not unless you promise I'm the only one for you.'

'I can promise that for this moment, if you want.'

'What does that mean? Nothing.'

'Take your pick. But look what you'd be missing.' He unzipped his flies and his rampant penis emerged, freed from the constraints of his trousers. 'See? Want it?'

Ginnie put out her hands to hold it and groaned – from sexual longing, but also because she feared she might not have been the inspiration for this particular erection.

A tap on the door made them jump apart.

'Sod! What now?' Xavier said, as he dived for his chair and, protected by the desk, rapidly rearranged his flies.

Ginnie stood in the middle of the room, her face flushed, hand to her mouth in the way of one caught shoplifting.

'Don't look so bloody guilty,' Xavier hissed at her. 'Come in, whoever you are,' he called loudly, with false bonhomie.

'Ah, here she is. We've been looking everywhere for you, Ginnie.' Bethina came into the room, a sad-faced Tessa behind her. 'See who's here.'

'Darling!' Ginnie exclaimed. 'What a wonderful surprise. How well you look – your face is so tanned.' Ginnie swept across the room, flung her arms around Tessa and hugged her tight, kissing her often and firmly. 'I'm so excited … This is my daughter, Xavier. My lovely, clever daughter.'

Tessa was alarmed. Her meeting with her mother on the stairs had been upsetting but this was even worse. Her mother had never gushed over her like this, never called her darling or smothered her in kisses. Her mother was acting and she didn't know why. The tension that Bethina had soothed returned with a vengeance and Tessa felt sick.

'Are you all right, Tessa? You look deathly pale,' Bethina asked.

'I feel a bit dizzy, that's all.'

'No breakfast, I bet. I know you young girls,' Bethina chided.

'Not dieting, surely, Tessa? There's no need for that. Not with a lovely figure like yours.' Xavier smiled.

Lovingly and with far too much interest, thought Ginnie.

Lecherously, thought Tessa.

'Too many late nights, more like.' There was a harsh ring to Ginnie's voice. 'Too many boyfriends. You know what the young are like, Xavier.' She giggled pleasantly, as if suddenly aware of her shrillness. 'I just can't keep up with my daughter and her different followers.'

'Mum!'

'You're only young once, Ginnie. Isn't that true, Tessa?' Xavier spoke in a tone like silk with a renewed spark of interest in his eyes. 'We should know.' But when he said that he was looking at Tessa, drawing her in, shutting Ginnie out.

Ginnie's mind raced wildly as she tried to think how to attract his attention back to her. But there was a blankness where plans should have been.

'Xavier,' she said simply, almost pleadingly.

It seemed an age before Xavier stopped staring at her daughter and turned to face her.

'Yes?' he asked, ice in his eyes.

'Nothing,' she said miserably.

But Tessa saw the look her mother gave him, of fear and longing and anger. Surely not, she thought. She must be imagining things. Not Mum! She couldn't possibly fancy him – she was too old for that sort of thing. It was disgusting. He was disgusting.

'I think I'd better sit down,' Tessa said. Suddenly everything made sense and she didn't like it.

chapter **fourteen**

1

Tessa looked anxiously across the table at her mother who, with her usual dainty precision, was buttering a small piece of toast.

'Mum, what have I done?' she asked.

'Nothing.'

'When you say that, all hell's usually about to break loose.'

'Do you have to sound like your father?' Ginnie flashed, and returned to the toast, scraping a minute amount of Marmite on it.

'What's happened to you, Mum? You've changed so much.'

'Of course I have. That was what you wanted, wasn't it? "Get a life," you told me. Well, I have.'

'But I didn't expect you'd change like this.'

'I'm sorry about that, but there it is. I'm a bit like the sorcerer's apprentice, aren't I? Once the change was made it would seem there's no stopping me.' She felt pleased with her analogy. Then she leant across the table, suddenly serious. 'I've never been so happy, never felt so free, never felt so whole. So, don't mess with me, Tessa.'

'I came to find you and see if you're all right. How can you be so upset about me being here?'

'This is my space, not yours. These are my people, not yours. And Xavier is mine – don't even think of it!' She pointed her finger accusingly at Tessa, who shook her head in disbelief.

'Mum! He's a dork. I wouldn't touch him, *ever*.'

'Fine, so long as you remember.'

'But, Mum. He's a creep and so slimy. Can't you see? How could you trust in someone like that? I mean—' She decided not to say what was on the tip of her tongue.

'How can I be sure he's not after my money? Is that what you wanted to ask? Did your father put you up to this? Of course, it's what he would think – after all, he wants my money, not me. A spiritual relationship is beyond his mercenary comprehension.'

Tessa wriggled in her seat. She was at a crossroads in the argument, she knew. She should continue blasting away at Xavier, trying to find out more about the cult to report back to Karl and her father on the phone this evening. She should find out how far its influence had worked on her mother.

'Dad's not like that. How can you say such things? He loves you, he really does. He's not having an affair, honestly,' she said instead, and immediately regretted that she'd been sidetracked.

'You forgot one thing, Tessa. You should have concluded that everything's in my imagination – my *menopausal* imagination,' Ginnie said sharply, and pushed away the plate of Marmite toast.

'I need to talk to you about what's going on here. I want to know.'

'I bet you do. I'm not stupid. Your father has sent you, I'm aware of that. I bet *he'd* like to know everything. Well, I shan't be giving him that pleasure!'

Tessa looked at her mother and hardly recognised her: her face was a mask of anger.

'I want to talk to you, Ginnie, if you'll excuse me, Tessa.' Jessica had arrived, unnoticed by either of them, and stood by Ginnie.

Tessa stood up.

'Sit down, Tessa. I want you here,' Ginnie ordered. 'It's got nothing to do with your daughter.'

Tessa wavered, not sure what to do. 'Sit,' Ginnie said, as if speaking to a dog, and Tessa obediently complied.

'Very well, then.' Jessica sat down too. 'What I really wanted to know is why you found it necessary to sneak on me in that manner?'

'Sneak? Oh, Jessica, you do show your age with the slang you use.'

'You did not have to rush to Xavier as you did, tittle-tattling. What were you doing? Trying to curry favour?'

'You're such a dried-up old husk of a woman, aren't you? I think you're jealous of me. I think you want him too. Well, listen to me, Jessica, and listen well. He's mine, and if you even once touch him I'll kill you, and that's not a threat, it's a promise.'

'Mum, stop it. This isn't you!'

'Isn't it?' Ginnie stared defiantly at her daughter.

'Ginnie, you're talking as if you're in some B movie, and a second-rate one at that!'

'Well, you should know, shouldn't you? You see the sort of spiteful person I'm having to deal with, Tessa? Is it any wonder I've had to change? I'm going to my room now. I'll see you in the morning, Tessa, when I suggest you leave.' And, not waiting for a reply, she sashayed between the long dining-room tables. She smiled in a superior but, she hoped, gracious manner at the other followers as she passed by. How she longed for them to know that she was the chosen one.

As she reached the door, Xavier walked in. Her heart fluttered at the sight of him, but he walked past without acknowledging her. Never mind, she told herself, she mustn't get upset. He was being discreet again.

In the hall she checked her duties for tomorrow. Kitchen again. She always seemed to be stuck in the kitchen. Yet Xavier had hinted that she'd soon be on more interesting tasks. When, though? Ideally she wanted to be Xavier's personal assistant, taking down his every word, typing it up for him. That would make her even closer to him. But for that to happen she had to get rid of Bethina, who regarded the archives as her preserve.

Ginnie had plans to make, schemes to work out, none of which would be helped by Tessa's presence. Maybe tomorrow she'd better be nicer, gentler to her, lull her. She'd been stupid today, ranting so harshly, but her nerves were all such a jangle it was hard to control herself.

A good night's sleep, that's what she needed, so that she was ready for Xavier's sexual demands. Just thinking about that made her skip up the stairs to her room.

In the dining room Tessa did not know which way to look. She felt so ashamed and mortified. A tear pricked her eye. She hurriedly wiped it away. That was the last thing she needed; if she turned into a weeping clod what help would she be to her mother?

'Don't let her get you down. She's not herself.'

Tessa smiled through her tears at Jessica.

'Please don't be nice or I'll cry.' She blew quickly into her hankie.

'It might be a good idea if you did,' Jessica heard herself say. Heavens, she was turning into a veritable agony aunt.

'Do you know my mother well?'

'Not really. To be honest, we never hit it off, I don't know why. But I have to admit that I've watched her change in the couple of weeks we've been here. She's on edge all the time. She makes no attempt to be pleasant. Being with her is like waiting for a volcano to erupt. Do you know Selina?'

'Where is she? I've looked for her. She knows Mum best of all.'

'She's gone home to Finchester. She got the flu.'

'That's odd. My father didn't say. I'd have thought she'd have been in touch with him ...'

'Ginnie asked her to contact him.' Jessica paused, wondering how much she should say to the young girl. 'Actually, it wasn't a friendly message. Maybe she decided it was kinder not to tell him. Yes, that's probably it.'

'I could swear my father said ...' Tessa shook her head. 'Still. Miss Lawley, will you be straight with me?'

'Only if you call me Jessica – formality from one so young makes me feel as old as hell.'

'Okay – Jessica. Do you think my mother's on drugs?' Tessa gazed at her earnestly.

Before answering Jessica looked about the room, checking that they were not going to be overheard. She need not have worried: the noise was high-pitched. There was an air of excitement, of anticipation as everyone chattered in groups.

'You mean that glittery look in her eyes? I thought that too, but Selina said no. It's true that when people get into something with the zeal that Ginnie has they get a look. Like born-again Christians or football fans. Selina said that when your mother had enthusiasms everything else went out of the window.'

'You can say that again!' Tessa laughed. 'Aromatherapy – the house reeked! Reflexology – none of our feet were safe. Then there was the tarot and she couldn't decide between tea and coffee without dealing the cards.' Tessa paused, thoughtful. 'But for all of those she was safely at home.' She looked around the dining room where followers were still chatting over cups of chocolate. 'We can't be here to care for her, if you know what I mean.'

'She's a vulnerable woman, that's one of the first things I thought about her.'

'She feels she's not loved or needed.'

'I've always thought being needed more important than being loved.' A sad little smile flickered about Jessica's mouth. Love, she knew, could be so transitory but being needed was a long-term thing – something that had always eluded her. She looked down so that Tessa could not see the expression in her eyes.

'Are you happy here, Jessica?'

'Yes. Certainly, I'm in less pain and that's changed my life. The rest? Quite honestly, Tessa, it leaves me cold. I've never needed to "find myself". I think the people here who are affected are the type who need something in their lives to fill a void.'

'But why should my mother? She's always so busy.'

'That's got nothing to do with it. But you said yourself she needed to be loved.'

'Jessica, can I speak honestly with you? I'm worried.'

'Of course,' said Jessica, while thinking 'if you must'.

'Do you think she's really in love with Xavier? It's the way she looks at him, the way she just spoke to you about him.'

'More likely she's infatuated – and that rarely lasts.'

'You think so?'

'I *know* so.'

'God, I hope you're right. You see, I've been sent to get her out and I don't know where to begin with her like this.'

'Try patience. But don't tell anyone else what you're about – it won't be too popular.'

'You won't tell anyone?' Tessa begged.

'Of course not. But ... well, Tessa, don't tell your mother either.'

'No – but,' Tessa laughed, 'it's funny really. Looking at my mother, being rescued is obviously the last thing on her mind. And I'm supposed to be rescuing you, too, and you don't seem to be in need of my services. And Selina's already gone. Redundant!'

'Me? Who sent you?' Jessica asked, although she knew what the answer would be.

'Your Humph. He's lovely, isn't he? Like one imagines Father Christmas to be.'

'I doubt if Humph would appreciate that. He rather fancies himself as a ladies' man.'

'Oh, a *sexy* Father Christmas – that goes without saying. What I meant is he's so in control and I felt so safe with him. He loves you a lot.'

'Did he say so?' She kept the interest she felt out of her voice.

'No, but it was there all the same. You know, an expression when he spoke of you. He's potty about you. Shall I send your love when I speak to him?'

'How will you do that? The phones in this place never work.' She broke off. 'Shush. Careful,' she whispered, seeing Bethina approaching their table.

'Tessa dear, you must be so tired. I've brought you some hot chocolate to drink. See, it's got cream in it.' Bethina placed the mug in front of her, smiling so beautifully that Tessa hadn't the heart to say she loathed it and dutifully took a sip.

'If you'll excuse me, bed calls.' Jessica got to her feet. 'We'll continue this talk in the morning, Tessa. OK?'

Later, in her room, Tessa sat on her bed and puzzled over the mobile phone in her hand. She'd checked it all ways, but still she couldn't get it to work; she couldn't dial out.

Before going to bed Jessica had to go to the kitchen: porridge making was one of her duties. She had to smile at that – how are the mighty fallen, she thought, as she heated the porridge in the giant saucepan on the hob before putting it in the warm oven to cook overnight.

'Anyone fancy a hot chocolate?' someone asked.

Jessica's hand stopped stirring. She knew that voice.

She remembered it well. Not seeing the face made it easier to identify. It was the voice of the woman at the original meeting in London. The old woman with hennaed hair, *'I can walk ... I'm walking,'* she had cried out as she stumbled across the stage.

'I'd love one, thanks,' Jessica said, as she turned to see the tiny, bird-like woman she had seen come out of Xavier's study. She had noticed her on odd occasions about the place. Her hair was dark, not red. She was young, not old. But it was her voice ... Jessica felt the room reel. Did this mean everything was a sham, including her own healing? She sat down quickly, afraid her legs would not support her.

'Here, you all right?'

'Fine, just fed up with kitchen duties.'

'Aren't we all? Let me, I'll finish the porridge,' the woman said kindly, and crossed to the cooker on slim, mobile, healthy legs.

Jessica willed herself to think she had made a mistake. Not the cures, please don't let there be anything bent about them ... She spoke silently to the God she had not bothered in years.

2

The relief with which H.G. greeted her made Jessica feel guilty that she hadn't come to see him for the last couple of nights.

'You needed time to think about me and decide whether or not I was just a raving, stupid old man.'

'No, of course not,' she said. He looked at her cynically. 'Well, yes, something like that. It just all seemed ...'

'Unlikely, I know.' His smile was genuine, beautiful

and lit his fine face with humanity, quite unlike the false, saccharine and vacant smiles she'd become uséd to in the past few weeks. 'Xavier is very plausible, isn't he? You did not talk about me to anyone?'

'No. I wanted to, but I decided I couldn't. If you had spoken the truth, it would have been too risky.'

'Excellent! So what has made you change your mind?'

'I'm good at identifying voices – not surprising, given my profession. I listen and I can identify where a person spent their formative years. It was a bit of a party trick – until tonight. I recognised a voice without seeing who was talking. I hadn't put the voice to the face before, you see, since the first time I heard her she was in disguise.'

'And?'

'I didn't like it.'

'That's all?' He made no effort to hide his annoyance.

'No, of course it was much more serious. I was – we were all conned. I feel so stupid to have fallen for it.'

'Then you're not alone. Xavier fools many people. He fooled me. If you don't want to talk about it ...' He shrugged as if he didn't care, but she thought he did.

'Maybe another time,' she replied. She was loath to talk about the false 'miracle' cure. She felt that if she did her own cure would disappear and the pain would be back. She was not ready to face that. 'There was something else. My friend – well ... rather, a person I thought was my friend has just upped and left.'

'Did you find it strange behaviour?'

'Quite honestly, yes. She seemed a polite person.'

'Maybe she hasn't gone.'

'She has. Xavier gave her a lift to the station.'

'Is that what he told you? Then ...' He raised an eyebrow questioningly.

'I believed him.'

'You were meant to.'

'I feel like one of those dogs tortured by that Russian,

Pavlov wasn't it? – one minute I'm steeped in suspicion, the next I think I'm imagining things. I'm like a yo-yo – and I'm not normally like this, I'm usually decisive.'

'Just up against an expert. Xavier can manipulate you any way he wants. This "con" that is bothering you so much. I can promise you he will explain it to you in such a way that you will end up apologising to him for doubting him. He's evil, Jessica. You must listen to me. You are at such risk. If you get sucked in, then your family and friends can say goodbye to you for ever. You'll be manipulated, degraded. In the end you'll no longer exist as you are now, you'll be a vacant husk, an automaton reacting as and when he wants you to. You have to get away from here.'

'But my hip.'

'You can get help for that.'

'But not like Xavier's. He's a genius.'

'Is he? Are you sure? And what's more important? Your hip or your soul?'

Jessica laughed – she had to at his use of such melodramatic words. If only she could call Selina, in Finchester, her mind would be put at rest.

H.G. watched her face intently, saw the swings between belief and disbelief and knew they had to act before Xavier was able to control her.

'I've a plan.' He leant forward eagerly.

'What's that?' she asked, but thinking, with a sinking heart, I thought you might. She should have stayed away and not let guilt and sentiment get in the way of her own safety. Yet her thinking that word *safety* told her that if half the time she liked to think all was innocence and light here, her subconscious was working on a different tack. 'Tell me your plan, I'm interested, really.' She'd seen the look of disappointment on his face and the flaming guilt interfered again. When this was all resolved she was determined to return to her old ways and never feel guilty about others ever again – it was uncomfortable and disruptive.

'I'm too weak to escape, that's obvious.'

She sighed inwardly with relief.

'I've got to build up some muscle so that I can stand – you can't carry me, can you?'

'Impossible.'

'Exactly. So my plan is blissfully simple. You see that tray over there on the secretaire? It contains the ampoules of the drug they give me. You pierce the ampoules at the top, siphon out the drug and replace it with distilled water. Then when they inject me I will pretend a paralysis. While I'm alone I can exercise my muscles, even lying here in bed.'

'Simple? You're joking! How do I doctor the ampoules? They're glass.'

'No, plastic. A sharp needle can pierce the top and they won't leak since they are kept upright in a small rack.'

'They'll see the hole.'

'Hardly. It will be a pinprick and the lighting in here is quite subdued, even in day-time.'

'And how long is this muscle-building likely to take?'

'I'm not aiming to run the marathon, simply to get myself to the side door and into the motor vehicle that you will have driven round.' He sounded as dignified as he looked.

'I'm sorry to be difficult, but how do I get a car?'

'You take one, of course.'

'I haven't driven in years.'

'That's no problem – it's like riding a bicycle, you never forget.'

'Then you drive.'

'I never learnt. Jessica, you put so many obstacles in the way that I begin to wonder if you really want to help me.'

'Of course I do. I come and see you, don't I? And if

even a little bit of what you say is correct than that is fairly foolhardy of me.' It was her turn to feel exasperated. 'And another thing, where do I get distilled water from at this time of night?'

'My bathroom. In the medicine chest you'll find a small bottle, enough for our needs. Now hurry! We haven't got all night!' And the querulousness of an old man was back in his voice.

His bathroom was sumptuous – so much, again, for his lack of interest in money! She opened the large glass-fronted cabinet and found an array of pills, medicines and creams. She found the water bottle fairly easily and was about to close the cabinet when her hand froze in mid-air at the sound of voices in H.G.'s bedroom.

She stood rooted to the spot afraid to breathe. Slowly she turned to face the half-open door. She preferred to confront whoever it was and the danger head-on.

'He's out for the count,' she heard a woman say. 'You sure he never wakes up? In the night?'

'No. Never.' It was Xavier. 'Shall we top him up? Just to be on the safe side.'

'And kill him? What would be the point?' The woman's voice was low and muffled. Was it Bethina? 'We need him to be alive, especially with the Yanks arriving this weekend.' It wasn't Bethina, but who was it? It was a voice she recognised and couldn't place – she was losing her touch, perhaps too much going on in her head. Then the woman sneezed and Jessica felt vindicated – a cold alters the voice.

'Poor old bugger. He never hurt anyone,' she heard Xavier say.

'Don't get sentimental on me now.'

'Christ, I'll be glad when this lot's over. That bloody woman gives me the creeps – she's got stretch-marks. What I do for money!'

337

The woman laughed. 'Not long now. Look, the bathroom light's on. Did you leave it on?'

'I'll see to it. You straighten him up.'

This is it! thought Jessica, heart pounding, sweat trickling down her back. Her mind was blank, she couldn't think of any excuse.

Xavier's hand appeared around the edge of the door. 'Hurry up,' he said to his companion, as he felt for the tapestry light pull and plunged her into darkness. He didn't bother to look in.

'You don't think the old cow will hear the noise?' he asked.

'No way. With the sedative I gave you to give her she wouldn't hear a bomb go off. Ready?'

'Should we knock on her door, check she's asleep?'

'No need.' The woman's confidence made Jessica smile. 'Old cow' indeed! But no longer could she ignore the truth ...

'It's OK, the coast's clear,' H.G. said softly. 'Now do you believe me? That they want me dead. That my days are numbered. That they are going to kill me.' As he enunciated each statement, he raised his voice until she feared that soon he would be shouting.

'Come on, H.G., calm yourself. You're getting over-excited.'

'Over-excited!' He looked as if he would explode with rage.

'Obviously they're up to no good—'

'The heavens be praised! She begins to see. I've a glimmer of hope!'

'Who was that with him?'

'I don't know her name – I've only seen her a couple of times before. She's hard.'

'What does she look like?'

'Young, plainish – does it matter? We've the ampoules to fix and you must work quickly.'

338

He was evidently used to getting his own way. He might at least say please, she thought as, despite her unpractised hands, she doctored the ampoules. She only hoped he was right and that they wouldn't notice. The interruption had shown her one thing; she was best off getting out of here – sharpish. She'd forget his half-baked rescue plan, she was sure they'd never get away with it. Far better for her to get herself away from Porthwood and go to the police – get them to raid the place. None of this was her responsibility. Why should she sort it out? Let them.

3

It was a sleepy-eyed Ginnie who glanced at her watch, noted it was nearly three in the morning and tumbled out of bed to go to the door of her room.

'Who is it?' she asked, before she opened it, hoping it was Xavier.

'Mathie and Morveen.'

She let them in. 'What do you want? It's so late.'

Mathie held up a richly embroidered deep-burgundy-coloured velvet cloak. 'You're to strip and put this on and come with us.'

'Why do I have to strip?'

'We do not ask questions when Xavier commands.'

'Of course. I'm sorry.' Rapidly she raised her night-dress over her head, wishing they would not stare. She hated others to see her body.

'Ready?' Mathie asked, and now Ginnie saw that both she and Morveen carried candles in sconces. Before they left the room, Mathie swung a censer from side to side releasing a soft plume of sweetly scented smoke.

In the corridor Ginnie found six other women waiting,

all holding candles, all with leaves and flowers twined prettily in their hair, all wearing ornate Venetian masks. They formed into a procession, four in front of her and four behind, Ginnie regally in the centre.

She held her head high. This was something important. Xavier had sent for her in this ceremonious way, with this lovely robe, because something was afoot – something grand. Perhaps she was to enter the movement officially. Or maybe he had chosen tonight to declare his involvement with her. She clasped her hands tightly at the idea. Maybe it was to be something like a wedding ceremony. The fact that she was still married to Carter floated across her mind and was dismissed. There were weddings and weddings. Her nuptials with Xavier would be a spiritual occasion. They had no need of the law.

She walked slowly down the stairs and along the seemingly endless corridors of the vast old house. It was too slow for Ginnie who wanted to speed to her fate, not plod along.

As they neared the long gallery a drumbeat began and Ginnie found herself walking in step with it.

The gallery was closely curtained, lit as before by thick cream candles. Logs blazed in the two stone fireplaces. The sweet smell of gardenia hung in the air.

The followers, robed and masked, stood in an oblong around the long, marble table, which was supported at each end by gilt eagles with outspread wings. It normally stood in front of the alcove to the side of the room, but tonight it was in the centre.

Someone, she could not quite see who for the room was gloomy, stepped forward and spread a white fur on the table. Another placed a white satin cushion at one end. The drumming persisted, gentle, sibilant, hypnotic. The group around the edge began to hum a resonant melodic sound, mesmerising too.

They reached the table – like an altar, she thought,

with mounting excitement. All it lacked was a golden cross and a Bible.

Mathie took hold of the collar of the cloak and began to remove it. Ginnie clasped it to her. She'd no intention of standing stark naked in front of everyone – whatever next! Mathie jerked at the cloak and an undignified tussle would have ensued if Xavier had not stepped forward. He was dressed, as always, in midnight blue, but tonight a white velvet cloak was draped around him, dramatically swept back over one shoulder so that the red silk lining flashed against the blue and white like a livid scar.

'You've nothing to be ashamed of. Now release it,' he ordered.

She allowed Mathie to take it and stood, naked, embarrassed and vulnerable, before the whole community. Instinctively she placed her arms across her breasts and crossed her legs but Mathie and Morveen prised her hands apart and forced her arms up from her sides until they were held horizontally away from her body.

'Stand with your feet apart,' Xavier ordered, and, of course, she did so immediately.

A white light flashed, blinding her momentarily so that she could no longer see anyone other than those in the bright spot with her.

Xavier held a gold cup to her lips and told her to drink. Not wanting to disobey and anger him, she did as he said. It was a good, rich wine.

'What's happening, Xavier?' she dared to ask.

'You're becoming one of us. Tonight we shall rename you and you shall be reborn.'

As soon as the chalice was taken from her two women stepped forward. One began to put flowers in her hair, the other to wash her. First her face, gently with warm scented towels, then her arms. She was followed by a second who attended to her hands, and a third her legs and feet. One stepped forward to attend to her back, another to her chest, gently cleansing her nipples, kneading her breasts. She jolted upright and nearly fell as she felt someone washing her genitalia, another her buttocks. An overly intimate washing, but one that was arousing her so rapidly, so shamelessly, that she feared she would not be able to continue to stand. She had consciously to stop herself closing her thighs together to trap whoever's hand was there, so pleasurable was it.

She found herself beginning to sway to the beat of the drum, to give herself over entirely to this pleasure, such sweet pleasure – readying her, she was certain, for Xavier, her man.

Strong arms lifted her and she was laid, reverently it felt, on the table. She lay naked, exposed, with a dreamy expression. She closed her eyes, enjoying the experience and felt rather than saw that someone had climbed up beside her and was astride her.

'Xavier,' she sighed, as she was roughly entered. And she writhed her pelvis up towards him, wishing they were alone – but then, oddly, discovering she was doubly excited at the idea of everyone watching their coupling. 'Xavier,' she repeated, and opened her eyes to see an ornate gold mask above her. But the hair around it was that of a blond man, who was riding into her, his head back and yelling as he came inside her. 'But ...' she began, but there was no time and another man was upon her and taking her and then another and another. The drumbeat and the chanting persisted and she lost count of how many there were.

The excitement in the room mounted as the others, aroused by what they saw, clasped and grabbed each other, mounting and entering. Some were with one sex and some with another, and Ginnie, still on her table, felt every one of her orifices filled with someone else. She found that not knowing who it was excited her.

And before daybreak she, too, had joined in with the

others as they drank, took drugs and pleasured each other, endlessly, through the night in every bodily position in every combination of couplings. All the time the video cameras relentlessly turned.

chapter **fifteen**

1

'Matt, could I possibly have a word?' Jessica grabbed hold of his arm as he stood in the self-service queue in the dining room where he was just about to have lunch. 'I've been looking for you all morning.'

'That's nice.' He grinned. 'Not now,' he said, under his breath.

'I don't know who else to—' she whispered urgently.

'Caleb – hi! What do you think the weather will do this weekend? More storms?' He was talking to the man ahead of him in the queue, who was piling his tray with the largest assortment of food.

'It's—' she began.

'Do you know Caleb, Jessica? He's our accountant, expert weatherman and Xavier's right hand.'

'Hello. What a strange mixture. You're interested in the weather, then? As a hobby?' she asked, hoping to cover her tracks.

'I've a small meteorological station on the roof. I've always kept records, ever since I was a child. You know, rainfalls, min and max temperatures, wind speeds.'

'How absolutely fascinating.'

'You're interested too?'

'In a minor way ...' The conversation about the weather creaked on and Jessica marvelled at how much the man could find to say about the subject. She wondered if he collected train numbers, too.

'It looks as if this afternoon will be fine enough for a walk. The snowdrops are a sight to see in the wood behind the tennis court,' Matt said, pointedly not looking at Jessica.

'A bit cold for me.' Jessica pulled her shawl around her.

'Are you not eating, Jessica?' Caleb asked, seeing she had no tray.

'I'm not hungry. I'll just have some tea.' She smiled her most professional smile at him and, like most men when confronted by it, he melted in its beam.

'You sit down and I'll bring it over.'

Not quick enough to think of an excuse, she reluctantly took a seat and waited for him. Perhaps he was interested in UFOs too.

An hour later she found Matt clearing undergrowth. As she approached, limping up the steep wooded hillside, she saw that he was not alone. Tristram, his back to her, was sitting on a log, smoking a cigarette. She bent to pick some of the snowdrops Matt had talked about to make her presence less suspicious. Matt saw her, jerked his head towards Tristram and frowned.

'Tut, tut! Smoking, Tristram?' she said, and, despite her nervousness, she injected an amused note into her voice. 'What would Xavier say?'

The young man leapt off the log as if stung, a look of horror on his face, his cigarette cupped in the palm of his hand, just as she'd hidden cigarettes as a schoolgirl.

'If you went behind that large oak tree over there then I wouldn't see you, so I wouldn't have to tell, and then, more importantly, I could rest awhile on your log.'

'Fine. Sure. You're a brick.' And obediently he did exactly as she'd suggested and moved a good fourteen feet away behind the vast tree trunk.

'Can he hear? Is it safe?' she asked.

'Nowhere is. I have a goon watching me all the time. I'll come to your room tonight.'

'What time?'

'I don't know. Is there a problem?'

She thought for a second of H.G. 'Before midnight would be best.'

He looked at her with uncomprehending annoyance, but she had no intention of saying anything about H.G. – not yet.

She and Matt discussed the snowdrops for a minute or two, then. 'It's safe now,' she called out cheerily to Tristram and made her way back down the hill. At least if Matt was being spied on she'd probably chosen the right person to help her.

'Nice walk?' Xavier asked her, as she entered the hall, cheeks coloured from the cold, eyes sparkling from the fresh air.

'Lovely. See, I've picked some snowdrops. I thought maybe you could have someone put them by poor H.G.'s bed.' She held them out.

'How very thoughtful of you. What a dear you are, Jessica.'

Beside him, Ginnie scowled at her as if she'd presented the flowers to Xavier himself.

'Good afternoon, Ginnie,' she said, thinking how awful Ginnie looked – pale, thin and with a haunted look in her eyes. Ginnie did not reply.

'Say hello to the nice lady, Heliotrope,' Xavier ordered. 'Heliotrope is Ginnie's new name.'

'Hello,' she said sulkily, which made Xavier laugh. Jessica tried not to. Heliotrope! What sort of a name was that?

'You'll have to excuse her, Jessica, she's in a bit of a grump today. Didn't get enough sleep last night, did you, Heliotrope?' This last sentence made him laugh again, as if he had said something highly amusing.

'Have you seen Tessa, Ginnie? I'd hoped she'd come on my walk with me.'

'No,' Ginnie said shortly.

'Asleep, probably – you know the young, Jessica.'

'But it's early afternoon!'

'She often sleeps all day and stays up all night,' Ginnie said.

'I was like that once.' Jessica smiled.

'We must find something to amuse her tonight, mustn't we, Heliotrope?' He grinned at her, and Jessica noticed how Ginnie tossed her head, as if tossing away the comment and realised there was a hidden agenda.

'Still, we must get going, Jessica. Things to do ...' And, still grinning, he led Ginnie by the hand into his study.

'Sit down. How are you?' he asked.

'Sore and ashamed.'

'I expect you are. My, how you enjoyed yourself.'

'I didn't.'

'You need not lie to me, Ginnie. It's me, Xavier.'

'It wasn't me. There was something in my drink. I wouldn't normally behave like that – you know I wouldn't.'

'I know no such thing.'

'But I love you, Xavier. You know I do. I'll do anything for you. Last night they said it was for you – that I couldn't be one of you without it. And I wanted that more than anything.'

'Then you'll want to please me?'

'Of course.'

'Anything I ask?'

'Anything.'

'A million pounds, then,' he said baldly.

'I'm sorry?'

'You heard,' he said coldly, and she shivered as if the coldness in his voice had touched her physically.

'But I don't have that amount of money in my account.'

'I realise that. I want you to phone your bank, write to

347

them confirming all the usual – to sell shares, property, whatever.'

'They'll want to see me.'

'They can't. They don't have to. What you do is your business. I'm disappointed, and here I was thinking you loved me.'

'But so much!'

'That's the price if you want to stay, if you want me to make love to you again.'

'I don't think I can. Imagine the trouble this will cause with my husband. I'll give you everything when I've divorced him and when ...' She was going to say when they were married but she lost the courage.

'I'd hoped you wouldn't make this difficult and I don't want to do this but ...' He crossed the room to the television. 'You see, if you won't give me the money a copy of this will be sent to your bank, your husband, and especially one to your mother-in-law. And, of course, I can send someone to wake young Tessa. Show her what her mother is really like. Now, you don't want that humiliation, do you? You don't want your in-laws to see how right they were all along and what a little slag you truly are.' He pressed the play button on the video recorder. The screen flickered to life.

Ginnie pressed herself back into the chair as if trying to distance herself from the images on the screen. Her fist shot to her mouth. 'Oh, no,' she wailed, at the sight of herself at last night's orgy. What distressed her most was the expression on her face – smiling, happy, laughing and, evidently, having the time of her life.

2

Jessica could not sit still. She was pacing back and forth – she couldn't have done it a couple of weeks ago before Xavier's work on her hip. It was one o'clock and Matt had not come. The old man must be in a terrible state. She was torn between going to him – scary though that was after last night's close call – and waiting for Matt.

At a gentle tapping on her door she rushed to open it.

'I said—' she began, but before she could continue he'd clamped his hand over her mouth, pushed her back into the room and shut the door, all in one swift movement. Jessica felt fear rush at her with the speed of a train and her legs buckled. She'd been wrong! He was one of them! Still with his hand in place he marched her towards the bathroom. Dear God, was he going to drown her? He kicked the door shut, leant over the bath and turned the shower jet on full. Only then did he let her go.

'Sorry about that but your room might be bugged – I know two that are.'

'Good God! I'm a wreck now. I said to come before midnight!'

'Forgive me!' he replied sarcastically. 'Have you any idea how difficult it's been for me to get here? I told you, I'm watched all the time.'

'Why?'

'They don't trust me.'

'How did you get here?' she asked suspiciously, lowering herself onto the bathroom stool.

'I got Tristram very drunk on a bottle of brandy I'd nicked. He's passed out and won't wake before morning – at least I hope not.' He sat on the lavatory lid.

'Why are you under suspicion?'

'Loads of reasons. The most important, for the

moment, is Selina. Xavier had warned us both off each other.'

'Selina didn't tell me.'

'She didn't have time.'

'She certainly left in a hurry.'

'Correction. She hasn't left, she's here.'

'You're joking!'

'Not about this. She's locked in a room in the cellar – they call it the Reclamation Room, it's used for their isolation techniques. It's a dreadful place. I managed to see her last night during the orgy – everyone was too occupied to notice that I wasn't there.'

'Orgy! Here!' Her eyes widened with surprise. 'The noise – of course.'

'Sorry?'

'Nothing. Just something I overheard,' she said guardedly. That must have been the noise that Xavier and his companion had been worried she would hear.

'I can't see Selina during the day. The minders never leave me.'

'But why is she there?'

'I'm not sure. I reckon she's signed over the shop to them and doesn't know it. Also she's concerned about Ginnie and Esmeralda. Maybe she asked one question too many. They know that if she left she'd spill the beans, especially when she discovers the shop isn't hers any more. As you know, she's a feisty bird so they're giving her the isolation treatment. It works on sense deprivation – no light, total silence or white noise, no food, no sleep. They want her to join.'

'But what use would she be if she didn't want to be here?'

'But she will if she stays there any longer. When they come to release her she'll be so relieved she'll think they're her guardian angels. She'll be begging to join them. Then she'll do anything they want. I've got to stop it. You see, they use women like Selina as whores. They're made available for important guests, people they owe favours to.'

'Dear God!'

'The local police are involved and I'm checking out if other constabularies are too. And, of course, there are the bank employees—'

'Banks?'

'Oh, yes, and doctors, civil servants – it's like a giant web. Someone shows interest in Fohpal and they run a check on them – their finances, medical records, the lot. These informants have to be paid and a bonk can be an extra reward.'

'Good God. Would they have done a search on me?'

'Undoubtedly. And Ginnie. That's why Xavier has focused on her. She'll be pleading with him to take her money by the time he's finished with her. They also use the women as bait for blackmail. If someone resists joining or contributing, they lure them into sex and video what goes on. If Ginnie was crabby and old and they thought she knew too much, if she was no longer useful to them, she'd disappear.'

Jessica shuddered visibly and wondered at what age you were considered old around here. 'Ginnie's daughter's here too – she's beautiful.'

'I saw her. She'll be one of them in no time.'

'Why, if you know all this and disapprove, do you stay?'

'My sister and her kids are in the movement. Nothing I say gets through to her so I'm building a dossier to get them closed down. Look, is all this necessary? We're wasting time.'

'Yes, I'm sorry, I think it is. Who are they?' All this was even more far-fetched than H.G.'s accusations. Was it a line? Was he a good actor? Was he trapping her?

'Xavier, of course, but he's the figure-head, not the leader. That's one of the women, I'm certain. Not Mathie, she's too lazy. Hesta's away too often to be in total control. My money's on Bethina. Look, I'm sorry, Jessica, you're just going to have to believe me. We've *got* to get Selina out. Do you drive?'

'I haven't for ages. My stiff knee makes it impossible.'

'It'll have to be possible tonight. I've wheeled one of the cars to that copse overlooking the sea. I'll fetch Selina now and meet you there. She needs a hospital – she's ill, pneumonia, I think.'

'Hang on a minute, I just said I can't drive.'

'You'll have to.'

'What about you? Why don't you?'

'I have to stay.'

'Why?'

'Haven't you listened to anything? If I put a foot wrong, my sister will be killed.' He spoke quietly, but emphatically.

'I believe most of what you say – the sexual abuse, the dodgy measures by which people are kept here. It's possible people are "persuaded" to release large sums of money – Ginnie for one. And I wouldn't be in the least surprised if Xavier has his fingers in the till. But murder? Oh, come on, Matt. Here? This is England, not Waco!'

'Jessica, millions of pounds are involved. When you're outside check me out – I'm working with an organisation which helps people get their families out of cults and deprogrammes them. Here, let me give you the number.' He scribbled it down.

'But why didn't you tell Selina? Why me?'

'I wanted her to know, but I was afraid if I told her she'd be in danger. It was hard not to. It hurt like hell when I could see she distrusted me. I'm terrified I've left it too late, that I should have got you all out sooner.

352

Something's afoot. You've *got* to go too. It's not safe for you either.'

'I'm safe enough. Not to put too fine a point on it, I'm too bloody famous for them to disappear me!' She snorted with amusement. 'And I'd refuse to co-operate in anything dodgy.'

'You won't have a choice. Your hip is much better, right? It's down to hypnosis.'

'No, it couldn't be. I'd know.'

'Then you don't know anything about hypnosis.'

'I know you can't be made to do anything you wouldn't normally do. I couldn't be made to murder someone if it's not already in me to be a killer.'

'Exactly, but a subject can be made to do virtually anything else. And hypnosis can certainly remove pain. My mother gave birth to me in a post-hypnotic state – she wasn't even asleep and felt hardly any pain. The pain was there, of course, she just didn't feel it. Hence your hip.'

'But he hasn't done that to me. I'd remember.'

'Not necessarily. Not if he told you to forget you'd been hypnotised, while you were still under. Told you to forget the crystal he uses.'

'The crystal!' Her hand shot to her neck. 'I remember the crystal.'

'Then he made a boob there. He's brilliant. The best. He had a stage show once, called himself Carlos de Santos. A young girl he'd hypnotised on stage went home and threw herself out of a window and was crippled for life. A court case was pending so he did a bunk to California. That's where he met H.G. and joined Fohpal – it was legit then. There's nothing wrong with the old man, he just lost control and Xavier and co. have cunningly built on his respectability.'

At the mention of H.G.'s name Jessica glanced towards

the door. Poor old man, what must he be thinking? – What could she do?

'Hypnosis and drugs – this place is alive with them. And people looking for that special something. It's easy. Heard enough? Are you on? Have I convinced you?'

'We might crash!'

'No, you won't. I'll be fifteen minutes. If I don't turn up after twenty, put your foot down and go like a bat out of hell. See you.' And he was gone.

Jessica turned off the shower, collected her handbag and stuffed the hexagonal-shaped papers of H.G.'s writing into a linen bag. She would have to leave everything else.

Once in the small stone-clad hall outside H.G.'s suite she struggled with the bolts on the old oak door, which were stiff from lack of use. Once she had finally pulled them back she glanced at H.G.'s door. She couldn't just disappear without saying goodbye. She silently opened his door and crossed to his bedroom.

'H.G. she whispered, and tiptoed to his bedside. She need not have worried – he was either asleep or drugged.

''Bye, old man. Sorry to leave you. I'll get help,' she said, and kissed his cheek.

3

Tessa raised her head from her pillow but lay back again as pain shot through her temples. There was a horrible taste in her mouth. Gingerly she sat up again, looked at her watch and saw that she had been asleep for nearly twenty hours – a record, even for her!

Sluggishly she got off the bed and crossed to the bathroom. Despite cleaning her teeth several times the taste would not go away. Her head throbbed, she felt sick and woozy.

She'd been drugged.

The idea made her stomach lurch. She hung onto the side of the basin as she studied herself in the mirror. She looked the same, but it all added up. The length of her sleep, the taste in her mouth, the pounding headache, worse than any hangover she'd experienced in her short drinking career. She felt ill and she was never ill. She sluiced her face with cold water.

When, though, and how? She'd eaten the same as everyone else. Had drunk from the same water jug. And then she remembered Bethina's hot chocolate – her special, she had called it. That was it. It had to be. And Bethina was so kind and sweet, which made it worse somehow. She suddenly felt intensely alone and wished she had not come. But, at that thought, she yanked the brush through her hair making herself wince. The pain stopped her thinking along those lines. It wasn't going to help anyone and would get her nowhere.

Back in her room she dressed in jeans and sweater. She squirted on some scent to give her courage, then sat on the bed and wondered what on earth to do.

From the chimney she took her mobile phone and, with a nail file, tried to take off the back but couldn't. Her stomach churned alarmingly and her palms dampened. She realised she had never been so scared in her whole life.

She slipped off the bed – this inactivity was making her feel worse and she needed to be doing something. It was cold so she put on her ski jacket, picked up her shoulder bag and, standing tall, made herself march from the room as if she hadn't a care.

All was darkness as she moved through the sleeping house. There was a low light on at the top of the wide staircase. In the hall she pulled at the red telephone kiosk door, but it was locked, as was the office. She wandered around several rooms looking for another phone, not really expecting to find one, but hoping all the same.

Back in the hall she wondered which wing Jessica's room was in – she knew it was on the ground floor. Still, she could hardly crash around barging into other people's rooms. But she needed to talk to someone, so she let herself out of the main door and walked, cursing the crunching gravel, around to the back where her MG was parked.

The car keys were not in her bag! She searched again systematically. She *always* put her keys in the side pocket, she never failed. Her mother spent ages each day searching for her own keys and Tessa, who had been given this car last birthday, had vowed never to be like that. So they'd been taken. But she smiled as she bent down and felt under the chassis for the small bag with a spare key, which she kept there in case her handbag was stolen. There were areas of Tessa's life in which she was so organised she amazed herself.

She free-wheeled the car down the slope from the courtyard where the others cars were parked. She would not drive through the estate: she'd seen a small road down by the seashore, she'd take that and see where it led – hopefully to the main road.

She drove slowly past a small copse and her heart leapt into her mouth at the sight of a car parked so that it was only visible from the sea. But she relaxed when she saw that no one was in it and pressed on.

Half an hour later she was banging on the door of the cottage. 'Dad!' she yelled, but it was Humphrey who answered it.

'Tessa, are you all right?' His concern was apparent. 'Jessica?'

'I'm fine. She's fine. I think they doped me and

buggered my phone.' Distanced from Porthwood she felt all her old confidence return.

'Come in. Sit down. Tea? Coffee?'

'Brandy?' She grinned at him. 'Is Dad okay?' She looked around at the chaotic sitting room, littered with empty glasses and bottles. The cottage had the musty smell of a summer-holiday house in winter.

'He's fine. Out like a light. I'll get him.'

Tessa sat sipping the brandy, feeling its comforting warmth slide down her throat and into her veins. She looked up as Humphrey lumbered down the narrow staircase.

'He's asleep,' he said.

'So? Can't you wake him?'

'I didn't like to.' It fascinated her to see such a large, confident man look embarrassed as if this state was the preserve of the young.

'More likely you couldn't wake him. He's drunk, isn't he?' She laughed. 'Don't worry, I'm not upset. He often is – it's his solution, poor old Dad. I'd better warn you, though, when he's like this he's out for the count so if this cottage caught fire you'd have to rescue him.'

Karl appeared, rubbing his eyes. 'I'll put the kettle on, then I'll feel a bit more civilised.' He stumbled in the direction of the kitchen, leaving Humphrey and Tessa alone again.

'Tell me about Jessica,' Humphrey said and leant forward eagerly. 'She's not hurt in any way?'

'No, she's fine – she's moving really well now. I think she wants to stay.'

'Oh.' He sat back despondently.

'Don't get me wrong. It's the treatment. She's not taken in by anything else – she warned me to be careful. As soon as she can she'll be out of there. She loves you, you know. It's in her eyes when she talks about you – they go all misty.'

357

'And your mother?' Humphrey's voice was suddenly gruff, as if he needed to change the subject.

Tessa looked about her furtively. 'If I tell you, you won't repeat a word to my father?'

'I promise.'

'I think she's in love with Xavier.'

'Oh dear.'

'He's the ultimate dork – I don't understand it. And she doesn't want me there, that's for sure.' A flicker of the rejection she had felt showed on her face. 'I asked Jessica if my mother was on drugs – there's a sort of hysteria about her – but she said she thought not. But after my chocolate was spiked – anything's possible. She wants to stay – there's no doubt about that.'

'Obviously we don't want your father knowing this at the moment – he'd rush in and make things worse. But I'd like your permission to discuss this with Karl.'

'Discuss what?' Karl asked, as he returned with a tray of tea. Humphrey looked questioningly at Tessa, who began to put Karl in the picture.

'This is what I feared. We've got to get them out,' Karl said when she had finished.

'What about the police?'

'Dodgy, Humph. Did I tell you that my contact is certain a member of the local police is involved? No, it's down to us.'

'But what if my mother won't come?'

'We're going to have to snatch her,' Humphrey suggested.

'Then what? You can't go around making an adult woman do something she doesn't want to,' Karl replied. 'Just imagine the legal complications that would occur from kidnapping her. The mind boggles!'

'You've done it before, you said,' Tessa pointed out.

'They were children.'

'If Tessa's right we would seem not to have much choice. I think Carter will agree to it. And, in any case, is it kidnap if it's her husband snatching her?'

'She'll resent us horribly – we'll be the enemy. But once the debriefing begins I'll be able to show her what a charlatan he is. It'll be hard for her because she's believed totally in him and the group and she'll suffer feelings of disloyalty. It takes time, you know, and she won't be totally back with you for weeks. Some subjects take months of counselling.'

'If we could get her to waver while she's there, she'd leave of her own free will. It wouldn't be so traumatic, would it?'

'Yes, Tessa, but how?'

'I could get Xavier interested in me – no problem. She might hate me for a bit but I could eventually explain.'

'Too dangerous.' Karl rubbed the stubble on his chin. 'He'd go too far, no doubt of that.'

'I can look after myself.'

'Quite honestly, Tessa, I don't think you should go back. They must be on to you – drugging your drink, putting the phone out.'

'I've been thinking about that. Maybe they wanted me zonked out so I didn't see or crash in on a meeting or something. And phones break, don't they?'

Humphrey's 'umm' sounded his doubt.

'She's our best chance, Humph.'

'In any case, I only came here tonight to let you know about the telephone. I intend to go back. I don't think snatching mum will do any good at all. But if you don't mind, I'm starving. Got anything to eat?'

'In that case,' Humphrey pulled a briefcase across the floor, 'you'd better take this.'

'It's minute!' Tessa looked at the Motorola Star TAC he handed her.

'Smallest there is. I'll have all calls to it interrupted so it doesn't ring. Use it to call us any time, night or day. We won't be repeating this.' He indicated the empty bottles.

'Steak sandwich do you, Tessa?' Karl asked.

'Awesome!'

4

Jessica found the car hidden in the clump of trees overlooking the sea. Sitting behind the wheel she practised pumping the brake pedal up and down, testing her stiff right knee. Each time it was a little easier. She had butterflies in her stomach – she hadn't driven for so long and was afraid she'd forgotten how to.

Alerted by the cracking of a twig, she looked up to see Matt carrying Selina. She leant backwards to open the door for him to place her on the back seat.

'Oh, my God!' Jessica said, horrified at her friend's condition. She was dirty, smelly and bedraggled.

'I know. I look dreadful, don't I?'

'How are you?'

'Grim and confused.' Selina managed a smile from her prone position on the back seat.

'Her temperature's down – I think she's far better than we had a right to expect.'

'She looks doped.'

'She might be but it's more likely the result of the disorientation. Another twelve hours and she'd be turned.'

'No I wouldn't. I'm tough!' she said, with pride. 'But oh, Christ, I'm starving.'

Matt gave them directions to get out of the estate, which Jessica was convinced she'd never be able to follow. She started the car.

'You said the grounds were alarmed?'

'It's okay. I switched it off.'

'Matt! Why aren't you coming?' Selina looked up at him, beseechingly.

'I can't. Jessica will explain.' He blew her a kiss, then turned and ran back to the house.

'Dumped again!' Selina said bitterly.

'I've got to concentrate on getting out of here, but then I'll tell you everything,' said Jessica, as she put the car into gear.

Jessica had thought she knew all about fear, but this bore no relation to the stage variety. She drove hunched over the wheel, grating the gears, the route lit only by a moon that constantly disappeared behind scudding clouds. But somehow she'd followed Matt's instructions for at last they reached the public road. They lunged between the gate posts, she straightened the vehicle, switched on the headlights and, with her foot down, they sped towards the city.

More confident of her driving now, Jessica settled in the seat. 'You mustn't think badly of Matt, Selina ...' She glanced in the rear-view mirror and saw that, despite the bumping and rattling and her dreadful driving, Selina was fast asleep.

Jessica had never been in an NHS hospital in her life: the London Clinic was more her style. She was not prepared for the busyness of the casualty department at this time in the morning. There were drunks, a tramp looking for some warmth, and they arrived at the same time as the victims of a multi-car crash on the bypass, which added to the chaos.

Furious at the off-hand attitude of the uninterested receptionist and fuming at the disorganisation, she found a wheelchair and pushed it out to the car.

'Selina, can you slide out?'

She was answered by a groan. 'Selina. Please. I can't lift you and I can't get anyone to help me. You're going to have to help yourself. Selina!' She bent down and yelled in her ear.

'Bloody hell! Where's the fire?' Selina laughed as if she hadn't a care in the world.

'Selina. Please. This is important.'

'Fine. Yes. I'll try. Where am I? I feel dreadful.' Selina shuffled across the back seat, her legs hanging out of the door, her face sleepy and confused.

'You're at the hospital. They'll look after you here. You're safe now,' Jessica said, gently this time.

'Jessica!' Selina stood up, looking dazed. 'Jessica! Oh, my God, it's coming back. I'm remembering ...'

'It's all right, I'm here.'

'Jesus!' Selina began to shake. She put up her arm to shield her eyes as if she could protect herself from her returning memory. 'I've been so scared. The noise! I thought I was going to die.' She clung to Jessica and sagged into her arms. Jessica steadied herself against the car.

'Try to stand on your own, Selina. I can't hold you up. It's okay. You'll be fine now. I promise. It's over.' She helped her into the wheelchair.

'Where's Ginnie? I must find Ginnie.' Selina began to get out of the chair.

'She didn't want to come, Selina. She's decided to stay.'

Selina shook her head as if to get rid of the cobwebs in her mind. 'Christ, Jessica. How did I get us into this mess? Why didn't I twig things weren't right earlier?'

'It wasn't just you – none of us wanted to and we shut off any warning signs. Now, I've never handled one of these things before. Hold on!' With difficulty she pushed the wheelchair up the ramp towards the casualty department.

'You're Jessica Lawley!' A blonde-haired, mini-skirted

girl with a bandaged hand and a ripening black eye pointed an accusing finger at her.

'Me? No. People say I'm like her,' Jessica said, in a broad West Country accent, and looked away.

'You sure you're not? You look as if you might have been Jessica.'

'Positive. I'm not. Wouldn't mind her loot, though.' She bent down beside the chair, oblivious to her knee, and took Selina's hand. 'Selina, listen. Do you hear me?' Selina nodded. 'I have to go – I'm getting recognised and I can't deal with that. Take this bag – okay? When you're recovered, read what's inside. It's H.G.'s diary. He's in terrible danger. You've got to rescue him.'

'But how? Can't you?'

'No. Impossible,' Jessica said briskly. 'Here, take this money. You might need it.' She stuffed a wodge of banknotes into the linen bag with the hexagonal-shaped papers. 'Selina, please let go.' Selina was holding her hand tightly, as if begging her to stay. 'I've got to get out of here.'

She stood up then, aware that several people were looking at her now, whispering her name. Not looking back at Selina – because if she did her resolve would shatter – she marched through the door, which had hissed open at her approach.

Safely back in the car, she turned towards the by-pass and the road for London. She had to get away from all that madness. She'd had a close shave back at the hospital when that woman had recognised her: '*You look as if you might have been Jessica.*' That was nearer the truth than the woman realised.

She *had* once been Jessica Lawley, but she'd stopped being her. She could so easily never have been her again. Now, though, her hip didn't hurt – so what if it was not cured? – and she could move. She would lose weight and get her hair tinted back to black, and she'd be Jessica Lawley again!

These thoughts cheered her as she left the city behind. As the miles slipped by she felt herself begin to relax. She'd panicked back at the hospital – that came from living on her nerves for so long ... But dumping poor, ill Selina, that had been typically selfish of her.

The lights of an all-night petrol station shone ahead and Jessica pulled in. She ordered coffee and thought about having bacon and eggs but decided, ravenous though she was, to wait until she was home and have Bun cook for her – Bun, home, normality. Wonderful!

In the phone booth she took the number Matt had scribbled for her, and hoped that the person would not mind being woken in the middle of the night but an answering machine picked up the call. She frowned: *that* wouldn't tell her if Matt was genuine. She disconnected the call.

There was no copy of the *Yellow Pages* to find the number of the police station so she'd have to dial 999. She picked up the phone. Her finger was on the nine ... She paused. Slowly she replaced the receiver. Hadn't Matt said that some police were involved and he didn't know in which regions? Better not risk it. Better to go home and forget it had all happened.

Back in the car she began to feel anxious. Her earlier euphoria had disappeared and her neck was stiff with tension.

'The future. Think of your future,' she said aloud.

H.G.'s face clicked in her mind. She blotted him out. The future!

Ginnie's face as she'd last seen her: white, wan and bolshie. That's it, bolshie cow, why should Jessica concern herself with her?

She'd telephone her agent as soon as she was back.

She'd book into Champneys for a month – a month there could do miracles.

A month. She'd been at Porthwood just short of a month.

H.G. slipped back in.

'No!' she shouted, and clutched the wheel so tightly her knuckles showed white. She saw him hunched and frail. She saw the look in his eyes …

'Why should I? What's it to do with me? I hardly know him! A few hours' talk and half the time I thought he was off his rocker. But he wasn't and everything he said was right. I don't want to be involved. Why should I? Why? Why?' she shouted, and banged her fist on the wheel.

She drove even faster, the car speeding through the night. She had her own mantra now: why me? She kept repeating it, forcing all other thoughts away.

At the Merrybank roundabout, west of Exeter, she drove the car too fast round the circle until she was facing the way she had come.

Why not me? She thought. Just my bad luck. But the bottom line was that she could not desert him. Not now.

chapter **sixteen**

1

Jessica feared that Matt would have switched the alarm system back on, but when she passed through the gates of Porthwood nothing happened. She allowed herself to relax. Then she thought that perhaps the alarm was indicated on a board in the house and was silent only to give her a false sense of security. She switched off the car lights and looked constantly about her expecting to see vehicles speeding towards her full of men ready to kidnap her, beat her up or murder her – she was convinced now that anything could happen.

Unable to remember the tracks she had used on the drive out she decided she would have to risk keeping to the estate road. On the journey she worked out what she could say if she was caught – as she expected to be – but, no matter how many times she rehearsed it in her mind it sounded implausible. She would say she'd stolen the car and rescued Selina on her own – there was no point in dropping Matt in it. She'd say Xavier's cure had worked so well that she'd been able to negotiate the steep steps to free her friend. But then they'd want to know how she knew where to find the Regeneration or Redundancy Room – or whatever they called it. Of course! She'd say Ginnie had told her. Why not?

The house was in darkness and Jessica drove cautiously round to the back, constantly on the lookout for lights to appear and alarms to sounds – but, to her astonishment, nothing happened.

She parked the car neatly with the others, edged the

door shut with a tiny click and moved with surprising speed through the dark – thank heaven it was winter with its late dawns – towards her wing of the house. Even if it *was* hypnosis making her feel so much better, there was no ignoring that a couple of weeks ago she could never have done this. No way.

Walking swiftly around the front of the house she stopped suddenly and listened. She thought she had heard a car, but there was nothing.

Moving along the grass borders rather than the gravel, Jessica negotiated the knot garden and reached the side door that led into the West Wing. It opened – she hadn't been discovered!

Inside, and longing for bed, she looked at her watch. It was five. She knew she was pushing her luck, but she needed to find out how H.G. was. She had to know if he had been sleeping last night or drugged into a coma.

Her heart was racing as she opened the door into his apartment. Her shoulders dropped with relief when she saw him sitting up in bed expectantly as she entered.

'Where have you been?' he asked, in a querulous wail. She resisted the urge to say a 'nice to see you' might have been better.

'On an adventure,' she said with a smile that she hoped looked reassuring. She explained quickly the night's happenings.

'That was very brave of you,' he said finally. 'Why did you come back?'

'My hip, of course. I'm not giving up on that now.'

'Jessica. You're not telling me the truth,' he said gently.

She looked away from him. 'Oh, all right. I came back because of you. And don't ask me why because I don't know.'

'I'm grateful. That was unselfish of you. The act of a courageous woman.'

'Oh, come on. Hardly!' She was deeply embarrassed.

'Have you told Matt about me?'

'No. I wasn't sure of him – not until I got right away. Then I believed in him. I must tell him now. He's our only hope.'

H.G. settled back on his pillows with a contented sigh. 'At last! The other night when you were trapped in my bathroom did you hear them say they expect the Americans to arrive here this weekend? Or was it next? I've been so stupid – I see what's happening. When they come we must move fast ...'

'Humph? It's me, Tessa.'

'Can you speak up? I can hardly hear you.'

'I'm under the duvet. I wondered if my room was bugged.'

'Very sensible. You're all right?'

'I'm fine. I got back here and saw Jessica flitting through the garden. I'm sure she'd just parked a car, too. The engine of one was still warm.' She sounded pleased with herself as she said this, surprised by her sleuthing skills.

'Jessica? What the hell's she been doing?'

'I followed her into a part of the house I didn't know and listened at a door. She was talking to H.G.! He's not ill like they said. She's got Selina to hospital. Humph, we're going to have to move quickly – this weekend probably.' She explained at length what she had overheard.

'Have you told Jessica you know all this?'

'No. I thought it best to talk to you first. She's no idea.'

'You're going to have to tell her. She obviously knows more than you and we've got to let her in on whatever we're doing. Which hospital did they go to?'

'She didn't say. There can't be many.'

'I'll try and track Selina down in the morning. Take care.'

A bathed and rested Selina lay beneath the tightly tucked-in sheet and looked up at the young doctor standing over her.

'You still don't want to tell us how you got into this state?'

'No,' she said firmly.

'You've been very lucky, you know. Bronchitis can so easily become pneumonia – and untreated that can kill you. Do you smoke?'

'Yes.' Selina rolled her eyes heavenward. 'You can cut the lecture – I know it by heart.'

'Very well – if you want to kill yourself.'

'I do!' she snapped, irritated at his assumption that she was so dim she didn't know how foolish she was.

'Your dehydration is almost remedied. The conjunctivitis should clear quickly. The weakness will respond to rest. Of course, I can't insist you stay but you should.'

'I know.'

'Don't, whatever you do, forget your antibiotics.'

'I won't.'

'And since you're discharging yourself against my advice, I must insist you sign this paper exonerating the hospital of responsibility.'

'Happily.'

'I think you're very foolish.'

'And I admire you, too.' She grinned.

'These clothes are a right old mess,' said the nurse, as she presented Selina with her filthy skirt and blouse, and an even dirtier mackintosh.

Selina checked that she still had Jessica's money. 'Is there an M and S near here? I'll pop in.' She smiled at the nurse, who gave her directions.

2

The formalities over, Selina was soon out of the hospital. As she walked out of one gate, Humphrey, Karl and Carter drove in at the other.

Ignoring the stares of passers-by, Selina followed the main road into the town. It was further than she wanted to walk for she was weaker than she had realised, but she wasn't about to give in. She tried to hitch a lift but could hardly blame the drivers for not stopping – she doubted if she would have risked picking up someone who looked like a vagrant. Which made her decide to go to M and S first and then to the police.

She wondered where Jessica was now. Back home if she'd any sense. If the diary on the papers Jessica had left was genuine – the bit she'd had time to read had made her hair stand on end – H.G. was in danger, and if he was so was Ginnie.

She'd reached the top of Lemon Street – half-way, she hoped. Suddenly she felt dizzy and leant against a wall. So weak. So cold. She paused, taking deep breaths until the faintness passed.

The traffic streamed by. Humphrey saw the young woman slumped against the wall – disgusting, a drug addict, no doubt.

Selina walked more slowly now. Pace yourself, she lectured.

In Marks and Spencer she picked up a pair of black leggings, a thick red jumper and a fawn wool donkey jacket. To these she added a white blouse and a large handbag in which to put the stacks of hexagonal papers. Upstairs she chose knickers, tights and a bra. They were out of stock of her normal plain sports bra so she selected the plainest satin one she could find, even if the cups were under-wired, then make-up and a hairbrush. She found the nearest public lavatory and changed, then stepped out into the street and asked for the police station.

The sergeant was kindness itself as he ordered tea and listened to Selina's tale.

'I heard H.G. speak once – at a gala here. Uplifting, it was. In danger? I'd hate anything to happen to that nice old boy. Mind you, you're better off talking to one of our inspectors who handles this sort of stuff.' He smiled, and she wondered if he believed a word she said.

The expression of horror on Matt's face when Jessica walked into the dining-room for lunch was a clear give-away. She smiled at him, hoping he'd understand that Selina was all right.

A whole morning had been lost as she'd overslept. When she'd left H.G., she'd collapsed on her bed not even bothering to undress and had slept nearly eight hours.

She picked up a tray and walked to the self-service counter. There was no queue and she picked up the last plate of salad and cheese, willing Matt to join her.

'Any more juice?' she asked the girl on serving duty, seeing that the jug was empty.

Grudgingly the girl disappeared into the kitchen and immediately Jessica sensed someone standing beside her. She did not turn but looked sideways. It was Tessa, with Matt beside her.

'Jessica, can I talk to you?' Tessa asked.

'Not now, I'm sorry.'

'But it's important.'

'I just said no. Now, will you excuse me?' Jessica said firmly.

'Suit yourself,' Tessa snapped, but felt in her pocket for the telephone and held it for comfort.

With Tessa gone Matt moved closer.

'She's fine, in hospital,' Jessica said, as softly as she could.

'Why are you here?'

'I've got to talk to you – soon.'

The girl returned with the juice, making further talk impossible. 'You too, Matt? You've had two glasses already.'

'Got a mighty thirst.' He grinned. 'It's working in the woods.'

Jessica looked for a space. Everyone was sitting about, chatting normally. Did that mean no one knew that Selina had gone?

A bell rang summoning them all to the usual energising session. No one stopped to ask if she was coming – just as well she'd refused to go all those times so there was nothing odd in her not going today.

The room emptied. She tried to eat her salad but found it impossible – every mouthful tasted like cardboard. She drank her juice instead.

Half an hour later she wandered out into the gardens, grateful it was a crisp winter's day so that a walk was the most natural thing to be doing. She went up the hill behind the house, forcing herself not to hurry, hoping Matt had meant this wood.

He was already there and, thankfully, alone.

'How'd you manage to get here?'

'I risked it. I waited until they were leaping about and slipped out. It was easier today – Xavier and the other dark blues aren't in evidence.'

'That's dangerous. Someone might have seen.'

'You're telling me?' he said tautly. 'Thank heavens you got Selina to hospital. You did warn her not to go to the police, didn't you?'

'Oh, hell!' Jessica's hand shot to her mouth. 'I clean forgot. Stupid. I panicked at the hospital – I had to get out.'

'Can't be helped. We might have to move sooner than I wanted. But what on earth induced you to come back?'

'It's H.G. He thinks they want to kill him. We've got to get him out.'

'You've seen him?' he asked, astonished.

'Yes, most nights …' And she told him everything she knew and about the diaries. 'But we don't know how long she'll be in hospital, how soon before she can get things moving. I don't think we should wait. I think we should get out now, don't you?'

'What? Tonight?'

'As soon as possible. I thought, walking up here, I've been so damn stupid. I'm sorry, Matt, I forgot to give her the telephone number of your associate – I couldn't get through.'

'Don't worry, Jessica. The way she looked she'll be in hospital for days. We'll be miles away by then.' He spoke encouragingly, but she knew he was only placating her.

'I hope you're right.' She decided to go along with him. 'Have they discovered Selina's gone? If not, it's very odd, isn't it?' she asked briskly, to allay her own fears.

'Maybe one of the goons who's supposed to be guarding her has and is too scared to admit she's gone. But it can't go on, not once things settle. We've been lucky in that all the top brass are involved with this American contingent due this evening.'

'H.G.'s worried about these Americans. Years ago he said he didn't want to be involved with the money side of the movement, then no one could ever accuse him of embezzlement or of using undue pressure on people. A trust was set up and these Americans are the trustees. Every five years they have a review of all expenditure and who's to control what.'

'Neat. So Xavier is going to get total control of the trust.'

'But how?'

'How did all of us get involved and enmeshed? Drugs and hypnosis! The old story. There's no reason for the trustees to be wary or afraid. The system has worked flawlessly for years – bloody hell.'

The truth stared Jessica in the face. Instinctively she clutched her neck as the horror mounted.

'After tomorrow, they won't need H.G. any more, will they?'

3

Selina was getting impatient. She'd waited a good two hours to see the inspector. At first she'd been quite content to sit on a bench in the front office and watch people trooping in and out with various problems, even two old ladies who'd lost their cats. But it soon began to pall.

She started to think about Matt again. His face kept slipping into her mind's eye and she wished she'd asked Jessica what he'd said about her. Her need and longing to see him, to be with him, were real and painful.

When eventually a young policewoman came to collect her, she jumped with surprise for she was miles away – with Matt.

'Miss Horner, my apologies for keeping you waiting,' the middle-aged, plain-clothes policeman said, as she was shown into his office. He shook her hand with a suspiciously over-firm grasp. 'Tea? Coffee?'

'No more tea, thanks. I've had rather a lot waiting for you.' She had not meant to sound critical, but the way he bridled implied that that was how he had heard her.

'I was busy, I'm afraid. I do have other things to do, you know.'

'I'm sorry – I didn't mean ...' But she knew there was

no point in apologising since he'd already made up his mind. The inspector, with his beer gut and florid complexion, began to shuffle papers on his desk in a preoccupied manner, as if she was not there. After a few minutes she coughed discreetly. He looked up with a false expression of surprise, as if seeing her for the first time.

'Ah, yes,' he said, and returned to his papers.

She had not liked the look of him when she had walked into his office, and so far his actions had not changed her opinion.

A few minutes passed before he pushed his papers together. 'Right, where were we?' He glanced at the note left on his desk by the policewoman. 'A complaint about the Fohpal people, I see.' He stared at her. 'And what, exactly, is your problem?' He looked stern, as if the investigation had begun – with her.

'They imprisoned me against my will.'

'Really?' He steepled his fingers. 'And for how long were you ...' he paused, '... imprisoned?'

'I'm not sure.'

'Not sure? Surely you would know how long you were locked away?'

'That's the point, I don't. I was in the dark, deprived of light, heating, sleep and food – you get a bit disorientated in such conditions, you understand?'

'I'm afraid I don't. I shall have to try to imagine.' He smirked at her, and Selina found her initial dislike of him mushrooming into loathing.

'What's today?' she asked, realising she had no idea.

'Friday.'

'Then I was there for three days.'

'Did anyone see you in this, ah, prison? Someone who could verify what you're saying?'

She paused. 'No one,' she said, deciding it would be unwise to give Matt's name.

'No one? Pity.'

'Look ...' She peered at the nameplate on his desk. 'Look, Inspector Somerset, I don't wish to appear rude, but if you insist on repeating everything I say we'll be here forever.'

'Was I? Three days, you say. Do you know why this happened?'

'Because I was trying to leave. And they stopped me.'

'Why should they do that?'

Selina looked out of the window behind him. 'I don't know.'

'You don't know?'

She gritted her teeth. 'It might have something to do with my shop in Finchester. I was selling it to them, you see.'

'And did you?'

'I don't know. I think I signed some papers – I'm not sure.'

'You think?' The slightest of smiles played around his mouth.

'Yes. I know it sounds odd, but I'm pretty sure they drugged me and made me sign. That can't be legally binding, can it?'

'Since you don't know what it is you signed, I wouldn't like to comment. And to accuse people of drugging you, well ...' He raised one eyebrow and Selina knew he didn't believe her.

'I'm worried about my friend. We went there together. And she appears to have been converted. She's become one of them.'

'One of Fohpal's members? What's wrong with that?'

'I think they drugged her too. She's very vulnerable, very unhappy. I think she could have agreed to anything. She's – how shall I put it? – different.'

'Her name?' His hand was poised with a pen.

'Ginnie – rather, Virginia – Mulholland, Mrs,' she added helpfully.

'Ginnie, did you say?' He looked up from the papers with a self-satisfied smile.

'Please, you must understand how worried I am.'

'I do. And how did you escape, Selina? How did you get here?'

What was the relevance of that, she thought, and who told him he could use her Christian name? She didn't want to involve Matt or Jessica, for that matter.

'My door was left unlocked – obviously by mistake. I slipped out at dead of night.'

'How fortuitous. So how did you get here?'

'By car,' she snapped. And then she realised that if she said she'd taken a car he'd want to know where it was now and the others would be implicated. 'I hitched.'

'That's a dangerous thing to do, Selina. Especially at night – a pretty little thing like you.' He was leering, and her defensive antennae, which had been on stand-by from the beginning of this interview, were now on alert.

'What are you going to do about it?'

'The keeping of someone confined against their will is, of course, a serious offence. Quite difficult for you to prove, of course ...'

'It happened!'

'And your friend – presumably she's an adult?' He pursed his lips. 'If that's the life she wants, you can't prevent her.'

'You don't believe me, do you?'

'I have an open mind, Selina. That's my job.'

'Do you know Xavier?'

'I might have met him, I can't recall.' She knew he was lying: Xavier stood out in a crowd and she doubted that it was only women who remembered him. 'Is there anything else?' he asked.

She sat clutching the bag containing the extracts from H.G.'s diaries. She knew that if she showed them action

377

would have to be taken. But she also knew that she didn't want him to see them and held the bag even tighter.

'No, nothing.' She got up.

'I could go over to Porthwood, show my face. I don't know if it would do any good but I could have a word with your friend Ginnie.' He smirked again.

'That would be very kind of you, Inspector Somerset.'

'Why so formal? Please. Call me Ken.'

4

Selina sat with a coffee in a small café opposite the great cathedral. She should have handed H.G.'s papers to the inspector. She should have told him about Jessica and Matt – that she wasn't alone in her fears and suspicions, that Matt, at least, had witnessed her imprisonment. But she just did not trust him. All through the interview she had felt him laughing at her. It was not that he hadn't believed her but that he had no intention of doing anything about it. Perhaps he was in cahoots with them. It might be a rural area, but that didn't make the police paragons of virtue. Bad apples existed everywhere, not just in the cities.

Once she was at home in Finchester she'd talk to the police there. It was a different county, it would be safer …

Safer. How wonderful to be safe again in her own flat. To sleep in her own bed and put all this drama behind her. But it wasn't that simple. She couldn't just abandon Ginnie. And although she had never met H.G., she had read his diary and she could imagine how she would feel if she should read in the papers that he was dead and she'd done nothing. And there was Matt. He'd called her 'darling', said he loved her, and yet he'd stayed. Why?

378

She ordered another coffee and while she slowly drank it she read the rest of H.G.'s diaries and then re-read the whole. His fear and terror leapt from the page – she understood his suffering now. And, able to relate to it, helped her finally to decide. It might be the last thing she wanted to do, but it was the only possible solution – she had to go back!

A fine rescuer she was – she had no plan. She would have to coast along and hope to get Matt, Ginnie and H.G. out. Hell! She pushed back her hair from her forehead as if that would help her think straighter. At least Jessica was safe.

She counted what was left of her friend's money. There was enough to hire a car – but she couldn't, she realised, because she had no driving licence. A bicycle, she'd find a shop which hired them and, failing that, she'd buy one.

Her coffee paid for, she crossed to the post office. There, she bought a large padded envelope, placed H.G.'s diary inside and addressed it to Carter Mulholland.

In the phone booth she called him to warn him it was on its way. She let the number ring a long time, but there was no reply. Frustrated, she called her own number.

'Porthwood Publications, can I help you?'

'Who is this, please?' she asked politely, her heart thumping.

'My name is Colley. May I be of assistance?'

'Thank you, Colley,' she said quietly. She replaced the receiver and felt as if the glass walls of the telephone kiosk were closing in on her. They had her shop! She hadn't dreamt the signing. She'd lost everything.

Selina opened the phone-box door, walked out into the street and collapsed onto one of the benches set on the cobbles of the Cathedral close. Fear and panic swirled in her brain.

Then she sat upright. They weren't going to get away

with this. How dare they cheat her out of her shop? How dare they reduce her to this wimpish jelly?

She stood up, and set off determinedly in search of a bicycle shop.

chapter **seventeen**

1

Tessa climbed the stairs to her mother's room and tapped at the door. She was now deeply afraid for her.

'Mum, it's me,' she said, from outside.

'Go away.'

'Please, let me in. We've got to talk.'

'I don't want to. I told you to go. Why are you still here?'

'I'm leaving,' Tessa lied, but it seemed the only way. The door opened slowly. Tessa fixed a bright, friendly smile on her face. 'Hi! I couldn't go without seeing you, could I?'

'That was sweet. Come in. There's really only the bed to sit on. What made you decide to leave?'

'Well, I think Dad's overreacting. You seem perfectly happy to me,' Tessa said, to lull her mother's fears, and was rewarded by a lightening of Ginnie's expression. 'In his defence, one does read awful things in the newspapers about cults and things.'

'True. And I suppose I should be pleased he showed some concern. Yes, that's right.' She smiled to herself as if she had a secret. 'I want you to feel free to come and visit any time. I've bought a room here and I'll check with Xavier that you can use it too.'

'That's kind of you. So you're really staying?'

'Of course.'

'Dad does love you, Mum.'

'I don't want to discuss it,' Ginnie said, thin-lipped.

'But you've been together—'

'Too long. I'm not prepared to talk about your father, okay?'

Tessa sighed. 'Whatever you say. Do you know where Selina is?' she asked, to find out if Ginnie knew what Jessica had done.

'Don't be silly. You know she left ages ago. Still, now she's given them her shop I don't know what she'll do. But she would never have fitted in here. She's not dedicated enough.'

'Wasn't she ill?'

'No. Hung over, more like. She smuggled drink in, you know.' Ginnie spoke disapprovingly. 'I've been thinking, I'd like you here when Xavier and I get married.'

'Married?' Tessa knew she looked stupid.

'I'm going to help him with his work.'

'Do you really believe in it all, Mum? I mean, this Inner Way stuff. You don't think you've been brain-washed?'

Ginnie laughed gaily. 'Of *course* not. You don't know how wonderful it can be – you haven't attended the meetings. You haven't experienced the release,' she said, with the enthusiasm of the convert.

'No, I realise. I told Xavier I'd go to the energising today.'

'You said you were leaving!' Ginnie looked at her sharply.

'I am, but not immediately. Look, Mum, I think …' Tessa paused, not sure whether to continue, but she loved her mother too much not to. 'I think …' she looked about furtively '… I can get you away from here.'

'I don't want to be got away. But I can tell what I do want, I want you to get out. I'm happy. I don't want you hanging around,' Ginnie said sharply. She didn't want to compete with her daughter for Xavier's favours.

'Don't worry, I won't.'

382

Having found Jessica's room, Tessa, frightened from her interview with her mother, knocked on the door. 'I'm sorry to bother you, but we have to talk.'

'Look, Tessa, I'm sorry about your mother, but—'

'I know you took Selina—'

With one hand, Jessica grabbed the girl's arm. She put a finger to her lips, held open the door and led Tessa to the bathroom. There, she turned on the shower, sat on the lid of the lavatory, and indicated the stool for Tessa. 'The room is probably bugged,' she explained. 'So, what can I do for you?'

'Bugged? So I was right. I spoke to Humph last night and I put my head under the duvet so they wouldn't hear me.'

'You've got a *telephone*?'

'Humph gave it to me.' She took it out of her pocket. 'We have to get in touch with them and arrange how they're going to rescue us. I've just talked to my mother – I don't know what to do. I'm frightened she won't come.' She brushed away a tear. 'I wondered if we took her to speak to H.G. perhaps he could persuade her—'

'H.G.? What do you know about him?'

'I followed you last night. I got back just after you. I'd been to see my father. They're close by – in a cottage.'

'Thank God. We've got to move fast. I've been trying to see Matt all morning, but he's always got a minder with him. Let's get hold of your father or Humph.'

Tessa dialled the number. At the sound of her ex-husband's voice Jessica found herself close to tears with relief. 'We have to move tonight, Humph. But the grounds are alarmed.'

'I can see to that – I've contacts.'

Jessica chuckled. 'Still the same Humph – always knows the right man.'

'Have they got guns?'

'I've no idea. I wouldn't be surprised. They have a contact in the police station so be careful.'

'We know that. Carter's here, wants a word. I'll have a word with Karl – he's our expert on Fohpal. We'll work out what we're to do. Hold on …'

'Jessica?' Carter's voice boomed down the line. 'Will Ginnie come with you?'

'I'm sure she will,' she said reassuringly.

'Karl says can you call back in a couple of hours? We'll have finalised our plans. He says not to worry it'll be tonight, and how many will you be?'

'Me and Tessa – Ginnie, of course,' she added 'H.G. and maybe someone called Matt.'

'Four, maybe five, fine.' The line went dead.

'I must say I feel a lot happier now I know they're galloping to the rescue.'

'I loved your ex – he's adorable.'

'So you said before,' Jessica replied noncommittally.

The group sat in the Long Gallery. They were subdued. Something was afoot and rumour was rife. Only Matt knew the reason for this meeting. He wished he could be anywhere but here; wished he didn't love his sister as much as he did; longed to be with Selina.

Xavier swept in, his expression one of barely controlled rage. He was followed closely by Bethina, her lovely features twisted with anxiety, Mathie, whose lips were even thinner than usual, and Berihert, massive and menacing.

'We've a traitor here!' Xavier began, without preamble and with no need to call for silence. 'Here among us! Is it you, you or you?' He thrust his arm towards the seated members, pointing accusingly at random.

The followers looked at each other. Questioningly. Accusingly. Guiltily. Fearfully. But mostly fearfully.

'That this should be beggars belief. What have you had

but love and support? What else do you need from me?' Xavier cried. The followers looked woodenly at the floor.

'Who has betrayed us?' he thundered.

'But what have we done?' A small voice at the back dared to ask. Everyone turned to stare and Ginnie blushed bright red, wishing she had not spoken.

'The one who is the traitor knows the crime. There is no need for me to explain. Until he or she steps forward, here we remain.'

Clever, thought Matt, admiring how Xavier had neatly sidestepped the need to explain about Selina having been sprung, which would have led to awkward questions. Most of the followers thought blissfully that they were free to leave whenever they wanted.

They were harangued for a good half-hour, Xavier lashing himself into an incandescent fury. Matt allowed himself to switch off and think of other things. It was the same technique he'd used for the past year to enable himself to remain uninfluenced by whatever was going on.

One of the older members held up his hand and asked permission to go to the lavatory.

'No, Silas. You stay here. No one leaves. If it's painful, don't blame me!' And the ranting continued.

'Any explanations, Matt?' Suddenly Xavier struck. And Matt, in his own world, was jolted back by a prod from Tristram.

'Sorry? I didn't quite catch that,' he called back, playing for time.

'I asked if you had any explanations. Can you shed light on what's happened?' Xavier said, in a voice so tightly controlled it sent shivers down the spines of the others.

'I'm sorry, Xavier, but I don't know what you're talking about – so, sorry, I've no ideas.' He shrugged his shoulders – nonchalantly, he hoped.

'Stand when you speak to me!' Xavier screamed. Matt scrambled to his feet. This was no time for heroics.

'Where were you last night?'

'In bed.'

'Don't play the innocent with me.'

'Ask Tristram here – he'll vouch for me. After all, it was you who asked him to keep an eye on me.'

'I never said that!' Tristram stammered. 'We slept in the same room.' He paused. 'When I was awake he was there.'

Matt didn't think this sounded nearly convincing enough.

'Nice one, Tristram! Thanks a bunch,' Matt said, under his breath. 'I repeat, Xavier, I don't know what your problem is. I repeat, I slept.'

'My problem is traitorous scum like you.'

The others looked at each other and muttered among themselves.

'My problem is the level of disloyalty, the depths to which you have sunk.'

The followers stared at Matt, their muttering louder.

'My problem is the pain you've caused me *here*.' Xavier slapped a hand over his heart.

'Traitor!' one voice shouted. 'Traitor!' Others joined in. '*Traitor*.' The call was noisy and loud. 'Kill him!' shouted one lone voice, and Matt's stomach turned to water. He knew full well that the call would be taken up by the others. That his time was limited.

He turned, pushed Tristram and Gervase out of the way, leapt up the short flight of stairs on to the mezzanine, and through the double doors, slamming them shut. He raced down the stairs and outside into the pouring rain. He knew the perimeter was wired, that the guards and their dogs were at this moment being alerted. Knew he had to get right away.

386

Jessica sat in her room and did not know how she was
going to contain herself for the rest of the day. They were
to be rescued at two in the morning and the nervous
tension she was experiencing made even the fear of last
night pale into insignificance. She had not packed – she'd
decided it was too dangerous. If anyone should enter her
rooms and find her cases ready the game would be up.
And if the rescue of Selina was anything to go by she
could not be lumbered with cases.

She wondered where Matt was now. He'd given her a
significant look as he went to a hastily called meeting
from which she'd been excluded as she was not a
member. Ginnie had looked proud that she was to be
there.

What to do about Ginnie worried Jessica. She was a
difficult woman and a silly one, too. But she'd led a
sheltered life, and in coming here she'd been a bit like a
lamb being led to slaughter. She wondered if she should
try one last time to speak to her. Perhaps if she told her
all she knew, tried to warn her of the dangers. But if
Tessa couldn't get through to her, chances were that
Ginnie would listen even less to her.

Hell, she thought, being involved in other people's lives
was such a pain. Everything had been so much simpler
when the only person she had to think about was herself.

There was a commotion outside. She crossed to the
window and peered out. A group of followers was racing
across the knot garden, shouting to each other. Now
what? Matt, she thought instinctively. He was in danger.

2

'It's all your fault! I go to France and leave you alone for a few days and all this happens. You're a fool, Xavier!'

Jessica stood in the frozen position of a child playing Grandmother's Footsteps. She wanted to leave, knew she should, but curiosity made her listen.

'Why was no one guarding the bloody woman? Why hadn't she been regularly checked? Answer me that!'

'It was an administrative muddle – it happens.'

'Thank God for Ken is all I can say. If he hadn't been there. And Matt – I never trusted that bastard. I knew he was up to something.'

'They're still looking for him.'

'What about the other one? How are you doing there?'

'Nicely. Writing cheques as if there's no tomorrow. Liz, you worry too much. Come here.'

'Piss off.'

'You know you don't mean that. We've been missing you – the big fellow here and me.'

Jessica rolled her eyes heavenwards. It didn't take much imagination to guess what 'big fellow' he meant. And the woman's voice had been Hesta's, but he was calling her Liz. She turned to leave the room and brushed against a small table. An ornament rocked dangerously. Swiftly she caught it, replaced it and exhaled with relief. She tiptoed across the room but her weight made a board creak alarmingly. Her wits about her, she turned so that she appeared to be entering the room, not leaving it, and was stepping forward just as she heard the female voice say, 'What's that?' Xavier came to his doorway.

'Jessica! Can I help you?' He smiled smoothly. 'Been waiting here long?'

'No.' She finished the word on an upbeat, eyebrows arched, all innocence. 'I was wondering if my session with you was at the same time, only you didn't say yesterday.'

'No, nor I did. Forgive me, Jessica, but yesterday everything was upside down. I'm not sure yet – with the guests from America arriving today. Might I let you know later?'

'Of course. You haven't seen Matt, have you? Only he's promised to teach me – chess.' She'd had to think frantically of something and hoped they hadn't noticed the slight pause before she'd said 'chess' and that he played it – he looked clever enough.

'Matt's a good player. He's around. I'll tell him you're looking for him.'

She had to admire his performance and hoped her own matched his.

'There's no hurry,' she said, as if none of it mattered.

Back in her room Jessica worried at how much Matt's presence mattered that night. The simple plan Tessa and she had evolved with Humph and Carter sounded all right but depended on too many imponderables for comfort. If the men were late, caught or crashed – she shuddered at the very thought of Humph being hurt, or worse, in a crash – it would be left to her and Tessa to free H.G. And she could not rid herself of a strange conviction that everything would go awry and that they would be on their own.

H.G. had told her proudly last night that he could stand – he'd been practising. She pretended an enthusiasm she was far from feeling: he might be able to stand for a minute or two but she doubted he could walk, and certainly not far enough to get away. Matt was so strong he wouldn't even notice the burden of H.G. in his arms.

But if H.G. was right and the key to his elimination lay in the American contingent due this evening, she had to prepare an alternative plan.

There it was again, that feeling that something was

going to go wrong – silly of her, she must keep reminding herself how often she was *certain* she'd forget her lines on stage and she never did.

And *why* had she chosen to help a crippled old man she was incapable of helping? What an old man, though! He had so much to teach her. He had such charisma, such charm. She'd become fond of H.G., a fondness she was pretty certain was love, not the sexual type that she had pursued with such keen devotion over the years, platonic, but none the weaker for that.

Two men. H.G., whom she'd met too late to be of any use to him, and Humph, whom she'd loved all her adult life but had been too proud and too cussed to tell him. Now it was too late – her awful pride would never let her.

'Oh, Humph!' She sighed.

Riding the bicycle from the town to Porthwood was harder than Selina had anticipated. The bronchitis made her wheeze as she pedalled and it was raining so that her new jacket was soon soaked. Fearing she might be seen she had taken the coast road which, though little used in winter, was further round than the main road. She had not entered by the gate, certain that a guard would be posted there so had had to climb the estate wall, haul up her bicycle behind her, hide it under bracken and then cautiously make her way through the woods to as near the house as she could get under cover. There she had waited for darkness to fall, huddled, wet, miserable and certain that at any moment she would give away her position by sneezing mightily.

At least by four it was dark and she thanked heaven that this was all happening in January. Stealthily she skirted the perimeter of the knot garden, unsure how she was to get into the house. Looking across the garden, she saw Jessica at her ground-floor window pulling the curtains. She ran, stooped low, across to the window, putting up her hand to tap at the glass. A thin shaft of light shone out as Jessica moved the curtains to peer out. The expression of surprise on her face as Selina jumped up would have been funny if the whole situation hadn't been so serious.

Recovering herself, Jessica pointed towards the side door. Selina waited, shivering, until the bolts were drawn and the door opened. Silently the two hurried back to Jessica's room.

'You're moving like Motor-Mouse—' Selina began, but Jessica put her hand over her mouth. She pointed to the bathroom and relaxed only when the shower was roaring in the background. 'Is it bugged?' Selina whispered.

'Possibly. I'm just taking precautions. What the hell are you doing here? I risked my sodding neck to get you out!' she said, sitting down on the lavatory lid. 'Still, am I bloody glad to see you …' Her voice trailed off. Exactly what *was* Selina doing back here? Had she been a plant all along?

'Don't worry, I'm not a spy. I'm here to help.' Selina touched Jessica lightly to reassure her.

'Sorry, it's the atmosphere in this place. You look moderately better than when I last saw you but not really fit enough for all this – and soaked! Here, take this.' She handed Selina her bathrobe.

'I'm fine. Honestly. Mostly I was weak from lack of sleep and that awful noise. The stuff the doc gave me zapped my chest infection.' Selina was stripping off her wet clothes as she talked, and Jessica remembered a time when she had been just as unselfconscious at others seeing her naked.

'But why come back?' She passed Selina a towel to dry her hair.

'I couldn't desert you all. Don't say it, I know it sounds

391

stupidly dramatic, but there it is …' To her consterna-
tion, Jessica began to cry, not noisily, not desperately, but
silently, as if the tears were a safety valve that had
suddenly been activated. 'Oh, my love, what is it?'

'I've been so worried.' Jessica dabbed at her eyes and
Selina landed her a box of Kleenex. 'It's not just H.G.
and Ginnie, there's Tessa too, and with no Matt, if things
go wrong I wouldn't know what to do …'

'Tessa's here? Oh, Lord, no. And Matt. Where is he?'

Face composed now, Jessica began to explain everything that had happened and in such a short time. 'It feels
like weeks and months of worry, not hours!'

'And you don't know where Matt is now?'

'There was an enormous kerfuffle after they found
you'd gone. There was a hell of a chase – out there. I saw
them, yelling and shouting, torches brandished. All they
lacked were bloodhounds.' She nodded at the window. 'I
fear they were chasing Matt.'

'The room! God, I wonder if he's down in that
godawful room. I'll have to go and check.'

'There's no way you're going back in there if you're
not completely better. Look at the state of you last time.'

'I've got to find him, Jessica. I love him so. And now I
know how brave he is …' She couldn't understand how
she'd ever doubted him.

'Selina, you must not go there. Promise me. Wait until
we've got Humph and Carter here – they'll bring help
with them.'

'Okay,' Selina said, but Jessica knew she didn't mean
it. 'How's H.G.?'

'Wonderful. He's so brave. I've nothing but admiration
for him. And he's a brilliant actor – he's fooled them into
thinking he's a drugged-out zombie still. He's so much to
offer us all. We've got to get him out.'

'You sound like a guru groupie!'

'There's worse things to be if it's someone like H.G.'

'And Humph *et al* are coming tonight? What time?'

'Two – well, thereabouts. The important thing I have to do is unbolt the little side door that leads into the knot garden for them. Tessa has a mobile phone – I'm to give them a ring that all's well. Then they'll come.'

'What about the alarm system?' asked Selina.

'Humph says he's got some people coming with him who can deal with that – he always knows the right man for the job. Then they plan to drive nearly to the house, but park behind the tennis court – I thought that was the best place. Then we can bundle H.G. out – one of the men carrying him if necessary.'

Jessica looked at her watch. 'We're having a double dose of energising today, with the Americans due later this evening.'

'But you never go to that.'

'I thought it was politic to become a reformed character and lull them into a false sense of security. You stay here. Don't make any noise.'

Selina sat with a book she was not reading. She'd come here for action, not this. But when there was a tap on Jessica's door, her heart jumped into her mouth and she scuttled for the safety of the long, full curtains.

Through a crack she watched, pulse hammering, as the door opened slowly and Tessa's head appeared. The sigh that escaped from her was audible, for Tessa looked up. Selina signed for them to go into the bathroom and repeated Jessica's shower routine.

'Have you seen Ginnie?' Selina asked, but immediately wished she hadn't as, with a resigned expression, she handed Tessa the Kleenex and settled down to listen as the girl told her of her fears, which were multiplying fast.

'We've got to go and see her and talk her out of this rubbish,' Selina said staunchly.

'She's probably in her room – she thinks I'm at the

energising. At tea she told me that if I went to it she wouldn't.'

'Oh, really, how pathetic! But this'll be a good time, then everyone will be occupied, won't they? Hang on, I've got to find something to wear.' Since everything of Jessica's was too big, she had to settle for her own leggings – not *too* damp – and a sweater of Jessica's that was rather baggy. 'I hope she doesn't mind. Right, come on.' And Selina, who was enjoying the drama, bizarrely, now that she was active, led the way.

3

Since their talk earlier in the day something Tessa said had been worrying Ginnie. '... *I can get you away from here* ...' That's what she'd said, sickening little bitch. It wasn't so much what she had said, it was the way she had said it, furtively, as if imparting a secret. And keeping on about Carter and how he loved her. It pointed to them having a plan to snatch her away from here. She'd read about such happenings, even seen a film on Sky about a woman 'rescued' against her wishes. Well, she'd see about that! She'd tell Xavier, he'd guard her.

She skimmed along the corridor to his rooms; he hadn't attended the energising, she'd checked. Neither had Tessa, come to that. Was she already putting her scheme into action?

Ginnie looked in Xavier's office, then in the meditation room. She had to find him, to warn him.

But Tessa wouldn't have instigated all this: it was Carter who had planned it, persuaded Tessa to come and spy on her. Afraid he was about to lose all her money, he was going to take her away from where she belonged. She couldn't allow it – she couldn't live if she was taken away from Xavier, the love of her life. She'd found him and she was not about to lose him.

Just recently Xavier had left her out in the cold again. She wished he wouldn't, it made her so afraid. But this news would change everything. It would make him aware of her. Speaking out against her own daughter could only endear her to him for ever. Even so, she felt apprehensive: she had not gone to his room uninvited since he'd shouted at her in front of Jessica.

There was no reply to her polite tap on the door. She pushed it open: the room was in darkness. He must be having a siesta – he worked so hard that his exhaustion was almost palpable. She was loath to wake him, but this was urgent – Carter could strike at any time. There was also the exciting prospect that he might invite her into his bed. She crossed the blood-red room to the door that opened into his bedroom, where he'd made her a whole and complete woman. Just thinking about those times aroused her. 'Xavier,' she whispered, edging into the darkened room. 'Xavier, it's me, Ginnie – or, rather, Heliotrope, I keep forgetting.' She giggled nervously. 'Xavier?'

'What the fuck! Who's that?'

'It's me, Ginnie. I've got something important to tell you.'

'Can't it wait? I'm sleeping.'

At that, a woman giggled. Ginnie's heart raced, her stomach lurched and she couldn't move, even though every fibre of her body wanted to escape from that feminine laugh.

'Some sleep!' the woman said, and the light was switched on.

'Hesta!'

'Hello, Ginnie. Snooping?' They were lying naked in the very rumpled bed. The smell of sweaty bodies and love-making was heavy in the air.

'But you're in France,' she said stupidly.

'No, I'm very much here – aren't I, Xavier? You'd better explain to our little friend.'

'I don't think I want to hear.' Ginnie put her hands over her ears.

'Sit down, Ginnie.' Xavier patted the bed. 'Hesta being here doesn't make any difference to us, you understand, we'll still play our little games.'

'You might as well know, Ginnie. I'm his wife.'

'No!' The word was long and loud. 'No, it's not true.'

''Fraid so, Ginnie. But I don't mind sharing him with you. In fact, you can join us now, if you want.' Hesta laughed cruelly.

'I want to go home!' She'd said it instinctively, but where was her home? This was her home.

'I'm afraid that's not possible, Ginnie,' Hesta said.

'You can't stop me.' But she didn't want to go. Never to see him again.

'Ginnie, please don't go.' Xavier smiled, put out his hand towards her. 'Come on, join us. Have some fun!'

Ginnie backed towards the door. 'I don't understand. I thought—' But she couldn't say what she was thinking, not yet. The pain was too great. She fled.

'Well, that was stupid. Why did you tell her we're married?'

'Xavier, it might have escaped you but I sometimes get a bit fed up with your screwing around. I wanted to establish my credentials, if you like.'

'I did it for us. You don't think sleeping with that old dog was a pleasure, do you? Now you've probably ballsed it all up. She won't pay up any more now, will she?'

'You'll find a way of persuading her, I'm sure. In any case, once the dust has settled we won't need her. We'll have enough money.'

'One can never have enough money, Liz. I'll have to go and talk to her.'

'Not now ... Come here ...'

Ginnie retraced her steps, head down so that no one could see her face, like a novice scurrying along close to the convent walls. She reached the sanctuary of her room and opened the door to find Selina and Tessa standing there.

'Selina! What the hell—' She slammed the door and leant against it.

'Ginnie, how are you?' Selina stepped towards her friend. She was shocked by Ginnie's appearance, and surprised that a few days could have made such a change. Ginnie, always slim, looked emaciated. Her hair was lank, her eyes dull and blank. 'You don't look well.'

'I'm fine. Really.' Oh, hell, she thought, I want to cry. I want to be left alone. She pushed herself away from the door, crossed to the chest of drawers and fussed with her hair. 'I'm beginning to get *centred*. I'm truly *rooted* now. You know, Xavier is really pleased with me. Exactly when are you leaving, Tessa?' she said coldly. Tessa looked at the floor. She didn't speak, there was no need: her sad face said it for her.

'That's great. It would have taken me for ever if I'd stayed,' Selina remarked lightly. She put her arm round Tessa's shoulders and hugged her, wanting to ease her unhappiness. She wondered how best to voice her concerns without putting Ginnie's back up. She decided that perhaps the bald approach would be best. 'How's it going with Xavier?'

'He's wonderful. Absolutely. I've never known what it's like to feel like this. It's as if I'm sixteen again.' She swung round to face them, her face rigid from trying to contain her emotions.

You don't look it, thought Selina.

'It was never like this with Carter.'

'Mum!' Tessa spoke, her voice reedy with pain.

'From what Tessa says, Carter is obviously contrite.'

'It's none of Tessa's business, as it isn't yours either. And who are you to lecture me on men, Selina? You don't know or understand men – you've never had a successful relationship.' Ginnie's tone was harsh, but she was rapidly losing control, and needed to be alone to cry.

'Have you?' Selina shot back, amazed at how quickly Ginnie could upset her.

'Yes, as a matter of fact I have – now.' She smiled and Selina had to acknowledge that she was doing quite well on the cultivated smirk.

'You're mad. Xavier won't stay faithful to you.'

'Jealous? Like everyone else.' She thrust her face forward aggressively, and Selina wondered if Ginnie had always been like this and had covered it up.

'Mum, Selina, *please*. This isn't getting us anywhere.'

'She's right, Ginnie. Look, we're only here to try to help you. We love you—'

'Don't say that.' Ginnie backed away from them, but with nowhere to go in the small room she was soon pressed firmly against the window-sill. 'Please ... I ...' Suddenly she clapped her hands over her face and began to sob. She was talking, mumbling through her tears, but the others couldn't make out what she was saying.

'Oh, my poor Mummy. Don't cry.' Tessa held her tight, stroking her fine hair, rocking her gently, their roles reversed. 'Tell me what the problem is. We'll solve it, whatever it is.' She led her mother to the bed and sat beside her, still holding her tight.

'I thought Xavier loved me!' Ginnie's faces was ravaged with misery. 'You're right about him, Selina. I don't know what to do or where to go,' she said clearly.

'I'm sorry. I'd have given anything not to have been

right.' Selina knelt on the floor and took Ginnie's hands, which were wet with her tears.

'Why is it always me? Why can't I be loved? I've so much love to give.' Ginnie began to sob. Selina and Tessa waited for her to regain her composure.

'Don't you think you'd be better off getting out of here? Go home. Back to Carter? You can patch something up between you. Make a new start.' Selina forced an optimistic tone into her voice.

'He won't want me!'

'But he would, Mum. He loves you, he really does. We'll help you get away.'

'How? Selina, you've heard the rumours, you must have. You can't get out once you're in – everyone says. But how I long to go home.' Ginnie's voice echoed her desperation.

'I did. You can.' Selina debated with herself how much to tell her. But as Ginnie was devastated it seemed safe to trust her. 'Tonight Carter is coming here to rescue us – see how much he loves you? He won't leave without you, I can promise you that.'

'He's coming here? For me?' For the first time since Tessa and Selina had arrived in the room Ginnie smiled genuinely, even if it was tinged with disbelief.

'You can speak to him if you like. Reassure yourself that he loves you and really is mounting a rescue.'

Tessa took out the telephone. 'He's close by, Mum, in a cottage.' She punched in the number.

'What do I say to him, after all I've done?'

'Just say you love him. Ask him to come and get you.' Tessa pressed the phone into her mother's hand.

4

Ginnie lay on her bed, meditation and study all forgotten as she wallowed in the misery of Xavier's betrayal. She berated herself for being such a fool. God, how embarrassing it all was – she couldn't even begin to think of some of the things she'd done, all for love of him. Carter wouldn't want her back if he knew. Such chaos she'd made. She wondered if she would ever recover; she felt as if her nerves had been stretched to breaking point. How would she keep calm until tonight? How could she wait, when all she wanted to do was to run away from this hateful place? Run as fast as she could from Xavier and his duplicity. If she saw him again she'd never speak to him. Never!

There was a knock at her door.

'Ginnie, can I come in?'

'Xavier? Go away!' she said, with firm resolution.

'Ginnie, please. I can't. I need to talk to you.'

'I don't want to talk to you.'

'I don't blame you. But I need to see you again. Beg your forgiveness. Please, Ginnie, allow me that.'

'But … I … please … go away.' Her voice shook.

'I've so much to explain to you, Ginnie. Let me. Your unhappiness is destroying me. Ginnie, I love you!'

'A moment,' she called back, mopping her eyes with an ineffectual tissue, quickly drawing a brush through her hair, checking her face in the small mirror. 'Come in,' she called. She offered up a small prayer that he really was here to tell her it had all been a misunderstanding, or a joke even, her earlier conversation with Selina fading fast.

'Please, my sweet little one, don't say I made you cry – I couldn't bear that.' He advanced into the room, hand outstretched – almost in supplication, she felt. She backed away from him. She must remain strong – even when all she wanted was to have his arms about her again. How she missed him. It was as if her skin needed the touch of him as hungrily as her soul.

'I've so much to explain. I have to apologise, my darling. How shocked you must be. How deeply hurt.' She was aware of his intense brown eyes, so deep, so impenetrable, so full of – what? Shame? Longing for her?

'I'm confused. And, yes, I feel betrayed by you,' she said, with dignity.

'Of course you are. I understand.' He touched her cheek and a jolt of pleasure seared through her. Had she wanted to back further away from him there was nowhere for her to go because once again she was wedged against the window-sill, this time, though, by his body. His thigh pressed firmly against hers, and he moved it so that he was prising open her legs. Then his hand thrust down between them, hoisting her skirt and probing until it found the place for which it searched.

She turned her head away as his lips sought hers. 'Not forgiven?'

'Hesta – is she – is—' But she found she could not ask what she needed to know.

'Is she my wife? Of course she isn't.' He forced his fingers past her panties. 'I do wish you wouldn't wear these – I want you always naked for me there,' he whispered huskily into her ear, his words exciting her unbearably.

'Then why did she say she was?' she said breathlessly, determined to find out the truth as she tried to control her mounting excitement.

'Hesta likes to make jokes.'

'I didn't find it funny.'

'No, you wouldn't. Neither did I.' His fingers were inside her, massaging her, pushing, searching. 'I punished her – it wasn't fair on you. I want you to be my wife, not her,' he lied, with consummate ease.

'But why were you in bed with her? How could you hurt me so?' She felt as if her legs would buckle and she leant on the window-sill for support.

'Isn't this wonderful? Am I pleasing you?'

She groaned, unable to control herself.

'I was testing you. Forgive me, it was cruel. I wanted to see how much it upset you to find me with another woman. Then I'd know how much you loved me.' She was aware of him unzipping his trousers.

'I don't understand you, Xavier.' He grabbed her hands and placed them on his penis while he continued the relentless massage.

'I don't understand myself most of the time, Ginnie, my darling. Oh, that's wonderful. More. Harder! I'm so insecure. I need stability. I need the love of a good woman. Like you. I need a wife like you!'

'You really mean that?' She stopped the steady movement of her hands. And leant back to look at him.

'What do you want?' he wailed in frustration. 'Should I kneel and ask for your hand?'

'No, no. It's just – it's what I want more than anything – I didn't dare to hope—'

'Sweet one.' His fingers dug harder.

'I love you, Xavier.'

'So I'm forgiven?' And he crashed his mouth down on hers, prising it open with his tongue while his hand delved into her. She was ready for him ...

'I spoke to Carter. Selina told me he's coming to get me tonight. But I don't want to see him. Not now. You do understand, don't you?' she said as, later, they lay in each other's arms and she felt secure again.

'Leave it to me. I'll tell him where to go.' He kissed her naked breast. 'Selina, you said?'

'Yes, she's back. Didn't you know?'

'What a joy!' he said, but she did not notice the sardonic inflection. 'When did you speak to Carter?' he asked, with what appeared to be only mild interest.

'This afternoon – after—' She blushed. 'You know what.'

'And how did you do that, my sweet one?'

'Tessa has a mobile phone,' she answered.

5

All was bustle and excitement in the hall as the entire group waited for the three Americans who were due any moment and who, Xavier had explained, needed to be cared for in the best possible way. 'Envelop them in our special Fohpal love,' he'd ordered.

Rumours were abundant, mainly on the theme that the American contingent had come to sort out who was to succeed as leader in the event of H.G.'s death. Everyone agreed that his heir was apparent in every way: Xavier. And the consensus was that, much as they loved H.G., it was time for someone new. Why, there were even members here now who'd never set eyes on the man.

The three Americans were sincere, enlightened and devoid of humour. All three were in late middle age and all knew H.G. of old and loved him dearly, as they said at regular intervals. Their task was a sombre one and not to be taken lightly.

Bethina was at her most serene and gracious, leading the weary contingent into the drawing room for a late tea, past the excited followers.

'Always such a lovely tea you give us, Bethina.' Mirabelle Forster sipped appreciatively at the Crown Derby cup.

'We like you to feel at home. And no matter the hour I know you'll want tea, dear Mirabelle.' She handed cups to Willow Makepeace and Clinton Williamson.

'We were wondering when it would be best for us to see H.G. We don't wish to intrude or to make things uneasy for him.'

'Perhaps early tomorrow morning would be best, Mirabelle. He's sleeping now and the least sound disturbs him. Mind you, when he's awake he won't recognise you – you are prepared for that?' Xavier's face was set in an expression of deep sadness.

'Personally I'm dreading it,' Willow said, with a flutter of her lace-trimmed handkerchief. 'To see such a man as he laid low will be hard.'

'At least we'll have the privilege of saying goodbye to him, not like most of the followers who'll have their memories alone,' Clinton said sagely, and with the hint of pomposity that his elevated position in the American fellowship had bestowed upon him. 'You say H.G. has left a will, Xavier?'

'That's the problem. It's not a will as such, not a legally binding document. He dictated his wishes to one of the followers, who typed it for him. Would that he had left a proper one, drawn up by a lawyer.'

'But he has signed it?'

'Oh, yes, Clinton. He did that. But still ...' Xavier cleared his throat. 'You must understand, it puts me in an invidious position since, you see, I'm named by H.G. as his successor. Far better that it's left to you three to sort it all out. I don't want anyone accusing me of usurping his position.'

'I shouldn't imagine anyone would think so of you, Xavier,' simpered Willow who, in a quiet way, lusted after him.

'Something's got to be sorted out, that's for sure. Someone has to be in control – I'm sure it's how H.G.

would want it. We trustees can look after the money with no trouble – it's an honour. But the overall position needs vision and insight.'

'The day-to-day running becomes more difficult – the bills ...' Mathie spoke for the first time.

'Understandable. Xavier obviously needs access to money.'

'You're all looking so tired. Perhaps you'd like a wash and brush-up?' Bethina asked.

'I just love your quaint expressions.' Mirabelle tittered.

'And later this evening, we've persuaded Xavier to give us a talk and a healing. We've a famous actress here – Jessica Lawley, you'll have heard of her?'

'Yes, of course.'

'Xavier has helped her arthritis immeasurably and we thought ...'

'She'll permit us to witness? How gracious.'

Xavier smiled contentedly. Everything was working out far better than he had dared hope. 'Now, if you'll excuse me? I've work to do.'

'Of course. Of course.' The Americans stood, and Bethina showed them to their rooms.

The Americans were taking a shower.

Ginnie was beside herself with happiness.

Jessica was as nervous as – what? She was not sure, except that every nerve seemed exposed, as if they had been rearranged on the outside of her body. She looked at her watch. Selina and Tessa would be here soon. She felt better when they were together.

6

Selina and Tessa were in Tessa's room. They felt secure since Tessa had found the bug under her bedside lamp and had cunningly covered it with a wad of chewing gum.

For the umpteenth time they were going over the plans for the rescue tonight. They had called Carter and Humphrey again, who had been reassured by their high spirits.

'Heavens, is that the time? I promised Jessica I wouldn't budge from her room – she'll be having kittens.' Selina slid off the bed.

'What if you're seen?'

'I'll use the back stairs. In any case, the Americans must be here by now, they'll be too busy fawning over them to notice me slide by like a wraith!'

Both women's heads snapped up as the door burst open. Shocked, they watched Xavier, with Hesta behind him, stalk into the room.

'Couldn't stay away, Selina? What a compliment to us all,' he said coldly.

'Something like that,' Selina stuttered. She was astonished that her heart could race as fast as it did and not explode.

'Tessa. Give me the phone,' Hesta ordered, as she pushed past Xavier, her hand held out. Xavier crossed to the fireplace where he stood still, watching the three women. He looked evil, thought Selina. How could she have ever found him funny? 'Give it to me!'

'I've got no phone. I don't know what the hell you're talking about,' Tessa replied, defiantly, while she felt her insides quake.

'Xavier!' Hesta barked and Tessa felt him pin her arms painfully behind her. Then Hesta stepped forward and slapped her face hard, then, as if she enjoyed it, she did it again. Tessa bit her lip to stop the tears, determined not to let them see her cry.

'Phone!'

'I just said –' The next slap was a thump.

'You aggressive bitch, leave her alone!' Selina shouted, and grabbed Hesta's raised arm. The woman turned her head and bit Selina's hand, forcing her to let go. Then, with one smooth movement, she kicked her hard in the stomach. Selina doubled up, gagging from the pain.

'I do love a cat fight.' Xavier laughed.

'You were such a mealy-mouthed cow. Wouldn't hurt a fly, would you?' Selina, almost winded, spat out.

'I was good, wasn't I? I knew I'd taken you in. I've often been told I should have been an actress. Now, in case you think you've made me forget – the telephone. Don't waste your breath denying it – Ginnie told us you'd got it and that she'd been talking to her husband and that he's coming to get her. See?' Hesta smiled with infuriating smugness. 'So, does Xavier search you, Tessa – no doubt he'd enjoy that – or do you give it to us?'

'If you'll let go of my arms, please,' she said, with heavy irony. She took the telephone from the pocket in the side of her jumper and handed it over.

'Right. Now dial your father and tell him he can't come tonight to get Ginnie – understood?'

'He won't believe me.'

'He will, if you say there's been a complication. Say the Americans are here and it would be too difficult to arrange tonight. Put him off, say you'll call tomorrow. Can you remember all that?'

'I won't call,' Tessa said, with a courage she was far from feeling.

'Yes, you will.' And, deliberately, Hesta hit Selina on the mouth and split open her lip. 'If you don't co-operate,

I'll give the cool, cold Jessica a going-over, and Ginnie too. I'll enjoy that.'

'What are you? A sadist dyke or what?' asked Selina, as she dabbed at her bleeding mouth.

'You can't insult me, Selina. Your opinion of me is of no interest. Now, Tessa, phone. And don't try any tricks.'

Her hand shaking, Tessa tapped in the telephone number. She wondered if it would help if she misdialled, but decided it wouldn't. She was purposely slow as her mind raced: could she get a message to the men that all was not well? Just as she pushed in the last number she thrust the phone into Selina's hand.

'I can't do it. I can't lie easily. Selina, you do it.' It was Selina's turn to think quickly. Could she say something odd to alert them? The phone was ringing and she could think of nothing. Even if she had it would have been useless since Hesta pressed her ear close to the telephone.

'Mulholland speaking.'

'Carter, it's Selina. I'm here. It's off.'

'Selina, are you all right?' he asked urgently.

'Never felt better.'

'Ginnie and Tessa, are they okay?'

'Fine.'

'Let me talk to them.'

'Not possible.'

'You sure you're all all right?'

'Honest, Carter. Don't worry. See you,' she said. And then, injecting a tone of hysteria into her voice, cried out, '... as soon as ...' But it came too late, Hesta had already pressed the button and the call was disconnected.

'Why didn't you say what I told you to about the Americans?' Hesta demanded.

'I forgot.'

'That's for forgetting.' Hesta raised her fist and Selina's arm was already up to ward off the blows.

'Stop it! Please!' Tessa screamed. 'I can't take this.'

'You're going to have to take whatever I decide, Miss Spoilt Brat Mulholland.'

'You'll both be dealt with – later,' said Xavier ominously.

'And Jessica?' Selina asked.

'Why should we harm Jessica? She's been a model guest and think what an endorsement she'll be!' Hesta replied.

'And Ginnie?' Selina asked, fearfully.

'We've got plans for her too. But a bit later than you.' Hesta smiled unpleasantly.

'What? When she's given you all her money? You bastards. It's not you, is it, Xavier? You're just the front, it's dear Hesta here who's in control – and the brains. Clever, I'll give you that. And I thought you were just another of his tarts,' Selina said recklessly, but, after all, she had nothing to lose.

Tessa stood, listening with mounting horror, as the realisation dawned of what they meant. 'Killed and hidden any more followers recently, Liz?' she said. It might be a stupid thing to say, but if she was going down she was going to go down fighting and, oddly, with this decision taken she did not feel nearly as afraid. And at least she had the satisfaction of seeing the look of anger mixed with horror flit across Hesta's face before the mobile phone was slammed into the side of her head and blackness engulfed her.

'You didn't have to do that, you evil cow. She's only a kid. Let her go.'

'What? And have her blab everything? Oh, no, Selina. We're almost there – almost got what we want – and you aren't going to stop us. By tomorrow we'll be gone and you'll be dead!'

chapter **eighteen**

1

Jessica could feel real fear bubbling inside. She had looked everywhere but could not find Tessa. Ginnie had been offhand with her and Tessa's bedroom was empty, although her things were still there. And where was Selina? Jessica was furious with her – she'd promised to stay put. Anything could have happened to her. Deep inside her Jessica knew that both had been found out, and if that was the case ...

Mathie waylaid her.

'Jessica, Xavier would like to see you in the gallery later.'

'What time?'

'About midnight. In half an hour there's our special welcome dinner. After that there's another chance to meet our guests at a camomile tea serving. Then there's meditation. Afterwards Xavier is holding a group meeting. He'd like to demonstrate his healing abilities on you for our American friends,' Mathie explained.

'So late?' Her mind floundered. If things went to plan, which was unlikely, she supposed, but they might, midnight would be too late. These meetings could be interminable, and it would never be finished by two. She pulled herself together – Mathie was staring at her curiously.

'Is there any problem? You look flummoxed. Are you planning on going somewhere?' Mathie grinned.

'A healing in front of everyone?' Jessica sounded aghast.

'You don't mind, do you? You should want to share the joy of Xavier's miraculous ability.'

'Of course. Selfish of me,' Jessica said, while raging inside at the idea of being made a public spectacle. 'By the way, have you seen Tessa? We were going to read from one of H.G.'s books to each other,' she said, she hoped piously.

'Is she with her mother? I haven't seen her all day,' Mathie said, as she bustled off. Jessica did not know why but she felt strongly that Mathie had been lying.

Just before dinner Jessica was introduced to the visiting VIPs and felt a little like a prize pig on display. But, still, she had to admit that she enjoyed the look of recognition in their eyes, their apparent pleasure at meeting her. Jessica missed her public more than she cared to admit, and these Americans were a pleasant-looking trio. She considered trying to get one of them alone and attempting to explain about H.G. and the diaries and Xavier being a crook, but they looked so happy here that she doubted they would believe her.

'We hear Xavier has been working his miracles on you,' one said, smiling broadly.

'He's wonderful,' she gushed, and it was not entirely false for whatever else was going on here she was grateful for her improved mobility. 'I could hardly stand without a stick when I first came here. I don't know how he does it.'

'He's a great asset to us at Fohpal. And his reputation expands.'

'I've been told H.G. is brilliant, too, and has many healings to his credit,' she said, testing their loyalty.

'Absolutely. He was so great. So very great.' The woman nodded sadly and Jessica noted that, like the rest, she had used the past tense, but decided not to say anything to them – not yet, anyway.

The food at dinner looked delicious, despite the

absence of meat and fish, and Jessica managed a bite or two, but was too wound up to eat more. She found it hard to concentrate on anything so she excused herself from the meetings – much to the two American women's disappointment – and went to her room. She longed for a drink. It wasn't true that alcohol clouded her vision: in the past a hefty Scotch had always helped her think.

With no Tessa and Selina, no Matt and no telephone, everything looked so bleak. She had no choice, she was going to have to take risks. Later tonight she would try to speak to the male visitor, Clinton; as always, she knew she would prefer to deal with a man rather than the women. Since they were from America the chances were high that Xavier had not got to them. Clinton looked about sixty. Hopefully, given his age, he would know H.G. well and thus would be steadier and above such scams as Xavier's. She would take him to meet H.G. and get H.G. to tell him everything in case he didn't believe her. Risky it might be, but she had no other choice. She had to have an alternative plan – the depressing feeling that something had gone wrong would not go away.

She felt much better with difficult decisions made. She washed her face and redid her make-up: perhaps she'd put in an appearance at the camomile tea serving – grim! Then, maybe, she'd be able to inveigle herself close enough to Clinton to talk to him.

She heard voices in the corridor outside her room. They seemed to be coming from the direction of H.G.'s suite. She crossed the room to listen at the door, turning off the light as she did so.

'Spot on.' She heard Xavier say.

'Willow and Mirabelle are sharp.' Her heart leapt at the accent – it was Clinton!

'Don't worry. We gave him a double dose. They can pop in any time, he'll be like the living dead. Shush, though, the old cow might be in her room. I saw her slip out from dinner. Not that there's anything she could do, but I'd better check.'

Jessica flattened herself against the wall and heard a light tap on the door. The door creaked open and Xavier looked in. 'Not to worry – she's not here.'

'Will she stay voluntarily or ...' She did not hear what the alternative was.

Her heart was beating so hard it hurt. She took deep breaths as she felt panic rise again. She must not let it swamp her. There was only one thing left to do. She had no option.

From her wardrobe she collected a black cloak, changed into a pair of flat shoes and, leaving the light off, slipped from the room and down the corridor. She paused in the hall and, looking over her shoulder frequently, slid back the heavy bolts of the door to the outside. She might as well – a miracle could happen.

Slowly she opened the door into H.G.'s drawing room, tiptoed across and peered cautiously into the bedroom. The coast was clear.

H.G. had evidently heard her for he lay as still as a brass rubbing.

'H.G. it's me, Jessica. You can open your eyes now.' But he didn't. He lay still. 'H.G.,' she whispered, and then tried louder, but there was no response.

What now? What should she do?

It was as if ravens were flapping in her head and she wanted to scream, release the pressure inside her before hysteria took over.

Calm down, she told herself, but her need for a drink now was paramount. H.G. had a tray of drinks next door. There were bottles of every description on a silver tray, but no glasses. She began to open and shut cupboard doors in her search, and finally found them. As she reached in to take one she noticed, to one side of the cupboard, a knife with a curved blade much larger than

413

its handle. She lifted it down. Its edge glinted evilly in the light and she felt remarkably comforted to have it in her hand. She felt even better when she had downed what must have amounted to a triple Scotch and then poured herself a second. Still holding the knife and the glass, she returned to H.G.'s bedside.

'Oh, H.G., how could you do this to me?' she asked the unresponsive man. She'd had a plan, admittedly vague, of supporting him to the door in the hall and propping him outside while she stole a car – like last time; hopefully the keys would have been left in it. She'd starred in films where people did clever things with wires to make cars go without keys but had never asked how it was done. If she ever got out of here, she'd certainly find out! Not *if*, *when*, she told herself firmly, as she sat by H.G., clutching the knife, full of Dutch courage, which was evaporating again by the minute.

Selina gradually regained consciousness. She had a pounding headache and a sore temple. Before her eyes opened, she knew exactly where she was. She balled her fists with frustration at being in this cell – they could call it whatever they liked but that was what it was. And they were going to kill her, she'd no doubt of that. This was crazy! This was Cornwall, England, the 1990s, not some Gothic horror tale or a movie, she told herself. She knew that there was no point in exploring the wall for a way out – there was no window, no air vents.

If only she'd something with which to pick the lock – she laughed at that idea, not much of a laugh but it made her feel more herself. How did one even begin to pick a lock? She'd read about it, seen it done in films. When she got out of here she'd damn well make sure she knew how to do it.

She pushed her fingers through her curls and wished she had a hairpin but she never used them – they only fell out of her unruly mop. In any case, it had been the first place Hesta had checked as she frisked her.

Now *there* was a thought. What on earth had they been frisking her for? Weapons? In her hair? Very unlikely. No, they were looking for hairpins – and why? Because the lock was pickable, no doubt about it, otherwise they'd never have bothered.

She felt a curious elation at this thought. Now all she had to do was find something ...

A soft groan sounded in the darkness and then another, louder one. A disembodied voice said, 'Gross!'

'Tessa, is that you?' she asked urgently. Tessa would never know how Selina's spirits lifted at the sound of that moan.

'Selina? I'm over here. What happened?'

'Xavier and Hesta knocked us out and if we don't find a way out – well, better not think about it.' She crawled in the direction of Tessa's voice.

'It's so black in here. I never knew darkness could be like this.' Tessa shuddered.

'At least the sound's off – that's something. That endless noise they play nearly drove me barmy last time.'

'You've been here before and you got out?' Tessa sounded excited.

'A bloke rescued me that time. I've not got any other handy fellows around.' The lightness of her tone disguised the fear she felt at their perilous state.

'Where is he?'

'Long story. I'll tell you when we get out.' Though *if* might be a better choice of word, she thought. 'If we could find something to pick the lock ...'

'I'll search one way and you search the other.'

'We'll start at the door, it'll be a reference point.'

'Where's the door?'

Selina groped for Tessa's hand. 'This way.' On hands

and knees they shuffled towards where she thought the door must be.

From there, they began methodically to edge their way around the floor, feeling for something metal – a piece of wire, a nail, anything. Selina thought they were probably wasting their time, but still, nothing ventured. She whistled tunelessly as she worked. Her probing fingers began to feel sore – the floor was rough cement. She touched something. She felt carefully. It was leather. It was a shoe.

'Tessa, is that you I'm touching?'

'What? No, I'm over here.' Tessa's voice came from the other side of the room.

Then what …? Gingerly Selina stretched out her hand and touched the shoe again. She felt the outline of the heel – it was lying on its side. Then she felt a foot in the shoe and her hand shot back. She gasped.

'Found something?' Tessa called.

'I don't think we're alone. Hi, whoever you are!' she said, into the darkness. 'I'm Selina.' There was no reply.

'Are they unconscious, do you think?' Tessa asked.

Selina ran her hands up the legs and found a skirt – a woman or a transvestite? She almost giggled. The woman was propped against the wall as she had been when she came round.

Who was it? She didn't like to feel further – it seemed rude and intrusive. After all, she wouldn't like a stranger of either sex fumbling about with her breasts. Faces were different. Tentatively she felt about where she thought the woman's face might be.

There was no face.

Her hands were sticky. She knew with what. This face had been beaten to a pulp. Selina felt as if a tight band had been tied round her chest. She fought to breathe and scrambled to her feet and, as she did, the woman slid to one side and there was a grunt of exhaling air.

'What's going on? Who's that?' Tessa began to scrabble towards the noises.

'No, Tessa. Stay where you are.' She could hear the shrill hysteria in her own voice. 'It's all right.'

'Who is it?' Tessa was beside her. 'Where?'

Selina grabbed in the dark desperately to stay Tessa's hand. 'Don't. Don't touch.' But it was too late.

Tessa screamed. The awful noise ricocheted off the dark walls. It was a sound that seemed to have no end.

'Stop that bloody noise!' Selina shouted. 'It's not helping.' She lashed out into the blackness and her hand hit Tessa's face. 'I'm sorry, I had to do that.' She backed herself away from whoever was lying – dead, she was sure – on the hard, cold floor. She could feel great waves of fear, like convulsions, shake her body.

The doorknob dug into her back, the pain sobering her. Oh, my God. She put her hand to her mouth, inadvertently tasted someone else's blood and gagged.

She hunkered down beside the door. She was not crying, but rocked back and forth in fearful despair.

'Selina, I'm so afraid.'

'Join the club,' she replied, as she began to shake from head to toe. No matter how hard she tried, she could not stop. Her teeth chattered, her limbs trembled. Think. Try to think. You're in shock. You've got to get out of it. She made herself breathe deeply, gasping for air, and as the oxygen flooded her system a measure of control returned.

'You all right, Tessa?'

'Who is it, do you think?'

'It might be a woman called Esmeralda.' A tear rolled down her cheek. It was her fault. She should never have left the letter.

She wiped her face with her arm, forcing herself to suppress her emotions.

They had to get out of here. They had to escape for Esmeralda too. People must know. If they didn't tell them she would just have disappeared and her family would never know what had happened to her – the worst cruelty of all.

Think logically, she ordered herself. Had she anything that might help? 'Have you got earrings on or something we could bend?' she called.

'They're studs – they won't do.'

Selina wriggled her torso: the bra she'd bought in Marks and Spencer was digging into her. She was wearing a ring, Indian silver with a topaz set in it, but it was too thick. She put her hand up to her side to release the pressure of this wretched bra—

The bra!

'Hang on in there, Tessa. I think I might have something.' Quickly she slipped her jumper over her head and felt behind her for the clasp. 'I haven't worn a bra like this, all satin and underwired, since my teens. I suppose we have to thank God for uplift!' she said, trying a joke, knowing that Tessa wasn't amused and that she herself couldn't raise a smile. With trembling fingers, she felt for the edge of the cup. She forced her teeth to stop chattering and began to gnaw at the stitching. She wished it wasn't so well made: her jaw ached as she chewed and tugged at it.

'How are you doing? Can I help?' Tessa was now sitting beside her.

'It's coming …' Finally the fabric gave – all she needed was the tiny hole she'd made to pull out the plastic-covered wire.

'Sod it. I've bloody well dropped it.' She searched the floor with fingertips to find it.

'I've got it. Here.' Tessa handed her the wire.

'Take this and work on the other cup, will you?' She gave Tessa the bra while she set to, concentrating hard, as she waggled the wire in the lock. But the lock was jammed by the key on the other side. Selina slumped against the wall and knew despair.

'What's happening? Why have you stopped?'

'The key's in the lock. There's no gap under the door.'

'Oh, Selina, what are we going to do?'

'Don't worry. We'll think of something,' she said, but Tessa was not fooled by the optimism she'd put into her voice.

Hesta stayed until the meditation was well under way but she could not relax. She had the strangest feeling of unease, which worried her since she was a pragmatic person.

'I've a feeling something's wrong,' she whispered to Xavier. 'I think I'd better check.'

'The old man's out like a light, so no need to worry there.'

'No, it's that bitch Selina.'

'You searched her.'

'I know, but I've this nagging thought we left the key in the door.'

'You mean *you* did,' Xavier whispered back.

Hesta left the group contentedly no-noing away. God, what fools they all were. Still, not much longer and they'd be free of this lentil-obsessed band of no-hopers. Just thinking of the huge sum of money they would soon be able to purloin, added to that which they had already salted away offshore, made her spirits lift. She'd talk to Xavier tonight and get him to persuade that silly woman Ginnie to come with them. Then they could milk her at their leisure. It would be one body less here. There was a mad glint in her eye. Certainly the bodies were piling up! Xavier did not know that Esmeralda was dead. She was not looking forward to asking him to help her dispose of the body. She frowned at that thought. It wasn't that he was squeamish – it hadn't bothered him when they'd had to kill the doctor, Dominic. No, the truth was he'd grown fond of Esmeralda, which was probably why Hesta had gone too far when she'd been punishing her. Killing her had been an accident, but she wasn't sure if Xavier would see it that way. Luckily he hadn't known he'd got the stupid girl pregnant.

In any case, it was his fault – Hesta had never minded in the past when he'd screwed around. In fact, she enjoyed hearing the details, later in their own bed. But Esmeralda had been different. He'd got too fond, too protective, and she couldn't have that.

He'd have to kill Selina, she decided. For a start it would make them even: if she helped him dispose of Selina he could help her with Esmeralda. They'd share Tessa. Yes, that was fair.

But it wasn't just the corpses she needed to get away from. She was getting edgy about Xavier. Once or twice he'd said there was no hurry, and nagging away in her mind was the thought that he was enjoying this guru bit and all the adulation too much. She suspected he was becoming addicted to it.

She sped along the cellar passageway. She'd been right – the key was in the door. A good job she'd checked. She unlocked the door.

'Are you there – bitches?' she spat out.

'Um ... Sorry ... Who's that?' A sleepy-voiced Selina replied.

'Rot in hell!' Hesta slammed the door. She took the key out of the lock and slipped it in her pocket.

Then, despite Xavier's assurances, she decided to check the old fool for herself. She moved quickly up the cellar stairs and ran across the hall. Best to check the old cow too since she hadn't seen her since dinner, and without knocking, she entered Jessica's room. She switched on the light. The bed was neatly made. She was about to leave when she saw Jessica's large handbag on a chair. The habits of a lifetime proved too strong and she went through it methodically for anything worth stealing. She was pleased to find a diamond-studded Rolex, fifty pounds and a cheque book. When Jessica began to screech that she'd been robbed, they'd have a full meeting and Xavier could rant and rage at them and they'd all look guilty, as they always did, which would amuse her no end.

Time to check H.G.

She turned off the light and walked rapidly towards his rooms, passing through the small stone hallway without glancing at the door that led to the outside.

She looked about the drawing room – rich pickings here eventually, she thought.

The door of the corner cupboard was open. Odd, she thought, as she shut it. She pushed open the door into H.G.'s room and was satisfied to see him lying as still as if he was dead already.

She stood a moment, looked down at him, 'Not long now, you boring old bugger,' and laughed. She swung round to leave but paused: in an angled mirror she caught sight of a petrified-looking Jessica.

'Not attending the meditation, Jessica? Prefer to hide behind the curtains?' There was no movement or response.

'You should have checked there were no gaps – sloppy that, Jessica,' she mocked. 'I suppose you were in a bit of a hurry when you heard me. Too nosey by far, aren't you?' There was no reply to her goading. 'You'd better come out – I've got all night.' Still Jessica did not move. 'Jessica, old girl, I'm picking up a spare pillow and I'm placing it on H.G.'s face and I'm leaning heavily down and I'm suffocating him and I won't stop until you emerge from your hidey-hole.' She spoke in a monotonous voice. The curtain twitched and Jessica stepped out. 'That's better.'

'I thought I heard a noise and came to investigate.'

'A likely story!' Hesta snorted.

'It's true.'

'Don't lie to me. Did you think you were cleverer than me? No one is – *no one*! Pity it was you, though, you might have come in handy. Now I'm going to have to dispose of you.' And she stepped towards Jessica, arm outstretched to take hold of her. From behind her back Jessica's arm arched up and out, the knife flashing in the subdued light as she aimed for Hesta's arm. 'Naughty! You'll pay for that!' Hesta grabbed at Jessica's arm. 'Give it to me,' she screeched. 'Drop this fucking knife now!' But Jessica hung on grimly, even though Hesta twisted her arm painfully back. 'Drop it!' she shouted, and H.G. stirred. She glanced at him momentarily, losing concentration sufficiently for Jessica to lash out at her. The knife sliced into the flesh of her lower arm. Blood gushed out.

'You cut me, you fucking cow! You hurt me.' And she leapt on Jessica like one demented, kicking and scratching. As they wrestled, her blood smeared Jessica and dripped to the floor. But even though Hesta was wounded there was no contest: she was fit, strong and thirty, while Jessica was unfit, fifty-four and disabled.

Jessica knew she was weakening, could feel the strength ebbing from her.

Suddenly Hesta's hold relaxed and, with a mighty groan, she dropped to the floor. Selina, herself smeared with blood, stood with a rather fine bronze of an elephant in her hand. She looked down at Hesta.

'I rather enjoyed that,' she said, unsteadily, and a wan-faced Tessa caught her before she fell.

2

'Where the hell have you two been? You promised to stay put, Selina, not go gallivanting around. As for you, Tessa, I've been looking everywhere for you!' An angry Jessica turned on them. Selina sat, white-faced, and Tessa stood like sentry, clasping her hands in front of her. 'Good God, what's happened?' Jessica had seen the gruesome smear of blood on Selina's cheek and glistening in her hair.

'Sorry,' Selina said, in a sing-song voice. 'They locked us up. We escaped.' She pushed back her hair wearily and then, realising it was wet with blood, shuddered violently. 'There's a woman's body in the cellar. I think it might be poor Esmeralda.' She spoke matter-of-factly, which made what she had said even more horrific.

'Dear God!' Jessica looked from one to the other. 'Are you hurt? There's blood—' And she pointed at Selina's face.

'No, I'm fine. That must be Esmeralda's blood.' And she started to shake again.

Jessica looked at Tessa who still stood as if made of stone. 'Tessa? Darling, are you all right? Sweetie. Sit down.'

At the kind words Tessa, too, began to shake. Tears tumbled down her cheeks. 'Oh, shit, this isn't going to help.' Angrily she wiped them away.

Jessica understood now why the girl had been clasping her hands so tightly: they were trembling like wind-blown leaves. 'Sit down, darling. You're all in.' Jessica took one of the quivering hands. 'I'll get you a drink – you look as if you need it.'

'We've got to get out of here, Jessica. We haven't time for drinks – they'll be missing Hesta.' Selina half stood, but suddenly, feeling dizzy, sat down again.

'See? We won't get anywhere unless you rest a bit. I'll lock the drawing-room door, that'll give us a smidgen of time. Now, stay put!' While getting the drinks, Jessica felt her old enemy, panic, hit her face on. Everything was deteriorating so fast. She looked at her watch – nearly midnight. They'd have to move before two or they'd all be locked up – or worse. There was no time to wait for Humph and the others.

She returned from the drawing room with glasses and a bottle of brandy.

'I hate brandy.' Selina sniffed it.

'I don't care, you're drinking it, I need your help,' Jessica said briskly, but with authority, and Selina downed the drink in one. Tessa drank hers holding the glass with both hands to guide it to her lips.

'There's another problem. H.G. is out like a light. Somehow we've got to carry him to a car.' Jessica was collecting his clothes as she spoke. 'It's a stormy night, we're going to have to dress him.'

'Jessica, I can't do it!' Selina looked up at her, her eyes full of remembered terror.

'Don't be a wimp! Of course you can.'

'Don't you talk to her like that – just don't.' Tessa stood up. 'She's been wonderful. I was useless, I went to pieces. She got us out of that place and it's all been too much for her and me!'

'I know, and it'll probably get worse, but getting this far and then giving up – I won't hear of it. Is that understood? Have another brandy, Selina, you'll feel better.' Jessica looked efficient and stern, but it was an act. She was falling apart inside.

'What am I missing? Goodness me, Jessica, you *are* sounding bossy.'

The women swung round to see H.G. struggling to sit up in bed.

'I thought you were comatose,' Jessica said accusingly.

'No, I was asleep. Why are you bossing?'

'Asleep! You slept through all that commotion? I don't believe it!'

'When I sleep I sleep. I'm renowned for it. You're early, aren't you? Didn't you say one o'clock? I'd have woken up for that time. I can, you know, just by thinking it.'

'You're H.G.' Selina said. 'I read your diaries. I wasn't sure whether to believe you or not, or whether Jessica was panicking unnecessarily.'

'Charming!' snorted Jessica, but she noted the sudden difference in Selina, as if meeting H.G. face to face had calmed her and put her back on track.

'I'm Selina. And this is Tessa.'

'How do you do?' H.G. said politely.

'Are the introductions over?' asked Jessica impatiently.

'Dear Jessica, you sound so grumpy. I'm sorry I didn't wake up for you.' H.G. smiled at her, and Selina understood this time why people followed him, for the smile was not the vacant, empty sort she'd become used to here: it brimmed with genuine charm.

'I overheard Xavier say they'd given you two doses. I presumed my water-filled ampoules had run out so I didn't try very hard to wake you.'

'He was here with the unspeakable Clinton. You know, I always had my doubts about him, from way back in the sixties, wrong motives. Self, you know. And a pot-head – never reliable people. Who's she?' He pointed to the body lying face down on the floor. 'She's not dead, is she?'

'It's Hesta. Selina knocked her out.'

'Not a nice lady – at all. Now, Tessa, come and sit here and talk to me.' H.G. patted the bed.

'It's all very well sitting here chatting, but three things are likely to happen. She'll come round at any minute, she'll be missed, and reinforcements will come to her aid.'

Jessica's panic had given way to irritation with the lot of them.

'She's right, of course.' H.G. agreed, nodding sagely. 'What time did you say the men were coming, Jessica?'

'We can't wait for them, H.G.'

'We were made to phone them to say the rescue was off,' Selina added. 'Can you walk?'

'With difficulty,' H.G. replied.

'We could prop you up on either side – support you. I'm feeling better. How about you, Tessa?'

'I'm fine.' But the shaking persisted, and neither Selina nor Jessica believed her. They left her sitting while they helped the old man dress. As Selina put on his shoes, Jessica helped him pull a sweater over his pyjamas.

'I don't like these shoes,' he said petulantly. 'I want my Ferragamo ones. And I'm all bundled up,' he went on. 'This jumper is rumpled, I'm particularly fond of it.'

'We haven't time to take everything off to iron it, H.G.' Jessica said grimly.

'So I'm to lump it, is that so, Jessica?'

'Now, which coat?' she asked, as she went to the dressing room, which she knew was lined with wardrobes full of clothes hung in colour-coordinated lines.

'The navy cashmere with the astrakhan collar,' he called. 'And I've a blue and gold silk cravat – I think that would be best.' Jessica did not know whether to be amused by his insistence on a degree of sartorial elegance in such bizarre and dangerous circumstances, to admire his courage or to be livid with him. When she returned with the coat it was to find him fussing about brushing his hair. She decided to be amused.

'What about you?' Jessica asked Selina in a business-like way. Selina had discarded the blood-covered sweater and wore only her shirt and leggings. 'You'll need something against the cold. Listen.' The wind was howling ferociously outside, tearing in from the sea with an angry force.

'You know, Selina, you look like one of them, but you're not. Isn't that so?' H.G. asked conversationally. Jessica felt fury at his inability to grasp the urgency of the situation.

'Yes. I'm not sure why, but then I've always lived life on the edges looking in – Xavier told me so.' She pulled a face.

'Then undoubtedly it's not true. I've another fine cashmere coat in my wardrobe,' he offered. 'A beige one – it would suit your colouring.'

'Could we *please* get a move on?' Jessica interrupted.

'Don't fuss, Jessica. We're getting there. Now, somewhere I've a particularly pretty silver-topped cane, which might help me.'

'God, what next?' Jessica exclaimed. 'You are an aggravating old fart!' she added, under her breath.

'What did you say?' H.G. paused.

'I said you're an aggravating old fart. And you are,' Jessica snapped.

'My dear Jessica. You can't know how happy you've made me. Such music to my ears. I've longed for someone to call me an old fart for so many years!'

This was too much and both women, despite the mounting tension, laughed with amused affection. Tessa did not join in.

H.G. was finally dressed to his satisfaction and the women warmly wrapped up.

'Tessa, can you help Selina with H.G.?' Jessica asked, but there was no response. 'Tessa, you're stronger than me. Oh, hell, Selina, it'll have to be you and me. Put your arms around our shoulders, H.G., we'll take your weight.'

'One minute.' H.G. held up his hand. 'Tessa, dear child, it's all going to be all right. Now you stand and

427

come with us,' he said gently, and Tessa, still in a daze, obediently got up. 'Right, ladies.' He smiled with the smile that, Jessica was sure, could galvanize whole armies.

They began to make their way slowly towards the hall, the unbolted door and freedom.

This isn't going to work, thought Jessica. They were only half-way across the drawing room, and already her hip was beginning to ache. She gritted her teeth as they moved on until, with a sigh of relief, she could lean against the wall beside the door into the hall.

'Can you make it, Jessica?' Selina asked.

'I'll bloody well have to. Where's Tessa?' She looked back across the room for her.

'As soon as we're free I'll work on that wretched hip for you. So sad for one so young and beautiful,' said H.G.

'Why, thank you, H.G. You certainly know the optimum time to hand out the compliments. Tessa!' she called.

Selina opened the door a crack and peered out, then shut it sharply and turned the key. She looked at the others, horror etched on her face as she fell against the door.

'What is it?' Jessica asked urgently.

'It's them. They've come to get us!'

3

'Who's out there?' Jessica shouted, over the insistent banging on the door.

'I saw Xavier and Berihert, I didn't register the others except it looked like a flaming posse. If only we hadn't stopped for that drink!'

'And if I hadn't made such a fuss about clothes. I'm sorry, Jessica.' H.G. looked downcast.

'You're not giving in. We can't do that. At least let's take some of the buggers with us. Here.' Jessica grabbed another heavy bronze elephant from a side table and handed it to Selina. For herself she found a silver inkstand.

'What about me?' H.G. asked.

'Just get back into the room and keep out of trouble,' Jessica ordered and, despite the imminent danger, H.G. smiled.

Jessica eyed the door: it was thick but if this battery persisted it would soon give way. Even as she thought this, she heard the first splitting of wood.

'You get the first creep through, Selina, and I'll take care of the second.'

Both women raised their weapons over their heads as, with a mighty heave from the other side, the door gave way. Wood splintered and the lock tore as Berihert crashed through, Selina, on tiptoe, smashed the bronze into his chest, which was as far as she could reach. The force of the blow made him stumble and Jessica brought her inkstand down on his head. He stood a second, an expression of surprise on his face, before he toppled to the floor like a felled tree. There was a delay, just long enough for Selina to retrieve her weapon as Xavier cautiously peered in. She threw it at him and the edge caught his forehead, cutting him. He was upright until he felt the trickle of blood, put his hand to his face to investigate and, on seeing the fresh blood, passed clean out.

At the sight of the two prone men, both women felt a resurgence of hope. But it was short-lived as Clinton pushed in, followed by Bethina.

'Bethina?' H.G. looked at her questioningly. 'Surely

not you? Not my little Bethina.' He felt for a chair and sank into it.

Bethina had the grace to look away. 'How sad,' said H.G., and Selina wondered if he was about to cry. 'Do you prove the adage, then, that "everyone has their price"?' Bethina did not answer but looked down, yet not before Jessica saw what looked suspiciously like a tear in her eye.

'Xavier! No!' a voice called from the doorway and Ginnie, pushing the others out of her way, rushed to his side and knelt down. She fanned his face, kissed his wound, called his name. 'Who did this?' She looked up at them, her face twisted with fury, his blood on her lips.

'Yo, friend!' Selina said ironically, and half raised a hand in salute.

'I'll kill you for this.'

'I love you, too!' Selina tasted fear as Berihert, consciousness returned, lumbered to his feet. He did not attack her, though, but took up a position in the centre of the room by H.G.'s chair, a stolid sentry.

Xavier groaned and Ginnie returned her attention to him. 'My darling, say you're all right.' Slowly his eyes opened and he sat up, rubbing his head. Pushing Ginnie aside, he hauled himself to his feet and looked about him wildly.

'You'll pay for that, you bitch,' he spat at Selina, who stood her ground and stared at him with such disdain that Jessica could have hugged her. Enraged, he stepped forward and slapped her hard across her face.

'Hey—' Clinton began, but was silenced by a wrathful glance from Xavier.

With a quiet air of dignity, H.G. remained in his chair as Xavier approached him.

'Where's Hesta?' Xavier demanded, pulling the old man to his feet in order to elicit an answer.

'Don't treat him like that.' Jessica stepped forward protectively.

'I'll treat him any way I want. He's excess baggage. Ginnie, Bethina, put the old fool back to bed and knock him out.'

'A moment,' H.G. said, and instinctively the women were still. 'Xavier, our relationship must not end this way.'

'It'll end how and when I want. I repeat, where's Hesta?'

'Xavier, if you won't talk, then I'll bargain with you. I'll give you anything you want, but just let these women leave now, peaceably. I'll stay. You can do what you want with me. What happens to me is no longer of any importance to me.'

'You expect me to believe that?' Xavier sneered. 'You always were a stubborn, vain old bugger. I know you! You want to live – everyone does.'

'Ah, Xavier, how little you understand me. I've faced my death so many times in the past months that it is no longer a stranger to me, more like a friend. There have been times when I would have welcomed it. I have no fear of death – you and your cohorts dissipated that. Do what you will with me but I implore you to let these innocent women go.'

Jessica felt such love for the man as he spoke in his beautiful voice and with such quiet dignity. There was a second's silence and she felt that everyone was holding their breath as they waited for Xavier's response.

'What? So that they can go and call the police?' he blustered.

'Your friend Ken? I met him. I wouldn't trust him to rescue my cat. We're not that daft,' Selina said, with spirit.

'You shut your mouth,' Xavier flared. 'Your problem, H.G., is that you've no bargaining power left. Don't you realise? After tomorrow when the trustees have inspected you and seen what a useless, sick old bastard you are and given me the power of attorney you'll be surplus to requirements – as will you all.' He smiled, a false, chilling smile.

'As you wish, Xavier. There's just one thing. I'm saddened by what has happened. It need not have been like this. But I want you to know that I forgive you, Xavier, for you are still like a son to me.' H.G. raised his hand – almost as if he was blessing him, Jessica thought.

No one was prepared for Xavier's reaction and they jumped collectively as he emitted a great roar. 'No! Don't fucking well say that, you old bastard!' And he put his hands over his ears.

'I know about Esmeralda,' Selina said boldly, sensing the struggle within Xavier. She was not quite sure what good it would do to say that, or even if it would make matters worse, but she had to grasp at the chance of weakening his resolve.

'What about her?' Xavier swung round to face Selina, a deep frown appearing.

'You know.' Selina shrugged as the idea dawned that perhaps he didn't. If she could keep him talking it might buy them a little time.

'You'd better tell me, Selina.' He lifted his hand menacingly again.

Selina did not flinch. 'Oh dear, has Hesta been keeping secrets from you?' She taunted him with the false courage of one who knows she has nothing to lose. 'That's not very cosy at all.' She was edging almost imperceptibly to her right, where a heavy silver box sat on a small table.

'What secrets? What the fuck do you know?' he shouted.

'Oh dear, oh dear. So you were the father of her child?' she went on, making a stab in the dark, amazing herself

432

at the things she was saying. It was as if someone else controlled her.

'Child?' He looked bewildered, then pulled himself together. 'Stop creeping towards that table and that box!' he yelled.

'So, Hesta was angry, was she? Didn't like the thought of little Esmeralda.' She hoped she still sounded confident. 'Didn't mind you screwing anybody else – like poor Ginnie here. But didn't like you getting too fond of Esmeralda – or had you fallen in love? Is that why Hesta killed her?'

'*She what?*' Xavier stumbled.

'See for yourself, in the cellar.'

'She's lying. Don't listen to them.' Unnoticed by them all, Hesta had appeared in the doorway from the bedroom. She held her arm, from which blood still seeped, close to her body.

'I'll get you a bandage.' Bethina glided towards the bedroom and the bathroom beyond.

'Don't you see, you fool? They're working on you, trying to get you to change your mind. She's a devious cow, that one.' Hesta pointed at Selina, who graciously inclined her head, like visiting royalty. 'Don't fuck it up now.'

A scream interrupted her.

'Bethina!' Xavier exclaimed, and moved towards the door, just as Bethina, white-faced and trembling, appeared. Behind her stood an even paler Tessa, a wild expression in her eyes, and in her hand the knife, still smeared with Hesta's blood and digging now into Bethina's back.

'Xavier, help me,' she begged.

'Tessa, my dear, what are you doing? You don't want to hurt Bethina – she's your friend. Come, my sweet one, give me the knife. We'll forget this ever happened and you can stay here with me, be my new darling.' He tried to caress her face but Tessa recoiled. The knife dropped to the floor with a clatter.

Tessa's eyes filled with terror. 'Leave me alone, I've had enough, I can't take any more of this. I can't. I want to go home,' she whimpered. Her legs buckled, no longer able to support her.

'Poor baby.' Xavier moved to put his arm around her.

Suddenly Ginnie, who'd been watching quietly, erupted across the room screaming loud and long, a blood-curdling sound. She pushed Berihert out of her way with extraordinary strength and hurled herself at Xavier. She leapt on his back, clinging to him like a limpet, pummelling him with her fists, scratching, biting, but all the time screaming. With as much ease as if he was picking an insect from Xavier's back, Berihert removed her.

'Oh my dear God, what have I done? Tessa, forgive me!' And Ginnie crumpled onto the floor.

4

Jerome and Gervase stood guard at the door of H.G.'s drawing room. They looked unhappy with their task and stared wide-eyed with awe at H.G., who still sat in the centre of the room. The others were on the floor at his feet, except for Jessica who was on an ottoman.

'Young man, would you mind if we poured small brandies for these poor women?' H.G. asked politely. Jerome and Gervase looked uncertain. 'Of course, you're welcome to help yourselves to whatever you fancy.' He gesticulated with his usual grace towards the bottles. Jerome glanced at Gervase; both men grinned, nodded and moved to the drinks tray.

Selina looked at the unguarded door with longing – but

if she leapt for it, how long would it be before she was caught? Even worse, how would the others be treated then?

The young men returned with the brandy, and a bottle each of malt whisky for themselves. Jessica downed her brandy quickly and gratefully. Selina sighed at being doomed only to be offered a drink she loathed. H.G. savoured his, and Ginnie and Tessa stared, unblinking, at theirs.

'Ginnie love, drink up, it'll help calm you.'

'Don't be so nice to me, Selina. It makes it worse.'

'I'm sorry, I don't know how else to be with you.'

'If you were angry it would be easier. Don't you hate me for being such a bitch to you, for everything I've done?'

'No, but I'll try if you like, if it makes you feel better.' Selina grinned.

'It's all my fault. If I hadn't been so stupid. If …' Ginnie closed her eyes in despair.

'In my experience, *if only* makes matters worse,' H.G. counselled.

'You're not your brother's keeper, Ginnie. We all have only ourselves to blame,' Jessica stated, and although she felt a measure of sympathy for Ginnie she found her sudden reversion to sanity a little too sudden to be genuine.

'Yes, but if only I hadn't—'

'Look, Ginnie, you can't hijack the guilt exclusively. What you did didn't affect me. Selina, perhaps – but the only person you've damaged apart from yourself is Tessa. She's the only innocent one here. Loosen up, for goodness' sake.'

'You still dislike me, don't you, Jessica?'

'I feel sorry for you, if you must know. You're probably going through hell right now. But it doesn't alter the fact that I feel guilty too. I saw things that were

435

not right here but I chose to ignore them and hoped I was wrong about them. I should have left, got hold of your husband, perhaps, and warned him. But I didn't. I was obsessed with Xavier healing me. You see, the big almighty ME. I didn't give a damn about anyone else – not, that is, until it was too late.' She smiled at H.G. as if in thanks to him for having awakened a selflessness she had not known she possessed.

'And if I hadn't been so obsessed with selling my business we'd never have been here in the first place. I can't ignore that.' Selina pulled her knees up to her chest and hugged them, as if for comfort.

'But you are all here now, at risk, because of me. I feel such despair at what I've caused to happen.' H.G.'s expression was sad.

'You know, we sound like kids in the playground saying my marble's bigger than yours!' Selina laughed.

'You amaze me, Selina. You can laugh even when it's darkest.'

'No point in crying, H.G., it only gives you wrinkles. In any case I'm sure we'll get out of here – I've got to. I must find my Matt so we can start again.'

'The how bothers me somewhat.' H.G. shifted position in his chair.

'They won't kill us, will they? Like that poor woman,' Tessa asked, her lip wobbling.

'No, of course not,' Jessica said with all the conviction she could muster. Humph would be here soon, she was sure. He and Carter must have grasped that all was not well when Selina spoke to them on the phone. An hour, that was all they had to *survive*. She stirred uneasily at this uncomfortable thought. Humph. She would concentrate on thinking of him. If she got out of here alive, she'd put all pride aside and tell him how she felt about him, how much she loved him. She'd explain how this experience had changed her, that she had learnt it wasn't so hard to put others first. She imagined him hugging her and, unconsciously, put her arms around herself and felt much better for it.

'Do you think if we asked—' Selina began.

'You've talked enough. Now stop,' Gervase roared, taking a long swig of whisky from his bottle.

'We're not doing any harm,' H.G. replied, worried now by the rate at which the two men were drinking. Being guarded was bad enough, but drunken guards would be worse.

'Xavier said.'

'Oh, we must do what Xavier says, mustn't we? Fancy him yourself, do you?' Selina snarled.

Gervase began to struggle to his feet.

'She was joking,' H.G. said quickly. 'Selina, I admire your spirit but be careful,' he said softly, and placed his hand on her shoulder to calm her.

Think positively, Selina told herself. She was in love, it wasn't all bad. In a bizarre way she was glad she had come here. They might be in a mess but being here had obviously changed her, hopefully for ever. Something at Porthwood had made her unblock her heart and allow love into it.

She looked at her watch. Not much longer, less than an hour, and Carter and Humphrey would come bursting through the door like knights on white horses and all would be well. All they had to do was hang on. She must find something else to think about ...

I've been too detached, too conscious of my image. H.G. frowned, not liking this truth and not liking himself much either. I have much to answer for, I must accept full responsibility for this catastrophe. Calm is what is needed most, I must conserve my energy ... And H.G. entered his mind and emptied it, temporarily, of these concerns. His pulse slowed, his blood pressure dropped as, effortlessly, he distanced himself in meditation.

Tessa was afraid and, try as she might to think of other things, all that filled her mind was the thought of the body in the cellar and the certainty that hers would be with it – unless her father got here first. She prayed now, long and hard, and hoped God was listening and forgave her for not having been in touch for such a long time. *Please let my daddy get here fast!* When she got out of here, she promised herself fervently, she'd be different, she'd be kinder, more considerate and she would let her mother know, every single day, that she loved her. She had thought *when* not *if*, she realised. She straightened her back and hope flooded in, nudging terror away.

Shame was uppermost in Ginnie's mind. Shame at the danger in which she had put her own daughter, at her own behaviour. How could she have done those things – the orgy, Ken? When she had seen Xavier touch Tessa she had known herself for the fool she had become. It was as if she had been blind and suddenly could see. She hated him and his control. She wanted him dead. But this was no way to think. Hate would be damaging and might anchor her here for all time, which she knew must not happen. She had changed when she came here, and now she had to try to change back to what she had been – except ... She could never be that Ginnie again. The woman she had once been had died here tonight in the violence. She had, somehow, to resurrect herself, make herself anew. If Carter loved her, she would be happy. If he could not forgive her, she would understand. She had had so much and she hadn't known it. Would she ever get it back again? Could she ever forgive herself? She sighed. She deserved to be punished ... She felt a hand take hers and squeeze it. Having heard the heartfelt sigh, Tessa wanted to comfort her. Ginnie smiled weakly at her daughter. Hate, she was full of hate. It would not go away and she no longer had the energy to fight it.

'Jessica, do you see what I see?' Selina pointed to the

door. On either side of it, like kapok-stuffed bookends, Jerome and Gervase lolled, the whisky bottles between them, half empty. Forbidden to drink alcohol by Xavier, and their systems unaccustomed to it, the spirit had been too potent for them: they were fast asleep, and the whiffling noises they made showed just how deep that sleep was.

Jessica called H.G.'s name softly and tugged at his hand. He nodded silently as he, too, saw the sleeping guards. Selina alerted Ginnie and Tessa. One by one they stood up and crept across the room to the door and freedom.

They froze and collectively held their breaths when Jerome abruptly sat up, opened his eyes and looked straight at them; but his brain was too befuddled for what he saw to register. They passed between them and through the broken door, with only one heart-stopping moment when Ginnie's long robe caught in the splintered wood.

'Pray God it's not locked,' Selina said, as they reached the side door.

'Ready?' Selina asked. 'Oh, no,' she said. H.G. was propped against the wall and sliding slowly to the floor, grey-faced, and Jessica was leaning on Tessa, obviously in pain.

'When I turned to hit Berihert I twisted my ankle – look, it's swelling. You go on, I'll be all right.'

'Not bloody likely – we've got this far.' Selina thought quickly. Two were incapacitated, which left three to carry them. Who should they take first? 'We'll carry H.G. a little way and then come back for Jessica – like leap-frog – and get them in stages out of the garden and round to the garages.'

'But it would mean leaving one alone, and exposed, while we got the other. It's got to be done in one run,' Tessa insisted.

'Take H.G. He's so thin the three of you can carry him between you. Leave me, please.'

'We'll take H.G. and come back for Jessica,' Selina decided.

'I'm too heavy, you'd never do it. Get going!'

'We'll get you outside and come back as soon as we can. Okay?'

With difficulty they helped Jessica out of the door and onto the ground. 'Don't bother coming back! The ground's soaked and I'll be dead of pneumonia before you make it.' She laughed, and felt quite proud that she could. 'Now go and get H.G.'

He was easy to lift and, a little better for his brief rest, was able to put his arms around the necks of Tessa and Selina as they made a chair for him with their linked hands.

'Ginnie, if you'll—' Selina looked behind her. 'Where's your mother?'

'She was right behind us.' Tessa loosened her grip.

'No, not now. We have to get H.G. to the garage and fnd a car. We'll look for your mother afterwards,' Selina said sharply, thinking, When I get hold of her again I'll *kill* her.

The storm still raged and the three were buffeted as they moved slowly across the knot garden. But the weather was their ally for windows and curtains were closed against it. It was unlikely that anyone would see them.

5

Sitting in the knot garden and slowly freezing, Jessica realised that at Porthwood there were degrees of fear and she was being put through the whole gamut. She lifted her watch to her eyes but, in the dark, could see nothing. It must be nearly two, she thought. Where the hell were they? She tried to listen but the wind, which was reaching even greater heights of ferocity, blocked out all other sound.

The garage doors were locked.

'There's my car.' Tessa pointed out the two-seater MG standing on the forecourt and explained about the second set of keys hidden under the wheel arch.

'That's the only good bit of news all night. Is nothing else going to go right?' Selina kicked the garage door. 'How the hell are we all going to get away in that?'

'There's a tiny space behind the seats, but I think even you would be too big for it. Or we could take the roof off and hang onto the boot somehow.'

'It's ten to two so let's just hope to God your father's *en route*. You take H.G. and hide him somewhere for the time being and I'll go and see if I can find a better place to put Jessica.'

'There's a copse up by the coast road. I'll hide the car there and double back.'

'I know the copse you mean. If I come up with any ideas I'll start heading that way with Jessica. Be quick.' They bundled H.G. into the front seat of the car. He was feeling much better now and protesting volubly at being the first to escape.

'H.G., do me a favour, will you? Just shut up.' Selina kissed his forehead as she spoke and waved to them as Tessa, throwing caution to the wind, roared away.

Like a wraith in her pale blue robe, Ginnie raced through the corridors of the old house. It was densely silent. The meeting in the Long Gallery must be over, or maybe it had not even taken place. She glanced at her watch. Almost two. Soon it would be morning. Soon the papers would be signed and then their fate would be sealed – as Xavier had threatened earlier.

Xavier! Her face twisted with bitterness. She left the hall and tore into the kitchens. She knew exactly what she needed.

'Tessa's parking H.G. in the MG and then she's coming back to collect you.'

'Don't you ever take anything seriously?' Jessica knew she sounded tetchy but could not help herself: she was wet, she was cold and she wished they had waited in the warm for Humph and his friends to arrive. 'Why did they pick on two in the bloody morning? Why couldn't they have come at a sane time like midnight?'

'Because they hoped everyone else would be asleep, I suppose. Christ, it's cold. Look, Jessica, I've had an idea. I know where the ride-on mower is stored. I'm going to get it and give you a lift out on that.'

'On what?'

'Jessica, dearest, this is no time to stand on your dignity. You'll look perfectly sweet on it. Shan't be a mo.' And she was gone, flitting through the garden, leaving Jessica longing to be young again.

'Xavier, it's me, come to get you,' Ginnie cooed, as she looked down on the sleeping forms of Xavier and Hesta. Xavier stirred but Hesta, drugged against the pain in her arm, slept on. 'I've come to tell you how much I hate you. How much I despise you. You've destroyed me and now I'm going to destroy you!'

Xavier woke. He struggled up in the bed, his eyes wide with horror as he saw Ginnie standing before him, a candle in one hand. 'No, Ginnie, no!' he screamed in terror, at the sight of the bottle of methylated spirits which she held in her other hand.

The ride across the gardens was bumpy. The mower was not built to carry two and their progress was agonisingly slow. At times the machine tilted alarmingly. Jessica gritted her teeth but Selina was laughing wildly, the wind catching the sound and hurling it into the night.

'You're bloody mad, woman!' Jessica screeched into her ear over the storm. She looked back over her shoulder, convinced that they must have been heard and were being followed. She banged on Selina's shoulder. 'Stop!' she yelled.

'Not now we've got going.'

'Stop, this minute. Look.'

At the urgency in Jessica's voice, Selina swerved to a halt. 'Oh, my God!' she said.

To Jessica, it resembled a scene from a horror film she had once starred in. The curtains at one of the windows were on fire and as she watched, the panes shattered.

'That's Xavier's room.'

'Good, let him fry. Come on, let's get going.'

'We can't do that, Jessica. We have to go back.'

'Life was so simple when I only thought of myself. All right, back we go. But it's ten past two! Where are they? Bloody men! Never there when you need them.'

Frantically they turned the mower and arrived back at the front of the house, just as Tessa came running round the side.

'Where's my mother!' she screamed at the sight of the flames, which were now pouring out of the window to be caught by the wind.

'Come with me, Tessa, quick! Jessica, ring the fire alarm and call the brigade.'

Ignoring the pain in her ankle, Jessica forced herself to walk into the house. By the time she reached the hall, Tessa and Selina, both lugging fire extinguishers, were disappearing from sight at the top of the stairs. Jessica broke the glass on the alarm and the klaxon rang out deafeningly. In Mathie's office she dialled 999. For once the telephones were working. Then, not sure what to do, she went into the hall.

'Matt!' She could hardly believe her eyes as he came running along the corridor leading from H.G.'s suite, followed by a crowd of policemen. 'Upstairs! Selina! Fire!' she shouted, and then, seconds later, 'Ginnie and Tessa!' as Carter and Karl rushed in. Humph was the last to appear.

'Sorry I'm late coming.'

'That makes a nice change!' Her delightful laugh gurgled.

6

The noise was intolerable. The followers milled around, pyjama-clad and tearfully confused. Police enthusiastically rounded people up, still angry at having discovered one of their own officers was bent. Firefighters trundled up and down the staircase. The ambulance arrived, and Jessica sat in the main hall with H.G., anxiously scanning the faces, afraid of what might have happened.

'You all right, H.G.? I'd get you some tea but I don't want to miss hearing any news.'

'I understand. I'm fine now. I think the excitement got to me earlier and made me collapse. So stupid of me! It makes me feel so feeble.'

'You probably did us all a favour. If I hadn't been on that mower at that moment and seen the fire ...' She shuddered.

'I can't describe the relief when your dear husband's face appeared in the window of that little car.'

'We're lucky they saw you there.'

'That was thanks to Matt. He said he'd used that copse

before and automatically glanced at it. And, of course, Carter recognised his daughter's car.'

'How come Matt was with them?'

'We didn't have much time for them to explain, but I gather when he escaped from here he went straight to Karl's cottage – he knew Karl had rented it and he planned to lie low only to find them there with their plan.'

'And the police?'

'Humph got in touch with the top man at Scotland Yard.'

'That's Humph, always knows the right person. And the alarm?'

'Humph again. They were deactivated by another friend of his – an expert in burglar alarms, I gather,' H.G. said, tongue in cheek.

'A villain more like!' Jessica chuckled. 'That's Humph, though, always knows who to turn to.'

'Officer.' H.G. half stood. 'Can you tell us what's happened? The stress of not knowing ...'

'There's two seriously burned.'

'Who? Is anyone dead?'

'I'm not at liberty to say, sir.'

'This is worse than not knowing.' Jessica breathed deeply in an effort to calm her nerves. It didn't work. She grabbed at the oilskin of a fireman who was passing. 'Any news?'

'Fire's out, mam. Here, aren't you Jessica Lawley?'

'Yes, Officer, I am. I'm surprised you recognised me.'

'With a beautiful face likes yours, easiest thing in the world.'

'You see, still admired. When all this is over, you will let me help you with that hip, won't you? Ah, at last.' H.G. and Jessica stood up as a sombre procession came down the stairs, led by two ambulance crews carrying stretchers.

'I can't look.' Jessica covered her face with her hands. Then she felt an arm go round her shoulders, a comforting, familiar arm. 'Humph, tell me.'

'A woman called Hesta and your friend Ginnie, they've got some nasty burns. Ginnie's the worst – she was burned pulling them out of the room.'

'Them?'

'Rescued that bloke Xavier. Told her husband she hated him but she couldn't let him die. Not when it came to it.'

'But I presumed Ginnie—'

Tenderly Humph put his finger on her lips. 'She did, but Xavier's taking the blame. He's told the cops he was burning some papers with meths and the fire got out of hand.'

'Why would he do that?'

'Maybe he hopes Ginnie won't give evidence against him.'

'He's been arrested? On what grounds?'

'At the moment I think he's been done for unlawfully detaining all of you. It is H.G., isn't it?'

In the midst of the chaos, introductions were made.

Carter was beside Ginnie's stretcher. 'Oh, my darling, my brave darling.' He bent and kissed her. 'I love you. Forgive me.'

'I love you too,' Ginnie whispered back hoarsely, her throat and lungs damaged by smoke. 'Tessa ...' Weakly she held out her hand. Tessa took it. 'I'm sorry.'

'Nothing to be sorry about, Mum. Just get mended quick.' And Tessa had to turn away as her eyes filled with tears.

'What do you think will happen with our friends Ginnie and Carter?' H.G. watched the scene at the stretcher.

Jessica sighed. 'Of course, one hopes for the best – but can you see someone like Carter changing? Even if he's been honest and hasn't had all those affairs, he must have neglected her dreadfully.'

'He appears to have forgiven her.'

'Yes, but will she ever forgive herself?'

There was a loud commotion and they looked up as Mathie, Clinton, Ancilla and Bethina were also being hauled off by the police.

'Are you sorry, Bethina?' H.G. asked, as she was marched past him.

She looked him coldly in the eye, 'No,' she said shortly, and, head held high, swept out into the night, shaking off the policeman's grasp as she went.

The last to appear were Selina and Matt who walked down the stairs entwined in each other's arms.

'If it hadn't been for Selina and Tessa it would have been a different story,' Humphrey explained. 'I just can't get over how brave you all were. Made our rescue bid superfluous, really.'

'It's the thought that counts.' Jessica stood on tiptoe and whispered in his ear.

'What's that? I can't hear,' he said with a grin.

'But if I say it louder, everyone will hear.'

'So?'

'I love you, Humph Lawley. Do you fancy giving it another try?'

'Yes, please,' said Humphrey, picked her up and twirled her round as if she was a young girl again, which was exactly how she felt.

Selina and Matt sat up half the night talking.

'I'd understand if you never wanted to see this place again – ever. I suppose you'll want to go back to your shop now H.G. says he's giving it back to you. But if you thought you could, then would you – perhaps just to see if you like it – well, would you think of joining me here? I think under H.G. it will be paradise. I had a word with

447

him and he agrees. But if you don't, we could always go somewhere else.'

'You're not going back to the outside then?'

'Being an architect? No. There was a lot that was good here, despite Xavier. I loved the gardening and I've decided to continue with that. And if …?'

'I think this place will do me nicely – with you, that is.'

The following day the followers congregated in the Long Gallery, their number augmented by many who, having heard the news of the fire on the radio and television, had come from all parts of the country to be with H.G. The house still smelt of smoke but Abigail had lit a hundred scented candles, whose perfume was slowly prevailing against the acrid odour.

H.G., in front of the alcove in which stood the sandalwood box, was sitting on the daïs on his rug, upon which he had not been permitted to sit for so long. He stroked it fondly with one hand and smiled shyly at his followers, lest they think him strange. He waited patiently as they settled.

'First, my dear friends, I have news of poor Ginnie. She is comfortable in hospital. She will be moved today to a specialist burns unit for treatment to her arms. The doctors are hopeful the scarring will be light. Tessa, of course, is with her and sends you all her love. Now, I think, we should show officially our gratitude to two remarkable women, Jessica and Selina, whom many of you know. Without doubt, had it not been for them I would not be here with you today and many of you would have been burned in your beds. They were on the point of freeing themselves from Xavier's wickedness but chose to return when they saw that fire. For such selfless courage my gratitude is boundless.'

Jessica and Selina looked suitably modest at the roar of applause and held on to their men for grim death.

'But, my friends, and this is why I have called this meeting, I have a confession to make. You see, dear people, I am not as I seem and as I have said these many years. I have been living a lie. I have deceived you. When I have finished my tale, if you regard me as a charlatan then I quite understand if you want me no longer ...' Slowly at first, stumbling over the words, H.G. retold the story he had hidden in the patchwork quilt. But, as the tale unfolded, his voice gathered strength and there was finally a strange pride about him and an excitement as if the telling was a great unburdening for him. When he had finished, there was silence.

Abigail stood up. 'For myself, H.G., this story, while fascinating and moving, means nothing. Whoever you are and wherever you have come from, you are still and, will always remain, H.G. to me.'

The roar of approval from the followers rang round the ancient room and many were crying.

'Don't forget, H.G., there are many of us here who chose not to ask, not to investigate too deeply. Many of us changed for the worse here and will have to live with that for the rest of our lives.' It was Berihert, shamefaced, who spoke.

'Before I came here today I read something about changing. This experience we have all suffered in various ways may have changed us, but for some, I know, it is for the better.' From the floor H.G. took up a dictionary of quotations and turned to a page with a marker. He coughed discreetly and put on his half spectacles. 'Washington Irving, the American, wrote, "There is a certain relief in change, even though it be from bad to worse ... it is often a comfort to shift one's position and be bruised in a new place." Let us regard Xavier's reign here as a new place. Now he is gone and we can return to the old and familiar, with a newness to us. Like the chameleon we, too, have changed.'

All Orion/Phoenix titles are available at your local bookshop or from the following address:

Littlehampton Book Services
Cash Sales Department L
14 Eldon Way, Lineside Industrial Estate
Littlehampton
West Sussex BN17 7HE

telephone 01903 721596, *facsimile* 01903 730914

Payment can either be made by credit card (Visa and Mastercard accepted) or by sending a cheque or postal order made payable to *Littlehampton Book Services*.
DO NOT SEND CASH OR CURRENCY.

Please add the following to cover postage and packing

UK and BFPO:
£1.50 for the first book, and 50P for each additional book to a maximum of £3.50

Overseas and Eire:
£2.50 for the first book plus £1.00 for the second book and 50p for each additional book ordered

---

BLOCK CAPITALS PLEASE

name of cardholder ....

address of cardholder ....

delivery address
(if different from cardholder)
....
....
....

....
....
....

postcode ....

postcode ....

☐ I enclose my remittance for £...........................

☐ please debit my Mastercard/Visa (delete as appropriate)

card number ☐☐☐☐☐☐☐☐☐☐☐☐☐☐☐☐

expiry date ☐☐☐☐

signature ....

prices and availability are subject to change without notice